CODE NAME: LUMINOUS

A Warrior's Challenge series
Book Four

Natasza Waters

Sensual Romance

Secret Cravings Publishing
www.secretcravingspublishing.com

JUL 2 2 2015

Y0-ACE-913

A Secret Cravings Publishing Book
Sensual Romance

Code Name: Luminous
Copyright © 2014 Natasza Waters
Print ISBN: 978-1-63105-544-7

First E-book Publication: November 2014
First Print Publication: March 2015

Cover design by Dawné Dominique
Edited by Tamara Hoffa
Proofread by Laurie White
All cover art and logo copyright © 2014 by Secret Cravings
Publishing

ALL RIGHTS RESERVED: This literary work may not be
reproduced or transmitted in any form or by any means, including
electronic or photographic reproduction, in whole or in part,
without express written permission.

All characters and events in this book are fictitious. Any
resemblance to actual persons living or dead is strictly
coincidental.

PUBLISHER
Secret Cravings Publishing
www.secretcravingspublishing.com

Dedication

For the warriors who dedicate their lives to a greater cause, and a greater good.
And to love, which shows them the way home.

Acknowledgments

No writer brings a book to publication without many moving parts. I love all of mine.

My family, who gives me the time I need to allow my stories to breathe life.

Tamara Hoffa, you are more than an editor, but I think you know that.

Justin Tatum, you are the face of Tony (Tinman) Bale, and I know you understand what a warrior is, because once upon a time you were one. From soldier to model, a new journey for you has begun. Good luck!

Waters' Warriors, thank you for your help and support.

Tonya Smalley and Sheri Fredricks, my BFFs who live too far away, but are never far from my heart, a thousand hugs. T.J. Mackay, you've made sacrifices that many don't know about, but that's what a brave woman does when she changes the world.

Once again, I thank the warriors around the world who stand boldly in the way of our enemies, but never lose grip of their humanity. May you all have loving arms waiting for you at home.

CODE NAME: LUMINOUS
A Warrior's Challenge series
Book Four

Natasza Waters

Chapter One

Lumin paced across the hotel room, stopping at the window to gaze at the mountains skirting Las Vegas. She squinted as the sun breached the peaks, spearing her eyes. A pre-recorded message on her phone droned on while fear chilled her to the core. She laid her palm against the glass. The heat of the July morning penetrated its thickness, but not the cold reality of the moment.

The voice directed the caller to press the appropriate number for different departments. None sounded right. Her fingertips slid down the glass as the little bit of hope she clung to evaporated. The bed sheet she held to her body drew taut as she twisted. Swallowing hard, her gaze swept over the man's body lying on the bed. Yeah, he was still dead.

"Press zero for an operator," the voice instructed. *Why did they always leave that to the end?*

"Naval Amphibious Base Coronado, how may I direct your call?" the woman on the other end asked.

"Please." She cleared her throat. "I need to find someone who works on your base."

With a healthy dollop of boredom, the operator inquired, "What department does he work in, ma'am?"

"His name is Tony Bale, he's a SEAL, uh, Team One, Alpha Squad. Can you please find him for me?"

"One moment, please."

Lumin squeezed the cotton sheet between her fingers and breathed out slowly while her heart thumped in her chest. How could she have gotten herself into this? She knew better. She was smart. Educated. In Las Vegas she'd learned to watch and listen, but never slip into the darkness that was an unseen counter-balance to the bright lights and tourists who lost their restraint in an adult playground indulgent of misdemeanors, if not sin.

"Ma'am."

The operator's voice made her jump. "Yes?"

"Petty Officer Bale is not on the base."

"Could you find him, please? This is very important."

"Ma'am, we do not give out personal information."

It sounded like the switchboard operator was going to hang up. There was no one else she could share the information with. She'd met Tony Bale last December when he'd asked for her help. Pedro Quadero, the head of a large cartel operating in Las Vegas, had kidnapped a little girl. She'd taken Tony and his friends, Mace and Nina, to Steven Porter, a powerful man in Las Vegas who helped them find Quadero. Steven Porter and his wife, Moira, were like Lumin's adoptive parents, but they couldn't help her now. If she involved them they might all end up dead. Tony was a Navy SEAL; maybe he would know what to do.

"Ma'am." She altered her voice, professional, calm, the farthest from what she was feeling. "This is extremely important. Mr. Bale told me to call him if I had information of a—" She paused. "A sensitive nature. You don't have to give me his number, but can you patch me through to him?"

A deep sigh penetrated the phone line. "One moment."

Lumin stepped to the room's control panel and checked the air temperature. She was freezing, and switched off the AC.

"Tony Bale." His voice enveloped her like a warm blanket. Optimism glinted like a shiny coin for the first time since she'd opened her eyes this morning.

"Tony," she whispered, holding back tears of relief. "It's—"

"Lumin?"

"I'm sorry, but I didn't know who else to call."

"What's going on?"

Loud music in the background, water splashing, and the laughter of small children and adults filled the airwaves between them. She bit her lip with doubt. They'd only spent a short time together last December. She pictured Tony in her mind, his image clear. A lean body with roping muscles and a chest any woman wanted to be held against dangled in her thoughts. Their meeting, although brief, seemed unfinished when he'd left her on the steps of Steven and Moira's home.

While every man in Vegas looked at her and saw a tall blonde whose legs they wanted to lie between, Tony had looked deeper. His eyes broke through her exterior and saw more, making her nervous and excited at the same time. Tony's actions, the way he talked about the little girl they were trying to find, and the way he carried himself proved to her he was brave, noble, but when trustworthy popped into her head she knew she'd hit on the right word. "I think I'm in big trouble. You need to tell me what to do." The signal cut out, and her heart leaped into her throat. "Are you still there?"

"I'm here, sweetheart, what kind of trouble?" he asked, his voice hardening. "Is it Quadero? Did he find out you helped us?"

The adult voices in the background ceased.

"No, it's not Quadero. Where are you?"

"In Mexico. Nina and Mace just got married. Are you in Las Vegas?"

Lumin hooked her fingers in a strand of hair, tugging to replace her rampaging fear with pain. She hesitated.

"Don't hang up," Tony commanded as if sensing her misgivings. "You can tell me, Lumin. I can hear you're scared. Whatever it is, you're not alone, okay?"

"Do you know what *Yersinia Pestis* is?" she blurted.

A deep rumble from Tony's throat preceded his answer. "The Bubonic Plague."

"Yes. In the Middle Ages it was passed through contact, but imagine if it were engineered into an airborne virus and mutated every thirty-six hours. It would kill millions of people." She licked her dry lips. "I think they've made one."

"The Bubonic Plague is a bacteria, and who is *they*, Lumin?"

"I—don't know who they are, but I think they know who I am." Her voice stuttered. "You must have contact with people who can look into this. I heard a name, Dr. Clifford Bjornson. That might lead you somewhere. I have to go."

"Wait! How do these people know you?"

Lumin dropped the sheet and reached for her dress. She pulled it over her head. Squeezing the phone between her ear and shoulder, as she did up the buttons she said, "Because Dr. Bjornson's partner is lying dead in my bed."

"Okay, listen—I want you to drive to San Diego."

"I don't have a car."

"Then get on a plane and fly to San Diego. I'll meet you."

"But you're in Mexico."

"I'm leaving now. Wait for me. Stay in the airport until I get there."

"I can't." Lumin twirled, looking for her flats. The tip of her shoe poked out from under the couch. She bent to retrieve it, and dug her hand underneath to grasp the other. "If they're trying to find me, I'm not going to draw their attention to you. I just wanted someone to know. You're the only Navy SEAL I've met." Her voice choked off in fear as her gaze slid over the carpet and came to rest on the dead scientist. "I don't know what killed him. He doesn't look sick, but he might be infected and now maybe I am too." Fear squeezed a tear from her eye, and rolled down her cheek. "I can't take the chance of infecting others if I am."

"Listen…to…me. If he isn't showing signs of the Plague than he died some other way. Get on a plane and wait for me in San Diego. I'm coming." Tony's voice softened. "Don't make me track you down, because I will. We'll lose time and it sounds like time is running out."

A bang on the door made her pulse jump. She waited to hear the words "Housekeeping" but they didn't come, only another hard knock. "Too late. They're here," she whispered, backing away. There was nowhere to go. She was on the thirtieth floor of the Grand Palms Hotel with no way out.

"Lumin." Tony's voice strained tight. "Sweetheart, do exactly what I say, and do it quick."

* * * *

Four hours later Tony hit the San Diego terminal gate at a full run. Nearly at the head of the lineup for Customs, he turned on his phone. Lumin had followed his instruction and luck helped. The men who broke into her room didn't want to stick around with a dead body on the bed, and he'd counted on it, telling her to hide between the mattress and box spring, concealing the edges with the sheets.

A couple with burns that screamed "give me Aloe Vera or give me death" were the only people ahead of him in the Customs lineup. Checking if he missed any calls from Lumin, he spared a glance at the agents, hoping he didn't get the old gal who wore a scowl like she had it out for the world. He thumbed the numbers in his cell till he found Lumin's number.

"Hello!"

"I'm just about through Customs. Where are you?" he asked.

"At the bus stop."

"Bus stop? Why—"

"I could pay cash."

Lumin might be scared, but her focus and good sense were intact. Keeping his attention on the kiosk, he suppressed a groan when the old biddy Customs agent became available. "I'm up next. Take a cab to this address."

"Where is this?" she asked, after he gave it to her.

"My condo. I'll meet you there in twenty minutes."

"Tony, maybe I shouldn't. Not until I know for sure if I'm infected or not. Getting on the bus was risky enough."

"Don't argue with me, Lumin. I know for sure. If you were sick, you'd be experiencing symptoms by now. Get in a cab. I'll see you in a few minutes." He plastered a charming smile on his lips. Old, young, didn't matter. He had the gift of drawing women's attention. For once it was going to come in handy for something besides a roll between the sheets.

Keeping his patience and his answers short, Tony tapped his foot. The old girl gave him the stamp of approval, and he took off at a fast run. He pushed past two businessmen and hustled through the airport doors to the taxi stand.

Cutting off a couple of young tourists about to step into a taxi, he apologized. "Sorry, it's an emergency." He grabbed the gal's bag from the back seat and thrust it at her.

"We can share," she said, smiling at him and raising her shades, giving him a once-over.

"Sorry, beautiful." He hopped in and closed the door, giving the cab driver his address. Traffic was light on the Coronado

Bridge. "Can you hurry it up, buddy?" he said to the Mexican driver.

"No speed. No ticket."

"Yeah, yeah," Tony gripped the door handle, his heart hell-bent on overdrive since departing the team in Mexico. Mace offered to come, as did the other guys, but he and Nina were on their honeymoon. They didn't have a lot of time before their next deployment and needed their time together.

The cab came to a neck-snapping halt in front of his condo, and he jumped out. Lumin stood in the entryway nervously watching her surroundings. His heart rolled over and sat on its haunches seeing her. Lumin's straight blonde hair coursed over her shoulders and rested against a divine body. Checking the area as he approached her, he noted all was clear. She spotted him, but didn't move. Fishing for his keys, he stopped within touching distance and stared into the blue eyes that had wandered into his dreams for months since he'd seen her last.

"I didn't know who else to call," she said as if in apology, her forehead rippling.

"You called the right guy. Come on. Let's get inside."

Tony cracked the door to his first floor condo and stalled to be certain the space was as he left it.

"Something wrong?" she asked, standing close enough to feel her aura chafing his.

He reached for her bag and slipped it from her shoulder. "Coast is clear. Make yourself at home."

Lumin followed him in and he turned up the AC. The July heat in San Diego could melt you into a puddle. A text bleeped its intention and he knew it was Mace.

Got her?

Roger that.

On our way.

Negative, I'll handle this.

Wife's orders.

Beads of sweat gathered on Lumin's forehead, and her cheeks flushed. He led her to his leather couch. "You feeling okay?"

She nodded and sat down.

"I'll get us something to drink and you can tell me what's going on."

"Just water, thanks."

Tony cracked the fridge. "I've got beer."

"I don't drink alcohol."

"'Kay," he said, throwing a few cubes in a glass and filling it. He sat down beside her and snapped the top from a beer for himself. "You're safe here. Relax." Encouragement didn't help, evaluating her straight back, hands tightly folded, and the tense air wavering around her. He wanted to calm her down. Her fear bothered him. "From the start, Lumin. Tell me all of it."

Lumin swiveled to look at him. The buzzing in his head when her gaze fell on him made it a little hard to hear. He shot back a healthy swallow of beer, and took a steadying breath.

"I—"

A knock on his front door stopped her. "Stay here." He waited until a second knock fell. Small fingers, he surmised. "Hello?"

"Tony, I saw you come home," a woman's voice floated through the door.

He opened it to see Marcie standing there in a see-through dress. He'd spent one hot night tearing up the sheets with her, and got a bad case of "run for the hills" when she moved in upstairs. "Hey, Mars, yeah, listen, I've got company."

"Oh." Her gaze stroked across him with disappointment. "I was just about to start dinner and thought…"

"Sorry, babe. My company's staying with me. Rain check, okay?"

"I suppose," she said, trying to peek around his shoulder.

"Talk later." He gave her a friendly smile before closing the door. His stomach clenched when he saw Lumin wasn't where he'd left her. *Okay, SEAL, get a grip.* "Lumin?" The patio door was open, and the curtains fluttered aside revealing his guest standing like a beautiful Greek statue adorning the postage stamp-sized space.

"I should go," she said, when he stepped onto the patio to join her. "I'll contact the CDC and tell them what I know. I should have done that before involving you. I wasn't thinking straight."

He offered her a raised brow. She was trying hard to not show her fear, but he could feel it as if it was rooted deep inside him. "You're exactly where you're supposed to be." *Wasn't that the truth.* Since December the team had been busy with workups, but he'd thought about her many times. At least five times he'd picked up the phone, but never finished dialing. He gently gripped her hand, and she let him lead her back inside. "Maybe you should lie down for a while." She refused with a slow shake of her head. When he had her settled, he said, "How did you get involved in this?" The nervous flit of her gaze put him on edge.

"I don't normally mix it up with tourists. They're only in Vegas for a few days, but my friend Star is always on me to take time off from studying."

"Studying what?" he asked.

"In September I start the third year of my law degree."

That surprised him. "You're an aerialist, aren't you?"

"I am now. My parents are performers, and they taught my brother and I everything they know."

"Where are they?"

"Europe. On tour. My brother has a family. I didn't want to take the chance I'd lead any trouble to him."

"Makes sense."

"Star convinced me to go out, but she didn't tell me she'd set up a blind date. Dr. Carmichael was introduced to me as a scientist. He seemed uptight, but decent enough. We took him and his friend out on the town."

Tony's mind romped ahead at SEAL speed, wondering how she'd ended up in a hotel room with him, and he wasn't sure he wanted to hear it. "Did he say where he was from?"

"Lebanon."

Tony took another swallow of his beer, nodding as he settled the bottle on his knee. "What happened next?"

"Star ditched me, and I was left to babysit. Halfway through the night he started hammering back the drinks. I suggested he return to his hotel. Dr. Carmichael could barely stand, so I helped him. When we got to his hotel, he threw up, and he did it all over me the first time. Instead of calling the hotel doctor, I stayed with him. I washed out my clothes and hung them to dry while I tried to keep him cool with compresses. He started talking about a plague. I thought it was drunken babble or delirium at first.

He began to beg for forgiveness, explaining he hadn't known what the bacteria would be used for. He'd been contracted to work with the Bubonic Plague, but alter it. Weaponize it, is the term he used. He thought he'd been hired by the U.S. military, but he found out it was a private backer. When he attempted to walk away, they locked him in a lab and threatened him."

"Did he mention names?"

"Just Dr. Clifford Bjornson. I think he was Carmichael's partner." Lumin shook her head and stared at Tony with a reflective expression. "I stayed with him because he begged me to. I fell asleep, and when I woke up…"

"He was dead."

She nodded.

"Have you told anyone else?"

"No, just you."

"Did he tell you where the lab was located?"

"Out in the Nevada desert. He didn't mention a town just that it was in the middle of nowhere."

Lumin stood up and began to pace the room. Tony's gaze tracked her lithe movements and graceful, long strides in her hip-hugging shorts. He was reminded of the first time he'd seen her hot-footing it across the lobby of the Grand Palms Casino in Las Vegas. Something had begun to race inside him then, and the key was still in the ignition.

"Have you eaten?" She continued to pace, preoccupied with her thoughts. "Chinese or Italian?" he tried again.

"What?" She stopped and stared at him.

His lips curved into a grin. "I asked whether you want me to order Chinese or Italian?"

"I'm not really hungry, Tony."

"Come here for a second." She kept her distance. "Lumin, you are not infected. Please, come here." She sighed and slowly approached him. He gently twined his fingers in hers and drew her down. Their knees brushed, and the touch sent a supercharged jolt through him. "You need to eat and rest." He stood up and adjusted the pillow, then pressed her shoulders to lay back. "Do me a favor and close your eyes."

"Tony, I can't sleep. My mind is running in circles."

"Just for a second." Her dainty, soft fingers gripped his calloused ones. Seeing her again was a little surreal. Holding her hand sent his blood galloping through his veins, but it wasn't lust, more like an incessant need to get closer.

Their time together had been brief, but it had a lasting impact. There were plenty of women to keep him busy in Coronado. Sometimes he didn't even remember the girls he'd screwed when they'd catch him in a coffee shop and say hello, but he remembered Lumin, and he'd never touched her. Not even a kiss.

She watched him with a cautious gaze as he lifted her hand and encased it with both of his. "SEALs learn how to fall asleep quickly. Many times we can only catch a few winks before we have to start moving again. Clear your mind." He smiled down at her. "Close your eyes." He waited until she did. "You're safe, Lumin. You're safe with me."

While he ordered a Chinese dinner for two, he darted a look at her. Her pale lips were parted a little, her breasts rose and fell in a shallow rhythm, and he knew she'd fallen asleep. Before he knocked, Tony met the delivery guy at the door. He grabbed, tipped, and closed the door. He set the food out and hovered at the back of the couch, reasoning in his mind that he was programmed to help people. Yet, it didn't explain why he wanted to simply stand and gaze at her sleeping form. High cheekbones, soft, inviting skin; everything about her challenged him to possess her. She reminded him of looking out across a blanket of newly fallen snow, absolutely pristine. If he touched her, he'd tarnish her. His desire begged to run full ahead and leave its mark. Good sense reminded him she'd sought him out for his protection, not to be mauled by a womanizing jackass.

He'd pulled her act at the Grand Palms up on YouTube. She amazed him as she balanced on the thin beam suspended high above the stage. Brave and agile, with an elfin beauty, she had the audience holding their breath. Like a lovesick fan, he played it at least fifty times. Even though he'd chickened out of calling her, the internet offered a small fix from a distance, but why the hell hadn't he called her?

"Are you just going to stare at me all night?"

He blinked and stepped back a little embarrassed. "Dinner's ready."

With a sweep of her long, tanned legs she strode to the table and settled down. The woman wore a pair of shorts like no one else.

"Smells good. I guess I am hungry."

She filled her plate, but pushed aside the chunks of chicken and beef.

"You're a vegetarian."

After slowly chewing a mouthful, she said, "You notice everything, don't you?"

He shrugged and loaded his plate. He was starving, but the hunger wasn't for food. "Depends on the subject."

She lowered her fork before it reached her mouth. "I'm sorry."

"Don't be. I told you. I owed you one."

"Not that. I didn't ask you how the little girl you were trying to find is doing."

He smiled. "She's doing great."

She mirrored his expression. "Good."

Tony remembered tracking Lumin into the nightclub in Vegas. "That guy that manhandled you in the bar, what happened to him?"

Lumin narrowed her eyes. "He was my show manager, but he was fired the next night. You wouldn't happen to know anything about that, would you?"

He shrugged innocently. When Steven Porter flew them back to Coronado in his helicopter after rescuing Squirt, Tony described the guy, and what he'd done to Lumin in the bar. He had a feeling Mr. Porter wouldn't like it much.

"Gordon was getting a little hard to bear, to be honest. I'm pretty sure he was high half of the time, and when he was, he got aggressive."

The thought of anyone touching Lumin gnawed at his belly.

"You said you were at Mace and Nina's wedding when I called."

"Yeah, one of those love at first sight things."

Lumin tilted her head and surveyed him. "And you? Am I going to make some girl angry for dragging you into this? I won't be here long. She doesn't have to be concerned."

He shook his head. "No, I…"

The door blew open and Lumin shot to her feet, her chair toppling over. He rolled his eyes seeing the herd of people stampeding into the condo. The loud chatter that accompanied them made him chuckle. Lumin's eyes were everywhere as the crowd put themselves front and center. "Lumin, this is Alpha Squad. Squad, this is Lumin Edenridge."

Gabbs crawled into his lap and slung an arm around his shoulder. "Hi, I'm Gabriella. Mom calls me Gabbs, and Uncle Tony calls me Squirt."

Lumin laughed. Her cheeks blushed as she righted the chair. "So, you're Squirt, huh?"

Gabbs nodded her head vigorously. "I'm hungry, Uncle Tony."

"You're always hungry, Squirt." He handed her his fork and she dug in.

"Lumin, it's nice to see you again. I never got the chance to thank you," Nina said, walking up to her.

"Your daughter is beautiful."

"Thank you, and you remember Mace?"

"Hi, Mace."

He gave her a two-finger salute. "Sorry, bud. The wife said we had to pack up our gear and follow you. We owe Lumin too."

Lumin's brow tightened. "You cut your honeymoon short? That's not right."

Nina placed a hand on her shoulder. "It's kinda like the Musketeers. All for one and one for all."

Lumin gazed at the rest of the crowd and Nina made the introductions. Master Chief Mason Briggs, who they called Fox, and his wife, Kate, had two beautiful girls, both redheads; Caleb, whose team name was Stitch, and his family; Clay, their electronics guy, and his wife; and finally, Nathan Young and Ed Saxton, who came solo to the wedding.

"Where's the Admiral and Captain Cobbs?" Tony asked.

"Right here, Tinman."

Admiral Austen strode through the doorway with his son, Adam, in his arms and Kayla at his side, followed by Cobbs, Marg, and Kelsey. Kelsey quickly pushed her way through the adults and scrambled up on Tony's lap, nudging herself next to Squirt. He laughed and reached for another fork. "Suppose you're hungry too."

"Do you have dessert, Uncle Tony?"

"No, but we'll get some."

Kayla and Marg pressed their way through the crowd and shook Lumin's hand. "Nice to meet you, Lumin. I'm Kayla Austen."

Lumin looked more than overwhelmed, but at least she wasn't scared anymore. "There's a lot of you," she said.

"We kinda run in a pack." Kayla smiled at her. "This is my husband, Thane."

Lumin raised her blue inquisitive eyes to stare up at him. "Hello," She paused then added, "Sir."

Ghost didn't waste a second. "Lumin, we need to know—"

"Thane," Kayla snapped. "Stand down and let her eat dinner first. I'll order more to feed the troops, Tony." She slung a diaper bag over Ghost's shoulder. "And your son needs a change."

The Admiral tossed an uncomfortable gaze at his wife. "Of course." He cleared his throat. "Nice to meet you, Lumin. Thane Austen." He stretched his massive hand out and shook Lumin's.

Tony suppressed a chuckle. The Admiral was so pussy-whipped since he'd married Kayla. That sure as hell would never happen to him. As his gaze fell on Lumin, she leaned over and brushed Adam's little hand, and he gave her a big smile. Tony knew what the kid was feeling. She warmed him from the inside out too.

Ed, the newest member of the team, edged closer, laying a heated look on Lumin.

"Edward Saxton, ma'am," he said, introducing himself.

Anybody in the room could recognize the cocky smile and hungry look on Ed's face, but when Lumin reached out her hand she seemed enamored. A quick quirk of Ed's brow and the intensity of his stare caused an odd electric sensation in Tony's stomach.

"Grab a plate, Cracker," he said, using his team name and drawing Ed's gaze away from Lumin.

"Thanks, T-man, don't mind sharing dinner with such a beautiful guest."

Lumin blushed and glanced away. She blushed? What the fuck? No way in hell was Cracker making a move on her. Over his dead body!

Chapter Two

Lumin ate quietly while Tony's squad surrounded her, battling for airtime and never ceasing their banter. They talked and joked like a big family over an evening meal. The camaraderie between them was palpable. She didn't know much about the Navy life, but it was evident the Admiral and Captain Cobbs radiated a sense of everything being in control, and she relaxed a little.

Kayla appeared stoic and hauntingly beautiful. Lumin didn't miss the way the muscular monster of an admiral looked at his wife and son. It reminded her of the way Steven Porter looked at Moira with a deep, enduring love. The Admiral and Kayla's son, Adam, was a tiny version of his father with blond locks and enormous pale blue eyes.

"How old is your son?" she asked Kayla.

The Admiral piped up as Kayla's lips parted. "Ten months." The pride ebbing from the Admiral when he held his son's hands as Adam balanced on his chubby feet taking wobbly steps between his parents was the same as Steven Porter with the twins.

"He looks so much like you," Lumin said.

"He certainly has his father's vocal cords and appetite," Kayla added.

The Admiral raised a brow at his wife and let go of his son's hands so he could take a few independent steps to his mom.

The only side of Nina she'd seen was when Gabbs had been taken hostage, but now she was a fiery, funny redhead who teased her husband Mace, any chance she got. Mason Briggs reminded her of a mountain man—gruff and grassroots. She liked it when they called him Fox. It was a little confusing because they called each other by a number of names, mixing up team names with first and last names, she tried to remember who was who.

They called Caleb Stitch, but she didn't know why. Maybe he knitted. He had a taut, lean form, and a serious expression, but when he looked at his wife and cradled his infant in his arms, the man was as sweet as they came.

Nathan kept trying to catch her eye, and she avoided contact because he made her uncomfortable. It didn't take much to see he was one of those confirmed bachelors who wanted a good, no-strings-attached time. Tony had called him Tadpole.

"What part of the country do you come from, dahling?" Ed Saxton asked her.

He certainly was a handsome, well-built man, and she liked southern accents. "Everywhere."

"I bet you really grab the crowd's attention when you're performing." He gave her a huge southern smile. It was as broad as his shoulders. "I visit Vegas a couple times a year. Maybe—"

"Maybe you better get seconds before it's all gone," Tony said gruffly, and shoved a box of Chinese food across the table which slid to a stop against Ed's forearm.

"Think I've feasted enough," Ed said, and gave her a wink.

Tony fired a dangerous look Ed's way.

She didn't have a lot of experience dating. None, actually. Living alone in Vegas she learned how to quickly avert the cheap come-ons by drunken tourists. School and her act kept her busy and focused. A few guys from her classes asked her out, but a memory of Tony had lingered since December, and she'd politely turned them down. Not that dating had ever been a priority to her.

Both she and her brother had been raised in a devout Catholic home. No matter where they traveled, Sunday mornings were spent in church. As a teenager, modest warnings about the other sex were religiously cemented into her upbringing.

Even with those warnings looping in her mind, she often replayed the moment when Tony stood on the stairs of the Porters' mansion saying goodbye to her. Every time she envisioned it, her heart squeezed a little tighter, and then she would berate herself for thinking he was anything more than a decent man doing a good deed. All she had to do to reinforce the thought was take note he'd never contacted her after that night.

SEALs were legendary for their skills and their valor. Seeing them now, acting like a big, fun-loving family, reminded her of how alone she'd really been for the last four years. She'd been raised on the road, shunted from one show to the next when her parents signed on for a new performance. They'd finally settled in Las Vegas, and her mother had put her foot down saying she wanted Lumin and her brother to finish high school in one place. A year after she graduated her parents received an opportunity for a show in Paris and they took it, leaving her under the watchful eye of the Porters.

"Hey, where are ya?" Tony asked. She started when his finger brushed against her knuckle.

She offered him a wan smile.

"Here, Lumin, have some dessert," Gabbs said, sliding a plate with cake smothered in ice cream in front of her.

"Thank you, Gabriella."

"You can call me Squirt if you want. Uncle Tony does, and since he's got a biiig crush on you, you can too."

"Ah—" Tony swept Gabbs up into his arms. "Take your matchmaker," he said, landing her in Mace's arms.

"My girl's observant. What can I say?" Mace laughed at him, and wandered into the living room. Squirt rested her chin on his shoulder and gave Tony an overdramatized wink.

"Oh man," Tony chortled. He bit down on his lip, embarrassed to be outed by a seven-year-old. "Sorry, she's incorrigible like her mom."

"Heard you, Tinman," Nina drawled, sitting on the couch with her back to him.

Lumin laughed out loud and felt her cheeks redden. The room was full of people, but her gaze kept slipping to the fair-haired man with sharp hazel eyes. She was used to fit men performing in the show, but there was something heroic about Tony that she'd never seen before, and maybe a little dangerous. He had very broad, straight shoulders and a molded torso. His T-shirt strained taut around his upper arms and bulged from the sleeves. *Capable* swept through her mind again. Tony could accomplish anything.

"Lumin?" Admiral Austen beckoned her to join the men on the patio.

"He's a little intimidating," she said under her breath.

"You're right, but he's a good man. You can trust the Admiral. You can trust any of us."

She nodded and was surprised when Tony slid his fingers between hers and gently prodded her toward the patio. Lumin noticed the women and children stayed in the living room talking

amongst themselves as if they knew the time for business had
come.

She squirmed in her chair when the Admiral's gaze fell on her.
The warm look that he shared with his wife had turned to solid ice.
Sitting beside him, Captain Cobbs placed his gray-eyed attention
on her as did the rest of Tony's team. Tony's hand gently gripped
her shoulder when she stiffened with nerves, keeping it there as she
retold her story to the men watching her intently.

"Admiral, how do you want to deal with this?" Captain Cobbs
asked when she finished.

"Carefully," he said. "Lumin, you mentioned you thought they
knew who you were. Explain that."

"I notice things and have a tendency to remember faces." The
Admiral listened, but she knew he was assessing her at the same
time. He'd been doing it from the moment he walked in the door.
"I—" She choked on her words. Tony knelt beside her chair.

"Lumin, this might feel like an inquisition, but we need to
know everything in order to come up with a plan," Tony reassured,
taking her hand in both of his.

"After I left the hotel room, I took the closest exit to the lobby
to get a cab. Two men watched me. I'd seen them the night before
when I was with Dr. Carmichael. They'd been watching us then
too. I caught sight of them at the second bar we went to. At first I
thought it was coincidence, but when I saw them again at the third
place, I began to worry. I think they have something to do with
this."

"You're going to stay here with Tony," the Admiral ordered.
"I'll find out if there's any chatter on this. If not, I'll start a case on
it, but it may not remain in our hands."

Cobbs pursed his lips. "If it falls into CDC hands they may
turn it over to CIA or FBI, then we lose control."

"I'll assess once we know more. Until then," the Admiral's
gaze dropped on her with a jarring chill, "you remain with Petty
Officer Bale. He'll keep you out of harm's way."

"Admiral, we're deploying in a week," Mace said, leaning
against the patio railing, muscle-ripped arms crossed over his
chest.

"Your mission may be to find a threat to the homeland," the
Admiral replied.

"Thane?" Kayla stood in the doorway with their son, Adam, pitching a very loud fit.

The Admiral pushed his chair back and rose to an impressive six-foot-three. "That's my cue, gentlemen." Kayla placed their son in his arms, and he raised him above his head. Adam stopped crying and gave his father a big grin, gnawing on his finger. "Giving mom a bad time, son?" He chuckled. "Chip off the old Frog."

"Get your ass in the car, no-good SEAL," Kayla ordered. She stepped aside, but couldn't dodge the kiss the Admiral planted on her as he passed. Kayla turned doe eyes on her. "You're safe, Lumin. Never doubt that with this team. They can accomplish the impossible. See ya, guys."

"Later, Snow White," the guys said almost in unison.

"Snow White?" Lumin queried, looking at Tony.

"That's her team name."

"She's a SEAL?"

"Nope," Tony answered, "but all our wives—I mean their wives, might as well be. They're as brave as we are. They are," he corrected quickly. "Not me, I mean."

"Heard that," Nina called from inside the condo.

Mace's shoulders shook as he laughed. "And they have great hearing."

Gabbs skipped outside and grabbed Mace's hand. "Time to go home, Dad. I want to see Lexi."

"Sure, Little Red." He picked Gabbs up in his arms then gave Tony a fist bump. "Later, men."

"Guess we better get out of here too," Cobbs said, rising. "You need anything, shout out, Tinman."

"Roger that."

Tony scooped a squealing Squirt from Mace by one ankle and dangled her upside down as he walked to the front door with Nina and Mace. Ed, who'd remained relatively quiet tucked in a dark corner of the patio during her questioning, stepped to her side once everyone had vacated. "I'm a little concerned, Miss Lumin."

"Why?" She had to crank her neck back to look up at the tall, impressive southerner.

"I don't like the accessibility of Tony's apartment, and I've got an extra bedroom at my place."

Tony held the front door open as Nathan exited. His head cranked around as if missing someone. Seeing Ed on the patio, Tony's expression turned severe as he marched toward them. "I think the Admiral's orders were for me to stay here."

Tony filled the patio doorway and his gaze landed on Ed with a sharp snap. Ed ignored him and knelt down on one knee. "My intentions are southern style honorable, Miss Lumin. I also live on the tenth floor. Not as easy access," Ed said directly to Tony. "You're on ground level, Tinman."

"Do you think someone is watching me?" Maybe she should move to a safer place, even though she felt safe with Tony?

Tony's hazel eyes grew not just angry, but predatory. "We're good here, Cracker, but thanks."

"The last twenty-four hours have been hard on her. She needs a bed, not a couch."

"Buddy," Tony growled. "Don't worry about the sleeping arrangements. Lumin stays with me."

"Maybe he's right, Tony. What if someone did follow me?" She stood, but Tony stayed her by wrapping his arm around her waist.

"Then I'll stay awake." Tony kept a hostile glare on Ed. "Speaking of rest, Lumin needs some."

"I don't want to bring trouble to your front door, Tony."

Ed shrugged. "I could stay. We'll split the night."

Tony jerked his head at Ed, and he followed Tony. Low, unintelligible words passed between the men, then she heard the door click shut.

Night had descended, and her gaze slid across the shadows on the playground. For the first time in a long while she felt safe. Even before yesterday, she was on edge. On her own, she always remained aware and it was tiring. Tony reappeared, drawing her from her thoughts. "Where's Ed?"

"Relieved of duty," he said, sitting down across from her.

"Tony, I really think you should take me to a hotel."

With a perturbed grunt, Tony sat back in his chair. "Is it because you don't think I can protect you?" His jaw cracked to a jagged angle, but his gaze relayed uncertainty.

"No, God no, not at all. I don't want you to get hurt because of me."

His brows popped and a silly grin crossed his firm, full lips. "I do dangerous for a living. Watching over you is an easy assignment."

Assignment? Of course that's how he saw her. Her adolescent daydreams of the handsome SEAL had created a romance good enough for bookstore shelves. SEALs were realists. Military men. Tony would watch her until Admiral Austen changed his orders. He hadn't shunted Ed out the door because he'd been flirting; he did it because he'd been charged with her protection.

"Sorry, I guess that must have been a little overwhelming meeting everyone like that," Tony said.

"They seem very—capable."

He chuckled. "Yeah, I'd bet my life on it."

"How long have you been a SEAL?"

"Eleven years. Mace and I went through BUD/S together."

"What's that?"

"Basic Underwater Demolitions training. Tough, but we both made it."

Lumin's heart seesawed a little. His eyes, filled with intelligence, centered on her as he spoke. He wasn't as large as Mace or the admiral; instead he had a lean, taut physique. She could imagine him being a strong swimmer. "Nina said Mace is a sniper, and Kate told me Fox is a senior Frogman, whatever that is. What do you do?"

Tony surveyed her for a moment, then explained. "I'm a heavy weapons specialist and Lead Breacher."

She raised her brows, not understanding.

"I go in first. That means I clear a path, sometimes using explosives. Basically, I'm a specialist on all mechanical and explosive entry issues."

"That sounds dangerous." Her blood chilled a little to think Tony was always the first to face danger.

Tony's gaze dropped to the table.

"It's very dangerous, isn't it?"

"Hazard of the job for any SEAL." Tony laid an inquisitive look on her. "Walking on a thin pole dangling mid-air doesn't seem very safe to me."

She shrugged. "It's second nature."

"Have you ever been hurt?"

"Once, when I was younger. Youthful exuberance. Broke my arm. Nothing serious."

"Think I like the idea of you being a lawyer. It's safer."

A niggle of nervous excitement erupted in her belly. "Mace mentioned deployment. What does that mean?"

"Means we're on the road for seven months, give or take."

"Away from home?" She was surprised by that. "How many times do you get to come home during that time?"

He shifted in his chair. "Never. We stay out until the deployment is finished."

"How do Kayla, Nina, and the other wives handle that?"

Tony's gaze darted toward the children's park that lay next to his patio. "It's not easy. Their kids grow up without a dad. We—they—miss all the important milestones. The wives are pretty tight. While a team is on deployment, often another team who is home will help out." Tony shrugged. "Lots of single SEALs because of the life we live."

Lumin read something in his eyes, but she wasn't sure what it was. He probably had plenty of girlfriends, not just one. "What will you do after?"

"After what?" he asked.

"After being a SEAL."

His brows rose as if he'd never considered it. "Haven't thought that far ahead."

Tony's cell rumbled on the tabletop. He picked it up, read the text, then put it down.

"Aren't you going to answer that?"

"No, I'm going to clean up the mess the kids made in my place." He left the table and she couldn't help herself. With a quick shoulder check, she fingered his phone so she could peek at the text.

Are ya home yet, baby? My wet girly parts miss you.

"Whoa," she exclaimed.

Tony appeared and snapped up his phone. Guess he wasn't lacking in the girlfriend department. If that was the type of girl he was used to, he wouldn't be interested in her. She gawked up at him even though her cheeks heated with embarrassment. "I'll help you clean up," she said, and hurriedly brushed past him picking up plates on her way to the kitchen, but she didn't miss him mutter, "Damn" under his breath.

* * * *

After Tony changed the sheets on his bed, knowing he would give it to Lumin, he returned to the living room. Once again she'd disappeared, and he wished like hell she'd stop doing that because it put his pulse into high gear. She wasn't on the patio, and it leaped into overdrive until he spotted her. "What the hell!"

Lumin had wandered into the kid's playground. He watched as she balanced on the horizontal crossbeam of the swing set, twenty feet in the air. Under the moonlight, her blonde hair shimmered. Her parents had named her correctly; she was luminous.

He rested his forearms on the railing and watched. Almost mystical, her slender frame gracefully stepped with precision, forward two steps, and then backwards. Maybe she needed the thrill. He could understand that. She'd shocked him asking what he'd do after being a SEAL. Was there such a thing? Once you've been a SEAL, everything else paled. He wasn't a nine to five kinda guy. Nothing would change that. Disappointment swelled in his chest. The guy who would catch Lumin would be a regular Joe. Her husband would come home every night thinking how fuckin' lucky he was to have her. Tony tried to shake the thought from his head, but it refused to leave.

Placing a hand on the railing, he jumped it and strolled to stand at the base of the swing set. "I'd say you'd better come down or you'll get hurt, but I know otherwise." He tensed, when she leaned over and then did a perfect walk-over like an Olympic gymnast on a balance beam. "Okay, that kinda bugs me."

Her sweet laughter fell on him like stardust and covered him in something warm and dreamy. Nina had ramped up his emotions and she'd always have a special place in his heart, but this woman intrigued him as well as made him nervous. Lumin reminded him of a butterfly that flitted between flowers, never landing for long. Kind of like Tinker Bell. "I hope you don't do that on top of the Stratosphere every night."

Lumin spread her filly-like legs, grabbed the bar with both hands and rolled forward. Tony sprung into action, and gripped her around the hips as she dangled by her arms. She let go and slid down his body; with every inch, sparks ignited inside him. When her feet touched the ground he wasn't ready to release her, even though she leaned away.

"Sorry, it's a SEAL's nature to come to the rescue," he said quietly, staring into her tropical-blue eyes. Long lashes whisked her cheeks when she blinked. Being this close to her stroked past temptation by a football field length and fell into the "must have" category. He wanted to touch her perfect, fair skin and graze his finger along her delicate features. Everything about her waved a red flag at him.

"Did you answer your text?" she asked.

Talk about putting his fire out. "I guess that made me look like a man-whore, didn't it?"

"A little."

Was he going to try and convince her he wasn't, because it would be a lie? Changing the subject would be the same as admitting he was. SEALs often avoided a straight answer, but mostly to protect their identity. He didn't want to lie to her. *Damn, damn, damn.*

"Everyone has a past, right? Doesn't mean the future plays the same hand." When all else failed, euphemisms worked. He did it all the time to the squad when things got too tense. Staring into her pretty features, tense wouldn't be the right word. Dumbfounded might come close. Would she let him kiss her? Should he ask? He never asked. What—was he fifteen? She nibbled on her lower lip, and the afterburners on his lust ignited. Sweet. Sincere. Smart...how many 's' adjectives could he come up with? Single? Was she? She would have run to her boyfriend if she had one.

"I think your past is a little more colorful than mine. Maybe you should answer her text, Tony. It's the polite thing to do."

Hope winked out of existence and he released her, feeling like a teenager rebuked. He cleared his throat. "Technically you're part of a mission, or you could be, and we don't get involved with people we're meant to rescue."

"I don't expect dinner and a movie. I don't need to be rescued. I just need a little guidance. By tomorrow I'll be out of your hair."

Lumin spoke intelligently, but seemed so damn innocent for some reason. Not likely. She worked in Las Vegas. City of sin.

"What?" *Leaving? She wanted to leave?* He shook his head as she sprung onto the kid's merry-go-round. "You can't go," he said, watching her step with bare feet across the beams that sectioned the platform into pie-shaped pieces.

"You know the whole story now. I'm sure your admiral will do something about it. You don't need me for anything."

He slowly palmed the beams of the round platform hoping to bring her closer, but she jumped from bar to bar as he turned it. The only way to reach her was to climb onboard. He gave the child's ride a push before he leaped on. With her willowy arms outstretched, she balanced on the small bar and bowed low before him like a lady from the 1500s. He couldn't help but smile at her performance.

"I am but the messenger, sir," she said with a British drawl.

"Not a 'sir.'" He vaulted over the beams quickly, catching her around the hips and snatching her from her perch. For the second time in five minutes she was in his arms. "Stop that. You make me nervous."

"I thought SEALs were brave men who remained calm in the face of danger," she teased.

"No, we pray we don't get our asses shot off, and use our training to make sure it doesn't happen."

Her dainty hands rested on his shoulders. Following the sway of her tiny waist and gently palming her hips had his thoughts jumping to this position without their clothes, and the ache in his groin intensified.

With a quick swivel and a hop, she leaped onto the bar once again. "Up you go," she said, gently tugging on his hand.

"What? You want me to stand on that?"

The ride spun in slow circles. Crazy, but he found his footing and rose with a few jerky movements. It seemed easy enough, but she was still holding his hand. When she released him he lost his equilibrium, or maybe that was just the effect she had on him.

"Stay there," she said, and jumped to the ground. Placing her hands on the bar, she pushed to make it go faster, then jumped back on the ride.

"Woman, are you crazy?" His arms twirled to keep himself upright.

"Crazy is going on dangerous missions and putting your life on the line," she said, reaching for his hand. "Walk."

"The Admiral is going to be pissed if I fall and break an arm."

"Head up," she instructed.

He did as she said.

"Now close your eyes."

"No way."

"Try it," she urged.

He closed his eyes and felt himself lose his balance. She gripped his hand, and he found balance again.

"Put your concentration on what isn't in motion," she said. She hopped to the platform and her hands circled each of his thighs. "You and I. Everything around us is moving, but we are the center. We are balanced."

It was the strangest thing. He closed his eyes and realized she was right, and the feeling he was going to fall evaporated.

"Where did you learn that?" he asked as the ride stopped spinning and he eased himself down to stand in front of her.

"My mother. It was one of my first lessons as an aerialist."

"My mother worked at a bar and brought a different guy home every night." The small smile she wore disintegrated, and he wished he hadn't said it.

"I'm sorry."

His hand rose to touch her cheek, and he couldn't help but wonder how many men had the honor of having her in their arms. "Don't be. It taught me to be self-sufficient. I had to figure things out on my own."

Before he could touch her face, she intercepted his hand and drew it to his side. "That sounds lonely."

He didn't have the best start in life, but it made him tough, and he needed that when he faced the challenges his profession brought. "It gave me good instincts, and those instincts are telling me you're not going anywhere."

"I think I'll turn in," she said, stepping from the ride and heading toward the condo.

"I changed the sheets on my bed." Hell, if he couldn't be with her, at least her scent would be left on his sheets.

She stopped. "I'm not taking your bed, Tony. I'll sleep on the couch."

"Ah, yeah you are."

"No, I'm not," she said, gripping the patio railing and springing over it like a deer.

He followed. With an easy sweep, he gripped her under her legs and swept her up into his arms. "Yes, you are." He marched down the hallway and gently dipped her onto the bed. He couldn't resist, and planted his hands on either side of her. "If I'm the man-whore you think I am, then you know that if I can't share my bed with you, I'll want a memory of you in it even if I'm not here."

With only three inches to spare between his lips and hers, she stared up at him, her hands palming his chest, but not pushing him away. Her eyes spoke differently; they weren't at half-mast with lust or flashing a sign of anticipation signaling *let's get down to hot and sweaty.*

He gave her a wolfish grin, but it quickly melted away because it was a façade. The one he used to get between a girl's thighs. He needed a canister of oxygen to clear his head and some distance between him and Lumin but instead, his mouth dipped an inch closer and the air thickened between them. Wanting to kiss her sweet lips overwhelmed him. A tremble of unharnessed need shot through him. It was just a kiss, but he desired it more than anything. Words came in place of his need. He said them just as he would have touched her lips—with a whisper. "I didn't want to leave you on those steps, Lumin. I've never forgotten you."

She barely breathed out the words, "Good night, Tony."

Her dismissal extinguished his hope, but his need surged as he backed up. Stalling in the doorway, he said, "Sleep well."

After he closed the door, he tugged at his jeans, the erection in his pants pulsing. He hadn't missed the swell of her breasts with him hovering above her. He would definitely not forget her scent or the flush in her pale cheeks. When he closed his eyes tonight, her image walking on the beam under the moonlight would replay itself over and over again.

After making sure the doors and windows were secure, Tony checked his Sig 9mm, then set it on the lower shelf of his coffee table. His phone charged and within grabbing distance, he laid back on the couch, never imagining he'd be sleeping on it. A wide grin crossed his lips. Maybe he could feign sleepwalking.

With one arm tucked behind his head, he stared up at the ceiling, his SEAL brain pacing the options ahead. He'd wait for Admiral Austen to relay any info he might find out, and then—and then what? Keep Lumin close, that's what, but the question was whether he could do it without breaking company policy. In other words, making love to her. Screwing her, damn it. Making love was for guys like his buddy Mace.

Kayla and Admiral Austen popped into his head. The Admiral had risked not only his job but his life, because he loved her. Nina would have traveled to the four corners of the earth to help Mace overcome his injury. Captain Cobbs was a cold, lethal son of a bitch, but when it came to Marg he turned over and put all four paws in the air. When the right woman came into a man's life, he'd risk everything to keep her, protect her. With his eyes adjusted to the darkness, he glanced around his bachelor pad. He liked his space. Variety and no lingering responsibilities worked for him.

Why the hell was he thinking about this shit anyway? Lumin had asked for his help, not his hand in marriage for Christ's sake.

An hour passed by, then two. He glanced at the clock just as the short arm was about to strike zero-three-hundred hours.

The shattering of glass and Lumin's scream vaulted him from the couch; he swiped the weapon from the table before his feet hit the floor. He nearly knocked her over in the hallway. He didn't wait, snagging her hand and running for the living room. Two options. How many men were there? Fuck it. Front door. With a gentle push, he held Lumin against the wall, at the same time feeling her fluttering heart on his arm. He opened the door ready to fire. *Clear*.

With a *thunk* a bullet shot through the drywall left of his head. Pushing Lumin behind him and swinging around he fired back, missing the dark shadow who careened back into the hallway for cover.

"Let's go," he whispered. Eyes everywhere, he ran for his car, digging for his keys. The second bullet passed him on the left and dug itself into the grass. They were aiming for him, not Lumin. She dove into the passenger side of his car. "Head down." Two more bullets struck the back window as the engine roared to life. He floored it, leaving a half inch of tread on the road. Lumin straightened, and he pressed her down again. "Not yet." He glanced in the rear view mirror. Headlights, two blocks behind him. Time for some evasive driving.

"Where are we going?" she asked, fingers gripping his leg.

"The base. They can't follow us there. Hang on." He took the corners hard and sharp. If he attracted a cop's attention, all the better, but whenever ya needed one...

The engine roared with his foot heavy on the gas as they slid onto the Strand. The lights weren't behind him anymore, but that didn't mean shit. Braking hard in front of the security gate, he showed his ID.

"And who's that?" the young security guard asked.

This guy had to be new.

"A guest." He darted a look behind him. A black two door Ford Acura crawled by.

"She'll have to get clearance, and…"

"I need in these gates. Call Admiral Austen for clearance."

"You know the Ghost?" The kid's face lit up.

"Kid, I'm gonna have your job in thirty seconds flat if you don't let me in."

"Sir, if there's a security issue, I need to know about it."

"I'm not a sir. Ah, fuck it." He hit the speed dial for the Admiral. A groggy Kayla answered.

"Tinman, what's wrong?" Before the sentence was out, she was fully awake.

"Bad guys came looking for Lumin. I'm at the base gates. The new kid doesn't want to let me in without the red tape."

A couple seconds later, the phone in the security hut rang and the kid answered it. "Yes, sir. Immediately." The kid hung up. "You're cleared. I'm sorry, sir."

"Told you kid, I'm not a sir." The bar rose, and he drove through with a sigh of relief. His cell rang. "You mind getting that?"

Lumin answered. "Hi, Kayla, yeah we're in. Okay, I'll tell him." She disconnected. "Kayla said we need to go to Admiral Pennington's office. Admiral Austen is on his way, and he's got information."

"We'll make a quick stop at the team boatshed."

"Why?"

Lumin had put things in perspective quickly. He liked the fact that she had her head on straight. He stopped the car and got out. "Come on."

They entered the boathouse, but since luck seemed to float between good and bad, the shed was filled with a class of recruits. They watched as he and Lumin strode in with him shirtless and her pant-less and a skimpy slip of a top. Of course, she was getting all the attention. "Eyes front, assholes," he barked at them. CPO Barber looked up and his brows popped. "Don't ask."

Barber gave him a halfhearted salute. "Put your eyes back on your gear, gentlemen," Barber ordered, but that didn't stop a few sideways smirks.

Tony cracked his locker and pulled out a shirt, and handed Lumin some pants. "Can't be meeting up with the Base Commander and the Admiral with those gorgeous legs to distract them."

"Thanks." She slipped them on and he chuckled seeing them drape from her hips.

He snagged a belt from his locker and slipped it through the loops, not minding the close contact while he worked it around her waist.

"I can do that, ya know," she said, followed by a quirk of her lips.

"What fun would that be?" He stepped away and let her buckle it. "Did you see them?"

"Only for a second."

"Caucasian?"

She wrapped the extra belt halfway around her waist, and tucked it in. "No, dark-skinned. At least the first guy who came through the window."

Tony buttoned his shirt. "Well, we know you were right about being followed. They must have been on your tail since you left yesterday morning."

"They tried to kill me," she said it as if she didn't quite believe it herself, swallowing and gazing up at him. "Thank you. I don't think I'd be alive now if I hadn't called you."

His fingers itched to palm her delicate jaw and draw her to him, but he couldn't, especially not with an audience. "You're a smart woman. Even on your own, I think you could have outwitted them. Ya ready to meet the Base Commander? He's a tough old bastard, but he's also one smart SEAL."

"Tony?" He nodded, taking a step to distance himself. "Do you think I'm going to have to hide for the rest of my life? Is everything I've worked for gone because of one lousy decision?"

"No, Lumin. I know you're out of your comfort zone right now. Most civilians would be, but you're not most women." He gently palmed the hollow in her back, guiding her out.

"But you have to leave on deployment soon. I keep asking myself, what then?"

He stopped her once they'd cleared the entrance to the boathouse and away from prying eyes. "One step at a time, my lady." His itchy fingers got their way and he brushed her cheek. So soft. "I think it would have been me who'd be lost if you'd been hurt." He held his breath, and when her gaze shot to his lips it was like a HALO, *High Altitude Low Opening*, jump from a plane. He dove for her parted mouth…and oh, heaven help him, it was more than beautiful.

His other hand snaked around her waist, crushing her against his chest. The sound of the sea close by went silent while a white surf surged inside him. His soul opened up and roared at him. With palms flat on his back, she clung to him. He'd felt lust before, but he'd never known thunder. With two steps, he had her pinned against the wall. His mouth and tongue had a mission of their own, and it scared him because every woman before her vacated his memory. The smell of her skin, the taste of her lips rallied together, overwhelmed him, leaving him senseless.

The sound of the men preparing to depart the boathouse rallied his senses. Opening his eyes, he allowed himself to drown in hers. She looked as overwhelmed as he felt. His heart thumped with an uneven beat as he drew her delicate hand into his. The impending meeting had better be quick. If her kiss could do this to him, making love to her would shatter both of them.

Chapter Three

Admiral Austen intercepted them as they entered the Base Commander's office. Lumin's bravery fizzled seeing the admiral's business expression which looked more like a man on a mission to kill. It turned out he'd been on the phone to Washington when Tony had called to request entry onto the base.

Admiral Pennington was already in his office waiting for them. After the introductions were made, they each took a seat. Lumin gazed around the room pausing on the pictures and awards tacked on the wall behind the large maple desk. Nothing was out of place, and every surface shone. Pennington greeted them with a serious expression on his aging face.

Admiral Austen settled in a chair to her left. The guy was huge. Lumin wondered how he didn't crush Kayla, a waif of a woman, when they made love, but what did she know about that? Nothing. At least not until a few minutes ago when Tony left her dizzy with his kiss.

"I called a friend in Washington to get details," the Admiral announced, breaking into her foggy thoughts.

Admiral Pennington leaned forward. "You called the President at this hour, Ghost? Christ!"

Austen deflected the comment. "They're three hours ahead of us, and he's up at zero-five-thirty to jog every morning. I asked him if he had been given any details on this threat."

"And?" Pennington sat back and waited.

"The answer was yes. For security reasons only he, Boiston of CDC and Harrelson at the CIA know the details, although they are scant. Miss Edenridge provided more information than the White House possessed. After what just occurred at Petty Officer Bale's home, I'd say the threat has merit."

"Agreed." Pennington turned his shrewd gaze on her. "Miss Edenridge, we'll put you in protective custody. Under Naval law we can do this, and keep you here for national security reasons."

Tony leaned forward. "Sir, I have offered to stay with—"

"You're deploying in five days, are you not, Petty Officer Bale?" Admiral Pennington's gruff words suggested Tony cease and desist.

Tony shot a look at Admiral Austen then said, "Yes, sir."

A muscle ticced in Tony's neck and Lumin's pulse stepped up the pace to match it. Tony was being ordered away from her.

Admiral Pennington's shaved head and perma-frown unsettled her.

"You'll be protected, Miss Edenridge, I promise you that," he said.

"Sol?" Admiral Austen stood. "I need Petty Officer Bale to remain with her. If she's a target, he has enough experience to keep her safe until we know more."

Pennington eyed Tony then her. Not flinching under his scrutiny was difficult. She knew absolutely nothing about the politics of the Navy, but she was thankful Admiral Austen was trying to keep them together. She wasn't sure who outranked who, but she prayed it was Admiral Austen.

"You can accompany Ms. Edenridge for a week, Bale," Pennington said. "I'd like to speak with Admiral Austen in private. You're dismissed, Petty Officer Bale. Thank you for bringing this information forward, Ms. Edenridge. I'll approve temporary quarters on the base for you."

"Petty Officer Bale?" Admiral Austen crossed his arms and gave him a long look. "I'd like you to relocate Miss Edenridge elsewhere."

"Why's that, Ghost?" Admiral Pennington asked.

Austen didn't even spare him a glance.

Tony stood, and she did the same. "Where, sir?"

"Where I found Snow White."

Tony didn't blink, and nodded shortly. "Yes, sir."

"Where's that?" Admiral Pennington asked, obviously not liking the evasiveness.

Austen turned his attention to the Base Commander. "Her old condo at the Landing." With a cold gaze he said, "You're dismissed, Bale."

"Thank you, sir." She and Tony left the admirals to their confab. When the tepid early morning air struck them, Tony gave her a tired smile. "I know where I can buy you a lousy cup of coffee."

She breathed out a short laugh, relieved she'd survived the intensity of the meeting. "Sounds good."

Grabbing a couple cardboard cups, Tony led her down to the beach and they found a log to settle against. They watched the sun rise. She'd never done that before with a man. There were a lot of things she hadn't done with a man, especially one like Tony. Her mind swatted at her mother's words warning of sin.

As the sun breached the horizon, a group of men jogged down the beach. "Why does the Admiral want me to stay at Kayla's condo? Wouldn't I be safer here?"

Tony's brow tightened. "That's not where Ghost found her."

"I don't understand."

"It means Ghost doesn't trust anyone. He didn't reveal all of the conversation he had with the President, which means this is far more complex than we thought."

"Was Kayla lost?"

"Long story, but he didn't find her at her condo. I have to take you into the mountains. Captain Cobbs has a ranch up there."

"Won't they follow us?"

He turned a small smile onto his lips, and she instantly warmed. Tony was such a handsome man. Something about him spoke loud and clear. He was capable, smart, and in charge of his destiny, something she'd lost in the last day, or given Tony to decide for her.

"We'll make sure they don't."

A shout drew her attention. "What are they?" she asked, seeing the group of men remained in formation as they ran down the beach.

"Phase Two class."

"How can you tell?"

"Color of their shirts."

"What does that mean?"

Tony hooked an arm around his knee. "Means they're luckier than most. By the end, there might be eight guys who make it."

"How many were there to start with?"

"Hundred plus. It varies."

"You're kidding."

"No, ma'am."

The men were ordered to stop a little farther down the beach, and they all dropped to do pushups. "How many passed in your class?"

"Ten of us."

"It's very difficult to become a Navy SEAL, isn't it?"

He turned to gaze at her. "Yeah, I don't want to sound like a conceited pr...bastard, but only the best make it."

"How old were you when you started?"

His grin broadened. "Are you trying to figure out how old I am?"

She jerked her head, caught in the act.

"I'm thirty, soon to be thirty-one."

"Uh-huh."

A sly smile made his eyes twinkle in the early morning light. "If I fessed up, so should you."

Seven years difference between them. That wasn't a lot, but he might think so. "I'm legal."

He chuckled. "I'd hope so if you're working in Vegas. Why don't you want to tell me?"

"Twenty-four," she said and watched his expression flick with concern. She'd hoped there would be none. He emptied his cup and crushed it with a slow squeeze of his hand and a long look out over the ocean. "Tony, I—never mind."

She jumped to her feet, and his gaze crept up her body, but a curtain dropped in front of him, cutting his energy off from her. She knew it by the tone of his voice.

"I never asked whether you needed to call someone."

"If I call Steven Porter, he'd go nuts. My parents asked the Porters to look out for me, and he takes the job too seriously."

"I meant…" he stood, his expression blank, "I mean, someone you're close to."

"Who?" She'd already told him her parents were in Europe.

Tony brushed a hand through his hair, and his jaw sharpened as if he didn't want to say it. "I should have asked if you had a boyfriend before, before, well…what I did."

"No, it's umm—I don't have one." She paused and felt her cheeks heat. "It's been a while."

"Are we talking a month or a year?" he asked.

She swallowed. "Umm, well, the last one was eighth grade. It lasted a whole day."

"Eighth…grade," he repeated, shock dawning across his sharp features.

"I moved around a lot, remember?"

"You've been in Vegas for a few years. You're telling me you never…no one ever?"

"Vegas is a short stop."

"But there are people who live and work there."

"I refused to be distracted from my schooling." She knew where this questioning was going.

"Lumin—" his mouth gaped.

"My father was very protective of me, and so was my brother. I wasn't allowed to date, and we moved around so much I hardly had time to make friends."

Tony blinked. "Have, have." He shook his head. "Have you even kissed a guy before?" The words rushed from his mouth.

She laughed and bit her lower lip. "Of course, an hour ago, or was it that bad you've forgotten already?"

Tony's jaw sagged then he sputtered, "Are you trying to tell me, I was—"

"My first kiss?" She locked her fingers behind her back. "Yes."

The shock flashed across his features like a lightning strike. "You have got to be kidding me."

She shrugged. "I was home schooled. When my brother Jed and I weren't learning the fundamentals of math and English, we were training with mom and dad." She debated for only a second. "My parents are very religious. I grew up with strict rules, especially when it came to boys. Why do you look so shocked?"

He shook his head to clear it. "I'm—I don't know. It's just not—common, I—"

"I get that after seeing your text message."

Tony's cell bleeped and he swept it from his belt. "It's time to go. We'll take you to Cobbs' ranch. I'll have one of the guys from Team Three stay with you." He gazed into the sand instead of at her.

"What do you mean? I thought you were staying with me." She actually took a step back when a cold and determined stare came to rest on her. This was the warrior, and he'd made a decision. One he wasn't including her in.

"No, Lumin. I can't."

A squeeze of failure or maybe inadequacy made her shy away. She'd thought this man was different, but he wasn't. "I get it. I don't send text messages telling guys how dripping wet my girly parts are." She turned away, but he caught her arm.

"If I go with you, I will take what doesn't belong to me. You don't understand because you don't have the experience." Tony's brow shot together. "I can't be around you."

"Why?"

"You want honest?" He shook his head slowly. An internal battle waged war inside him, and the determined SEAL was winning. "Sex is all I think about when I stand too close to you. I don't deserve you, but that won't stop me from trying to possess you. I don't do virgins, Lumin. You're twenty-four; our age difference is enough, but you most definitely can't give me what you should only give to the man you fall in love with, and I'm not that guy."

Rebuked, her heart shriveled. The man she'd dreamed about, maybe worshipped a little, pushed her back across an invisible line. She nodded then straightened her shoulders. At least he was honest, but it didn't stop the canyon of disappointment that cracked open inside her. She couldn't help but wonder whether his decision would be different if she weren't a virgin.

* * * *

Six hours and one award-winning decoy later had Lumin safely on Cobbs' ranch. She stood on the wrap-around deck, and Tony stood on the ground staring up at her. The moment was identical to the night he'd left her in Las Vegas. The difference this time was he knew for certain he was walking away from something special, and seeing her uncertainty made it harder.

Mace nudged his shoulder. "What the hell are you doing, Tinman?"

"What do you mean?" he said, giving her a nod good-bye and heading toward the vehicles. He was going to lock himself inside and handcuff his wrist to the door.

"You're letting Ross stay here to watch her?"

He turned his gaze on his friend. "It's safer that way."

Mace's brows rose. "Safer for who? You? Her? I'm not saying Ross won't keep her safe, I don't know if you've noticed, but the guy can't stop gawking at her. You leave them here alone, and—"

"Nothing will happen, believe me. Besides, Ross is cool. He's a good man."

"Look at me." Mace hammered him on the arm. "What the fuck is that supposed to mean? You're not? Get a grip."

"When it comes to her, the truth is I won't be able to keep it in my pants, all right?" He stalked away, but Mace kept stride.

"So what? She obviously likes you."

"She's a bloody virgin. I kissed her this morning, and it was her first kiss for fuck's sake."

Mace stopped, and gripped him so he would too. "Seriously?"

"Yeah. Seriously. I guess I assumed living in Vegas she was like every other hot-blooded woman and had a past. She's been very sheltered up until a few years ago, and by the sound of it, her mother breathed fire and brimstone about the debauchery of the male species." He shook his head. "And she's right. I wouldn't even know what to do with a virgin, and staying with her is too much temptation. Besides that, she's only twenty-four. Almost seven years difference between us."

"She's twenty-four, big deal. What's the real reason?"

The question stunned him. "What do ya think?"

"How about you might have feelings for her, and that's why you're concerned about her innocence. That doesn't make you a prick. It means it's time you take a look at yourself and see what everyone else sees."

Tony shrugged.

"Don't fucking shrug it off. You fell for Nina. You went the distance for us, even though it might have meant our friendship would have been severed. For some reason you've always thought less of yourself, and the women we rolled around in the sheets with who gave it up freely were the only type you deserved. You're wrong."

"Problems?" Ghost's throaty timbre broke the tense stare between him and Mace.

"Yeah, he's being a stupid shit," Mace spouted.

"I ordered you to watch over her, Petty Officer Bale, not Ross. Why is he putting his gear in the ranch house?"

"Because I told him to. I start deployment in five days."

"You," Ghost growled. "Do as ordered. The President has viable information that the bacteria was not only weaponized in the U.S. as Miss Edenridge confirmed, but it might have fingers extending into American cooperation. They need to follow the trail until the lab is found, along with someone who will talk. Alpha Squad is the only group of men I will trust with the information."

"We can trust Ross."

"Everyone remains outside of the circle until proven otherwise. Get your gear and tell Ross he's taking the drive back to San Diego. Now."

"Admiral—"

"Now, Bale."

"Yes, sir." Tony marched away from Ghost and Mace like a man on his last walk to the gallows, trying to convince himself he could resist his desire for the woman who watched him from the porch. No big deal. He would just keep his distance. Treat her like a friend. He heaved his sea bag over his shoulder and headed for the house.

"You're staying?" Lumin asked, nervously watching him approach.

"Apparently, I've been ordered to stay," he said, not looking at her as he strode up the steps.

"Tony, I didn't ask—"

"I know you didn't."

Mace followed him in, carrying a box of groceries and sat it on the kitchen counter. "I'll let you put these away."

"Tinman," Ditz called from the kitchen table, stepping away from a laptop he'd connected. "I've set you up. You've got scrambled communications through a satellite link. If you select this icon, it will send a message to all our cell phones on the squad, simultaneously."

"For what?" he asked, and strode over to see what the squad's communications guru, Clay "Ditz" Sacks, had invented now.

"A distress signal," Ditz said, running the cursor over the alarm bell icon.

Smartass! "Thanks, Ditz, but I'm sure we'll be fine," he said, staring out the back window to the deck and fire pit that sat in the backyard.

Ditz surveyed him and said, "What the hell's the mood about? You're shacked up with a beautiful woman with nothing around but ducks and beavers. I've sure as shit never gotten a mission like that."

Tony shot him a patronizing glare.

"Clear out, men," Ghost called from the doorway. He checked over his shoulder to make sure the place was empty. Lumin had retreated upstairs. The Admiral advanced on him with a look he didn't understand. "Until I give you the word, you protect her. It will be you and you alone that keeps her alive, Petty Officer Bale. Your deployment has begun, and this is your mission."

Tony bit down on a retort and breathed heavily through his nose to square himself off. "It doesn't have to be me."

Ghost gripped his shoulder and burned him with a gaze. "I know my men. I know you, Petty Officer Bale. On these same floorboards I found heaven and faced hell. I hope you don't have to go through what I did, but it's time you dig deep. There are things that have held you back. Things in this," he said, pinning a finger to the side of Tony's head. "We all have a past to reconcile." Ghost searched his eyes. "You are one hell of a SEAL, but you are also a leader who hasn't stepped forward yet. We don't conquer if we don't challenge. It's one of the first things you learn as a SEAL. Every man who wears a trident wears his past and everything he does in warfare."

Tony dropped his gaze to the floor concerned what Ghost could see, but he saw everything; that's why he was still alive while too many other men were feeding worms.

"Lumin called you for help. She sees, even if she doesn't understand, that you are a man who will protect her and lead her through the fire. I can guarantee you, you'll face fire, and I expect to see you both on the other side without a singe. Whether you know it or not, that woman upstairs will teach you something about yourself that you need to learn."

Ghost turned his mountainous presence away and walked out of the house without a backward look.

Why the hell did his guts feel like they'd been twisted so tight he'd never be able to process a pea? He let out a stuttering breath, assimilating what Ghost had just rammed down his throat.

"He's pretty scary when he wants to be." Her voice drifted down shaky and meek.

Tony's gaze darted to the landing above, where Lumin gripped the railing. He didn't move. Didn't feel like he could. Lumin glided down the stairs and approached him carefully, stopping only inches away from him.

"Are you all right?" she asked, looking scared as a rabbit, as if Ghost had ripped her skin off and exposed her underbelly instead of him.

He cleared his throat and nodded. "Yeah."

"Why do they call him Ghost?"

Not really something he wanted to share with her. Their worlds were too far apart, and with her sheltered existence it was like dipping angel wings in blood. "We all have team names."

"I noticed. You're Tinman because," she paused, thinking. "Because you work with heavy equipment and explosives?"

"That would be a great explanation, but," he chuckled and scratched his cheek. "That's not the case." She waited for him to explain. "Ah, truth is on basic I had a bad habit of always screwin' around with my knife. I'd open everything with it, including tin cans...I slit my thumb open three times. Needed stitches every time. After the third time, I got tagged with the name Tinman."

She broke into a hearty laugh.

He couldn't help himself. When she laughed her light encompassed him, and he laughed right along with her.

Gaining control, she asked, "And Ghost?"

"I don't want to tell you, Lumin." He swayed his head.

"I'm not made of fine china, Tinman." She chuckled using his name.

She was to him, but he wasn't going to tell her that. "Captain Redding gave it to him. He was Ghost's lieutenant for many years. He called him Ghost because he said the Admiral could kill a man before he even knew his life was over."

Lumin nodded. "You, I suppose, have done that as well?"

Tony drew in his bottom lip. She'd see him in a totally different light and he didn't want that for some reason, but he nodded anyway. "We're trained to lead in an environment of constant stress and chaos. Sometimes," he glanced at her, seeing her rapt attention, "sometimes that means taking a life." He swallowed heavily.

"So...you don't let doubt stop you." She squared her shoulders. "You finish the mission. You don't let anything stand in your way," she said, her voice hitched to enthusiasm.

He cranked a brow at her, not really sure what she was getting at. "Yes," he drawled carefully.

"That's good to know," she said brightly.

"It is?" Now he was confused. Women were strange creatures.

"I have a mission."

"You do?"

"Yes."

"Should I ask?"

"Yes, you should."

He scratched his chin and the days' stubble reminded him he needed to find his razor. "Are you going to tell me?"

"You're going to take my virginity." She did a dramatic about-face, marched across the vast great room, up the stairs into her room, and shut the door with a *thunk*.

His mouth smacked shut after gaping for a few seconds. Blinked. Blinked again. "What?"

Chapter Four

Tony hammered on the door she'd disappeared behind. "We talked about this, Lumin. I'm not the one."

Lumin grinned to herself. He thought he was so darn smart. She didn't survive Vegas without having some brain cells, nor two years toward a law degree. She quickly removed her clothes, brushed her fingers through her hair, squeezed her cheeks, and then waited next to the door.

"Lumin, I mean it," he yelled from the other side. "We're on the same side here. We'll, we'll…hang out, play cards, go for walks…"

Swiping the grin from her lips, she yanked the door open. "We can do all of that when my mission is complete."

"Oh! Oh, shit," he shouted, and slapped a hand over his eyes, taking a step back. "For the love of God, woman, give me a break."

"Remove your hand, Petty Officer Bale."

"No," he barked. "Please, put your clothes back on."

"Are you trying to tell me I'm ugly?"

"No, damn it." He spun around. "I'm going downstairs."

She grabbed the back of his pants and he jerked to a stop. "Turn around, SEAL."

"No. No. Fuck no." His jaw cinched tight. "Sorry."

"What is the matter with you? Tell me exactly. I might not live to see tomorrow and I don't want to die a virgin," she chirped at him. "Why is it so wrong that I want to know what sex feels like?"

Tony shook his head vigorously.

"You're the one acting like a virgin. Did you send the message about dripping pussies to yourself?"

Tony grabbed his head with both hands before whipping around, snapping his eyes closed. "Please, just do what I say, and stop using that language. It's not you."

A hefty grin popped onto her lips and she smothered it. Gripping his wrist, she tried to pry his hand from her arm, but although he held on, he didn't hurt her. "Let go."

"Why?"

"Let go."

Slowly he released her and she guided his hand, but as soon as he realized where it was headed, he pulled it back. "Lumin, stop," he ordered with a firm voice, and opened his eyes to glare at her. "I'm not saying you're not beautiful. You are," he stuttered. "I'm not saying I don't want you. I'm not. I'm telling you I can't. I won't. All right. Now stop fucking around, and put your clothes back on." He flinched. "Shit, sorry. Aw, damn it."

Her heart sank with the heavy-handed words and the stern look he poured all over her. Deflated. Definitely embarrassed, she stepped away.

"Lumin."

She closed the door, cutting him off from her. Maybe she didn't know people as well as she thought. She'd seen desire in Tony's eyes, but it wasn't covered in a cheap plastic coating like it always was in the men drifting through Vegas. She quickly dressed and swept up her backpack, adjusted it, and secured the belt around her waist. Pushing open the window, she checked her surroundings. A large tree grew next to the house, and she stepped onto the ledge and grabbed hold. Carefully, she clambered down and jumped the remaining four feet to the ground. Giving her pack a quick wiggle, she headed for the highway. It wasn't more than a mile or so. Maybe she could hitch a ride. She didn't want to go back to Vegas. Maybe she'd head north to her brother's place.

It didn't matter. Staying with Tony after he made it clear he didn't want her, not to mention embarrassing herself, was impossible.

* * * *

Tony stood at the door two hours later, hoping she'd cooled off. He knew he'd hurt her, but it was the only option to put things into perspective. She didn't know what she was asking. Lumin was the kind of woman who needed to offer her innocence to the guy who would love her till death do they part. He was most definitely not that guy.

"Lumin, come on out. We'll talk." He rolled his eyes with the silent treatment. "Lumin, I'm coming in there if you don't come out. If it's so damn important, I'll explain myself. Open up."

He ran a hand through his hair, and then reached for the knob. It turned and he grinned to himself. So she wanted him to come to her. Fair enough. He might have to grovel a little...but... "Lumin? Where are you?" A quick scan of the bedroom made him sprint for the bathroom. The curtains fluttered across the open window next to the bed. "Shit. No. Lumin!" He practically threw himself out the window. She'd escaped using nature's fireman's pole.

God damn it. He vaulted down the stairs, snagged his keys off the coffee table, and ran for the front door.

Sitting in a hick town, three hours later, he absentmindedly spun his cell in circles on the restaurant tabletop.

"Refill?" the waitress asked.

"Can I get it to go?" Tony asked.

"Sure, be right back."

He picked up his cell, and then put it down again. He'd done it several times already. How the hell was he going to explain he'd lost his mission in under thirty minutes? *Fuck.* He fisted the table. He'd texted her, and received one back, it said *Forget I called.* He'd sent fifty so far and it went from ordering to begging to enticing and back to begging. His cell buzzed and he snapped it up. Shit!

T-man, how's it going?

Was he going to admit to Mace he'd lost her? No. He would find her. He was a friggin' SEAL. He could find a lizard in the damn desert. He sure as hell could find a beautiful woman in his own backyard. He texted back.

Great.

A thumbs up was Mace's response. While holding his phone another text came in.

I'm safe. Your mission is over. Stand down.

He chuckled with the terms she used. She paid attention.

He texted back. *Unless you're with me, my mission is not over.* He bit his lip waiting. *Talk to me.*

Over.

Not. I care about you. Not over.

The seconds ticked by as if covered in sap.

You're lying.

He let out a breath. *Will you please answer my call?*

He dialed her number. She answered but didn't say anything.

"Please, Lumin. Where are you?"

"I'm safe, Tony. You can go back to San Diego."

"No, you're safe when you're with me, but you're not."

"I've lived on my own for years. I'm quite capable."

He sighed and tried to hold onto some patience, but it was getting harder to do with this woman. In a lot of ways. "I know you are, but there are people looking for you, and I know how to protect someone. I'm the SEAL, you're the beautiful, delicate…" His fingers drummed on the table. "Why me?" It came out of left field, and it was a stupid question.

Her breath hitched. "Because you never looked at me like a thing. Because I thought you saw me, not just—the cover." She paused and then said, "Because you make my heart race and that's never happened before. I'm not totally ignorant. I read books. I just never experienced it until I saw you for the first time."

The waitress placed a large to-go cup in front of him. "Your coffee, sweetheart."

He nodded his thanks. What could he say? Truth—for a change. "Lumin, I'm exactly the opposite of what you think I am. I'm a guy who plays the field and never revisits where he's been, if you know what I mean. I'm the biblical textbook asshole your mother warned you to stay away from. It wasn't that long ago I was sitting on a beach thinking that I didn't want to end up like those old retired single SEALs sitting in front of a TV with a wifebeater on and a fridge full of beer. It lasted all of a week before I was deep inside another woman, and the next night a different one. That's who I am. That's—who my father was. We're the same. That's just the way it is. You make my pulse beat hard too, but it won't last, and I'll hurt you, and I don't want to hurt you."

Ball was in her court. The line remained open, but silent. He drummed his fingers, waiting.

"No, it's not. I can read people, Tony. That's how I've stayed out of trouble in a town that's nothing but trouble. My mother taught me to listen. She told me I could learn things, even things that aren't spoken out loud."

A small smile crossed his lips.

"You're smiling now, aren't you?"

He blinked with surprise. "Yeah, I am."

"When I look in your eyes, I don't see a sailor or a SEAL. I see a man with a heart who's trying to hide it from everyone."

Tony sat back with a plunk against the bench seat. "Why do you think that?"

"Because of the way you took the admiral's words to heart, and they scared you. I saw your expression, and how deeply his words affected you. The way you are with Mace and the other members of your squad. They have your loyalty until the end of your days. That tells me you're a man with a huge heart, not a cold one."

A billowing silence filled him, and it stilled years of clattering doubt that never seemed to shut down. "My father left us when I was five. I found him again in my twenties and asked him why he'd left. 'I was having too much fun, kid. I like the ladies. What can I say? Didn't want the party to end.' He was a cold, heartless bastard."

"Maybe he was, but you're not. My parents are performers through and through. They'll walk the wire until they can't anymore, but that doesn't mean I will. I want to help people. People who don't have the money to hire an expensive lawyer, but need justice. I am a performer, but I choose not to remain one."

A wave of acceptance settled in his chest. Like lying in a pool of warm water, the thin walls he'd erected to keep her away dissolved.

"Are you hungry?" he whispered.

"Yes."

"Can I take you out for dinner?" He barely breathed the words while his nerves jumped inside him.

"I'd like that."

He chuckled with relief. "Why don't I pick you up and we can grab something? I know this great ranch. It's got a lake. A perfect place to have a picnic under the stars. I'm not saying I've changed my mind about—things, but…"

"I'm in Lakeside."

Shit, so was he. "Where? Lumin?"

"Look to your left behind that big trucker with the funny hat."

He vaulted out of his seat. She smiled at him from a booth on the other side of the restaurant. God, she was beautiful. He wove his way through the tables and slid in across from her. "I didn't want to hurt your feelings."

He looked to the ceiling as if there might be some help up there. A soft, small hand covered his and he looked down at them and then into her eyes. The sea had nothing on her. He could drown in them and love every minute of it. With a gentle brush, he stroked her hair across her shoulder, and leaned over the table to steal the breath from her soul, because Lumin had turned the light on in his.

* * * *

The creatures of the night created a symphony for them as they lay on a blanket staring up at the stars beside the lake. Lumin's eyes followed the green laser beam of light that Tony rolled across the heavens, pointing out the different constellations in the sky. It pierced the heavens and seemed like it actually touched each star.

"The Navy certainly teaches you a lot of stuff," she said, and rolled her head to smile at him.

"I used to wonder why they filled our heads with stuff, too, but eventually I used it in some way." He rolled onto his side and propped his head in his hand, letting his other hand trace her chin, her cheek, and eventually her lips. Since they'd returned to the ranch three hours ago, he'd given her many first kisses, and he was a lifetime away from stopping. He could sense her impatience, but he wasn't going to rush a damn thing. Mainly because he hadn't figured out how he could make the experience pleasurable for her. She was waiting for him to lead the way. "Why do you want to lose your virginity now? I want you to wait." The next words out of his mouth shocked the shit out of him. "I can wait."

She clutched his finger and brought it to her lips and kissed the tip. "I told you why."

He chuckled. "You're not going to die tomorrow. Or the next day."

"You don't know that." She rolled onto her side to mirror him.

"Yes, I do." With a slow brush, his finger traced her collarbone and caressed her sleek arm. She was lean, but her muscles were developed from the strap act she performed.

"Did the Navy teach you how to be psychic?" she teased.

While his fingers skirted her arm, he let his thumb graze the fullness of her breast. "In a way. It's called confidence. Believe in yourself. Believe in your skills. Believe in your team. That's how you create the future."

"Tony, I'll admit I'm a little nervous, but I want you to show me what to do."

This time when he passed his hand down her arm his thumb swept against her nipple, rounding it with a gentle caress. "Tell me what you feel."

Her eyes shuttered with his touch, the response under his thumb made him impatient and needy.

"It aches, but in a good way."

He was actually loving this. There was no need for speed, and although he'd been lying there with a stone-shattering erection for the last two hours, he wouldn't let it possess him or her until she was ready.

"That ache is going to become a sizzling need, Lumin," he said, placing a deep kiss on her mouth. With a gentle prod, she opened for him and he let his tongue roam her sweetness. She was uncertain, but not tense. Hesitant for only a few seconds, then she began to explore herself.

When she laid her head back, he followed. He nibbled at the edge of her mouth and kept tasting until he found the pulse in her neck, licking the strong beat of her heart with his tongue.

A niggling thought crept into his mind. *She is yours.* As if she read his mind, she sat up and with one swoop removed her top, then turned her back to him. His hands actually shook as he reached for the clasp. He brushed her wisps of blonde hair away, and slowly unhooked the claws. She vaulted to her feet and drew her shorts and panties to her ankles then stepped out of them.

His pulse fired on all cylinders, and his heart drummed heavy in his ears. Under the moonlight with the rays catching her straight locks of hair, his eyes had no hope but to become addicted. Totally, overwhelmingly addicted.

Full breasts like teardrops, a flat stomach with the tiniest hint of tone narrowed to rounded hips and taut thighs. Like Adam and Eve, they had the garden all to themselves. A warm summer breeze blew with a whisk of mountain air to keep them cool, but he still couldn't get enough oxygen into his lungs.

"I've seen many beautiful women, Lumin, but I've never seen exquisite until now." He rolled to his feet and drew his T-shirt over his head, flinging it to the ground. His body flexed, and her breath hitched in her throat. "I sure as hell hope you know what's in these pants."

She laughed. "Pretty sure I remember a little bit about the birds and bees."

He reached for his button and hesitated. Maybe he should keep them on. His need, their need would become primal. Something wild was growing inside him. It wanted to fuck the daylights out of her, but he wouldn't allow it. For the first time, he was going to make love.

"Why are you stopping?" Her eyes were like blue cups of light catching what the heavens cast down on them.

"Because we do this slowly. Come to me." He swallowed seeing her step without hesitation at his command, and he'd never felt like more of a man than in that second. He began at her neck and his hands glided a breath away from her skin, not touching her, just letting the thought seep into her mind that he was close and he would have her. She shuddered, impatient and excited. Finally, his thumbs made contact across her nipples, puckered and perfect.

She sucked in her breath, her eyes widening even more. Would he find what he hoped he'd find if he carried on? He bent to one knee and raised his eyes to watch her. She followed his hand as it drifted down her body, stopping just above her mons.

Releasing her gaze was hard, but he leaned forward and brushed his tongue across her fold. With the lightest touch, he circled her flesh, and tasted her excitement. His heart swelled and so did his shaft when she exhaled a perfect little moan. Forking both her hands in his, he laid her down on the blanket and this time showed her the pleasure of his mouth on her breasts.

Another sigh escaped her lips and she arched into him, squirming as he circled her nipple and sucked it slowly into his mouth. Kissing his way to her thighs, he probed once with a quick kiss on the beautiful nub jutting from her fold, and her fingers dove into his hair.

"Oh, God," he hissed. She was so wet her silk dripped down her cheeks in streams. He was going to have to lose his pants soon or he'd have a permanent zipper mark on his skin. Rising to his knees she sat up with a start, and he laughed, kissing her back to the blanket. With a quick hand he freed himself and tossed the pants. "Listen to me," he kissed her again. "This part is up to you. I'm going to make you feel things you've never felt before, but it's you who has to tell me when you want me."

"How will I know?"

He smiled down at her. "You'll know. Trust me."

She offered him a sweet smile, her hair framing her like a golden mane, and he had no other recourse but to kiss her again. Long and hard. She broke the kiss when his thumb began to strum her wet bundle of nerves and she gave a little cry, closing her eyes. "Look at me, Lumin." Her eyes flashed open, filled with a sexual fury that drove his heart into hard, pounding beats. He knew what was coming, but she didn't. Nature was in control, and its need to fuel a man and woman's prime directive pushed away all thought and allowed touch to steer the course.

Lumin's arms snaked around his neck and she pulled him toward her. Wild but innocent, she devoured his lips. He withdrew, and traced a path down her body till he found his target again. A long, slow lick across her fold and her thighs opened to him. His hands folded around her hips and palmed her ass. With a deep sucking pull on her slick flesh, he moaned.

She cried out and bucked. "Oh shit, oh shit."

His tongue kept her in a passionate balance as his finger probed into her channel, slowly, carefully he stroked her. Oh damn, she was tight. Really tight. There was no doubt she was a virgin when he met the resistance. He kissed his way back up her body, lingered on her breasts and met her mouth with his.

She palmed his cheeks. "I want to touch you."

He was barely keeping himself on this side of sane. "But you have to stop when I tell you," he said rolling onto his back, bringing her with him.

"Why?"

"Because guys are made a little different than women. We don't have the willpower." *Nope, none whatsoever, especially with her trim form lying on top of you like a warm, silk blanket.*

She sat back on her haunches, and the second her fold swept up his cock, he jolted. The heat scorching through him nearly paralyzed his brain. Her hands strayed down his abs, tracing the indentations, and he watched her curious touch. His shaft stood like the bloody obelisk in Washington. She palmed it with gentle uncertainty, then stroked it.

"It feels like metal wrapped in silk."

Without making it obvious, or at least as little as possible, he folded his hand over hers and squeezed her hand tighter.

"Really?"

He grinned, but gritted his teeth as she slid down his legs and her hair draped across his stomach. A groan crawled right out his throat when her wet mouth slid over his head and she sucked. The moan from her vibrated through him when she drew him in, and desire tightened in the base of his spine.

"Stop, Lumin, stop." He unglued his eyes from the back of his head and drew her up his body. "Lean back on your palms," he said hoarsely. His chest heaved with heavy breath and determination, but he was dangling from a fine line, and it was about to snap. With his thumb he strummed her. A primal urge gripped him as her hips began to rotate against his. He opened the condom he'd slipped under the blanket and rolled it on quickly. Throwing herself forward, she rubbed her nub against him, covering it in a warm, wet acceptance.

"I need you."

He gripped her neck and drew her mouth to his. "Not nearly as much as I need you. Go slow. Relax, and take me inside you," he breathed, and possessed her mouth while his finger circled her slick nub. Her thighs clenched him, and he felt her soft wet core cover his head. He swallowed and rocked his head back determined not to thrust himself inside her, knowing he'd lose his mind.

"Hurts." She closed her eyes.

"Only for a second I promise, and then pleasure," he reassured her.

She nodded and tore through her hymen with a small cry, her velvet sheath taking him deeper. His head throbbed, wanting her wet channel to clamp around him.

"Be still," he said quietly and kissed her gently. "No rush, my beautiful light, there's no rush. From here on in, it's only pleasure. You and I." He kissed her sweetly on her mouth, on her nose and each cheek. "Your body will accept me." She swiveled her hips to test the waters, and he circled her breast, teasing the tip, and then savored each one, flicking the pebbled peaks.

"Oh yes," she cried and her ass began to rotate in a sensual rhythm, Mother Nature and lust taking each other's hands.

"Oh God, you feel like heaven," he growled, watching a blissful expression crown her features. He was buried deep in her, and she rotated her hips. He encouraged her to rise up and ride him. She liked it, and before long the dance became a race to the finish line. He had to wait. He had to see it and feel her come around him, and it didn't take long. Her eyes shot open and then slammed shut, her muscles clenching him and a cry escaped her, setting him off in his own orgasm as his balls tightened and he released himself with a roar of pure, raw satisfaction.

She draped herself against him, her warm breath skipping across his chest, and he curled her tight in his arms. His heart swelled. No woman had ever trusted him like this before. He tipped her chin. "Are you okay?"

She nodded. "A little sore maybe."

He carefully pulled out of her, trying not to jolt with the sensitivity. He winced when *she* did. "It'll be better in a couple days," he said, ridding himself of the condom.

"Days?" she said wide-eyed.

"Yes, Lumin, you have to heal, and then..." He kissed her chin. "And then, well...you'll see."

He needed her body pressed against his and drew her tight. Their legs remained entwined, and her lids closed, heavy with sleep. Under the moonlight, under the stars, he prayed she was right. The thought of being like the man who donated his sperm to bring him into the world made him sick. He didn't want to be that man. Grabbing the edge of the blanket, he wrapped it around them and nestled his cheek against her warm breast. Her silky skin calmed his fears. She was like a soft little kitten curled into him, and even though she was at peace safe in his protection, she wasn't close enough. This was one mission he would never, ever forget.

Chapter Five

Tony woke with the sun warming his cheek. He stretched and ran his hands through his hair. With a start, he sat bolt upright and blinked. Where was Lumin?

"Lumin?" He rocked to his feet and snagged his jeans, jumping into them and his boots, noticing her clothes were gone. "Lumin?"

His gaze darted around the lake and through the tree line. He ran the trail, ignoring the slap of a few branches against his face. Before darting from the forest, he cleared the area with a surveying gaze and then ran for the house. When he hit the stairs, his heart began to beat again. An enticing smell wandered from the house to meet him on the steps. He entered the great room. *Pancakes!*

Lumin glanced up. "Good morning." She put down the flipper she held and walked toward him. "Hungry?"

The air seemed different this morning, like there was an invisible fibrous line connecting them. She looked—different. Softer, if that were possible. He cleared his throat as she reached him.

"Kinda woke up with a start. You weren't there."

She tipped onto her toes and kissed his mouth. With the dainty brush of her lips, his erection jumped to duty and his hands curled around her ass, tugging her closer.

"You were sleeping so peacefully. I didn't want to wake you."

"That's a rarity for me. I don't normally sleep very well."

Her eyes shined when a smile coursed across her features. "I'm making breakfast, but I'll apologize now."

"Why?"

"I follow the directions, but it doesn't matter what I make. It tastes like crap." She broke into a laugh. "You can use a lot of syrup."

"I'm sure it's not that bad."

They sat down on the back deck. *Holy shit, how can you make a pancake taste this bad?* "Good," he said, taking another mouthful after adding syrup.

She barked with laughter. "You lie." She shrugged. "I don't know why I can't cook. I'm hexed."

He put his fork down and downed the glass of orange juice she'd sat by his plate. "Can't be good at everything."

"You are," she said, pushing her plate away. "Ick, this is awful. You don't have to eat it."

"Coffee's decent," he said, taking a mouthful to wash down the pancake stuck in his throat. He grinned at her. "Don't really mind when it's prepared by such a beautiful woman. How are you feeling this morning?"

She blushed and her crystal gaze swerved away from his inquiring eyes. "A little sore." She played with her fork before meeting his eyes again. "It was the most incredible thing I've ever felt. Being in your arms, I mean." She let out a breath. "I don't think I'm supposed to say that. Guys get all weird, don't they?"

"I'm not all guys." He stretched his arm across the table and grasped her hand. "It was pretty incredible. If you want the truth, the guy's guy inside me can't wait to make love to you again."

Make love. He said it, and it didn't feel weird. Why was that?

"Obviously, I don't know what I'm doing."

He rose and pulled her to her feet. "That's the sweet part. You don't. No man has touched you except me, and I think I could get a little possessive over that." She glanced up at him with doubt. "As in, I don't want any other man to touch you but me."

She backed away from him. "I better clean up the dishes."

"Leave them. Let's take a walk around the lake." He drew her behind him and they took their time, listening to the rustle of the wind in the trees and birds calling out to each other. He held her hand and darted glances at her at least a hundred times. Every nerve ending sparked with excitement. Even though he'd taken her innocence, she still radiated a purity that made him crazy. He couldn't look at her without a charge of warmth streaking through him.

"Are you going to tell me Ghost and Kayla's story?"

It took most of the walk to fill her in. When they'd reached the point where they'd started, she said, "Kayla doesn't look sick."

"I wouldn't call her sick," he said, sitting on a fallen log and drawing Lumin onto his lap. "I think of it more as a fight to survive. The choice to mend over mind."

"I like that," she said, casting her gaze across the lake. "The choice to mend over mind, kind of says it perfectly. I don't know if I could have survived all of that. She must be very strong."

He chuckled. "The strong part comes into play with the Admiral. You should have seen them try to wrestle each other to the ground mentally before they gave in to love. Every time they had a fight, Ghost would take it out on us. Kayla was the first woman to prove herself working in Base Command. She's a code cracker and a warfare analyst. That got under Ghost's skin big time and he rode her hard, but I think it was because he was trying not to fall in love with her."

"What does a warfare analyst do?"

"She strategizes the moves of both sides like a chess game. She can think ahead and see the likelihood of the enemy's intentions."

"How does she do it? It sounds interesting."

"You'll have to ask her. Must have something to do with understanding people first. Since history repeats itself, there are formulas, tactical maneuvers that can be altered and reinvented. I don't really know. Both she and Ghost have this kinda eerie way of knowing what's going to happen before it does."

"What about Nina? She works there too, right?"

"She does. Kayla trained her, but she's more of a communications expert. She coordinates and multitasks the teams' movements and their missions. In the middle of chaos, she's filing her nails and keeps it all up here," he said, tapping his head.

Lumin eyed him. "You sound different when you talk about Nina."

He shrugged. "She's got it together, and she keeps us laughing."

"Guess I better start Googling Navy SEALs to understand what you all do."

He chuckled and wrapped his arms around her waist, resting his head against hers. "What do you want to know?"

Lumin draped her arm around his shoulder. "Tell me what happens on a mission."

"Hmm."

"Is that secret?"

"Parts of it, I suppose. Do you know what SEAL stands for?"

"No, not really."

"Sea, Air and Land. We're trained to operate in all three environments. There's two groups. One is located in Coronado, the other in Virginia. Teams One, Three, Five, and Seven deploy from the west. Each team is broken down into platoons and squads. In each one you have men who are specially trained like Mace, who's a sniper. I'm called a Lead Breacher. Then there are frogmen, another name for divers. We all dive, but some of us specialize in underwater demolitions. Stitch is a corpsman. When we get torn up, he tries to put us back together again. Some skills, like diving and parachuting, are common to all of us."

"But you're not all officers?"

"No."

"You told the young security guard not to call you 'sir.'"

"I'm enlisted, not an officer."

"Will you be?"

He narrowed his eyes at her. "Does it make a difference?"

"Yes."

He jerked back. "It does?"

"You should be, and obviously the Admiral thinks so too. I heard him say you haven't taken on a leadership role yet. He seems to think you should."

Tony scratched an itch at the back of his neck. "To become an officer I'd have to enter officer training school. Most enlisted guys stay enlisted."

"But you'd be a good leader."

"How would you know that?"

She blushed and traced her finger along his cheek. "You taught me last night."

He laughed out loud. "That's a little different, Lumin."

Her gaze softened. "I don't think so. You were patient, taught by example, let me try to find my own way, guided me when I wasn't doing it right, and rewarded me with words of encouragement when it was over."

He swallowed deeply as she hit every key factor of being a leader on the head. "Leading you into my web of pleasure is a little different than leading a bunch of alpha warriors into combat."

"But you can't deny the fundamentals are all there."

He leaned back and gazed at this intriguing woman. "I think you're going to be a force to be reckoned with in the courtroom."

"More words of encouragement," she teased.

"No, I just want in your pants again." She swatted him, and he laughed, watching her cheeks color.

A text bleeped from his phone.

Is she still a virgin?

He deleted it quickly.

"What did it say?" she inquired.

"Nothing."

"Another booty call?" She slipped from his lap and eyed him suspiciously.

A girl questioning him about his texts used to make him uncomfortable. Lumin's question was curious without being possessive. It didn't bother him at all. "It wasn't a woman."

She wandered away from him, pulling her shirt over her head.

He wasn't going to interrupt and continued to gaze as she shimmied from her clothes and beared a course for the water. He sat in glorious, stunned warmth as she waded into the lake. At night she was an elfin creature; by day, water nymph. Good thing water was his element too. Turfing his clothes, he joined her with a quiet slice into the lake and rose up in front of her. Gazing at her unabashed beauty, it hit him this wasn't a mission for Uncle Sam, this was like a—a vacation or maybe something more permanent like a—*nah*. Up to their chest in water, her legs wrapped around his hips, and she draped her arms across his shoulders. His hands swept to her ass and he nestled her closer.

"Tell me," she probed.

"Tell you what?" he whispered and tasted her lips. His submarine was going to full battle stations wedged between their bodies.

"What did the text say?"

"It was Mace checking up on us. That's all."

"No it wasn't," she argued, beginning to sway her hips in a delicious rocking motion.

He knew making love in the water wasn't what books and movies made it out to be. Water washed the natural lubrication of a woman away and made it uncomfortable, but he was enjoying the dance their bodies shared for now and wasn't about to stop it.

"SEAL's honor." He stole a long, lingering kiss. And then another.

"I like being here with you, Tony." She nuzzled her nose into his neck, kissed his shoulder and rested her chin on it. "Thank you for protecting me."

He leaned back. "I'm not doing this out of duty, believe me. I want to be here." *Where the hell was all the honesty coming from and why was it coming out of his mouth?* "You are so beautiful. So honest and open. I like that. I like it a lot."

She pinned a smile on her cheeks. "This is honest." She pressed her flat belly gently against his oversized hard-on. "Do I do this to you?" she asked, her lashes whisking her pale cheeks.

Her innocent question made him laugh. "I'd control it if I could," he teased, "but I doubt that's going to happen around you."

If she wanted honest, he could do that. Hiding his feelings had become second nature, but pieces of something perfect were falling into place with this woman. He wanted her to know him, even the dark parts.

Lumin leaned her forehead against his. "When you hold me, I feel all nervous and jittery, and it's hard to breathe."

Good to know he wasn't the only one feeling that way. "I know you're telling me the truth, but it's so hard to believe you never let anyone close enough to hold you or kiss you."

Lumin released his shoulders and her gorgeous body arched back, floating in the water. He kept his hand beneath her bottom and she stared up at him, her blonde locks drifting on the surface. Again, she reminded him of some mystical creature. If he'd found her out at sea, he'd swim a hundred miles to catch her. Her nipples hardened, and so did he as if they were connected by some kind of psychic link.

"They tried. Mom told me that men wanted sex, but most would be gone afterwards. My friend Star told me how great it was and that love didn't matter. I guess I wasn't in a hurry to find out."

He leaned over, slipping his arms around her slender waist. Kissing her became an all-consuming need. Within a minute, his mind became fuzzy and he was carrying her in his arms toward the shore. She clung to him with ease, and he laid her on the soft moss. Her fold was slick and ready. "It's too early, my lady, but I don't have to be inside you to make you feel good."

With one sleek move, she disappeared beneath him and her lips mouthed the head of his shaft.

Holy Jesus, God in heaven. He held himself up on his hands and knees, and closed his eyes to let only the touch of her lips and her tongue circling his head, rampage through his body. She was a quick learner and she had him suspended in a place he'd rarely been. It was a hypnotic passion. Slow. Sensual. One that made his chest expand and his innards tremble with every suck. She'd covered her hand in her own moisture, then squeezed his sac as she worked him down her throat with deep thrusts.

He swung around and wrapped his hands around her thighs, opening up her sweetness to him. Licking her tenderly drove her crazy. She squirmed and mewled under him, giving her the same rhythmic kisses and licks she bestowed on him. His body was hard as a rock, his desire spinning down to the final seconds. He wanted her to come with him and sucked her nub deep into his mouth, flicking at the tender tip. His orgasm made him yell out as he tried to pull from her mouth, but she was coming at the same time and sucked him even harder, throwing his body into convulsive jerks.

Slowly, he opened his eyes, and rolled to his side, then lay flat on his back breathing heavily. With sweet little kisses she worked her way up his legs, skimmed his knees and eventually hovered above him, her wet hair raining down with a curtain of little drops falling around their faces.

He palmed her cheeks and kissed her lips. "My lady, I think it's time for a nap."

She laughed at him. "Nap, huh?" She scooped their clothes into one arm and gave him a wicked little smile. "What's the matter, old man? Getting a little slow in your old age?"

"What?" he growled. He lunged upward and she took off running in all her exquisite naked beauty through the trail. He'd let her get to the house, but he'd corral her there and take charge of the rest of their day, and it was going to be spent in bed.

Halfway up the stairs, his cell rang. "Can you answer it, Lumin, my hands are full," he said, carrying her to the second floor. He was only a few surefooted steps away from paradise.

"Hello?" She paused, and then pointed to the ground hurriedly when they reached the second story. "Yes, Admiral. One moment, please."

"Yes, sir."

"Bale, are you close to your computer?" Ghost asked.

"No, sir. Standby." He ran down the stairs, Lumin close behind him. "Go ahead."

An incoming CDC brief appeared on the screen. He and Lumin both rose with a jerk, finishing the synopsis at the same time.

An isolated town in the southern region of New Mexico reported an outbreak of what appears to be the Bubonic Plague this morning. Four residents of the town are reported dead. The town has been quarantined as the CDC investigates.

"This is a test," Tony said into the phone.

"I believe so, Petty Officer Bale," Ghost replied. "Nina, Kayla, and the children were put on a military aircraft an hour ago, bound for Canada."

"I'd do the same thing. What are my orders, sir?"

"Bring her in."

"What? Why?"

"Because we need her to lure the men who were tracking her."

His guts squeezed tight with protectiveness. "With all due respect, sir, no!"

"If they are testing already, we are out of time. They will launch this on the United States of America if we don't bring them down now. I have the President's order sitting on my desk. We have been tasked to find them. This mission is now in the hands of JSOC, *Joint Special Operations Command.*"

"Sir, you refused to use Kayla to lure the Shark. You expect me to put Lumin on the end of a pole to go fishing? I'm not doing it, sir."

The line went deadly silent. He was so God damned court-martialed; he just wondered how many years he'd get or, worse yet, if he'd have to find a new job as a civilian.

Instead of blasting out of the stratosphere, Ghost said, "Tinman, I understand why you want to protect her, but this is different. The Shark was one man against all of us. This is an airborne weapon that could potentially kill millions. Lumin is our only link."

Tony clenched his eyes closed. His SEAL mind understood the logistics, but he never expected his heart to outweigh that nor rebel against his duty to his country. "Sir—I can't."

"What can't you do?" Lumin asked.

Tony shook his head. "I can't, Admiral, don't ask me. There has to be another way. Maybe a decoy. A Marine from the base who looks like Lumin. I'll come back, but I'm leaving Lumin here."

Ghost paused, considering his request. "If it doesn't work, we lose them. They'll know we're tracking them. They'll scatter, and our only hope to find our target will be gone."

"What do you expect Lumin to do? Let them take her?"

"Yes."

"No, sir."

"I'll do it," Lumin said, backing away.

"No, you won't. You'll end up dead. I guarantee it."

"They've already released it once. Where will they release it next time? Can you imagine how many people will die, Tony? If I'm your only chance to find them, I have to try."

"Bring her, Tinman. Bring her now."

"Yes, sir," he said, disconnecting the call. "Get dressed. I'm going to put you on a plane bound for Canada. I'll say you slipped away."

Lumin shook her head slowly. "No, Tony."

He ran a shaking hand through his hair. "This is not an act, Lumin. No second chances. Life and death, and more than likely death. I will not let you do this. You have zero defenses against them. They want you dead because of what you know."

Lumin backed away from him. "As a SEAL, you'd die to protect your country. I don't have to be a SEAL to do the same."

He swallowed heavily as she turned and strode across the vast great room toward the stairs. The scenarios his mind had conjured of his beautiful light waiting for him after a deployment extinguished. A heavy weight hung in his chest as he watched her exquisite body ascend the stairs. He'd just begun to know her. They needed more time, much more time—like maybe growing old together.

* * * *

Lumin tried to lighten the stifling tension in the car as Tony drove them back to San Diego. Miles passed without his severe expression lifting. Once they'd rolled to a stop, arriving at the base, she tried to leave the car, and he gripped her arm.

Tony took a deep breath and turned to her. "I'm not like my father. I know that." Her heart melted seeing the truth in his eyes. "I watched the guys on the squad fall in love with their wives. They told me when you meet your forever girl, you'll know." His rugged jaw flexed with tension and his gaze riveted itself to her, making her heart hammer in her chest. His forehead pinched together. "You shared something with me, trusted me, and I'm honored." His gaze snapped to their hands as he brushed hers with his thumb. A small smile lifted the edges of his mouth. "Maybe I shouldn't tell you that. Girls get a little nervous if a guy throws his heart down too early," he continued, rephrasing what she'd said to him up at the ranch. "I care about you. I don't want you to do this. Tell me now and I'll drive straight out of here."

She leaned over and kissed him on his cheek. "I'm scared. Really scared, but there's no backing out. I trust you Tony. I know we haven't had enough time, and Star would say I'm crazy, but I don't need months to figure out you're a good man."

He drew her into his arms and buried his face in her hair. "I don't want to lose you, Lumin."

She clung to him, loving the way he nearly squeezed the life from her. Their noses brushed.

Tony possessed her mouth and her heart. His fingers twined in her hair and deepened the kiss, his tongue playing with hers. She'd trusted him with her innocence, now she had to trust him with her life.

He palmed her cheeks and gazed into her eyes. "You're my lady, and I won't let them hurt you."

She nodded quickly and swiped a tear away. They walked arm in arm toward the Base Commander's office. Part of her felt like a sheep being led to slaughter, but she knew Tony wouldn't abandon her.

Chapter Six

A text popped up on Tony's phone. He reviewed it quickly and altered course, steering her toward the water.

"Where are we going?" Lumin asked.

Tony kept scanning his surroundings as if there was a concern. Within a few minutes they arrived at a building with a coded lock on the front door.

"It's our Loadout room."

"What's that?"

"We keep our gear in here. Before a mission, this is where we come to gather our equipment."

Tony's team stood in a loose arc surrounding Admiral Austen and Captain Cobbs. When they entered, all eyes turned. Ghost nodded and he gave Tony a sage look.

"Reporting, sir," Tony said through clenched teeth. Mace had his arms tightly crossed and he didn't look happy. She shifted uncomfortably, and Tony's arm tightened around her shoulder. "Whatever the plan is, I'm not leaving Lumin's side. Court-martial me if you want. Throw me out of the SEALs. I don't give a shit." Tony glared at the Admiral.

"I understand, Tinman," the Admiral stated patiently. "We won't be far away, but she has to leave the base and our protection. They are watching."

"Are we watching them?" Tony shot back.

"Yes," Ghost said slowly. "There are two teams of two men."

"They want her dead, Admiral. They'll kill her, then head for cover."

Admiral Austen set his attention on her. "Lumin—"

"No," Tony said, stepping in front of her. "Listen to me. We can accomplish the same thing without risking her life if we use a Marine from the base. If they catch on and run, we'll be behind them. That's what we want."

Captain Cobbs took a slow pace to stand ahead of the Admiral. "Petty Officer Bale, the percentage is high that they won't kill her, but take her with them instead. If that happens we trail them and find the nest. It's a risk she has to take. Ghost has received more intel from JSOC. They've known for a year of the potential threat, but couldn't locate the cell. He convinced them to allow Alpha squad to become the primary team, DEVGRU, *Develop Group that which used to be called SEAL Team Six from Virginia*, is being tasked as well to work this mission. It is now on *us* to stop a national disaster. This is the largest threat U.S. citizens have faced in years, if not ever. Time is running out. Ghost just received the first report from CDC on the Plague. It killed all the residents of that New Mexico town in twelve hours."

"I thought there were only four dead," Tony said.

"The last one passed away an hour ago. The symptoms of the plague are the same, but far more aggressive with a zero survival rate. The terrorists have attached the genes of a bacteria to a virus. It makes it far deadlier. This hybrid carries both Ebola and the Bubonic Plague. Lumin, the doctor told you he had engineered it to mutate every thirty-six hours." Ghost held a folder and offered it to Tony.

She swallowed heavily and lowered her eyes when Tony flipped it open. A picture of a little girl, her eyes gazing upward in death, made Lumin's stomach churn. The lymph nodes in the girl's neck and near her arm pits had exploded. Blood seeped from her mouth and nostrils. Lumin looked away, her stomach rolling with nausea, and she raised a hand to cover her mouth.

"We have one thing in our favor. Although the plague has been screwed with, it has been beaten before. There is a vaccination against the initial bacteria. CDC is working with what they found in New Mexico. The danger is the speed at which this thing will mutate. No scientist can work that fast to find an antiserum. Millions will still die," Ghost said. "Antibiotics will not stop this strain."

A tear rolled down her cheek and she began to nod. "What do I have to do, Admiral?"

Ghost nodded at Caleb, their corpsman. "Stitch is going to give you the first of two inoculations. In case they inject you with the virus, this may slow it down."

"You better have one of those for me." Watching Caleb withdraw an injection and swabs, Tony's lips seamed into a tight line.

Ghost took a deep breath. "Petty Officer Bale, I need you with the team."

Tony started to shake his head slowly. As Stitch reached out to swab her arm, he clamped a hand on the corpsman's wrist to intercept.

"Tinman, this is for her protection," Stitch said sternly.

"She doesn't need protection because I won't allow her to go." Tony turned to face the Admiral and Captain Cobbs.

Before he could say another word, the Admiral stepped up to him. "Petty Officer Bale, I am putting you as lead on this mission. Fox?" he barked.

"Sir," Master Chief Mason Briggs answered.

"Master Chief, you and Petty Officer Bale will lead the squad. Your new lieutenant has not arrived yet."

"Who is it, sir?" Mace took a position beside Tony.

"You've heard his name before." The Admiral glanced at Cobbs, who arched a brow but remained silent. "Lieutenant Abraham Lewis."

"Whoa!" The guys took a step back in unison.

"Get the fuck out," Nathan said, showing his shock with an F-bomb which he rarely used.

"Who is he?" Lumin asked from the corner of her mouth.

Tony blew out a breath. "Just the biggest egomaniac in Virginia. He's got a rep of never listening to his men. SEALs work as a team. That's how we stay alive. Eight brains all thinking at once. Lewis is known for deciding unilaterally and getting guys killed."

"Wasn't my decision, men," Ghost explained. "Give him some time."

"Time to get us killed," Caleb said with a sour look on his face. "Why the hell are we getting saddled with the son of a bitch?"

"Because you had a vacancy."

"And Virginia wanted to get him the hell outta there," Ditz said, winding a cable around his hand, his boy-next-door features looking ill at ease.

Within a few seconds all eyes fell on Ed Saxton. Tony had told her he'd come from the East Coast. Ed eyed all of them in turn. With a slow southern drawl, he said, "Yup, he's a dick. I switched from Team Two because of him. None too pleased to hear this, Admiral."

"If there are issues, there is a chain of command. Use it, but I'm hoping you men can change the way he does business."

The guys grumbled discontent, but nodded.

"Lumin, this is dangerous. I wouldn't ask you if there was another way," the Admiral said.

"I want her to join Kayla and Nina," Tony demanded, pulling her a step back with him.

Lumin forked her fingers through Tony's, and he clutched them tightly. "Tony, there isn't a choice. Go ahead, Caleb."

Tony glared at Stitch as he swabbed her arm and his brow furrowed when she winced as the injection broke her skin.

"Why did you send Kayla and Nina to Canada?" Tony asked.

"He didn't," came a woman's voice from behind them.

"Kayla, what the fuck are you doing here?" the Admiral boomed.

She blinked and calmly threw a look at Nina who stood beside her, hands on her hips. "The children are safe, Admiral," Kayla said. She and Nina advanced. "Get that god damn scowl off your face. I have a job to do, and so does Nina. We're part of this team."

"Is Adam—?"

"Safe at my parent's place. They've already arrived," Nina said.

Lumin grinned, seeing the shock on the Admiral and Mace's expressions.

"Gonna fire me?" Kayla said, eyes snapping a challenge at the Admiral.

"Should have done that a year ago," he growled back.

She put a hand on Lumin's shoulder. "You're going to be fine. This is the best SEAL squad in the country. We're going to track you and think three steps ahead of the bad guys and end this."

Lumin snuck a look at the Admiral, and he wore about the scariest expression she'd ever seen on a man. He could crumble buildings with that look. Kayla ignored him. Seeing the maps tacked on the wall, Kayla wandered over to them and the team followed. Nina stepped up beside her.

"Lot of area?" Nina gazed at the map.

"If they didn't want to attract attention, and Lumin says it was in the middle of nowhere, what does that mean?" Kayla asked Nina as if testing her.

Nina gazed at the map. "Underground," she said, her eyes darting back to her mentor.

"That's what I think too." Both women turned. "This is where the New Mexico town was hit. It's called Ramah, population three hundred and eighty-five."

"Population is zero, now," Nina said churlishly.

"It sits between two Indian reservations and nothing but desert around it. If the lab is in Nevada, there is a reason they used this isolated town."

"They're located in eastern Nevada," the Admiral said.

"I believe so. If you look at a map of Nevada, and I just finished staring at one for an hour, it's the most likely scenario."

"Why not Arizona or Utah?" Mace asked.

"A buffer," Nina surmised. "If you're guilty of murdering someone, you don't stand beside the body. It's human nature to put distance between you and your target or your guilt. I checked the population data. For the most part, Arizona and Utah's smallest towns are still higher in population than New Mexico."

"Or they could have two labs," Fox suggested.

"True. That would not be good, but it would make sense. If one is found, the other could still deploy the virus," Kayla added.

The Admiral stepped up to the map. "If there are two labs we need another squad besides DEVGRU. Who do we bring in, Petty Officer Bale?"

"Recon specialists," Tony answered immediately.

"What are they?" Lumin asked.

"They do the same as Kayla, except they're out in the field. They explore enemy territory ahead of the main operation to supply as much information as they can."

"Where would you put them?" Lumin asked. "There's a lot of ground to cover."

"Fox?" Tony leaned into Lumin. "He's the best tracker on both coasts."

Fox stared at the map for a good, long time. "Snow White, north or south Nevada?"

"My gut tells me north, but that means nothing," she answered.

The Admiral stepped to Kayla's side. "Why, baby?"

The Admiral surprised Lumin by calling her that.

Kayla's gaze seemed vacant for a moment. "I'm Dr. Carmichael. I've created an airborne plague, one I'm pretty sure they're going to release. I want to get as far away as possible. A place where I can hop a plane to just about anywhere. If the lab is in the north, I'd go south. I'm not certain, but I think the prevailing wind direction in Nevada is westerly."

All eyes in the room traveled northward on the map waiting for Fox. "Highway 80 intersects the northern part of the states. They'd use it to feed into secondary highways after that. We'll need four teams set up here, here, here and here," Fox pointed to each location on the map.

"How many men, Fox?" Tony asked him.

"Two on each point."

"What will you look for?" Lumin spoke her thoughts out loud, and when Fox turned his attention on her, she said, "Sorry."

Fox gave her a wink. "No law against thinking out loud. We look for anything that doesn't fit."

"Oh," she breathed. To her it seemed like a needle in a haystack, but if Fox was the best, he must know how to turn the haystack into bales and find what he was looking for.

"It may not be that difficult," Ditz said. "We'll put a GPS tracking unit on you, Lumin."

"What's that?" she asked, edging into Tony.

"A very small chip and a transmitter, sweetheart," Tony explained. "We can easily hide it in your clothes or in jewelry. Even if you disappear from our view, we'll know where you are as long as the satellite sees you."

"I thought that was movie BS."

"Look at me, Lumin," he ordered, turning her chin toward him. "This is important and you have to remember it. The range is excellent, but you have to stay visible. The satellites are roaming around up there." He pointed upward. "I want to know where you are at all times." His gaze strayed to her mouth and his air escaped him in a staggered breath.

Lumin looked around nervously when Tony stepped back, and she noticed Nina's brow raised, an inquiring expression on her face.

Ghost walked up to Kayla and gazed down at the little woman who was his wife. A small grin crossed his lips and he looked like he wanted to kiss her. Kayla gave him a well-what-do-you-think-now-bigshot look. "I am so fucking glad I married you."

The guys burst out laughing.

Ghost raised his gaze from his wife. "It's your show, Bale. Who else do we pull into the mission?"

Tony scrubbed his chin with one hand while the men waited. "Sixteen more men. One squad for Nevada, and one for New Mexico. When does she get the next injection, Stitch?"

"We're going to rush the process a bit. Six-hour intervals. When I say rush, I mean by a week. Lumin, if you experience any side effects you need to tell me immediately."

"Why didn't they take Lumin between Las Vegas and San Diego?" Mace muttered under his breath. Everyone stopped and waited.

Ed narrowed a look on her. "Good question. They trailed you. They could have taken you on one of the stops between Vegas and here, but they didn't. Why?"

Kayla approached her. "Lumin, you said Dr. Bjornson was Dr. Carmichael's partner. Did they say how they left the lab? Did they escape? Were they released?"

Lumin closed her eyes and tried to remember the doctor's slurred words. Between begging for forgiveness and how he'd been tricked, he told her he and the other doctor had been held captive. Had he said how they got away?

Lumin opened her eyes when Kayla's hand rested on her shoulder. "Was Dr. Bjornson the man who was with him in Vegas?"

Lumin shook her head. "No. The other guy was a friend, as far as I could tell. Someone he knew from Lebanon. None of it made a lot of sense to me. Once I got Dr. Carmichael settled in bed, he was delirious. He'd pass out for a few seconds and then start talking again."

"Does it make any sense at all, that this guy would be partying in Vegas if he was trying to hide?" Ed asked the squad.

"He was nervous all night," she said, curling her brow. "He kept looking around, and that's what made me pay attention. That's when I noticed the two men watching us."

"What if they were trailing him?" the Admiral added.

"Why?" Lumin asked.

The Admiral squared a look on Kayla as if working it out. "Come on, babe, we've got pieces to the puzzle. What does it show us?"

"Carmichael is a viral specialist. They wouldn't let Carmichael go unless he'd finished his job, and then they released him but gave him a slow-acting drug to kill him. It's not the plague because Lumin would have seen the symptoms. Two men watch the doctor then trail Lumin here without taking her. They don't try to grab her until she arrives at Tony's." Kayla's gaze shot to the Admiral's. "Bjornson got away. He didn't finish, and they thought the other doctor would lead them to him. Carmichael spent time with Lumin. They're trying to find him."

The Admiral and the rest of the team nodded. "It's plausible," the Admiral said. "In fact, it's likely. Lumin, when they take you, you're going to have to keep yourself alive. Keep them dangling as if you know where Dr. Bjornson might be."

"And you don't think they will torture it out of her?" Tony asked sharply.

"Not at first," the Admiral said, offering Lumin a sympathetic smile. "We won't be far behind. We have to find the lab. We might even find who is behind this."

"Why aren't we having this meeting in the Base Commander's office?" Ditz asked what Lumin had wondered all along.

The Admiral flashed a look at Captain Cobbs. "The White House believes whoever is behind this had help. You can't walk into a drug supply store and ask for a specimen of the Plague. It had to have come from a high security lab. That can only mean intervention from the highest level," Cobbs stated.

"Someone gave them the Plague to play with?" Mace said. "The terrorists have a high-ranking American in their back pocket?"

The Admiral nodded. "That's why this stays within our squad. Only I give the reports to JSOC, and they will be misleading."

"You think there's a traitor in SPECWAROPS?" Stitch queried.

"Who knows where he or she is, but the White House is certain there is one," Admiral Austen supplied. He wrapped an arm around Kayla and nodded. "Check your gear, men. We go hot in twelve hours. Load out. As soon as Lumin is given her second injection, we deploy."

"Sir?" Nathan's expression was tentative at best. "You said 'we.'"

"You're two men down," the Admiral explained, sharing a look with Captain Cobbs.

Kayla groaned loud enough for everyone to hear. "Thane, you have a job. It's in Hawaii."

"Mrs. Austen," the Admiral growled back. "You have a job, it's raising our son."

Kayla rolled her eyes, and Lumin couldn't keep the chuckle in. Tony leaned toward her ear. "Just like old times."

The rest of the men broke the circle, shaking their heads as they aimed for their lockers.

Kayla's voice tightened. "I swear, if you go with the squad I will divorce you." With her hands riveted on her hips there was no mistaking this woman was a match for the surly Admiral.

Although a foot taller, Ghost paused. "No, you won't."

"I sure as shit will."

"Baby—"

"You gear up, so will I."

"Like hell you will. You're retired, sort of."

"You need Nina and me on this mission. Who did we agree makes the decision on whether I retire or not?"

Ghost rolled his lips and darted a quick look around. "You do," he said quietly.

They were standing toe to toe, both glaring at each other.

"Well then?"

"What good are we to Adam if we're both dead?" Ghost hurled at her loudly, losing his patience.

"This will be a pandemic. It will kill our son if we don't stop it together."

Ghost towered over her and Kayla didn't even blink. "I—need—you—*alive*, woman. You can do what you need to do from Base Command. That's as close as you're getting."

"Don't count on it, Admiral."

"That's right," he yelled. "I am a god damn admiral, but you seem to forget that."

Lumin stood cemented to the spot, watching them volley back and forth. "Aren't you concerned," she asked Tony.

"About what?" he asked, absently watching the men.

"Them." She motioned toward the Admiral and Kayla.

"That? Christ no, they haven't even gotten mad at each other yet."

Lumin cranked her head in shock. "That's not mad?"

Tony chuckled. "Nope. That's just posturing."

"I'd hate to see mad."

Tony slipped an arm around her shoulders. "You'll know it. Kayla starts shouting in French-Canadian and if she's really pissed she'll chuck shit at him. Apparently, she's got great aim. Right now she's just annoyed, see—her hands are on her hips."

"Wow, you guys know each other that well?"

"Those two bark at each other like dogs, but it sounds worse than it is."

Lumin saw Mace and Nina standing beside each other shaking their heads at the same time. Mace said, "Your turn."

"Nope," Nina shot back. "It's yours."

"I'm pretty sure it's yours," Mace said.

"Fine." Nina raised her fingers to her mouth and gave a short hard whistle. "Hey, anyone around here want to stop a pandemic? I know, crazy thought, but instead of bickering, why don't we all play nice and save the world. 'K? 'K."

Ghost and Snow White stopped arguing for a split second and glared at Nina, but it didn't last long.

Ghost raised a finger at Snow White. "You're not going into the hot zone."

"I'm going where I'm needed."

"Kayla, I'm putting my foot down this time. The last time you came on a mission, you nearly died."

"That wasn't my fault."

"I don't care whose fault it was. The Taliban almost shot you. They did shoot you. Now get your ass home."

"My ass is going to Base Command. Come on, Nina. We have more research to do."

"Fine, stay at Command, but you're not coming."

"Guess again, no-good SEAL."

"It's Admiral," he shouted.

"Admiral no-good SEAL," she shot back as the door to the Loadout room slammed shut.

Nina gave her husband a playful wink and strode after Kayla. Lumin felt a little better knowing Kayla and Nina would be close by.

Nathan hung by the Admiral's side. "That woman never, ever listens to me. She's the only person on the planet who doesn't do what I say. Why is that?"

Nathan's brow cinched up and he said slowly, "Cuzzzz she's the only person on the planet who isn't scared of you."

The Admiral panned a look as if he'd just seen a purple giraffe cross in front of him.

"Come with me." Tony tucked her under his arm, leading her toward the door.

"Where are we going now?" She clung to him because she needed the extra courage. They reached a row of buildings and he held a door open. The space was empty of human inhabitants.

"This is the teams' Mess," he explained, as they maneuvered around a set of weights, skirted a foosball table and he led her to a couch. A fridge and small bar sat along the far wall. "Something to drink?"

"Sure, a soda."

He opened the fridge and twisted the top off a Sprite, handing it to her. With a gentle hand he brushed her cheek. "I will do everything I can to keep you safe. Even if you can't see us, I'll be close by." She lay back against the headrest of the couch and stretched her legs out. Tony ran his hand up her calf. "You have the best legs I've ever seen, and I want them back." He got up and went to a cabinet and pulled out a blanket, returning to cover her. "Try to get some rest. I'm going to head to the galley and get us something to eat. I'll be back soon."

"If I'm sleeping, wake me up."

"You need to sleep."

She sat up. "Would I sound like a silly female if I said I want to spend every second I can with you until I leave?"

"I'll be right here." He gently prodded her to lie back and kissed her.

She didn't want him to go quite yet and wrapped her arms around his neck, holding him close. "Thank you for being my hero."

Tony's arms squeezed her possessively. Resting her head against his chest and listening to his heart made her feel better.

"I'm not a hero, Lumin. Just a guy doing his job."

Her heart sank a little. "I'm a job?"

His eyes darted upwards and he shook his head. "No, you're not. Nowhere near, but I have to think sharp the second you're out of my hands because I want you back in my arms as soon as humanly possible."

"I don't have the training you have. All I've got are a few street smarts."

"That's all you need. We'll do the rest. I believe in you, Lumin. I need you to believe in yourself." He kissed her forehead and then her mouth. "If your gut tells you things are going in the wrong direction, I want you to run. Don't take any more risk than necessary. Use every skill you have."

"I wish I had the abilities Kayla and Nina have. It's like they can see into the future."

Tony folded her hand within his. "You have other skills. You have agility, and the skill to see and recall things. Everyone has a strength. Use yours to stay out of trouble. Now, get some rest. I'll be back soon."

He headed for the door. "Tony—" She paused and waited for him to turn. "I believe in you too. That's why I called you. You might not see yourself as a hero, but you are. To me, you are."

He hovered in the doorway. "Hard not to fall for a woman who tells you something like that," he said, so quietly the words barely reached her.

"Do warriors believe in love?"

His shadow shifted, his shoulders straightening. "Honestly, it's mostly lust. Least it was for me, although I thought I fell in love once before."

Nina popped into her mind. The way she'd looked at them gave Lumin concern. "Was it Nina?"

He nodded once. "Yeah, it was Nina, but Mace and she had sparks from the word hello, and I just wanted in her pants. It wasn't love. It was infatuation. She would have ended up on the cutting room floor like all the rest."

"There's something pretty amazing about her. I think I understand. Kayla too. They're both really strong women. They fit in so well."

In the doorway, with a muscled arm stretched above him, his hand gripped the frame. Tony's certainty of who he was and what he could accomplish was always present. His confidence had a sexy energy, and she loved it. Honorable and brave with an addictive persona, he was everything her mind had conjured up since he'd left her in Las Vegas. Even his voice made her tremble with excitement.

Before he turned to leave, he said, "Some guys aren't attracted to strong, Lumin. Some guys, like me, are attracted to the light."

Chapter Seven

Callum Dafoe strode through the main underground artery that led to his quarters. The reinforced walls stopped the sand from filling in the six-foot-wide tunnel that separated the living quarters from the lab. He reached the end, and slipped his card through the lock, allowing him entry to his private domain. He needed to think, and headed for the bar, pouring himself a healthy finger of whiskey. The east wall was made of glass offering an uninterrupted view of the desert plateau. Sitting down, the cool leather of the chair seeped into his skin. Nestled in the center of a rug with a timber-pole side table, it was his place to reflect.

The alcohol burned its way down his throat and quieted his anger. Another day down, and no closer to finding Dr. Bjornson. Carmichael was dead, and the woman he'd spent the night with in Vegas was being held by the Navy in Coronado. He had no idea what Carmichael relayed to her before his last breath, but it could have been Bjornson's hiding place.

A knock landed on the door. He picked up a remote control and unlocked it.

"Sir?"

"Any word, Billings?" he asked, not turning to look at his laboratory manager.

"I'm afraid not, sir. The men have reported in and advised she is still at the Naval Amphibious Base as far as they know."

"We have to assume she knows something. She's probably told that sailor she ran to everything."

"We don't know what that is," Billings said, rounding the chair to stand in front of him.

"She'll give us what we need, and if she knows nothing, kill her. We have kept this operation under the Americans' noses for the last year without a leak. We are nearing completion."

"Do you still wish to deploy the launch without Dr. Bjornson?"

"If we must. I'm not waiting a day longer than what we projected." He clutched the glass with a death-grip, anger and hate churning in his stomach as it had for three years. "My wife and son have waited long enough for justice."

He placed a hard gaze on Billings as he stood before him with his coke-bottle thick glasses, unruly hair, and white lab coat. The man looked the same every day of the year. "Apprehend that Vegas slut. Take her to the decoy factory and question her there."

"You want me to do it? I'm a scientist, not an interrogator."

"Azeel can question her, but I want you there."

"Yes, sir." The soft pad of Vincent Billings' loafers and the click of the door closing told him he was alone again. He reached for the picture on his side table and stared into the face of his beautiful wife and the broad smile of his five-year-old son. "America took you from me." He kissed the glass, as he did every night, and placed it gently beside him.

Three years had passed since the love of his life died in a pile of rock and fire. Three years of grief propelled his one and only task. He poured millions into creating this lab and the one in New Mexico.

Afsana used to complain he spent too much time with his business and not enough with her and their son. He wanted nothing but to give them every comfort. To provide for them. He didn't give a shit about the war between America and the Middle East, but he used it to make millions. He gave the Americans the weapons they wanted. He sold the same to the Afghanis. They could blow themselves to kingdom come for all he cared, but that's not what happened.

Instead, the Americans' missiles landed on his family's estate, and took his beloved and his son. Afsana was raised in Kabul and refused to leave the war-torn country, no matter how many times he'd begged her. He wanted to bring her to America where he had been raised, but she was adamant. His parents had been so proud to be Americans when they immigrated.

The day she died, he vowed he would give her the justice her death deserved, and that meant the death of every living American. They would suffer like she had, slowly, painfully for twelve hours. He'd walked in horror amongst the rubble until he heard her cries and his son's. They had been together. The workers dug but couldn't reach her, and finally her cries were no more. He ordered them to keep digging, and when they pulled her lifeless, torn body from the brick and stone, she clutched their son in her arms. Even in death, she was beautiful. She haunted his dreams.

Callum drew in the last drop of the whiskey, then set his glass down watching the sun stride across the desert plain, chased by the galloping shadows of the night. The virus which they called EA2 would do the same to the great nation of the United States of America. Every soul would die, their life force extinguished in a bloody, painful death, just like Afsana.

* * * *

Date: 07.25.2014
Time: 0200UTC (Coordinated Universal Time)
Case: Active
Mission: Code Name Luminous

Twelve hours and one more injection later, Lumin stood beside Nina and Kayla as twenty-five men rallied in the Loadout room.

"Operation Luminous," Mace said, and grinned down at the floor.

"That's right." Tony had written it in big letters on the white board. "We need to acquire one very lethal virus and bring Lumin back to Coronado after she leads us to the laboratory. That's our mission," Tony said, walking toward the maps tacked on the white board. Twenty-five SEALs and two liaisons, Kayla and Nina, stood watching him. "This is the largest terrorist threat to face this nation in recorded history. The White House and JSOC have tasked us to stop a pandemic before it starts. No further outbreaks have occurred since the quarantine of Ramah. If this plague is released, the clock starts ticking, and we only have thirty-six hours before it mutates. Worse than that, it kills in twelve hours. Everyone on this mission has now been vaccinated with an antiserum of the original strain of the Bubonic Plague. It is doubtful it will save you against the new virus, only slow it down. The kill ratio is one hundred percent. More than likely, the Tangos will have a vaccine for the current strain."

Tony glanced at Ghost, who surveyed him with a mentor's eye. "There is zero room for failure. We fail, we die, and so does every citizen of this country, then it will cross oceans and borders and kill everyone in its path." He gazed at the SEALs in addition to Alpha Squad who had been brought in for their specialties in reconnaissance, demolitions, chemical and biological warfare, and land navigation. "We will give the men who have been patiently waiting for an opportunity to apprehend Lumin their chance. At this point we have no intelligence on who the terrorists are, thousands of miles of desert to find one, possibly two labs cooking up our demise, and stop the imminent dissemination of a plague. Are there any questions on your taskings for this mission?"

The crowd of expressions melded into one of determination.

"July twenty-fifth, eighteen hundred hours. It's time to roll, SEALs."

The squad broke up and headed for their gear. Vehicles were waiting outside, and everyone had been assigned their duties. He craned a look in Ditz's direction. With a quick jerk of his head to the affirmative, Ditz put his attention back on the mobile computer he carried. Alpha squad surrounded him. The Admiral and Captain Cobbs fell in as well.

He saw Ghost glancing around. "Where's Lumin?" he asked. Tony remained silent for a moment until Ghost's steely-eyed gaze dropped back on him. "For that matter, where is that pain-in-the-ass wife of mine?" Ghost adjusted his pack. "Aren't you escorting Lumin from the base?"

Mace slid a step closer to stand beside Tony. "No, sir. The mission is hot." Ghost cocked his head, waiting for more. "Lumin is on her way." He shot a look at Ditz.

"Exiting the base gates," Ditz informed him.

"I thought you were accompanying her?" Ghost queried.

"No, sir. The men waiting would be suspicious of a trap. You said I was leading this mission, so I took the best idea and implemented it."

"Which was?" Ghost said sharply.

"Snow White," he explained calmly, "suggested it would look normal if the ladies took Lumin off the base."

Ghost's hand shot out and clamped down on his windpipe. Like a thundercloud growing in the sky, Ghost's frame grew to an angry anvil head ready to strike him down. The squad jumped on the Admiral and yarded him back.

"Kayla is with Lumin?" he shouted.

Tony coughed and gasped trying to get air into his lungs. He straightened and coughed again. "Lumin has no military experience. She wouldn't have stood a chance. Nina and Kayla understand how we operate. They can protect her."

Ghost vaulted for him and it took the entire squad to hold him back.

Tony stood his ground. "Nina has hand-to-hand combat experience. Kayla will extrapolate every option and help them pick the best one."

"Sir," Mace said with a low warning in his voice. "Admiral, my wife is there too, but Tony is right. Lumin would never survive unless Nina and Kayla were with her. I trust both of them."

Ghost quit struggling and glared at Tony. "You know what Kayla has lived through. She has no fear, you fucking idiot. No fear of death. No fear of making the wrong move. No fear of sacrificing herself."

"It was her idea, and it was a good one, sir. The terrorists will take all three, and they won't kill any of them, thinking one of them knows where Bjornson is."

Ghost brushed the men's hands from him and stepped into Tony's airspace. "If she dies—"

"Kayla's vehicle has stopped on Orange Avenue," Ditz interrupted.

Ghost's head swiveled. "At a stoplight?"

"No, sir, movie theatre, and they are walking away from the theatre." Ditz lowered his head and placed a hand to his ear. "Roger, good copy, Alpha Four." Ditz's head rose. "Confirmed. They are with three men, getting into a vehicle. They've been taken."

"Keep the visual," Ghost ordered, and ran for the door, the rest of the team behind him.

Tony communicated on the comm set, "All Alpha units, the light has been taken, Alpha Four and Five follow."

The 'rogers' came back from Fox and Ed, each of them leading a squad of men assigned to track the women. Tony, Ghost, Mace, and Captain Cobbs jumped into a black SUV and Ghost floored it. He said nothing, and the grave expression on his face implied he wouldn't be forgiving Tony any time soon.

Comm chatter was kept to a minimum. The women each wore a piece of jewelry that held a tiny transmitter. The GPS chips were tracked by satellite and their signals fed to several laptops. Mace held one of them. The radius for tracking was endless. As long as the jewelry remained with the women, they would know where they were. The drawback was the satellite. If the women entered a building, or went underground, the satellite would not pick up their signal.

Ghost cranked a hard right onto the Strand. "Where are they, Mace?"

"Northbound, toward the San Diego Freeway."

Ghost picked up a handheld radio. "Base Command, this is Alpha One."

"Alpha One, Base Command, go ahead."

Tony recognized Gord's voice. He had arrived in Coronado with Kayla and Barry. They'd been hired together. Gord had one duty, to monitor the satellite and track them.

"You have a pinpoint on the light?"

"Affirmative, Alpha One. The light took the westbound entrance onto the freeway."

"Airport?" Captain Cobbs suggested, sitting next to Mace in the back seat.

Tony turned to see Mace's gaze glued to the monitor. They'd run the plates of the vehicle belonging to the men who'd been tracking Lumin. It was a rental issued to a guy with a fake ID of one Richard Smith, residing in North Pekin, Illinois. These guys were just the couriers. More than likely they knew nothing, and weren't worth apprehending.

"Shit, they aren't going to make this easy," Mace muttered. "They just exited the freeway, bound for North Harbor Drive."

"Airport," Tony confirmed.

"Alpha One, this is Alpha Four," Fox called.

"Go ahead," Tony answered.

"Light is being taken to the private terminal."

"Roger that, ID aircraft," Tony ordered. If they got the ident on the aircraft they'd be able to follow, but he'd already assumed they'd take this route. Someone was in a hurry to question Lumin. The question he needed answered was who and where?

"Base Command this is Alpha One," Ghost transmitted. "Standby for AC deploy."

"Roger, Alpha One."

Two helicopters were standing by for the SEALs. The teams' SUVs slowed and converged at the airport, remaining in the shadows.

Ghost threw the vehicle into park. Without turning his head, he said, "You made the right call, Petty Officer Bale, but you better hope to fucking God we don't lose them, or you're going to learn how to fly from ten thousand feet."

"Sir."

"Kayla is pregnant," Ghost said, his eyes fixed out the front windshield. "It's a girl."

Tony's guts rolled. Damn her. Why the hell hadn't she said anything? "I didn't know, sir."

Ghost's blue eyes glittered with the light from a nearby building. "We're calling her Sloane."

Mace trusted him, but Tony could see he was scared shitless. When Kayla and Nina approached them with their plan, Mace was dead against it, but they couldn't talk Nina or Kayla out of it.

Fox called in. "Niner Mike Lima four eight five. Lear jet."

Ghost relayed the information to Base Command and ordered, "Find out who owns that aircraft." The SUV doors opened and closed, the SEALs darting for the darkness and the tarmac where the helicopters waited.

* * * *

"Buckle up ladies, wouldn't want anything to happen to you," the dark-skinned man who Lumin heard the others call Azeel ordered.

"Do we get champagne on this flight?" Nina asked, taking the window seat of the small corporate jet they'd been herded into.

"Red, you got a mouth on you."

"Course I do, part of the human anatomy. You have one too, even though you're missing a brain," she said, grabbing the buckle and clicking it into place.

"Shut it." Azeel waved the gun he'd been pointing at them since they'd been taken.

Lumin couldn't keep from shaking, but Kayla and Nina seemed as cool as could be. Azeel took the seat across from them. "It's a short flight, but we have time to talk."

"About the weather?" Nina asked, crossing her long legs.

Azeel's eyes ran down her trim pipes to her ankles and back up again. Lumin and she were about the same height and built almost the same way. She couldn't help the thought that Tony liked his women tall, trim and physically fit. Kayla was a small woman with delicate features, and her skin had a hint of olive with big dark eyes that sucked you in when she gazed at you. She probably already knew what Azeel liked for dinner and what he was planning on having tomorrow for breakfast. She remained quiet while Nina took up the slack with one-liners.

"One or all of you have information that we need. Let's start with you," he said pointing the gun at her. Her pulse kicked up into scared rabbit beats.

"If you're looking for a certain wayward scientist, you're pointing that gun at the wrong person," Nina said, fiddling with the arm rest. "Does this seat recline?" She searched until she found it, and pushed back.

"She was with Dr. Carmichael, not you," Azeel said, resting back in his seat.

"Means squat. You know women, we have this knack of sharing everything." She paused. "Do we at least get peanuts?"

Azeel's mouth seamed into an angry slit. "I'm going to have a good time pounding some manners into you while I get the information I want."

Nina scratched her chin with the tip of her fingernail. "No peanuts then."

Kayla pursed a grin. "Dr. Bjornson won't be found if he doesn't want to be found," she said. "Don't you think he would have gotten the hell out of Dodge with you on his tail? He's not exactly happy with what you made him do."

"I didn't make him do anything, it's Dafoe's party, I just get paid well to give him what he wants," Azeel said. "And one of you has information on Bjornson's location. At least you better, or all three of you are dead."

The jet engine on the Leer began to wind up, and the aircraft slowly turned toward the runway.

Nina eyed him. "Ya know, Azeel, we headed out to see a movie and ended up on your fancy Leer jet for destinations unknown. It's all pretty exciting." She gave him a blinding smile and he scowled. "Gonna give us a hint as to where we're going? I didn't pack my swimsuit."

"You won't need it buried in the desert."

"Desert, huh?" She turned a look on Kayla. "Least I'll get a tan."

Kayla chuckled. Lumin looked out the window and prayed to God that Tony and his SEALs were out there. Soon these guys were going to get mean, and she didn't know how long she could take a beating before cracking.

Once the aircraft left the ground and leveled off Lumin asked, "Could I have some water, please?" Fear had turned her tongue into sandpaper.

"Sure," Azeel said, unsnapping his belt. He nodded to one of the other men and then went to retrieve a bottle. He waved it in front of her when he returned. "All you have to do is tell me where Bjornson went."

Nina watched her carefully. She should have known better. Engaging them, asking them anything would have strings attached. "Do you even know what you're a part of?" she asked. "No reason is good enough to release a plague."

Azeel sat back in his chair. "Ah, so you do know something. Too much by the sounds of it." He unscrewed the cap and took a drink, smacking his lips with pleasure. "I have nothing to worry about. At the end of the day, I can live in a mansion in Florida, or take over the Taj Mahal if I want." He shrugged. "Everyone else will be dead."

"And you want to live in a world with decaying bodies and canned food you manage to scrounge up? The world as we know it will end. What kind of world is that to live in?"

Azeel dropped the bottle of water in the seat beside him, and leaned over. "One without three hundred million Americans."

"Hey, smart guy," Nina spouted. "The Plague doesn't stop at twenty-four degrees latitude, you idiot. It will cross every ocean, infiltrate every country including your own, whatever that is."

"My family is taken care of."

"For the first thirty-six hours," Lumin said, seeing this moron didn't have a clue. "Once it mutates, no one is safe. There is no antiserum for that."

Azeel's expression darkened.

"Ah, your boss forgot to mention that, huh? Bummer. Don't worry, you'll have plenty of real estate to bury your family," Nina growled.

"Jihad is not about this life, but the one after. We fight to the end for our belief. Americans fight for nothing."

"What does Dafoe believe in?" Kayla asked.

"Justice," Azeel said sharply.

"You're going to kill us when we tell you what you want. Why should we?" Kayla persisted.

"Because Mr. Dafoe is like you."

"Like me. You mean he's American?"

"You're going to die anyway," Azeel said, taking another long, gandering look at Nina. "Now or later, but if you tell him what he wants to know, then it may be later, and you can scurry into a hole and hope for the best." He picked up the bottle of water and handed it to Lumin. She stared at it, not knowing if she should take it. Nina swiped it from him and handed it to her. "Let's start with something simple. Who's the blond guy you ran to in San Diego? Obviously he's military. What did you tell him?"

Lumin wet her lips, and desperately wanted to chug back the water, but hesitated when he asked about Tony. "A friend. He has nothing to do with Bjornson."

"What did you tell him?"

"I needed a place to chill for a while."

"Is that why he took you to the base for protection? Come on, Lumin. Lying is an art form. You understand art, being a dancer."

"I'm not a dancer."

"No, you're a Vegas showgirl. Far less talent, but you keep a smile on men's faces, don't you? Probably by spreading your legs."

Lumin shook her head in disgust. Azeel's hand was lightning fast when he gripped her arm, digging his fingers into her flesh. "What did you tell him?"

She winced and tried to pull away, but he pinched harder.

"Does it matter what she told him?" Kayla intervened, leaning forward and glaring at Azeel. "The United States Special Operations knows what we know. The question is whether or not you'll get to Bjornson before they do. What will happen if the good guys get there first?"

Azeel dropped her arm and his large frame leaned forward to match Kayla's. His deep, black eyes swam with a crazy light. A thin sheen of sweat layered his dark-skinned brow. "Then we don't need you anymore, and I'll have the pleasure of torturing you the way I want to."

Lumin's stomach twisted into a knot.

Kayla didn't blink, but women can sense danger and unease like a storm front looming in the distance. "Is torture part of Jihad? Do you get pleasure from that, Azeel? You're singing to the wrong bird."

"Your admiral husband and the rest of the SEALs will follow us, Kayla. We have something very special waiting for them. I have a personal vendetta against SEALs, and I can't wait to see them scream in pain as the plague turns them into bloated flesh."

Lumin's fear skyrocketed. They knew who they were, and that the SEALs were coming.

Kayla's voice dropped ten decibels. "You think you're smarter than my husband. He's going to stack you and your men like cordwood. You're the ones who will be buzzard bait."

"I doubt that, Mrs. Austen. Your husband has power and he wants you back alive. If you tell us what we want to know, he'll have you back. Nothing will stop what we have planned. I'd suggest if you know where Bjornson is, you tell me now, and you won't have to endure my skills."

Nina sighed loudly and Azeel's eyes slid to her. "You're getting boring, Azeel. You sound like every other terrorist playing the same record over and over again." She offered him a contemplative gaze. "It's not the SEALs that will kick your ass, it's us. You walked right into the middle of a shit storm, and you don't even know you're neck deep."

Azeel sneered at her. "I know everything, Mrs. Callahan, but most importantly I know where your daughter Gabriella is. I'll make sure my man sends me a live feed when he injects your daughter with the plague."

Nina's leg shot up so fast it was like a blur, and so was the ricochet of Azeel's head, with the pointy end of her boot snapping it back. Blood sprayed from his nose and he roared with anger, vaulting out of his seat and swinging a powerful fist aimed for Nina's face.

Chapter Eight

Date: 07.25.2014
Time: 1200UTC 0400hrs PST
Mission: Code Name Luminous

"Where are they?" Vincent Billings asked, walking into the abandoned facility outside of Kingman, Arizona. This was a waste of his time. He should be back at the lab trying to finish Dr. Bjornson's work, but disobeying Callum Dafoe was not an option. The man was psychotic about giving his dead wife and son the justice he believed they were due.

Vincent's hate for Americans had deep roots as well. In Iraq, when they'd come in and destroyed everything in their path, he hoped one day he'd see justice. It hadn't taken much for Dafoe to convince him to manage his lab while they re-engineered the Plague. Once upon a time, Vincent had been Kasim Al-Saadi. His parents had been in favor with the ruling power and lived a comfortable life. They sent him to England for his education, and he received a doctorate at Stanford for infectious diseases. He didn't have the experience Carmichael and Bjornson had, but he knew what they were doing and his role was to keep progress moving.

"They're separated," one of Dafoe's security officers informed him. He jerked his head toward the back of the building.

"Which one is Lumin in?"

"Door number two," the guy said.

When he entered, he saw two security men standing in opposite corners of the room. One took a long drag on a cigarette and then flicked it on the ground. "I want to speak with Miss Edenridge—alone."

The men shoved off the walls and exited with a disdainful look as they passed him. Lumin looked like a scared rabbit who was trying to keep a brave face. Her right cheek was red and inflamed. Her hands were tied behind her back, sitting in the center of the room. Slowly, he closed the door. "Lumin, these men will not stop hurting you until they get answers." She stared at him, tears welling in her eyes and dripping down her cheeks. He didn't really care if they skinned her alive, but he had to make her believe that he did. He hunched down. "Lumin, I know you were dragged into this, but you don't have to be involved. Just tell us what Carmichael told you before he died."

"Who are you?" she whispered, choking on a dry throat.

"I'm Dr. Billings." He looked over his shoulder as if checking to make sure no one else was around. "I'm as cornered in this as you are. I'm just trying to stay alive. Dr. Carmichael and Dr. Bjornson were my friends. Now Carmichael is dead and I'm afraid Cliff is as well. I want to find him. I need your help."

"I want to leave," Lumin said, closing her eyes as another tear squeezed out. "Let me go."

"I will, my dear. I promise, but you have to tell us where Cliff is."

"You're going to kill everyone."

"I don't want to kill anyone. If I could stop this I would, maybe I still can, but not without Cliff."

Lumin opened her eyes and blinked to clear them.

"Please, they won't give me much time alone with you. Lumin—please."

"Dr. Carmichael died even though he helped you."

"That was Dafoe, not me."

"You didn't save him."

Vincent was losing his temper. He couldn't tell whether or not she was stringing him along or on the verge of spilling what she knew. *Patience.* "I am in a position to get you out of here. You have to trust me."

"My friends, what about them?"

If he promised her everything she'd know he was lying. "I'll try." She shook her head. "If they talk before you do, I can't help you. Dafoe's men will kill you." He patted her on the leg. "I'll get you some water. Be right back."

Vincent exited the room and looked for Azeel. He heard a woman threatening someone and he headed for the next door. One of Azeel's henchmen had a tiny brunette around the throat, squeezing the air from her. "Let her go," he demanded. She staggered and reached for the chair, but fell to her knees before she reached it. He strode across the room and helped her. "There is no saving this country. Why don't you tell me where Bjornson is and end your suffering?"

The woman raised her pretty face and stared at him with dark, benign eyes. She concealed her pain deep inside. "Your plan is already screwed. Are you Dafoe?" she said, through a blossoming lip where someone had fisted her.

"No, I'm a scientist. I worked with Clifford Bjornson. I need to find him."

The brunette's gaze lowered to the floor and her head drooped. "Good luck with that."

He grabbed her hair and yanked her head back. "Listen to me. I'm losing my patience. One of you is going to talk or two of you are dead."

* * * *

Azeel slowly paced around the table Nina was pinned face down on. It took two strong men to hold her there. She was definitely a fighter and that turned him on. He leaned over and looked into Nina's eyes blistering with hate. "Would your husband still touch you if I took you myself, or would he be sickened at the thought?" She struggled, but the men held her down by cranking her arms behind her, way past the point of pain. "Stand her up." He ripped her top open, the buttons flying off and bouncing on the cement floor. With a knife he pulled from his pocket, he cut through her bra front and once through each shoulder strap. With a flick of his hand, he revealed her breasts. "I'm going to fuck you dry, Red."

"How do you fuck someone without a dick?" she spit at him.

He gripped the band of her skirt and yanked it down, exposing her black satin panties. "Very sexy," he said, running a finger across her shoulder and then around her breast, playing with the tip of her nipple with his thumb. "Believe me, I have enough to fill you and more. Probably the best fuck you'll get for the rest of your life, considering that's imminently short."

The door burst open. "What's going on in here?" Dr. Billings shouted.

"Come to watch the show, Doc?" He stood behind Nina and grasped both of her tits, pulling her against him. Dr. Billings looked unnerved. "I'm going to fuck the truth out of this one." He bit her shoulder hard and she suppressed a cry of pain. "Oh, sweetheart, look you're bleeding," Azeel said with a mocking tone.

"Where is Dr. Bjornson?" Billings said, stepping in front of Nina. "Tell us or I'll let him do what he wants."

Azeel grabbed her face roughly and dug his fingers into the hollows of her cheeks. "Look at the man when he talks to you, Red. You got an answer for him or not?"

"Bite me," she hissed.

And he did, digging his teeth into the already swollen openings of his last mark. Nina screamed.

Gunfire erupted from the main area. Billings stiffened. "What's that?" He forgot he was within striking distance. Nina kicked him in the nuts, doubling him over, and used his falling body to spring back against Azeel. He stumbled back, and she swiveled without pause and kicked him in the groin. He nearly blacked out with the power of her long leg. The door flew open and a soldier with a weapon at eye level entered the room.

"Nina," the soldier yelled. "Look out."

A little late for the fiery redhead though, and Azeel plunged the needle into her shoulder and pumped the contents into her body.

The soldier gripped her to his chest protectively and yanked her away, pulling out the needle and dropping it on the floor. "Do we need him?"

"Tinman? Don't tell Mace, please, Tony."

"I can't do that, Ninja Girl."

"He won't be able to do his job. Promise me."

"Do we need him?" The soldier's eyes were cold and calculating.

Nina nodded and then gasped out, "Yes."

"Too bad, soldier boy. Have to kill me another day I guess."
He didn't expect the bastard to come down on the trigger and fire
into his knee. Before he blacked out he heard Red say to the
soldier. "We definitely need that other guy."

"Don't shoot me," Billings screamed.

* * * *

Mace parted from Tony and headed for the farthest closed
door. He kicked it open and then rammed himself against the wall.
Taking a careful look inside, there was only one chair and one
occupant. "Kayla?"

She raised her head and he ran to her, undoing the ties behind
her back. She threw her arms around his neck. "Thank God."

He gently touched her lip.

"I'm all right, Mace. Where's Nina and Lumin?"

"Other rooms, I think. Come on." He wrapped an arm around
her waist and helped her to the door. "Ghost is going to shit a brick
when he sees you."

Kayla choked out a laugh. "Tell the Admiral to keep his
knickers together. We've got information. Not all of it, but more
pieces to the puzzle."

"Ya really think that's going to help when he sees you like
this?" he said, walking through the doorway with her.

Mace looked to his left and saw Tinman come out of the other
room with Nina. He'd covered her with his camo jacket. Her face
was bruised, and his anger drove his good sense to the brink.

"Nina," he called. She looked up, and blew him a kiss. God,
the woman made him nuts. "Where's the Admiral?" Mace asked.

The rest of the Tangos were under control and on their bellies
on the floor. A single shot coming from the last room made
everyone's head crank up. A few seconds later Ghost appeared
with Lumin draped in his arms.

"Secure the area," Tony shouted.

"She passed out," Ghost said, laying Lumin on a table.

Mace slung his weapon to his side and moved toward Nina.
Tinman raised his hand as if he wanted him to stop, and Nina
stepped behind him. What the hell was going on? Ghost reached
for Kayla, embracing her with a concerned look.

Tony left Nina's side and hovered above Lumin, searching her face. Her cheek was puffy and red. Someone had worked her over, but she was breathing and that's probably all that mattered to Tony. He gently pulled her hand against his heart. "Lumin, wake up. You're safe."

Lumin's head rocked and her long lashes fluttered. "Tony? Tony," she said, and then flung herself into his arms.

He rocked her, holding her tight. "It's okay. Everything is going to be okay."

"Who got the worse end of the stick, you or them?" Mace asked Nina, taking another step toward her and stopped when she distanced herself. "You look like hell, baby." Nina wrapped her arms around herself. "What's wrong? What are you doing?"

"I love you. I'll always love you," she whispered, but her face was a mask of barely restrained emotion.

Nina's body began to tremble. "Hey, it's okay, babe. The cavalry is here. Everything's under control," Mace said.

"Sir," one of the squad members from DEVGRU waited for Ghost to turn around. "I found this on the floor. It's empty."

Ghost's brows shot together and then his eyes widened with concern. All three of the women stared at Ghost. "Which—" he paused and his jaw grew taut. "Which one of you?"

Mace's heart started to thump hard in his chest. "Is that what I think it is?"

Lumin stood, protected in Tinman's arms as his gaze went from the needle to meet Nina's eyes. Mace's blood ran cold. "No," he said sharply. He vaulted toward Nina. Tinman tried to stop him, but he tore from his grip and wrenched Nina to his chest. "Nina, no."

"I'm sorry." Her brows crumpled. "I'm so sorry, Mace," she tried to push away from him.

Mace's gaze bounced off of every face, until he found the one he wanted. He had the guy with the white lab coat against the wall by the neck. "Where is the antiserum?"

The guy offered a seething glare. "She's as good as dead. Just like my family. The ones you Americans slaughtered in my country."

With his first swing, the bones in the guy's nose shattered. "Where…is…the…antiserum?" Mace hollered inches from his face.

The guy spit out a piece of tooth when he said, "Twelve hours. You can watch her die in front of you, and it's agonizing."

Mace got one more strike in before he was pulled away and watched the man slide down the wall, unconscious.

"She has to be quarantined," Ghost said quietly, letting go of Mace's arm. "Ditz?"

"Sir," Ditz said, giving Mace an uneasy look. "I'll advise USAMRIID, *U.S. Army Medical Research Institute*, for transport."

Mace took a step toward Nina, and Ghost stopped him. "Nina?" Ghost warned.

She nodded briskly, swiping the tears from her cheeks, understanding that no one could come near her anymore. "Mace, promise me—"

"No, I won't promise a god damn thing. You're going to live. You hear me? Gabbs needs you. I need you," he said hoarsely.

Nina's face pinched together with agony. She raised her hand to her belly.

Kayla sucked in a breath. "Oh, Nina, no," she said, with a rare showing of emotion. "Please don't tell me you did this with—"

Mace was confused. "With what? What? Nina." He saw she still protected her stomach, and then it dawned on him.

"It was a surprise." A gust of air came out with fresh tears. "I was going to tell you on our last night in Mexico, but then…"

Mace felt like he'd been enveloped in a cloud of numbness.

Nina nodded and gave a half-hearted smile. "We'll be all right," she said, clutching her stomach.

He scrunched his eyes closed and let out a deep breath. "I will find the antiserum," he vowed, forcing away the hopelessness. "I will search every hole in this desert to find it." He lifted his gaze to his friends, his family. "I'm going to be a father."

Ghost gripped him around the shoulders and held onto him. "Yes, you are, Mace." He paused and said, "Meeting in there." The Admiral pointed to the middle room.

* * * *

Tony's arm propped Lumin up, and she needed his help. They filed into the dilapidated office she'd been held in, but as soon as they entered the room he left her. Only the members of Alpha Squad were present. Ghost faced the wall for a moment and then slowly turned to speak to them. One fist was clenched tightly, but that was the only sign he was unnerved. Lumin couldn't keep the tears at bay. Nina could die, and it was because she'd protected her. Tony must hate her, and she wouldn't blame him. She'd brought this to them, and now Nina was infected. Ghost tried to speak, but then his head lowered as if he was trying to keep it together. When he rested his gaze on them, Lumin was shocked to see tears in his eyes.

"In war, we understand when we fight for this country it may mean we die for this country. I have no explanation why someone like me escaped that end and others have not." His lips pressed together for a second and then he spoke again. "We put it on the line to protect our families and what we believe in. Nina is like a sister to me." He scrubbed away a tear and kept talking. "That woman has a fire that burns in her and will until her last breath. Mace, I will not stop until we have the antiserum in our hands, but we have less than twelve hours to find it. I will use everything in my power to keep Nina alive." He put his gaze on his wife. "Kayla?"

All eyes turned to her, and she nodded slowly and took a deep breath. She filled the team in with every detail she had gathered since they'd been taken.

As Kayla spoke, Ditz searched data files. Filling them in when he found what he was looking for. "Callum Dafoe is a businessman and producer of small and medium-sized arms. He sold his weapons to the highest bidder and then sold more to the next highest. His wife and son, as Kayla suggested, were killed in a bombing in Kabul three years ago."

"I don't give a shit about his motivation. Where is he?" Ghost growled.

Ditz didn't flinch with Ghost's sharp response, and kept reporting. "He disappeared after that. Border services have a record of him entering the States three years ago. He's an American citizen, but was born in Afghanistan. His parents immigrated thirty-five years ago."

"Other relatives in the U.S.?" Ghost queried.

"Searching that now, sir," Ditz said.

Nathan and Ed brought in a table, and Fox flattened a map on it. Tony had moved away from her and concentrated on the map. He wouldn't look at her and Lumin knew her suspicions were correct.

Ed stepped to her side and gave a comforting smile as he wrapped his arm around her and squeezed her shoulder. "It's not your fault, Miss Lumin," he whispered.

Tony looked toward them, but nothing registered in his eyes. Tears threatened, but she held them back.

"Before I question our scientist out there, and Ghost goes to town on that bastard Azeel, where is the lab, Kayla?" Fox asked.

Kayla's gaze snapped to the map on the table. "Ditz, does Dafoe own property in Nevada?"

Ditz sat back and nodded. "Found it. Lots of it," he answered. "Arizona, New Mexico, Nevada, and he has a residence in Los Angeles."

Kayla ran a slow hand through her curls. "I still believe the Nevada lab must be in the northern part of the state. Azeel didn't give us anything on the location. They would keep the scientists and the others sequestered to avoid leaks." She blinked and looked to her husband. "I've got an idea, but it's going to take time. I'll call Base Command and tell them what I'm looking for."

"We're out of time," Tony said. "They are too far ahead of us. The only reason Dr. Carmichael is dead is because he finished his part of the puzzle. I think the deployment of the Plague is imminent."

"Time to find out," Ghost said. "I'm going to have a little talk with Azeel." Kayla moved as if going with him. "No, Kayla."

"Nina is my best friend. You need me in there while you *talk* with him. Call it therapy."

He jerked his head in approval. "Fox, put your teams into position before you question Billings. We need to find Dafoe."

"Aye, aye, Admiral." Fox stretched his neck and flexed his fingers. On Nina's behalf, Fox would seek justice as well as information from Billings.

Tony said, "Ed, Nathan, Stitch, question the other prisoners."

They all nodded, but Ed didn't leave her side. Cobbs joined Stitch, and they departed.

"Find a corner and get some rest, Lumin," Tony said, and turned his attention back to the map. The room emptied except for her, Ed, and Tony.

"I'm sorry," she said weakly. "I know it's not enough in light of what Nina is about to face. I never imagined this. I'd take it back if I could."

Tony kept his attention on the map. "We lose people in our line of work," his voice gravelly with emotion.

Ed remained beside her. "This is not your fault, sweetheart," he said.

Tony's head snapped up and his gaze popped between them.

"I don't know Nina all that well myself," Ed continued. "But I know she's a brave lady, and so are y'all."

Tony watched silently.

"Nina isn't just people. You love her," she said to Tony.

Tony's brow flexed, his gaze riveted on the table. "I do. We all do. She's part of our family."

Lumin heard the words he didn't say, *But you're not.* "Maybe the vaccines we received will slow it down."

"I doubt it. They want people to die. They've re-engineered it to be immune. If we don't find the antiserum, Nina won't make it." A harsh line of worry crossed his forehead.

Lumin removed the space between them and clutched his arm. "I'll help you." Tony held her with a vacant stare. There was no warmth in his eyes, and she couldn't blame him. "Use me again."

"No, Lumin. When Billings doesn't return, Dafoe will know we've captured him. You dying, as well as Nina, won't stop the virus," Ed said from behind her.

Tony walked away from her, and so did hope. What could she do? A man screaming made her nearly jump out of her skin. The Admiral had to be *talking* with Azeel, but she knew they didn't have the time for the Admiral to wear a man like him down. Azeel's hate ran too deep, and he'd die before giving up any information.

She and Ed watched Tony walk toward the door without another word. "I don't know what to do." she said, hoping Ed would.

"Hey, you've done enough." He drew his arms around her. "You're a brave lady, you know that."

She wasn't brave. She wasn't a warrior, and she felt alone even though Ed was obviously trying to comfort her. Her heart fell when Tony halted at the door and said, "Cracker. Outside. Question the prisoners." It came out harsh and cold.

Ed faced Tony and nobody could miss his agitation. "You really are an asshole." Tony took a threatening step into the room. "Stand down, Bale. I'm going to get her some water first."

Tony seemed to draw back and nodded. "Fine."

"I'll be right back, Miss Lumin." Ed walked past Tony and their gazes were locked on each other in some kind of silent combat.

"Tell me what to do, Tony. I'm out of my element," she said, when Ed had left the room and Tony stood there as if undecided to stay or go.

He shook his head. "Nothing. Stay away from the prisoners. I'll arrange transport to get you back to San Diego."

"San Diego isn't my home." She swallowed deeply, digging for some bravery that Ed thought she had. No way was she going to crumble in front of Tony. "I don't know anyone there."

Tony's jaw flexed. "You can stay at the base. You'll be safe there."

She straightened her shoulders and wiped every emotion from her face. If he could do it, so could she. Not that many hours ago he wanted her to stay at his apartment, now it was the base. Although the rising sun heated the roof making it crack as it expanded, her heart shriveled with the knowledge Tony's concern was all wrapped up around Nina. She couldn't blame him. Love had eyes of its own, and it always looked up when danger threatened someone you loved.

"Thanks, but I don't belong there." She gripped her hands together for her own security. "I'm sorry, Tony, but I know you'll find the vaccine, and Nina will be okay. She has to be."

He gave her a short nod, and left her alone.

Chapter Nine

Minutes turned into two hours. Nina was quarantined to one of the rooms they'd been held in, and Lumin slid down to the floor with her back to the door. "Nina, how are you feeling?"

"Fine," Nina's voice drifted back. She must have been sitting on the other side of the door.

Lumin folded her hands into a tight ball. "Are you lying?"

"Yes."

"What is it?"

"Fever and my muscles ache. Lymph nodes are starting to swell."

"I can't believe this is happening." She heard Nina shift her position.

"Considering I was sunning my ass a couple days ago in Mexico and just married the most handsome man in the world, I'd have to agree."

"Why did you do this if you were pregnant?"

"Couldn't let Kayla have all the fun now could I? Kayla is pregnant as well. She's expecting a little girl."

Lumin's eyes welled and everything blurred. "Tony's really upset this happened to you."

"Tony looks like he's kinda smitten. I'd do anything for that man. I'm so happy he's going to settle down."

"He's really scared for you."

Kayla appeared, sat down beside her and covered her hand, giving it a squeeze. "Some stinkin' virus isn't going to hurt Nina," she said.

"Hey, boss," Nina greeted.

"How ya doin', ya old married boot?"

"Feel like shit," Nina said and chuckled.

Lumin found comfort in Kayla's warm hands. They were dainty, but the woman exerted some kind of powerful field. Lumin felt safer when she was around. "She's got a fever and aching muscles."

"It's blistering hot outside and after kickin' Azeel in the face, I'd say that earns aching muscles," Kayla responded.

"Thanks for the lie, boss."

Kayla turned her head and winked at Lumin.

"How's the search going?" Nina asked.

"I've got Gord looking for routine movements in northern Nevada on the satellite. He'll find it."

"What are you looking for?" Nina asked weakly.

"Supplies. We humans are animals of habit. If the Tangos have a group of people sequestered, they have to feed them."

"Sounds like a plan." Nina sighed. "How's Mace?"

"Fucked up," Kayla said. "But he hasn't known you as long as I have. He knows you're ornery. I know you're undefeatable."

Nina choked out a laugh. "Not sure I can win this one." She paused, then said, "Kayla, I have a will, and I changed it and named you guardian for Gabbs. I know you and Mace can work it out, but if he wants to keep Gabbs, then—"

"Stop, Nina. I hear you, but I don't want you thinking about this shit. It's negative crap."

"It's reality, Kayla. I've got ten hours and the symptoms are coming on fast."

"I wish you wouldn't have come," Lumin said, more tears spilling.

"Shit happens," Nina said. "You wouldn't have made it by yourself. We spread the love around and gave 'em a run for their money. We have more information. That's how this works. If someone falls in the process, it's part of the job."

"You're not a SEAL. I blame myself and I think Tony does too."

"Say what?" Kayla and Nina said at the same time.

She stared into Kayla's questioning gaze. "I'm pretty sure he loves Nina."

"Oh, bullshit," Nina spit from the other side. "Listen, little sister. Tony's a big, old, bad man-whore, but I think that might have changed recently. Even when we were in Las Vegas, Tinman kept sneaking looks at you. From the way he acted when Ghost wanted to use you as a guinea pig, I'd say he's got a bit of a heart palpation for you."

Kayla nodded at her. "Think she's right. Tony's just like the other guys. Their jobs leave them restless when they get home. Women flock to them, and what guy is going to say no to sex? Tony has always been a love 'em and leave 'em kind of guy. If he didn't care about you, he wouldn't have put up the stink he did when Thane wanted to use you to find the Tangos."

Lumin hiccupped through her tears. "I suppose."

"No supposing about it," Nina said. "Those big lugs all have heart, even though they have to stash it when they're out on a mission. Tony's one of the harder cases, but I think even he's starting to settle down and look into the future. You came along and he's got that glazed puppy dog look in his eyes."

"Tony's—different."

"Oooh, would ya listen to this," Nina sung out, followed by a whistle. "Sounds like the new girl has a bit of a crush on our Tony. What d'ya think, boss?"

"Think she's exactly what he needs," Kayla said, swiping Lumin's hair over her shoulder.

Lumin liked both Kayla and Nina. Not having a big sister, something she'd always wanted, she felt like she'd been adopted by them. "I did something stupid."

"Do tell," Nina spurred her on. "It might make me feel better, since I'm holding a first place position in stupid today."

"I kind of, well—I kind of asked Tony to take my virginity. He didn't want to. Maybe that was a mistake."

Kayla tried to resist a laugh, but it came out anyway. "You had to seduce Tony? Is…is that what you just said?"

Nina chuckled from the other side of the door. "See, miracles do happen."

"I think my age bothered him. We're seven years apart."

Kayla grinned at her, and Lumin was surprised at how beautiful she was when she smiled. "If Tony had reservations about taking your innocence, I guarantee he's got a serious crush on you."

"But he looked like he hated me after Nina was injected with the virus."

"That's not hate, Lumin." Nina sighed. "That's Tony finding Tony, and what you saw was him connecting with the fear of losing you. He and Mace are like bookends. Brothers of war. He feels what my husband feels, and it scared him. He's never let himself get close to a woman before."

Kayla nodded. "These men don't do anything halfway, Lumin. That's your first lesson in falling for a SEAL. They live hard. Fight hard. And when they fall in love, they fall hard."

"Tony told me your story, Kayla. What happened to you and how the Admiral saved you."

"Pfft, Kayla saved Ghost, not the other way around."

Kayla looked into her lap and wore a haunting smile. "No. He did save me. In many ways. I thought I'd healed myself." She eyed Lumin. "Thane shook up everything and helped me rebuild all the trust I'd lost in men. He never quit on me, even though I put him through hell." Kayla offered her a warm smile. "They say still waters run deep. These SEALS, who live their lives in sea and sand, never give in."

"Look at the cost. Nina's sick because you tried to help me."

"Not going to argue that sucks. Just wish I could have kicked Azeel in the nuts again. It might've made me feel better," Nina joked.

All of them laughed.

"The guys will find the antiserum," Kayla said, when the seriousness of the moment threatened to probe at them.

"I really wanted to see that movie too," Nina joked. "We'll have to catch it when we finish saving the world, and for the love of God stop crying, Lumin."

Lumin swiped at her eyes. "I can't help it. I wish our places were reversed."

"Don't sweat it," Kayla said, twisting on her hip and repositioning herself on the floor. "Nina likes being a martyr."

"Fuck you," wafted through the door.

"Bite me," Kayla growled back and they both laughed.

"My throat is screaming at me right now. Think I'll try to get a cat nap," Nina said.

Kayla rested a flattened palm on the door. "Rest. Everything is going to work out. Even if the clock runs out, I know you'll hang in there. You have to. No giving up," Kayla said to the door. She blinked away a tear. "We made a promise, remember?"

Nina let out a high-pitched sigh. "Yeah."

Lumin didn't ask what that promise was, but she could see it was one made by best friends who would do anything for each other. Kayla nodded and brushed her cheeks, then stood. "I'm going to check in with Base Command. You okay?"

Lumin nodded. "I think I'll take a walk outside." She watched Kayla disappear into a circle of SEALs as she pushed herself to her feet. The sunlight made her wince when she stepped outside. A few of the SEALs were grouped together, Nathan being one of them. He wandered toward her.

"How ya doing?" he asked, rearranging his weapon to his side.

How did they stand in the heat with all the clothes and gear? She'd be a puddle of melted goo by now. "Just talked with Nina."

He nodded. "She's sick, isn't she?"

She nodded and bit back her guilt. "Yes. What's going to happen to her?"

"Areomedical techs are on their way." He turned his head and looked toward the long empty road that led to the factory.

"Are they doctors?"

"No, they're a transportation team. Ghost had already spoken with USAMRIID before we started the mission. They were on standby. The C-130 is waiting at Luke AFB."

"Where are they going to take her?"

"To an institute in Maryland. They have a containment facility."

Lumin swiped away the sweat beading on her brow with an arm. "That doesn't sound very good."

"It's a specialized team that's coming to get her. The doctors in Maryland will be working double-time to save her."

Far in the distance, Lumin saw dust rising in the air. "That looks like a vehicle," she said.

Nathan turned and spoke into a small mic on the end of a wire. "Admiral, incoming. Looks like Nina's ride."

Every head in the group of SEALs turned. It wasn't just one vehicle, it was five. One was a large military truck, the others were SUVs, a jeep, and one panel truck for the prisoners. Several men came out of the building, and one was Tony. She could pick him out easily, even though they all looked the same in their fatigues. The Admiral and Captain Cobbs appeared and the Admiral ordered something to the men who nodded and moved away from the entrance. Lumin wanted to be there when they took Nina away, but Nathan stopped her.

"Admiral has given orders that we all remain clear until Nina is placed in the containment stretcher."

"What's that?"

"You'll see," was all he said, his expression severe.

A commotion and shouting came from inside the factory, and Lumin recognized it as Mace's voice. The Admiral immediately headed inside. Lumin's heart squeezed tight. Mace must be going out of his mind with worry, and yet he had to stay with the squad. She waited with the rest of them and watched as four men in biohazard suits emerged from the truck. They carried a stretcher that had a square plastic container with inverted sleeves for working on the patient. Lumin covered her mouth to restrain a cry. This is how Nina would have to be transported. Mace wouldn't even be able to hold her when he said goodbye.

The minutes ticked on until they finally appeared. Lumin choked back a moan. Nina lay encased in the bubble, and Mace walked beside her. His hand stuffed in one of the many sleeves. The Admiral and Kayla escorted them on the other side. Tony ran to them, and so did she. They reached Nina at the same time.

The men in the suits lifted the stretcher into the back of the truck.

"Baby, I'll see you soon," Mace said, his words shaky with emotion.

"I love you, hot stuff," Nina's words were muffled from inside of her small plastic prison.

"Don't give up." Mace stuffed his other hand in one of the sleeves and gripped hers tightly. "Say it."

Nina tried to smile, and then her brow furrowed, and tears finally came from the brave woman's eyes. "I don't regret anything, Mace. Not a second."

She turned her head away to hide her tears from her husband. "Tony?"

Tony leaned over the plastic covering. "Right here, Ninja Girl."

"Don't you let him do anything stupid. Watch my husband's back."

"Always do. This is just a speed bump. You hang in there for a couple hours and we'll get that serum to you."

She nodded quickly. "Take care of Lumin."

Tony didn't take his eyes off of Nina. "I will."

"Hey, you know I love you for what you did for Mace and me. I'll never—"

Tony darted a worried glance at Mace, and pushed his hand through a sleeve. Nina's hair was plastered to her sweating skin and her cheeks were a rosy red. He brushed her cheek. "Don't start giving me goodbye speeches, Ninja Girl. I want to see you on the mat when this is all over. We'll go a couple rounds and you can kick my ass."

She closed her eyes with a slow blink. "I love you, Petty Officer Callahan, and I love my daughter. She needs one of us." Nina swiped the tears away. "Remember that before you go all crazy SEAL."

Mace leaned forward and kissed the covering that kept him from holding his wife. Lumin could feel the depth of their love as the aeromedical team pushed Nina's stretcher farther into the truck. Mace and Tony watched the door close, cutting them off from Nina. Mace couldn't hide his pain any longer and he palmed his face, shaking his head.

Tony gripped him in a hug. "Don't even think it, buddy. That's not the last time you'll see her. Hey!" He pulled Mace's hand from his face. "You hear me?"

Mace's chest heaved. He jerked his head in a nod and stared into the heavens.

* * * *

Lumin backed away, feeling like she didn't belong. Tony hadn't even spared her a glance. At the moment she probably couldn't look herself in the mirror. She thought about what Nina and Kayla told her, but they'd been wrong. If only she'd called the CDC and dropped it in their lap, Nina wouldn't be in the back of a truck. She pondered her mistake until she reached the factory and sat down against the wall. The hot metal burned the skin on her shoulder blades. There had to be a way she could help. She stared up into the sky. The night she and Star went out with the two men played itself over and over again. The SEALs needed more pieces of the puzzle. She bolted upright with a thought, and reached for her phone, forgetting Azeel's men had taken it from her, but someone had to have one. She saw Nathan milling about and approached him. He gave up his phone without question, and she quickly put distance between them as she dialed.

"Hello?"

"Star?"

"Where the hell have you been, Lumin?"

"Are you okay? Do you feel all right?"

"I don't know if I'd call being held against my will in some fucking hole in the ground, okay."

"Lumin Edenridge," a man's voice said calmly into the phone.

"Yes, is this Mr. Dafoe?"

"So you know who I am. That is a problem."

"It isn't a problem if you let Star go. She wasn't with Dr. Carmichael, I was." Lumin watched as Dafoe's men were herded into another truck with armed SEALs making sure all of them stayed in line.

"And did the good doctor tell you where Clifford Bjornson is hiding?"

"Yes, and I'll tell you if you let Star go."

"I sent men to collect you, but it seems you've brought the Navy SEALs along for the ride."

"I'll do what you want, just let Star go. When she calls me telling me she's safe, I'll tell you what you want to know."

"I have a better plan. I want you to come to me without the SEALs, and if I see one sign of them Star will have twelve hours to exist on this earth."

She nodded. "All right," she said and listened carefully. She finished the call and approached Nathan. "Nathan, the Admiral says he doesn't need me anymore. Do you think I could borrow that Jeep? I'm going to go into town and get a room and some rest."

"I'll drive you, Lumin. Ghost isn't finished interrogating the prisoner, and Fox hasn't gotten very far with Billings, either."

Small pebbles and sand ground beneath her sneakers as she turned. "It looks like you have enough transportation. I just want to get a shower and deal with some...you know, lady things."

Nathan shuffled, looking quite uncomfortable. "I see."

It never failed, single guys never liked talking about a woman's monthly issues. "Here's your phone."

"Keep it," Nathan said. "Tony will want to be in contact."

Doubt that. "Will Mace be okay?"

Nathan adjusted his weapon, cradling his forearms on it. "He'll hold it together. If anything, he'll do it for Nina." Nathan said, "Keys are in the ignition. I'll let Tinman know where you are."

"He knows," she lied. She needed time to widen the distance between them, and time to find the antiserum. She just needed to get it and get out without being killed.

She waited outside, watching the movements of the team of SEALs. Her pulse skipped with nervous beats. Most of them had filtered into the building for some shade. She stayed away from them and skirted to the shady side of the building. There she waited, hoping they would forget about her. She heard the crunch of pebbles under a heavy foot.

"Lumin?"

Stupid. She wanted to look up and see Tony, but instead Ed knelt down on one knee in front of her. He removed his helmet and set it on the ground. A concerned look penetrated his blue eyes and a taut jawline edged his handsome features.

"Stop beating yourself up," he ordered gently. "What happened to Nina is not your fault. It could have been any or all of you who ended up with the same fate." He covered her hand. "I would have never drawn you into this mission. Even if it meant losing a lead on the cell, you shouldn't have been involved in this."

She shook her head. "You know more now, and that's the only good thing that came out of it. I hope you find Dafoe."

"That's what we're trained to do and we will." He brushed her hair aside and said, "Why don't you come inside and we'll get a drink of water. It's too hot out here, even in the shade."

"I'm fine." She snagged a stone from the ground and clutched it, wishing it was magic and she could cast a spell to end all this. The crunch of pebbles made them both look up. Tony appeared, then stopped, seeing them. His hazel gaze tore into Ed.

"Fox wants you," he said sharply.

"Trying to convince Lumin to come inside," Ed said. "Come on, Lumin." He pulled on her hand.

"I'd rather stay here. Thanks, Ed."

He nodded. "Convo," he said to Tony, but Tony didn't move. "Later."

Ed stalled, but then carried on around the corner.

She stared out at the endless desert instead of Tony.

"Have some water," he said, offering her his canteen.

"No thanks." She wanted him gone so she could get to the Jeep and on the road.

"Ed's right. I should have never allowed them to use you."

"And then Nina wouldn't be infected. I know."

"Lumin, I'm going to call Steven Porter. All our resources are tied up right now. I want him to come and get you."

"No," she said sharply. "I don't want them to know."

"He can protect you. Stay with them until this is over."

Finally, she lifted her gaze to meet his. If she argued, he might take away her chance to help Star. "Fine. I'll do that. He can send someone to get me. Bye, Tony."

His brows shot together with concern for a quick second, and then he nodded as if coming to the same conclusion as her. Once again it was like that night when he left her on the Porters' steps. This time, she'd never see him again. Quite unlikely she'd get sucked into a terrorist plot for a second time, she thought sarcastically.

The desert air wasn't only hot, it was stiff with meaning. She'd ended up on the cutting room floor just like all the other women Tony had taken to his bed, but it didn't mean she couldn't help her country. Her friend Star was in trouble and she could find the vaccine to help Nina.

"Lumin, look—"

She raised her hand and centered the courtroom stare that she'd learned from practicing in the mirror. "You have a job to do. Go do it." She pushed herself to her feet. Tony opened his mouth to say something, and then closed it again, looking pensive. She swallowed deeply, but didn't veer from his gaze.

He pulled his phone out.

"Don't need it. I have Nathan's."

Tony's jaw flexed. "When this is over…"

"Don't do that," she said, trying to hold her emotions in check. "We both know I won't see you again. Don't try to placate me."

His gaze dropped to the ground and he took a step back. "I won't."

It was a bittersweet moment. One she knew she'd remember her whole life. He'd always be the man of her dreams and her hero, but he also played the lead role in who knew how many other women's memories. She mentally placed the love story she'd created for her and Tony back on the bookshelf as she walked away.

Chapter Ten

Tony watched Lumin round the corner of the building, and every instinct told him to run after her. She'd asked him what he would do after being a SEAL, but there was no *after*. He would always be a SEAL. Missions, duty, training, dragging her into his world meant she'd be left alone for months on end. Lumin deserved the white picket fence. A family. She was a beautiful young woman with the potential to change the world and have a normal life. SEALs didn't have normal, so he let her walk away and reminded himself it was the right thing to do. He rubbed his chest as he entered the factory. It hurt. His heart actually hurt.

Two hours passed with the squad hanging over the maps. Options and ideas were contemplated as they put their attention on finding Dafoe's lab. Kayla paced the floor, deep in thought. He needed a break. As soon as he didn't focus, his mind leaped to Lumin. He should talk to her before Steven Porter sent someone. He left the room and looked around the factory floor. All he saw was camouflage. Was she outside again?

"Hey, Tadpole!" Nathan stopped his conversation with Stitch and turned to him. "Where's Lumin? Did a chopper come in for her?"

Nathan looked at him strangely. "Chopper? Did you arrange a pickup instead of her taking the Jeep into town?"

"What the hell are you talking about?"

"Admiral knows, he gave her permission to take a Jeep and head into town."

Ghost spoke with Captain Cobbs near the factory entryway. "Sir, when did Lumin leave?"

Ghost gave him a shrug. "Left? Where'd she go?"

A sickening feeling ebbed inside Tony's gut. "You didn't clear her to take a Jeep and head into town?"

"No, why the hell would I do that?"

Tony ran outside, pulling his phone. He dialed Nathan's number, but no one answered. "Hey," he yelled at one of the guys from DEVGRU. "Have you seen Lumin?"

"The blonde gal? She left a couple hours ago."

"Oh, fuck." He dialed Nathan's number again as he ran back into the factory. "Nathan," he yelled. "Does she still have your phone?"

"Guess so. I told her to keep it. What the fuck's the matter?"

Kayla appeared. "What's going on, Tony?"

"She's gone."

"Said she was heading into town to stay at a hotel," Nathan added, joining them.

"Kayla, will you check the local hotels in Kingman?" She nodded and headed toward Ditz, who was always attached to his mobile computer.

The Admiral and Captain Cobbs walked up to him. "What's going on?" the Admiral asked.

"I think Lumin has gone to find Dafoe on her own."

"How the hell is she going to do that? We don't know where he is."

"Maybe she does," Tony said, fear grinding its gears in his belly.

The Admiral and Cobbs shared a look. "You think she held something back from us?"

"No." He scrubbed his face with his hands in frustration. He'd missed something. Dafoe couldn't contact her. She had Nathan's phone. Who did she know? He paced back and forth while the men watched him.

"Maybe she's in town, let Kayla find out," Nathan offered.

"Not in town," Kayla said walking up to join the circle after a few minutes passed. "I just called all the hotels. She's not there."

He grabbed Kayla's shoulder. "Help me, Kayla. Who are we missing in all this?"

Kayla shot a harried look at her husband. "Ah, we have one dead scientist. One missing scientist. Um, Lumin was in Las Vegas when this all started. Dafoe wouldn't be able to contact her. The only other people are her friend Star and Dr. Carmichael's friend from Lebanon."

Tony's head shot up. "Star. Her friend!"

"We don't know where she is," Kayla said.

"No, but Lumin could get hold of her. We protected Lumin. We didn't protect Star." Everyone was silent. "He's got her. Dafoe has got Star. Lumin must have called her. She's going to Dafoe. It's the only possibility."

"Oh, no, she wouldn't be that stupid," Kayla said, shaking her head.

Tony dialed Nathan's cell again. "Shit," he yelled, and stormed away from the squad. "Don't do this, Lumin," he said to himself as he stepped into the sunlight. A hand landed on his shoulder and he whipped around. Kayla stared at him with big eyes. "This is my fault. From the word go. I never should have let Ghost use her." Kayla remained silent while he raved about his stupidity. He should have known better. Lumin felt responsible and he'd done nothing, absolutely nothing to squelch her thoughts.

"Are you done beating yourself up?" Kayla asked quietly.

"No." He sucked in a stuttered breath.

"Maybe she's driving back to Las Vegas. She's probably fine."

"She's not fine," he yelled. "Fuck." He whirled around.

"Tony, what is this really about?"

"I'm an idiot. I got scared, Kayla. Mace, he—" he clamped his eyes shut. "He might lose Nina, and he knows it. It's tearing him apart because he loves her so much."

"Of course he does," Kayla said. She gave him a quirk of a smile. "And you're falling in love with Lumin and it scared you."

He jerked his head with a nod. "I think I am. At least I can't get her out of my head. I nearly lost it when Ghost brought her out of that room draped in his arms. I thought...I thought..."

"I know what you thought. Did you talk to her? Does she know any of this?"

He rammed the cell in his pocket. He shook his head. "I held her back. I shut her out because—"

"Because you don't want to feel like Mace," Kayla finished for him. "Love doesn't make you vulnerable, Tony. It gives you strength."

Kayla wrapped her arms around him and gave him a hug, and he crushed Ghost's wife to him for support. "She's all alone."

Kayla palmed his cheeks and looked into his eyes. "Until she makes contact, there's no way to find her. If she's doing what you suggested, she'll have dumped the GPS tracker. If she does call, you better do some fast talking. Now send her a text, and keep sending them."

"A text? Oh fuck, duh." He pulled the phone and did just that.

Kayla rested a hand on his shoulder. "God takes care of the innocent."

His breath stuck in his throat. "But she's not. I took that from her, then I let her go."

"Have you?" She smiled at him and returned to the factory.

Tony walked a trench into the desert floor, sending text after text, but she didn't answer. After thirty minutes of trying, he rejoined the squad. They had to find Dafoe, and if they could find him they would find Lumin.

* * * *

Tony's cell rang and he answered it without looking at the caller ID, hoping it was Lumin.

"Petty Officer Bale, it's Gord. I think I've found something. Is Kayla there?"

"Wait one, Gord. You're on speaker, go ahead." Tony sat his cell on the table. His guts twisted tight with fear. Lumin was sticking her head into the lion's mouth, and she was going to die. He had to find her. Both Billings and Azeel were extremists and refused to give up information. Azeel took the beating of his life, and was barely hanging onto it after Ghost had lost his cool.

"Kayla, I think I might have found something. I did what you asked using the satellite data and went back for an entire month in the history."

"Spill it," Kayla said, leaning over the map. She pointed to the northeast corner of Nevada before Gord said a word.

"There's nothing there," Ghost muttered.

"I watched a southbound delivery truck take Route 93 and then head west along a back road to a point almost due south of Humboldt National Forest. It made the trip every Wednesday, arriving at fifteen hundred hours from Twin Falls, Idaho."

Tinman shook his head. Kayla's finger was pinned less than an inch from that spot.

"A delivery of supplies," Captain Cobbs suggested.

"Possibly, but there's nothing there. No homes. No structures. Nothing. The truck disappears from view for one hour and then reappears," Gord added.

"They're underground," Kayla said absently.

"There's something else," Gord said, and all eyes swayed to the cell. "I checked the subterranean water systems. There is a large one. A very large one that reaches the Colorado River."

"Let me guess," Tony stated. "It runs past that point."

"Underneath it," Gord confirmed.

"But the doctor developed an airborne contagion," Mace said.

"Just something to note. It may have nothing to do with disseminating the Plague," Gord added.

"Or everything to do with it. Dr. Carmichael said he was developing the airborne virus. He didn't explain Dr. Bjornson's role. We assumed he was his partner."

"We need intel on Dr. Bjornson and what his specialty was," Tony said. "Ditz?" Ditz was already tapping furiously on the keyboard. Everyone waited. It didn't take long.

"Shit." The Admiral groaned, reading over his shoulder. "Dr. Bjornson, marine bio scientist specializing in disease and viral microbiology."

"They're covering their bases," Ed said with his slow, southern twang. "One by air, two by water—"

"Gord, where exactly did the truck go in Idaho?" Kayla asked, staring intently at the map.

"A wholesale food factory."

Kayla's gaze rose to her husband. "It's not delivering supplies. It's taking them."

"Probably both," Ghost said. "That's the cover. Deliver food, and return with the Plague." Ghost pointed sharply to the map. "He's right fucking there. Let's move. Ditz, call in a security quarantine around that wholesale food factory."

"Yes, sir."

Twenty-five SEALs jumped into two helicopters. It wouldn't take long to reach the location, but five minutes was too long. The wind snapped through the open doors of the Black Hawks as they whirled their way on a beeline for northern Nevada. The team fast-roped to the ground and broke into five squads as they neared the point Gord had seen the truck deliver the supplies. The topography grew with gentle slopes. No structures were evident.

"Fox, what do you see?" Tony asked.

"Nothing. No movement."

Ghost stepped up to his right side. "Spidey sense is going off. Something's not right about this."

"Captain Cobbs, approach the area from the north with your team."

"This smells bad," Cobbs came back in their headsets.

Ghost agreed. "I'm going to take my squad to the south. Watch your step."

"Roger, out."

"Nathan, Ed, Mace, Stitch, you're with me. Nathan take point," Ghost ordered.

"Yes, sir."

Tony remained with the rest of the men ordering a one hundred meter clearance. They watched Cobbs and Ghost approach with extreme caution. The minutes ticked on with limited chatter from both leaders to the men following them, using mostly hand signals to communicate.

"Found an entrance," Cobbs reported.

"Standby," Tony instructed. "Admiral?"

"We've found it all right. Nobody breaches the facility. Tinman, south side."

Tony worked his way toward Ghost's team, keeping low and watching the ground for IEDs. He rounded the slope and saw Ghost gesturing to someone. Was it Lumin? He ran the last few steps. "What the fuck?"

The squad gazed into a comfortable, but sparse living quarter. The window had been shaped and fit into the sandstone hill with a twenty foot wide and ten foot high view of the plateau they were on. One dim light shone over a woman who'd been trussed to a chair. At her feet sat a cooler. With a sick sense of humor, the word *Antiserum* had been penned across the side.

"You can bet this is wired." Ed said what they all surmised.

"Is there anyone left in there with you?" Ghost asked, and only loud enough to reach her, but not wake the dead or any lingering security.

The young woman with dark hair shook her head slowly. They didn't have to read lips like Ghost to make out the word, "Bomb" as she mouthed it.

"Who are you?" Ghost asked.

"What did she say? I can't hear her," Nathan asked.

"Her name's Star."

"Lumin's friend. Lumin has to be here. I have to find her." Tony scanned the ceiling, walls, and floor. He didn't see any detonators, but he had no doubt they were there.

"Is the vaccine in that cooler?" Ghost asked.

Star's eyes blinked closed, and she nodded then said something.

"I know, sweetheart. Hang in there."

"What did she say?" Tony asked.

"She said it's a trap. Bomb is under her chair and strapped to her back."

"It's got to be more than that," Ed said, placing a hand where the glass met the rock.

Tony scrubbed his face and shunted the pack from his back. Mace had remained quiet, his attention on the cooler and nowhere else. Tony glanced at his watch; eight hours had passed since Nina had been infected. Mace called the hospital every thirty minutes. The last time Nina was too sick to speak.

"Hey, we're going to make it. Nina is strong. She's hanging on."

Mace nodded as if he was in a trance. "I'm going to get that serum or die trying," he said.

"Can't use C4 or the compression could set off the other IEDs. Admiral?" Tony said.

Ghost narrowed his eyes, following the seam where the glass had been fitted into the rock. "There's always the good old-fashioned way." He tapped the glass with his finger.

Tony checked again. "Agreed." He took the butt end of his weapon, hauled back and hammered the glass. They stood still, waiting for the proof of a wrong move as the glass shattered. Mace stepped inside cautiously, but Tony could feel his impatience.

"Wait," Tony said, searching the floor. He carefully raised the rug where Star sat. An IED had been planted in front of Star's chair.

"Please, get me out of here," Star begged, and began to wiggle.

"Ma'am," Ed laid a hand on her shoulder, and she turned terrified eyes up to him. "Stop moving, or we're all dead."

She swallowed and sat still.

"That's a girl," Ed drawled. "I'm going to step behind you and get this off, all right?"

"You do and I'll be your sex slave for the rest of my life," she said.

Ed chuckled and moved around behind her. "Hmm, how can I refuse an offer like that?"

Ghost slid onto his back and looked under the chair. "Thank fucking God," he said, reaching under the chair.

It must have been a rudimentary bomb. Probably set up in a hurry. Tony turned his eyes away for a second and when he turned back, his hand shot out and stopped Mace from opening the lid on the cooler. "We're almost there, buddy. The girl first."

Mace curled his lips tight and knelt down in front of her. "Star, do you know if they put explosives in this cooler?"

She shook her head. "I don't think so."

"How do you know there's serum in there?" Mace asked, his hand resting on the lid.

"That man, Dafoe, he opened it. I saw a few glass cylinders."

"Describe them." Mace was keeping her engaged while Ghost and Ed worked on the IEDs.

Star did her best to remember.

"Sounds like serum," Mace said, as Ed backed away with a pack loaded with C4 in his hands.

"Be right back," Ed said taking the IED with him.

Ghost slid from under the chair. "It's defused."

Tony nodded. "Star, when did Dafoe leave?"

"I don't know." She rung her hands together. "Maybe three hours."

"Was Lumin here?"

"No. Are you that SEAL she always talks about?"

Tony's chest tightened. He never should have let the months pass without picking up the phone and calling Lumin. Star's question bore a hole of regret inside him. "I'm an idiot." He looked at Ghost uneasily, realizing he'd said it out loud.

Star's brow tightened. "Dafoe tricked her. He told her he'd let me go if she came to him. He's going to kill her. I know it."

"Do you know where he is?" Tony asked.

Star gave him the directions she'd heard. "I think he's in New Mexico."

"Cooler," Mace said abruptly.

Tony held his hand out to halt Mace. "Get up slowly." Star put a death grip on his fingers, and she stood. The team gave a barely perceptible sigh when nothing exploded. Ed returned.

"I'll get her out of here. Miss Star, come with me." Ed gave her one of his toothy, wolf grins and her gaze locked on him. Now that she wasn't loaded with explosives her brain saw the good-looking man in front of her.

"We're not going to pick it up," Tony warned.

"I'll open it," Mace said. "Get out of here."

"Buddy, I'm staying here," Tony said, gripping his shoulder.

Mace shook his head. "Nina is dying. If this isn't the serum, then I want to meet her in heaven when she gets there. Go find Lumin." Mace raised his gaze to meet him.

They'd been in a lot of tight places, near misses, but over the last eleven years no moment seemed to touch this one. "Why would he leave this here for us?" Tony had to ask.

"Because there was the chance we'd focus on it and Star, instead of the IED under the rug."

"Star?" Tony shouted before she got too far away. "Did you see any wires when he opened up the cooler?" She clutched Ed's arm and shook her head. Tony turned just as Mace opened the lid, and he shut his eyes not believing that it could be this easy. He felt the air move and realized it wasn't a compression blast, but Mace running past him.

He heard Ghost order into the comm set, "Alpha Air One, Petty Officer Mace Callahan en route, take him to USAMRIID, push it to the max."

"Copy that, Admiral," the pilot radioed back.

Mace ran like the wind, a fistful of vials in his hand. "He'll make it," Tony said to Ghost and Nathan.

Ghost gave him a look he wasn't sure how to read. Was there doubt? "Let's go find Dafoe and Lumin."

They hurried back to the remaining helicopter. Cobbs waited for them. "I've radioed in this position. CDC is en route. We're leaving five men to clear this building."

Tony relayed the coordinates to the pilot and found a place on the floor. The chopper lifted into the air and he gazed into the horizon. Was she dead already? Was she infected? He touched his pocket where he'd taken one of the vials for himself. Every mile brought him closer to her, but he was afraid of what he'd find. His memories slid back to the lake. She floated in the water, unashamed, innocent and sensually beautiful as his hand hovered beneath her body. Right now, her existence floated just beyond his touch. Soft skin, perfect, rounded breasts, slender legs twined around his hips, all lingered to remind him of his light.

He'd never felt closer to a woman in his life. He didn't want her memory to fade like all the faces of the women he'd taken to bed. Casual, no-strings sex had fed his need, but there was nothing casual about Lumin. Her life was tied to his, and he wanted a permanent knot.

He hadn't realized it at the time, but he'd erected a barricade against her back at the factory. He didn't blame her for Nina's misfortune. Lumin had sensed the emotional wall he threw up, but it was to protect himself. Caring about someone hurt. It hurt when she left his protection and the base. It hurt every single second she was out of his reach. It hurt to see her in Ed's arms, and it hurt to hear her say she believed he loved Nina.

"You've done a good job leading the team," Ghost said, just loud enough to rise above the sound of the blades and the wind. "Once we have this mission in the bag and saved the world, I'm submitting your paperwork to officer training."

He didn't lift his gaze from the horizon, and heard Lumin's voice in his mind. "Lumin thinks that too. She's going to be a lawyer. I used to hate those guys, but she wants to help people who don't have the funds to help themselves."

"Can't see her being cutthroat," Ghost said.

"She's not, but she's wicked smart." He paused. "And beautiful and sexy, although she hasn't got a clue. Her innocence is hotter than anything I've…" A thickness collected in his throat. He glared at the roof of the chopper to stop himself from imagining her any other way than laughing and balancing on a slim pole suspended in the air under the moonlight. "She trusted me. I had a whole line of reasons why I shouldn't drag her into a life with a SEAL, but the truth is I freaked out. Dafoe has her. My fault."

Ghost rested his forearms on his bent legs. "We don't give the women we love enough credit. We're so used to saving the day, we forget they saved us. We'll find her before Dafoe does."

"When did you know for sure you loved Snow White?" he asked.

Ghost see-sawed his hand slowly across his jaw. "There were a few first times, not just one. The first time she looked at me. The moment I feared I couldn't have her. The first time I left her for deployment. Every time she had a close call and I almost lost her. And now—every time I come home at the end of the day and see her there waiting for me with our son in her arms. I've thanked God a million times over for sparing her life and mine."

Tony smiled to himself. "You really have it bad, Admiral."

"You got that right, Petty Officer Bale. She's like a drug to me, and I will never kick the addiction."

"I think I'm addicted to Lumin. I saw her the first time crossing the lobby of the Grand Palms casino. She stood out as if there was a beam of light shining down on her, so I wouldn't miss her, but there was no way I could miss her. But I keep asking, 'Why her?'"

"You want my honest opinion?"

"Hell yeah," he said turning to face his mentor.

"Soul mate."

"You believe in that stuff?" Tony asked, surprised to hear the most dangerous, but grounded guy he'd ever known give that answer.

"I do now. Besides, I love pissing Kayla off. She's the sexiest thing I've ever seen when she's mad at me."

Tony grinned and bowed his head. "Sir, that's a little twisted."

Captain Cobbs' silver eyes settled on him. "You're both rookies. Try pissing off the same woman for over twenty years."

"How did you know, Captain?" Tony asked.

Cobbs spared a wicked smile. "Did you sleep on your back or wrapped around her?"

The heat on his cheeks intensified. "Umm, well, wrapped around her."

"What does she take in her coffee?"

Tony chuckled. "One milk and one sugar."

"What doesn't she like?"

Tony turned a sideways smile at Ghost. "Alcohol and meat."

"And most importantly, can you remember the face of one woman you screwed before her."

Tony chuckled again. "I was just thinking about that. I can't."

"Then—Mr. Bale—you have found Mrs. Bale." Cobbs' grin split his face and he looked off into the distance.

Had he? Or would God take her away from him after teasing him with perfect? "It's a risk," he said absentmindedly.

"Because you know if she's taken from you, you'll lie down and die just to be with her." Ghost gave him a fatherly smile.

He nodded. "Yeah."

"She's Mrs. Bale, all right."

Chapter Eleven

Each mile that separated her from Tony made the weight of sadness and regret heavier on Lumin's heart. She wasn't part of Tony's family of SEALs. She wasn't seasoned or knowledgeable like Nina or Kayla. A square peg in a round hole, she didn't fit in Tony's world.

She had to make amends and help find the antiserum that would heal Nina. Three hours passed as she drove eastward on Highway 40 following Dafoe's instructions. After the fourth hour, she was driving under the blistering sun and took Highway 491 toward Farmington. After thirty minutes she slowed, looking for the sign he'd told her to watch for. He said a gravel road with one rock pyre approximately five feet high marked the turnoff. She came to a skidding stop when she passed it. The horizon was bare of structures. The cell phone Nathan had given her rang for the fiftieth time. She knew who it was. There were several texts, and she quickly spun through them until she reached the last two messages.

Stop, Lumin. Please stop. Don't go to him.

Are you trying to break my heart?

She quickly tapped out a message and sent it.

I won't let Nina die. Trust me.

Tony had figured it out and like any good SEAL, he'd do anything to keep her safe. The phone rang, then it rang again, and again. What the hell was the matter with him?

"What?" she said, answering it because he was waking up the desert.

"Wherever you are, turn the vehicle around and drive back to me," he said harshly.

She'd dumped the GPS tracking unit on the highway in case they tried to follow her. Her location was a secret, and she'd keep it that way. "I don't want Nina to die. She means a lot to you. I brought this to your doorstep."

"Lumin, you'll get yourself killed. I'm coming, just pull over. Wait for me."

"No. If you come, my friend Star is dead."

"We found Star. She's safe. Mace has the vaccine and he's on his way to Nina."

She closed her eyes in relief. "Good."

"Where are you?"

"Almost there and I'm going to keep going."

"What?" he shouted. "Like hell you are. He's a terrorist, Lumin. He won't let you live."

She swallowed heavily, grinding the gear into first and the jeep jerked into motion with a little gas. "He said if you or the other SEALs showed up he'd release the virus, but if I go I can stall him."

"He's lying. These guys don't stop until we stop them."

"Then I have to hurry."

"God damn it, Lumin." Tony was seriously pissed.

"I'm going to help you. I know you don't think I can, but I'm going to try."

"So, you're just going to let Dafoe take you from me."

"I'm not yours, Tony. I'm sitting in a pile of throw-aways with the rest of the women in your life. I can live with that, but I screwed up coming to you, and I can do something to fix it. I can help."

"I don't want you to help. Stop, damn it." Lumin knew for certain Tony was seriously pissed. "If you'd stop running away from me, I could concentrate on my job instead of you."

"It's mind over matter. I don't mind and I don't matter, Tony. In the greater scheme of things, neither of us do. You told me I have skills. I plan to use them."

"Balancing on a beam a hundred feet in the air is dangerous. Lumin, you're walking into a terrorist cell. It's suicide."

"It's me who owes you one now."

Tony roared at her, "If you fall, there is no one to catch you. There is no tomorrow for us."

His words hit her square in the heart. "There never was."

"That's not true."

"Try to get here as quick as you can, I'll do my best. Good-bye, Tony."

She hung up and concentrated on the road. It was groomed, but she hit enough potholes to jar her teeth. A shiver ran up her spine. A big bug landed on her chest and she screeched, swatting at it, giving her even more shivers. She remembered the first time she'd put her hand through the strap, and they hoisted her high into the air. She'd been scared then too, but it hadn't stopped her. Fear was life's warning bell to pay attention. She squinted, seeing dust rise in the distance and it was travelling toward her. Showtime.

* * * *

Lumin lay in the desert after abandoning the Jeep and waiting for the oncoming vehicle to pass by. Two men got out. They searched the jeep and the surrounding area, but they didn't find her. She would go to Dafoe, but she wanted to arrive unannounced. Once the men had gone, she began to walk. She couldn't see any buildings ahead. Time needed to stop. Anxious, she put it into a jog. After a mile or more, she finally saw a structure growing out of the sand. Soaked from fear and the hot sun, she stopped to think and catch her breath. Would he have exterior cameras? Maybe he knew she was there already.

He probably didn't expect someone to cross the desert on foot. She hunched and watched. Crossing herself, she kept low and ran around the side of the building. The large home with steep roofs and a wrap-around porch appeared out of place in the middle of the desert. Peering around the corner into a window, she saw three men sitting at a dining room table. Sullen expressions and slumped in their seats, they looked bored. She ducked down and waddled toward the back end of the home on her haunches. There were less windows and it looked like an enormous garage. Keeping herself tight to the wall, she stole a look and exhaled with relief. She'd found the lab. Two men in white coats worked at a counter, peering into microscopes and moving about with a deliberate pace.

Her cell rang, and she fumbled to answer it, her heart pounding in her chest. Her gaze skittered to either side, but no one appeared. "Stop calling me," she hissed.

"Lumin, bloody hell, woman. Where are you?" She heard movement around the corner and her blood chilled. She had to go up or be caught. With a running jump and the help of a planter box, she gripped the edge of the roof and pulled herself up quickly. Just as two men rounded the corner, she threw her legs over the side and lay flat.

"Nothing. You're hearing things," one man said to the other. "I need a coffee. I'm heading inside."

The other man remained quiet, but she heard their footsteps round the house and enter a door. She lifted the phone to her ear. "You almost got me caught," she hissed.

"Where are you?"

"On the roof. I found the lab," she whispered.

"I swear to God, woman, if you die so will I. You like your coffee with milk and sugar."

"What are you talking about, Tony?"

"It means I want you to believe me when I say you're important to me. I know I acted like an ass at the factory, but there's a reason." A yip of a coyote in the distance broke the silence. "Lumin, did you hear me?"

"Yes."

"Do you believe me?"

"No, now stop phoning me."

"Don't move," a voice commanded from behind her.

She closed her eyes. A man hung out the second story window with a weapon pointed at her. Her hand was only an inch away from the gutter and she nudged the cell into it. "I'm here to talk to Dafoe," she said.

"Crawl toward me."

She did as he asked. When she reached the window, a hand grasped the back of her shirt and he yanked her inside. She'd been pulled into a spacious bedroom with a king bed and honey-colored wood floors. The door opened and a tall man of Middle Eastern descent walked in.

"Have a seat, Miss Edenridge," he said.

The security man motioned with the gun for her to follow his instructions. She sat down on the couch.

"You can leave," he said to the security guard.

The man wore suit pants and a comfortable dress shirt. He poured a glass of water from the mini bar and handed it to her.

"Thank you."

"I'm Callum Dafoe," he said, sitting down across from her.

Lumin saw a painting on the wall and she stared at it.

"That's my wife and son," he said, watching her.

"I'm sorry they're dead," she said. There was no point concealing she knew what happened to them. "Azeel told me."

"Sorry won't bring them back."

She shook her head. "Neither will killing millions of people. I understand your grief, Mr. Dafoe, but I don't understand your wrath."

"You wouldn't unless you've lost someone."

She looked into her glass for a moment, then drank it all. "I'd grieve. If someone I knew was killed by a drunk driver I'd be angry, but I wouldn't want to kill everyone who drives a car."

Callum Dafoe settled an inquiring look on her. "I am not a holy man like many in my homeland. I don't care about a never-ending war over grains of sand and inches of earth. Justice for my wife's death is within my power, and I will see it done," he said calmly.

She didn't have to find the serum anymore, but maybe Dafoe would give away the Americans who helped him.

"You told me Star was here. I want to see her." She knew full well Star was already safe, but she had to pretend she knew nothing.

"No, I said I would release Star if you came to me. Where is Dr. Bjornson?"

"You have the airborne virus. What more do you need?"

"The airborne virus dies off. We created a second virus. A stronger one that could mutate after thirty-six hours, but Bjornson escaped and he has the only antiserum." Dafoe rose to his feet. "Make no mistake. I will release it, whether it means I have to die as well, but I'd prefer not to. Where is he?"

"Why can't your American partners who helped you get the Plague in the first place find him?"

Dafoe's sharp gaze drilled into her. "Carmichael shared a lot with you, didn't he? Obviously the poison we gave him didn't work fast enough."

"Why would the Americans who helped you want to kill millions of people?"

"Why else, Miss. Edenridge? General Caufield is greedy. He sits at the President's elbow and he wants the President's position. Without money he can't accomplish that, but he has plenty of it now, and he can aspire to be what he wants."

At a knock on the door, Dafoe said, "Enter."

One of the scientists she'd seen downstairs in the lab came in.

"Tell me where Bjornson is, Miss Edenridge, or the next twelve hours of your life will be agonizing."

Tony wasn't going to make it in time. "You're going to kill me either way," she said, staring at the syringe the scientist held in his hand.

"While you succumb to the virus you will have time to change your mind. Your life depends on you telling me where Bjornson is." Dafoe leaned over to within a breath of her. "I'm betting as death approaches, you will." He swiftly walked toward the door. "Inject her."

Dafoe opened the door and two of his security detail walked in. They held her steady while the scientist stabbed her. She watched the syringe empty as the virus was set free inside her. She didn't deserve this; no one deserved this.

The guard grabbed her arm and pulled her to her feet. "Where are we going?"

"You're going to do us a favor and infect a lot of people. We're taking you home," Dafoe said.

"What? No!" She fought but they restrained her, yanked her downstairs and pushed her into a vehicle.

The guard gave her a dark, determined look in the mirror as they drove away from Dafoe's compound. "While we release the next test in three cities, the CDC will be chasing their tails trying to stop it. By the time we reach Las Vegas, you will be sick and very infectious. We will deposit you in the heart of the tourists. Everyone within five yards of you will become infected, then they will scramble for their planes taking it with them and depositing it all over the world. Anyone who comes near you will die."

* * * *

Date: 07.26.2014
Time: 0000UTC 1600hrs PST
Mission: Code Name Luminous

"Good luck, man," the pilot said when Mace jumped from the helo before the skids hit the ground. He ran like hell was behind him. Twelve hours had passed since Nina had been injected.

"Where is she?" he shouted as he skidded to a stop at the reception desk. "Nina Callahan, my wife, where is she? I have the antiserum."

"Follow me, sir. We were notified you were en route."

Mace ran behind the security guard, weaving their way deeper into the institute. They reached a section that required the guard to brush his security pass through the reader. Two men in lab coats looked up when he bolted through the door.

"Where is my wife? I've got the antiserum for the virus."

"I'm Dr. Lambert, Petty Officer Callahan. We have your wife in the quarantine suite. I'll take the antiserum. Follow me."

He walked behind the doctor but he wanted to grab him and run. They reached a room that looked very much like a hospital room, but it was completely contained. Someone in a bio suit hovered over Nina. She lay there, not moving, her eyes closed. He placed his hands on the window. His heart burst seeing her swollen neck and pale complexion. "Is she—is she?"

"I'm sorry Mr. Callahan."

"Sorry! Sorry," he yelled. "Give her the vaccine."

"Mr. Callahan, it's too late. We're just trying to make her comfortable."

"No!" he shouted. "Get me a syringe. Now!"

"I can't do that."

Mace grabbed him by the throat. "Listen to me, she might be a lab rat to you, but she's a mother and my wife. You don't know her or what she's made of. Let me in there."

"Petty Officer Callahan, I'll call security and have you removed if you don't back away."

"Give me a god damn syringe."

"You'll be infected."

"Then I'll be infected," he shouted in the doctor's face. He'd break the lean little doctor in two if he didn't do what he asked.

The doctor remained wide-eyed, but resistant. "I've brought more serum. You can give it to me after you give it to Nina. Let me in there."

The doc didn't move and Mace yanked the card pass that dangled around his neck with a snap. He turned and sliced it through the reader. The light clicked to green and the door opened into the pressurized anteroom. Quickly he slid it through the next reader and the door unlocked.

"Get me a syringe," he ordered to the man inside the suite. The guy turned toward the window and Mace saw the doctor nod his head. He watched the guy load it, and then snatched it from his hand and gently pierced Nina's arm.

Nina could barely open her eyes. Her skin was on fire when he touched her to empty the syringe. "Baby, I'm right here. You're going to be okay. I've given you the antiserum."

"What are you doing so close? Get out. You'll get sick."

She forced her eyes open, but they couldn't focus on anything. She blinked and shivered when he rested his hand against her cheek.

"I'm not leaving you."

"I don't know if you're real or not."

Mace's laugh rumbled in his throat. "Mrs. Callahan, I'm real, and I love you."

She smiled and took a shallow breath. "I feel like shit."

There was no way to order a virus to get the hell out of her body, but his beautiful wife would do it if she could. He could see the dark, dead skin surrounding the buboes. "You'll have some scarring, but we both have that."

She groaned when she tried to move. "I like your scars—sexy," she said weakly.

Every word was a strain for her. He kissed her forehead and clutched her hand. He would not let the Reaper take her. "You have to fight now. Fight for Gabbs and for me, and for our baby."

"No…fight…left," she murmured.

Mace gripped her slender fingers and squeezed. Her wedding ring had slipped to the side and he straightened it. He'd bought her as many diamonds as he could because he wanted it big enough that no man would miss it. "Nina, you never gave up on me. I'm going to keep pushing and pulling, and I'll carry you if I have to." His words choked in his throat and tears welled. "Please, I know you don't want to leave us. Please hang on, baby, I've got you. Fight, fight it off."

"Mr. Callahan?" the muffled voice came from the guy in the bio suit.

"Yeah, Doc," he answered, but kept his eyes on her.

"If the serum is working, we should see a change within the hour," the doctor said.

"House calls?" she mumbled.

Mace brought her hand to his mouth. "You're gonna make it, Nina."

"The baby?" she asked.

"Don't know. We can make another baby, but I can't do that if the love of my life isn't with me."

"Bad guys?"

He wanted her to rest, not talk. "Not yet, but we'll find them."

"Outbreaks. Dafoe?"

"Baby, would you please stop thinking."

"Tell...me."

"None. He might be on the run."

"Not running, Mace." She blew out a strained breath. "Lumin okay?"

He didn't answer, instead he kept his sharp eyes on the rise of her chest, and prayed it would keep moving.

"Mace?"

"Dafoe has her."

"What happened?"

"He had her friend Star. Least that's what he told her. We found her in the Nevada lab. She's safe, but Lumin's not."

"Go. Team needs you," she whispered.

"Nina, until you prove to me you're going to beat this, I'm not leaving nor will I take the vaccine until you show me you'll fight to survive."

She had no strength left, but she clung to his thumb. "Tony's in love." She smiled. "I'm gonna have a new sister."

The doctor hovered behind him and offered a cup with water and a straw. Mace brought the straw to her mouth. "Drink this."

She tried to swallow and sputtered the water.

He wet his fingers and drew it across her lips and she sucked it in. "Come on, baby, I know you can do this."

Nina opened her crystal green eyes and focused on him. "Put a bullet between Dafoe's eyes for me, hot stuff." She squeezed his thumb. "Go."

Her hand slackened and his heart jumped out his throat. He quickly felt for a pulse. Faint, but there. He turned a look over his shoulder. "Is there anything else you can do?"

"I'm sorry, Mr. Callahan. I hate saying it, but it is in God's hands now. We'll keep her hydrated. Her temperature has dropped a quarter of a degree. It's a good sign."

He prayed for an hour and watched his wife's slow, shallow breathing. Eventually, he could see she wasn't struggling for air, and he sat up. Over the last hour, her temperature had dropped another degree. The doc injected him with the antiserum, and he nodded his thanks.

"Thank you for bringing these," the doctor said, holding three other vials Mace had given him. The doc stood beside him. "She wouldn't tell me how she was infected. There seems to be a big lapse in information. The Plague shows up every once in a while, but I've never heard of it acting so quickly."

"That's because it's a weapon, Doc. Ebola and the Bubonic Plague."

"And—we're not the ones in control of it, are we?"

Mace shook his head. "Not yet, but we're closing in."

"Will we see more cases?"

"Only if we fail." Mace extended his hand. "Thank you for taking care of her."

"Of course. I think you may have gotten here in the nick of time."

"What about our baby?"

"I can't answer that. The fetus hasn't aborted yet, which is often the case, although the data is hundreds of years old. Not many people survived when the Black Death was romping around Europe."

"For now, all I care about is seeing her get well. We'll deal with the rest together."

"You're a SEAL?" When Mace nodded, he said, "She talks a lot in her sleep. Are you going back out there?"

"Yeah, I promised the love of my life I'd put a bullet between the guy's eyes who's responsible for this." He paused. "I always keep my promises."

He walked to the door and stopped when the Doc said, "Make sure you kill him. I don't want to be forced to save his life if he ends up here."

"Count on it, Doc."

* * * *

Admiral Austen and the rest of the squad lay low in the desert sand watching the vehicle leave the house. There wasn't another dwelling for miles. Ghost waited with his cell tucked to his ear.

"Kayla, you back at Base Command?" He paused. "Good. You got an eye on the car that departed the subject area?" He nodded. "Roger. We'll follow at a distance. Any early guesses where they're going?" Ghost rose to his feet when it was safe to do so and the rest of the squad did the same. He listened, then darted a look at Tony. "Roger that. I hope you're wrong, but we have to make sure Dafoe is the man in charge. I'm going to split part of the team and send them to contain the house and whatever is in it. Dispatch CDC here. Think they're going to find everything that wasn't in Nevada." Kayla said something and then the Admiral's harsh features softened. "Love you, sweetheart."

The Admiral stored his phone while Tony patiently waited, but the Admiral wasn't quick to share. "What's her analysis, sir?" he asked. "I want to stop that vehicle and retrieve Lumin."

"I know you do, Tinman, but we have to be sure he's the main operator and not taking her elsewhere."

Tony mulled it over for a split second. "That's not what Kayla thinks. What did she say?" His gut was telling him something else, and if it's what Kayla thought as well, he was going after that vehicle now.

"No. She has another theory."

Tony's tension grew, but he remained still although his heartbeat had shriveled to non-existent.

Ghost raised his gaze to somewhere over Tony's head, deliberating his thoughts. "It's only a theory, Tinman."

The other SEALs milled about and checked their gear, talking quietly in smaller groups. Captain Cobbs took a position beside him, soon to be joined by the rest of Alpha Squad.

"I want to hear her theory, sir," Tinman said, bristling at the thought the Admiral held the information back.

Ghost inhaled deeply and said, "It's possible Lumin has been infected."

"Where are they taking her? Why leave the house?" He asked the questions, but the answer already sat like a slow burning torch in his stomach.

Captain Cobbs' lethal gaze landed at his front doorstep. "They've infected her, and they're going to release her in a populated area."

The Admiral watched him with a steadfast glare to see his reaction. If he lost his cool, it meant he wasn't in control. A mission was a breathing entity, and he had to keep altering course and thinking ahead. "We have to intercept if that has occurred," he said calmly. "If Dafoe isn't the head of this operation, we may have lost that opportunity, but the alternative isn't in question." The Admiral continued to watch him. What more did he want? The rest of the squad sensed it as well, and waited. "We've got fourteen men. Seven men to secure the house and get the answers, while the rest of us follow Lumin."

The Admiral and Cobbs shared a look and the Admiral nodded. "Proceed."

Tony called the men and explained the plan. Alpha Squad would trail Lumin. Another platoon of SEALs from DEVGRU had reported in from the Wholesale Food Factory. They'd found crates with vials of the Plague. The factory owner admitted he'd been given a large sum of money to store and disseminate the goods. Those locations were being investigated. The owner professed to not know what existed in the crates. He'd just been prepared to send it in trucks to the locations as instructed. None had left the factory, which was good news.

Kayla called back and advised the vehicle had a course laid for Nevada. Maybe Dafoe was returning to his other lab, but he doubted it. With certainty, Tony's dark thoughts swam closer to Kayla's theory. They'd have to stop the vehicle by any means of force if it was bound for a populated area. Doubt seeped into his mind, and he wished Mace was here to smack him upside the head. Leading the squad was one thing, but did he have the courage to stop the vehicle if it meant taking Lumin's life?

His gaze strayed to Ghost. The man had never veered from his duty to his country. Tony had seen him do things that had stopped him in his tracks, questioning if the man had a soul. In close quarters situations he was ferocious. He'd seen pure terror in an enemy's eyes when Ghost took aim. The Admiral was lethal, a killer with control and purpose. Would he kill Lumin?

Captain Cobbs took a life without a flinch of emotion, his grey eyes keen as a wolf and his strike just as deadly. Ed, Nathan, Stitch, and Ditz; would one of them kill Lumin? Tony released a deep breath. He had to hunt the woman he'd fallen in love with.

"Tinman?"

He turned his attention to Ditz.

"They're westbound on I-40."

Tony's eyes strayed to each face. "They're bound for Las Vegas. We have to stop the vehicle."

Ditz broke off to communicate to someone else. Tony's band of brothers were geared up, waiting for his command.

"Wait one," Ditz yelled out. He spoke again to someone on the radio. As he listened he nodded and his eyes met Tony's. "Tinman, Admiral, the team has secured the house."

"Any information we need?" he asked.

Ditz nodded but looked toward the ground when he said, "It's confirmed. Lumin was injected."

"And we have the serum. Let's retrieve her."

"No, Tinman. Ah, shit," Ditz said, and then cleared his throat. "One of the viral specialists said she was injected with a new strain." Ditz shook his head. "We were wrong about Bjornson. He was working on the antiserum to the newest strain."

"There are two viruses?" Ghost asked.

"Bjornson escaped as we thought, and he has the only vaccine to the new strain. The first one has a shelf life. It dies off quickly, but the second one…nothing will stop it. That's why Dafoe wants him."

Tony's soul careened. "Are you sure Lumin was injected?"

"I'm sorry, Tinman. Dafoe is gone and they don't know where. The people in that vehicle are the weapon and they're planning to infect as many as they can."

Tony gave the order to fallout and for everyone to board the helo. There was no sense in chasing them by vehicle. Fox alerted DEVGRU to deploy and search for Dafoe. The chopper lifted into the air. The squad at the other lab was given orders to prepare to block Highway 40 where it branched into Highway 93 headed for Las Vegas. Every man in the squad sat silently in the aircraft, and stared at anything but him. Dafoe had turned Lumin into an unwitting enemy, and she had to be stopped.

The helo touched down in the desert off Highway 93. Military vehicles waited in the darkness for orders to stop all traffic. Tony watched the headlights on the highway as they approached. None of the vehicles tried to veer off. They kept coming. How would he stop himself from taking her into his arms? Why had he agreed to allow her to be used by the Navy?

"Tinman, the vehicle is under a klick away," Fox said. "Don't worry man, we'll get Lumin out of there."

He waited with twenty other men. His squad and two others from DEVGRU had joined them.

"Half a klick," Ditz called out.

"Lock down the highway," Tony ordered.

Flares, trucks, and men swarmed the highway, stopping traffic. To the oncoming vehicle it would look like an accident. Before they realized it was a trap, they'd be secured. As the vehicle rolled to a stop, the entire squad surrounded it, weapons pointed at the occupants.

Fox yelled, "Out of the vehicle. On the ground."

Three of the four doors cracked open. The driver got out with his hands in the air. "On the ground," Tony yelled, and others did the same to the men who appeared.

Lumin was still inside, and he held his breath. There was a scream, and a weapon fired. The back window cracked with the impact and blood splattered against it. One of the Tangos released a wail of grief and dove back into the car. He reappeared with a limp body in his arms wailing in another language, "My brother. My brother." Tony recognized it as Dari, one of the most common languages of Afghanistan.

"Don't move." One of the men from DEVGRU took a couple steps toward the vehicle and looked inside. "Get out of the vehicle, lady," he yelled.

"Hold fire," Tony ordered. The SEAL could make an easy kill shot. "Lumin?"

"Don't come near the car, Tony. Please," she cried out.

He dropped his weapon and signaled for the other men to do the same. Putting one foot in front of the other, he positioned himself away from the vehicle but able to see inside. "My lady, I'm here. It's okay."

"Tony move back. Five yards. You need to keep away."

Defeated, her bright blue eyes shone with fear.

"There's no vaccine for what they put in me, Tony. That's why they were looking for Bjornson. He's got it."

Tony lowered himself to his haunches. "We know, Lumin." He'd never wanted to hold a woman so bad in all his life. Every muscle in his body strained to go to her. "Are you feeling the symptoms yet?"

She nodded, and let out a sharp breath. "But we stopped it, right?"

"Yeah," he lied. Dafoe was a fanatic. He wouldn't give in. He'd have a backup plan and access to more of the virus.

Lumin covered her face. As her tears fell, the feeling of loss overwhelmed him. Even as a boy with a mother who cared more about opening her legs to the stragglers she brought home from the bar than she did about her own son, nothing had ever affected him like this.

"Lumin, I won't let you die." He said the words and at first he didn't know if he was lying or not, but she raised her head and stared at him.

"How? There's no cure."

"Sure there is," he said. "Love."

"What?" her voice warbled.

"I love you, and when a SEAL loves a woman, there's nothing that stands in the way of that. Not another man. Not doubt. Not even a virus. I will find Bjornson. I will save your life, and maybe you'll agree to go to dinner with me again, and if I'm a lucky man, you'll fall in love with me."

She smiled through her tears, and he smiled through his.

A warning shout from several men came only a breath before gunfire started. Men in body armor rushed from three SUVs behind them. Glass, metal, and sand erupted with bullets ricocheting off every surface. The SEALs dove for cover, but there wasn't much. "Get down, Lumin!"

They hadn't counted on this, but the Tangos obviously had, and they were ready. The SEALs fired back. He saw Ditz holler, grab his leg and fall to the ground. The firefight turned a corner when the muzzle of a grenade launcher appeared over the door of the first SUV in the line of cars on the highway.

"Take cover," he yelled. Dafoe's men took out the transport vehicles which exploded into a fireball of flame as the gas tanks ignited. "Ditz is down, Admiral." Ghost didn't come back. Jesus fucking Christ. "Captain Cobbs, report." Tony quickly checked his comm gear. "Fox, you copy?"

Nil response.

"Drop your weapons," a voice called out that didn't belong to the good guys.

Tony's guts untwisted when he heard Ghost say, "We can stand off all night, but within an hour you're going to have the entire Nellis Air Force Base up your ass. Put your weapons down and surrender."

"We don't surrender to Americans."

"Then stand clear of the vehicles so I can kill you faster."

"We want the woman."

Ghost's voice came from a different angle. Tony knew what he was doing. He had no comms, he had to trust that Cobbs was instructing the squad to take an offensive position.

"Lumin, stay down. I'll be back." She didn't respond. "Lumin?"

"Here."

She'd scrambled into the front seat. "Stay on the floor until I come back for you."

Tony slid on his stomach toward the next car, keeping himself hidden. If they wanted a firefight, they'd get one up close and personal.

Ghost kept them engaged. "My men are prepared to die just like yours. Stalemate, friend."

Tony reached the right side of the car ahead of Lumin's and saw Fox. They signaled to one another.

"Aw, fuck," Tony swore when three men showed themselves, each with a hostage in front of them. A woman and her two children stood rigid with fear as the terrorists held a gun to each of their heads.

"The woman in exchange for their lives. Lumin's dying already, but you can save this family."

The *whip* of incoming choppers, at least five of them, approached. Reinforcements had arrived.

"Times up," Ghost said from the darkness. "Cavalry has arrived. Step away from the woman and her children."

A vehicle roared to life and Tony knew it was Lumin's. The car lurched ahead, made a sharp U-turn and headed south. The terrorists all opened fire on her vehicle and Tony with the rest of the team launched to their feet and fired on Dafoe's men. They dropped one after another. One of the SEALs from DEVGRU started to fire on Lumin's car and he yelled a cease fire.

"What's she doing?" Fox asked, watching the tail lights grow smaller.

Tony dropped his weapon to his side. "Creating a diversion and taking herself out of the formula." He grinned to himself. She was a warrior after all.

Chapter Twelve

Date: 07.26.2014
Time: 0300UTC 1900hrs PST
Mission: Code Name Luminous

Lumin floored the gas pedal. Staring into the beam of her headlights, she concentrated on staying between the lines. Migraine-strength pain thumped so hard in her head it felt like her eyes would pop out. She snapped up the cell phone she'd picked out of the dead guy's hand in the back seat. She swerved once, and shook her head to clear it. Darting glances downward, she dialed Tony's cell number.

"Lumin, where do you think you're going?" he answered.

"Away—from everybody, but I need to tell you something. When I was with Dafoe, he said General Caufield helped him. He said he was close to the President."

"Okay, sweetheart, got it. Now turn the vehicle around. Everything is under control."

"No, Tony."

"What do you mean, no?" he said sharply. "Lumin, get your ass back here. We need to get you to USAMRIID."

"There's no point. There's no vaccine. No cure. I'm going to find somewhere to hide. Away from people."

"You can't hide, Lumin. I'll put a chopper in the air now. You can't outrun it."

"Don't be stupid, Tony. I'm infected. There's nothing you can do."

"I care about you, woman. Turn the fuc—flippin' car around."

Lumin shook her head. The lines on the road began to slither like snakes. "Tony, I know I've said this enough, but I'm sorry. Sorry I brought this to you. I should have never called you."

"I can't do my job if my lady is in danger."

"Tony, how many women did you screw between last December and now? I might be—unskilled in the bedroom, but I'm not stupid." Tony covered the phone and spoke to someone.

When he uncovered the phone he cleared his throat. "Maybe, but it's not like I didn't think about you, a lot. I just didn't know what to do about it. We were together for a few short hours. I had workups for the deployment, and—shit, I know this sounds like excuses."

"That's what it sounds like. Do me a favor and call Moira Porter. Tell her what's happened. But she can't tell Steven. He'll go crazy trying to save the day."

"Maybe he should have been a SEAL."

"I'm sure he would have made a good one." Lumin broke off and clutched the wheel with both hands, trying to blink away the dizziness.

"Lumin? Lumin!" he shouted.

"Please don't follow me. I'll make sure I go far away from people. I promise."

"What? You think I'm going to let you crawl in some hole and die alone? Why are you doing this?"

"I'm a realist and you have to get real too. I'm going to die. Phone Moira. That's all I'm asking you to do. Don't make this into a big deal." She could hear Tony running.

"It's a big deal to me. Now turn that fucking car around."

The sound of helicopter blades whirling got louder in the phone. "I don't want you to get sick. Don't follow me, Tony," and she hung up.

She had to ditch the car, and soon. There weren't a lot of places to hide in the desert, but she could double back to Kingman. Maybe she could borrow another vehicle, but she had to do it without running into someone. The cover of darkness helped, but the clock had now started for her, and she wouldn't survive.

She reached the outskirts of Kingman and drove slowly until she spotted a Travel Lodge sign and turned into the parking lot. Getting out and striding across the lot, she looked toward the front of the building. Sound moved freely in the desert, and she heard the blades of a helicopter in the distance. Could she actually steal a car and get away with it? She needed an RV, not a car. In Las Vegas she'd seen RVs parked in the Walmart parking lot.

Trotting back to the car, she headed for the downtown area. She couldn't ask anyone for directions, and pulled over. Searching on the phone, she found its location and headed toward the address. She rolled into the parking lot with a slow crawl. The moon climbed the night sky and shed an eerie glow. She was hungry. When was the last time she'd eaten? No wonder she had a headache. Her muscles hurt like hell, as if she'd run a Tough Mudder race. Spotting a bottle of water tucked in the door pocket, she took a big gulp. Warm or not, wet went a long way to quench her burning thirst.

A car drove in the opposite parking lot entrance and she slouched low in her seat. A young girl emerged from an old Honda Civic and quickly sauntered toward the front doors. Lumin watched the RVs, hoping a revelation would strike with a bolt of brilliance. If she stole one, a call to the police would have them chasing after her and she was surrounded by miles of open desert. Kingman wasn't a big city, the authorities would find her. Options were narrowing, but she didn't want to spend her last hours on earth in a plastic bubble in USAMRIID. She wasn't irresponsible. No one would die because of close contact, but she had to think of something. The virus was taking over her body, and it seemed to be getting worse with every minute. How long would she have before she couldn't think straight anymore? She was an hour away from Kaibab National Forest. Could she make it without being seen? She was so damn tired. Slipping her fingers across the bottom edge of the seat, she reclined and closed her eyes for a moment. The phone in her palm jingled and she clutched it.

"Tony, give it up. Find the men responsible for this. Stop calling me."

"Lumin," Kayla answered.

She sighed, glad that she wouldn't have to fight with the SEAL that had whisked her heart away from her. "Kayla, I know he told you to call me."

"Yes, he did, and for a good reason."

"You'll understand, even if Tony can't, but I don't want to die in an air-tight room surrounded by doctors watching me like a lab rat."

"Neither did Nina, but she's there, and you're not going to die. The squad wouldn't let that happen. My husband won't let it happen. You don't know us, and I'd probably feel the same as you, but I want you to trust us."

"There's no cure for this second strain. Dr. Bjornson has fallen off the map. He might even be dead. Finding him will be impossible. If Tony finds me, he'll get sick. I can't let that happen."

"Didn't I tell you Alpha Squad can accomplish the impossible? If you run from us, we won't be able to save your life. Tinman's going all SEAL crazy to find you. Let him."

"Tony doesn't have to sacrifice himself for me. Please help me find a place to hide, Kayla. I don't want to make anyone sick. The SEALs need to find Dafoe. He's out of his mind. There's nothing but vengeance inside that man, even if it means he has to die."

Kayla inhaled deeply and said, "I can't do that, Lumin. Tony won't stop until he knows you're safe. He, Mace, and my husband are made from the same man-cloth. Stubborn and brave. When their hearts take up the call of duty, there's no turning them back. Nina is getting stronger by the hour and Mace has rejoined the squad. They're wasting time looking for you when they should be searching for Dafoe."

"Then tell them to stop. Convince them, Kayla. They'll listen to you." Lumin gulped down the rest of the water. She was so thirsty she'd drink from a mud puddle.

"Lumin, I don't want you to die. If you hide from us, we can't get the vaccine to you."

Her heart dropped to the pit of her stomach realizing she'd never see Tony again. It was a mistake falling in love with him. "I should have never called him. I hate that I can't take it back."

"Love is never a mistake. I'd bet my life on the fact that Tony is the man of your dreams and the man you'll grow old with. Trust him."

"I know he wants to save me, but he can't, Kayla. I'm infected. He'd say anything."

Kayla adjusted the phone, hearing the whisper of hair being brushed aside. "Like what?"

"He just told me he loved me, but I don't believe it."

"Why not? As far as I know, he's never told a woman that. That man walks around with a shield of valor, but his past keeps him as the underdog when he should be flying. Some things are a sacrament to a SEAL, truth being one of them. Those three words are never said unless they're real."

"We barely know one another. It can't be."

"Don't you feel the same? He's special and you know it. Don't deny it." Kayla released a deep breath. "You're his chance to find his wings. He'll become the man he's supposed to be if you give him a chance, he'll prove it to you."

"Kayla, I know you went through a lot in your life, and you got a second chance with the Admiral, but I'm not like you."

"No, you're not, but you're exactly what Tinman needs. Stand beside him."

"If there was a drop of hope, I would try. Believe me I would, but there isn't. Will you tell him something for me?"

"I will."

"I'll always be his light, and I love him too."

Lumin cut the call. Kayla had kept her talking too long, and she didn't know if she could track her cell phone, but she wasn't going to risk it.

* * * *

Thane, accompanied by Admiral Pennington, stepped out of the helo that landed on the south lawn of the White House. A security team escorted them into the world-renowned structure whose first cornerstone was laid in 1792. He kept the grin from his face remembering Kayla rubbing the war of 1812, when the British set it on fire, into his backside. Through a rear entrance, they followed security into the main hallways and toward the West Wing and the Oval Office. The guard tapped on the door, and the President himself opened it. He extended a hand and Thane gripped it. He liked this President; they had become friends over the last four years, but they'd known each other for much longer.

"Greetings Admiral Pennington. Thane," the President said, "Coffee, admirals?"

Thane needed it since he'd been up for a couple days. He'd snagged a few winks in transit to the East Coast, but he was still tired as hell. "A couple gallons will do, John," he said.

A Presidential aide quickly brought the coffee to the table, and they made themselves comfortable on the opposing couches.

The President poured himself one, but didn't relax in his chair. He began, "I'm assuming you wanted to meet here to talk about the virus. For you to fly all this way, I'd also have to assume that you want to speak about how a protected strain of the Bubonic Plague ended up with a terrorist in the United States."

Thane noticed the President's hands didn't shake, but they squeezed the cup he held with a Presidential symbol embossed on it.

Gulping back the first cup, Thane nodded. "John—"

Another knock landed on the door and the aide opened it. They all stood. Admiral Felix Hoskins, the Commander of the Special Operations Command and the highest ranking SEAL in the country, strode in. Behind him the Commander of JSOC, Admiral Cagney, entered. Admiral Hoskins oversaw the various Special Operations component commands of all the United States Armed Forces. When an operation required all the forces to work together, the command of the operation fell on his shoulders. A plague about to be launched on the world definitely fell into that category. The President rose to greet both men.

"Mr. President," Hoskins and Cagney responded, then took a seat.

The President turned to his aide. "Please advise General Caufield, Secretary of Defense—"

"Not yet," Thane said harshly.

The President blinked and his chin dropped. "Why not, Thane?"

Admiral Hoskins' black gaze held Thane's. Being the ranking officer it was his responsibility to pass on the bad news, of which he'd already been informed.

"Sir," Hoskins began, "Callum Dafoe, the man responsible for obtaining the Plague, had help from inside the White House."

"What?" The President put down his mug and his expression deepened with concern. "That's not possible if you're intimating it's Darrin Caufield. He is a decorated General. He has served this country from the day he joined the forces. I know him personally."

Thane clasped his hands together and grilled the President with a look that spoke of apology, but no bullshit. "Caufield gave the plague to Dafoe. The intelligence is not wrong. We wouldn't be here if it was a hunch, John."

The President rose while shaking his head. "He is the Secretary of Defense, this country's most important asset in protecting its people. He served on my Intelligence Advisory board. I've known him for thirty years."

"Mr. President," Admiral Cagney, a twenty-year SEAL veteran and one hell of a warrior, leaned forward. "We all have a weakness. Your position is his."

"Are you saying he wants to be President?"

Thane nodded. "Yes. Obviously he didn't consider what would be left after a virus of this deadly magnitude devastated the globe. The survival rate is zero. There would not be much left to lead, unless he saw it as a history-making moment to rise from the ashes and rebuild a country from what's left."

"No, Thane. I won't accept it. He's put this country first, always. He's a man of honor."

"Aren't we all until greed twists its way into our soul?" Hoskins said.

"What proof do you have?"

Thane filled his mug for the third time. "Lumin Edenridge was taken by Dafoe and injected with the virus. He admitted Caufield supplied him with the bacteria and he did it for money to begin his campaign."

"You're here to arrest him," the President said, putting his attention on Thane.

"We've lost Dafoe. He's carrying a second strain of the virus. The first one had a flaw. It dies off quickly. The second strain does not." Thane glimpsed his phone when he felt it vibrate, and closed his eyes. A sickening tightness balled in his gut after reading the message.

The aid answered the door and took the paper he was handed, presenting it to the President. He read it quickly and breathed out heavily. The other admirals in the room looked to Thane. "Three towns now reporting plague symptoms."

"How do you know?" Hoskins asked.

Thane lifted his phone. "My wife."

The President nodded. "CDC brief." He handed the paper to Admiral Hoskins. "Kayla's still working? I thought she retired."

"She's lending her efforts and we need her on this mission. She found the lab in Northern Nevada with the help of Base Command staff." Thane blew out a deep breath. "If this is the second strain, we need to quarantine these towns, but it's probably too late. They are larger than Ramah, but still somewhat isolated."

"How do we find Dafoe?" the President asked.

Thane nodded slowly and stood up. The other Admirals did as well. "Now, it's time to call in Caufield."

General Caufield strolled into the room, then jerked to a stop seeing every set of eyes on him. "Mr. President, gentlemen."

No one acknowledged him except the President. "Come in, Darrin," he said, taking a seat behind his desk. Thane sat in a chair, while his counterparts sat on one couch, which left the other for General Caufield.

Caufield wore his uniform and ribbon rack of medals like a suit of armor. He was a barrel-chested, short man with a strong but quiet persona. Thane had met him several times, and appreciated the man's intelligence and his level-headed approach to warfare. As far as he knew, Caufield had been a respected and confident advisor to the White House.

"I take it the news on the virus is not good," Caufield said, sitting down.

Admiral Hoskins once again took the lead. "Darrin, for forty years you have served this country without fault."

Caufield didn't bat an eye waiting for the punch line.

"A terrorist by the name of Callum Dafoe has been uncovered. For three years he has poured his money into creating a virus with a one hundred percent kill rate to seek justice for a bombing that took out his wife and son."

"Is he in custody?" the General asked.

Thane glanced at his peers. Everyone's game face was on. "General Caufield." The General's dark blue gaze slipped to him. "The virus has been launched in three more towns. American citizens, people you've dedicated a lifetime to protect, are now dying. When you walk out of this office, you will be arrested, tried, and more than likely imprisoned for the rest of your life. I don't really give a shit what you say outside these walls, but right now you are going to tell us how to find Dafoe and anything you know about Dr. Bjornson." Thane rose and stepped toward the General. He knew fear and it radiated from Caufield. He leaned over the General. "I will bar those doors and you won't have to worry about a trial, General. Innocent people are dying because of your greed.

There is a second strain, and the antiserum you no doubt possess is useless. Where—the—fuck—is Dafoe?"

Caufield shifted in his chair and turned to look at the President.

John shook his head slowly, poorly hidden disgust painting his expression. "Tell him, Darrin, so we can stop this before we have a pandemic."

Caufield lowered his head.

Thane balled his hand. He didn't see shame, he saw regret at being caught. "Where, Caufield?" he growled.

Caufield stood and faced him. "I don't know. Our transaction and communications were finalized."

"Tell me about Bjornson."

Caufield ran his hand down his face as if rubbing away the moment and the nightmare he'd started. "Dr. Bjornson is retired. When Dafoe needed experts in virology, I offered his name. Clifford and I had crossed professional paths many times over the years. He moved his family to California when he retired."

"Where?" Thane barked. Patience was becoming a lost commodity.

"San Diego. He and his wife Ariana wanted to be closer to their grandchildren. His son-in-law is a Marine."

Admiral Pennington spoke. "I'll dispatch a squad to visit his residence." He reached for his cell and wandered away from them.

"Send Petty Officer Mace Callahan to do it. If there's information, he'll get it," Thane said. Caufield took a step back when he turned his attention on the General. "Bjornson hasn't shown himself since he escaped. He may be dead. If he is, your death sentence is sealed in cement with every other American citizen. You won't have a headstone that says President of the United States, you'll be in a mass grave with every other rotting corpse."

Caufield strode with as much pride as he could garner to stand in front of the President. "Since the day I agreed to Dafoe's offer, I have regretted it, but there was no going back without implicating myself and hurting my family."

The President reached for his phone. "Send a security team to the Oval Office immediately." He stood and faced Caufield. "You are a traitor to this country. You declared war on America when you gave Dafoe the plague." The door to the Oval Office burst open and a team of security officers came through. "Arrest General Caufield. Admiral Cagney, will you escort them?"

"Yes, Mr. President." Cagney gripped the General's arm and led him out of the office.

"Thane, Felix, can you stop this before it gets out of control?"

Thane's cell rang and he saw it was Kayla. "If you're calling, you have something."

"Thane, there are quarantines around each of the towns."

"That's good news."

"No, it's not."

"Sweetheart, you sound scared."

"Dafoe's second strain can live in water. The city's water systems were shut down and they automatically diverted to the water towers. That's where he put the virus."

"How many people left the towns before they were quarantined?"

"We don't know. They're investigating now."

"If we get them all, it's contained."

"No, Thane, it's not. People use the bathroom. People wash their hands, shower, and it all goes somewhere. All three of these towns were situated near underground river systems. The virus is free. It'll find its way into streams, lakes, and reservoirs. It will find its way to the cities."

"Is there any mention of this in the media yet?"

"I'm monitoring the largest news sites. Nothing yet, but if this gets out, there will be pandemonium."

"I'm on my way home."

"Okay," she said, her voice shaky, and that made him scared because Kayla didn't get scared.

"Leave one person in Base Command. Get everyone else to go with you and buy as much bottled water as you can. If hell breaks loose, I'll need you to be able to remain in the Ops Center."

"I'm leaving now. I'll call you when I'm back."

He lowered his voice and said, "Kayla, I love you, but I have to see this mission through. We're sending Mace on recon to Bjornson's residence. I'm going to join the team and we'll track down Dafoe. Lumin has six hours left. We have to find that antiserum."

"Maybe I should go with Mace?"

Jesus help us. "I didn't spend the last year and a half chasing your crazy, sexy ass down to be mine forever to lose it to some bug. I trust you to keep our unborn daughter safe. You're the woman of my dreams, and my son is the pride of my life. I can't lose any of you, but I believe in you, Snow White. Find Bjornson. He's the only one who can stop this."

"Thane Austen, I won't let God himself break up our family. Find Dafoe, and kill that son of a bitch before he kills us."

"Roger that, my beautiful wife. Call me before you head out with Mace."

"Bye, darling."

Thane swiveled and his brows puckered seeing the admirals and the President staring at him. "She'll find Bjornson, but in the meantime, we have a bigger problem."

The President prompted, "Sounds like it. Water. How do we stop people from drinking water without letting them know the real reason and starting a national panic?"

He brushed a slow hand through his hair. "We can't, Mr. President. You need to be quarantined. The Commander and Chief has to live."

Chapter Thirteen

Date: 07.26.2014
Time: 0600UTC 2200hrs PST
Mission: Code Name Luminous

Lumin needed gas and water. Sweat rolled down her back even though the air conditioning was on high. Scoring some aspirins to fight the fever would help. A fuel and food sign clung below a Route 66 marker. Another few minutes passed before a dilapidated gas station came into view. She parked in front of the pump and stuffed the corporate credit card she'd found in the glove box into her back pocket. A young guy sauntered from the gas station. Her eyes followed him as he rounded the front of the car. Luck helped with dim lighting over the pumps. She didn't want to try and explain why dried blood was splattered across the back window.

"Evening, ma'am. Fill her up?"

She nodded. "Do you have any water and snacks inside?" she said loudly.

"Yes, ma'am we're full service."

She waited until she heard the nozzle inserted then got out of the car. The musty-smelling store had a few shelves with mostly chips and fast food. The floor looked as if it hadn't been washed since the store opened, and the cracked linoleum gave away the building's considerable age. Pulling her sleeve over her fingers, she grabbed some bottled water and a few bags of chips. She dropped them on the counter, left the card and put some distance between her and the cashier's desk.

"All of this on the card, ma'am?" the young man asked as he rounded the counter.

"Yes, please." She hovered by the canned goods while the guy rang up her order. "What?" she asked, seeing him eye her.

"Five bottles of aspirin. You must have one helluva headache," he said, putting the last bottle in the bag.

"Migraines."

She had to sign the receipt. Taking a deep breath, she hurried back, swiped the pen from his hand, scribbled her name and snagged the bag from the counter.

"Your receipt, ma'am, and you've got my pen," he said when she had the door halfway open.

"Do you mind if I keep it? I lost mine."

"Sure, lady." He pushed the receipt to the edge of the counter.

Damn it. "Don't need it. Everything's electronic these days." She ran back to the car, threw the bag on the passenger seat, and gunned the engine.

Tucking the bottle between her thighs she cracked the cap with one hand, and drank the whole bottle down. She fiddled with the aspirin but couldn't get the cap off so she pulled over, and quickly sprang three pills and downed them. With a shoulder check, she got back on the highway. Time to find someplace to wait this out.

She slowed when she saw a sign cross her headlights that said *Kaibab Recreational Site.* Turning the wheel, she took the forestry road. The pine, spruce, and fir trees would keep her hidden. Driving slowly, she noted only two camp sites were occupied. A couple of outhouses sitting on uneven ground next to each other made her ponder how she'd go to the bathroom. She'd have to contain her bodily fluids. Pulling into the last site, she parked the car. Checking her cell service, the phone rang. The number was blocked.

"If this is a United States SEAL, I want you to hang up."

"Lumin, you sound tired."

Tony's concerned voice struck her in the heart. She closed her eyes, but it didn't stop the tears. A harsh squeeze in her chest threatened to make her bawl like a baby. "I'm okay."

"No, my lady, you're not. Before you hang up on me, I need to tell you something."

"I'm not dying in a cold cement room with a guy wearing a baggy suit hovering over me, Tony." She tucked her hand underneath her armpit to coddle the thrumming pain. The lymph node was swollen, and she remembered the picture they'd shown her at the base. Fear had taken up a solid residency in her stomach. Six hours to go before her expiration time. She stared at the passenger seat, at the bottles of aspirin sitting there. Could she do it if things got too bad?

"Then talk to me, because I want to hear your voice. I want you to hear mine."

"Later. I'll call later."

His voice hitched. "When it's too damn late, you mean. When I can't save you. Don't hang up, please."

She snuffled and rubbed the tears away. "I know you can stop Dafoe. I know you can do anything you want to do."

"I want to hold you in my arms. More than anything I've ever wanted."

"That wouldn't be smart. I thought SEALs were smart."

"I'm a man, and right now my heart is going a hundred miles an hour. If everything falls apart, if the team can't stop this, I want to be with you."

"I'm scared." The air hitched hard in her throat and she choked out a sob. The wall of hope she'd surrounded herself in crumbled.

"Please, Lumin, tell me where you are. Don't make me run in circles. You're making me nuts."

Lumin nearly jumped out of her skin when someone knocked on her window. A young couple with knapsacks peered inside. "Are you okay, lady?"

"Yes."

"Roll down the window," the girl said, winding her hand.

She shook her head. "I can't."

A flashlight beam punctured the glass and swept through the car, settling on the seat beside her. The girl's eyes strayed back to her. "Whatever it is, it's not worth that."

"Please back away from the car. I'm okay." The guy pulled on the girl's arm, drawing her away. They took another look over their shoulder before disappearing down the road. They had to be in one of the campsites she'd seen driving in.

"Why did she say that, Lumin? What's not worth it?"

"Tony, you need to stop calling me. Do your job. Dafoe is insane. Find him."

"It's too late to stop him."

"What do you mean?"

"Three towns are now quarantined. The population is infected. He released the second strain into the town's water source."

"Water!" She gripped the phone tighter. "Can it make it to the Colorado and other major rivers?"

"That's a likely scenario."

"The second strain can survive in air and water?"

"We don't know about air. They were taking you to Las Vegas to infect others. We assume so, but we don't know, and we can't know until I find you. Kayla and Mace are trying to find Bjornson and the vaccine. I have to know where you are so I can give it to you. Hiding from me will only waste time."

"Don't be mad at me. I'm not hurting anyone else."

"You're hurting me."

"No, I'm not." Her voice wavered with emotion. "We barely know each other." Her lip quivered and she couldn't stop it. Her right hand gripped one of the pill bottles and she closed her eyes, knowing it wouldn't be much longer before thinking straight would be a chore.

Tony sucked in a short breath. "I'm fucking begging you not to give up on me, Lumin. I thought you trusted me."

She smiled through her tears as the ache in her heart twisted tight. In spite of the agony she was about to face, the fear was swallowed by the memory of his arms around her. "I have a huge crush on you, Tony Bale. I have ever since you saved me from Gordon in the bar. Every night since then, I dreamed about the moment you left me on the steps of the Porter's home. I play it over and over again like a moment from an epic love story." She coughed out a laugh. "Stupid, but it's the truth. My heart raced when I saw you for the first time. It races now thinking about you." She swept her forearm across her cheeks and took a big, stuttering breath. "I'm probably not the first to tell you that, and I most definitely won't be the last. You are an amazing man, Petty Officer Bale." The phone was absolutely silent for so long she thought they'd been cut off from each other. It broke with a strangled cry. He was crying? "Tony?"

"I'm going to find you, woman, and when I do you're never going to run from me again. So hide all you want, because I'll be damned if I'll let my soul mate die alone. Come hell or high water, I'll be with you to the end. So, tell me where you are!"

A small beep sounded and the background noise went silent. She yanked the cell from her ear to see the battery was depleted. The tears came, rolling like a giant wave, and she leaned her forehead against the wheel, the phone falling from her fingers to the floor of the car. Pain, heartbreak, they stirred together in a cauldron of loss.

* * * *

Date: 07.27.2014
Time: 1400UTC 0600hrs PST
Mission: Code Name Luminous

The anteroom door to Base Command cracked open with a suck of air. Mace, geared in his fatigues, strode through it. "Ready to roll, Snow White?"

"Affirmative. I've got the address for the Bjornson residence. It's at the end of Telegraph Canyon Road near Otay Lake."

"Let's go pay them a visit."

Kayla grabbed her purse and slung the strap over her shoulder. "You don't think they're there, do you?"

"We're going to find out."

Kayla stared up at the clock and her brows knit together.

Mace shook his head at her. "She's already out of time."

"No," Kayla spit out. "She's young and strong. The virus will act differently with everyone. Let's go."

It took them twenty minutes to reach the well-kept acreage with white fencing and a modest rancher sitting on a knoll above the road with an unobstructed view of Otay Lake.

"What do you think?"

Mace's eyes scanned the front of the house and the surrounding area. "Stay here for a second." He cracked the door and reached for his Sig. Running for the house, he put his back to the wall when he reached it and scanned the property. He waved and she got out of the car. He pointed toward the side of the house. She nodded and followed.

The back yard was beautiful, with a huge green lawn, a hip-high fence and a large brick patio. An outdoor fireplace and loungers completed the outside living room. A kid's swing set and an oak tree with the beginnings of a tree fort sat snug within its noble branches. She followed Mace, and they both peered in the back window. The TV was on. Mace edged his way down the wall and reached for the patio door. It slid open with a pull. He signaled for her to join him.

"Your show, I'm just the muscle," he whispered in her ear.

"Hello, is anyone home? Ariana Bjornson, please come out."

"Who are you?" A worried voice came from the hallway leading to the kitchen.

A small child whispered in an overly loud voice and was hushed by an adult female.

"We're here to talk to you about your husband," Kayla said.

A head of white hair appeared from the hallway. "Please don't hurt us. We don't know anything."

Kayla stepped inside the comfortably furnished home. "My name is Kayla Austen. This is Petty Officer Mace Callahan, United States Navy SEAL. We need your help. People are sick and we know your husband has the antiserum. I'm not here to arrest him or hurt anyone. I need to help my friend, and the residents of three towns now infected."

"Stay there," Mrs. Bjornson whispered to someone behind her.

She stepped into the kitchen. "Your grandchildren are safe. They can come out."

Ariana Bjornson was a slender woman, maybe sixty years of age. A young boy and girl followed her, but she kept them behind her. "I don't know anything. I can't help you."

"We have to find your husband. He has the only vaccine to the virus that's been released by a terrorist. If you don't help us, we're all dead. The virus is making its way toward us. It's in the water. All we can do is get the vaccine, replicate it and start vaccinating people. Even then, thousands will probably die." Ariana was a mother, and most likely an innocent victim in all this. "I don't want my son to die, and I want this little girl to be born," she said, placing a palm on her stomach. "Please help us."

Ariana blinked and glanced at Mace. Kayla hoped like hell he didn't have his scary SEAL face on and his weapon was secure.

"That man, Dafoe, he's looking for my husband."

"We know. We have to find him first." The kids made a break for it, and Ariana tried to grab them. "It's okay," she reassured.

Kayla eased herself into a kitchen chair. Cranking a look over her shoulder, she made sure Mace got the hint. "Mrs. Bjornson, we know your husband was caught up in this. The other scientists were tricked as well."

Mace gave her a sympathetic look, and he was good at them.

"You're a SEAL?" she asked, coming to the table and sitting across from them.

"Yes, my wife was infected with the first strain of the virus, but we found the serum. We have to stop this if we can. Once it gets legs, it's going to kill thousands of people."

Ariana clasped her aging hands, wrinkled and covered in blue veins. "Clifford didn't realize in the beginning what his work would be used for. He'd been contacted by an old friend, and asked if he'd like to come out of retirement for a project. He thought it was backed by the U.S. military. They confined him to a lab in New Mexico, and when he realized who the man was behind the project, it was too late. He was a prisoner."

"Just like Dr. Carmichael," Kayla added.

"Yes. They had him for an entire year, and threatened our family if I went to the authorities. This man, Dafoe, he promised Cliff would be released when he'd finished his work. Yesterday Cliff called me. We've been living at my sister's place in Colorado for the last year. We only came back today."

Mace jerked his head toward the living room. Kayla had seen the luggage as well. "He's hiding."

Ariana nodded, her eyes dull with worry. Kayla reached across the table and gripped her hand. "Please take us to him. He is our only chance to stop this."

"Christopher. Maddy. We're going to see Grandpa, get your bags." The kids ran from the room. "Cliff isn't far. We have friends on the other side of the lake."

"We'll follow you," Kayla said, and she and Mace squeezed each other's hands under the table.

"They'll be watching this house," Mace said under his breath. "We've got to come up with a decoy."

"Roger that, thinking the same thing." She moved to the window and looked out over the lake. "There might be one way." Mace stood behind her and gave her a big hug, gazing over her shoulder.

"Congratulations by the way," he said, and kissed the top of her head.

She shifted and wrapped an arm around his waist. "A little girl. I always wanted a little girl."

Mace smiled down at her. "Are you stopping at two?"

She chuckled. "Thane wants four, but we'll see how he does with his daughter. I think she'll be turning him inside out with worry and love the second she's born. He'll protect Sloane ferociously."

"No doubt there."

"I talked to Nina just before you picked me up. She sounds good. Not exactly the best way to find out you're going to be a father."

A beaming smile spread across Mace's handsome face. "My family is more important than riding high on a mission. We've been talking about making a change. If I can get a transfer, we're considering moving to Hawaii. We want the kids to grow up together."

Kayla stood on her tiptoes and kissed his cheek. "Everything has changed so much in the last couple of years. Until now, it was all for the better."

"It still is, Kayla." Mace gave her a quick squeeze. "Let's find Bjornson and get the antiserum to Lumin."

"Tony must be going out of his mind with worry."

"She's three hours over now. She must be in bad shape. Tinman lost contact with her. Her phone died."

"When?"

Mace darted a look at her. "Midnight. You had enough to deal with."

"Mace." She gave him a glare. "There are more people than me in Base Command. All hands are on deck." She unlocked her phone and dialed the base. Barry answered and she gave him instructions. When she hung up, Ariana appeared with the kids, and she explained the plan.

The wind was warm as it brushed her face. At high speed, she and Ariana crossed the lake in their boat. Mace balked at the idea, but he had the kids and was driving around to meet them. If someone was following, they would follow Mace instead of her and Ariana.

"That dock over there," she shouted and pointed toward the west.

Kayla nodded and slowed the craft until it was gently drifting a few feet off the dock. She took a quick look at the rise of green lawn toward the back of the house. Dr. Bjornson had to be watching. Hopefully he'd see his wife and present himself. She secured the ropes to the cleats and they walked up the steps cut into the hillside. Ariana wore a worried expression.

"Is something wrong?" Kayla asked.

"I'm not sure," Ariana said, walking beside her as they approached the house.

The patio door was open, and Kayla saw something that twisted her nerves into a tight 'be wary' ball.

"Oh, no," Ariana cried, and began to run toward the house.

Kayla caught her. "Stay here. I'll go." She ran the rest of the way, but cautiously. An arm was draped out the door, and she saw a grey head of hair on the frame. "Dr. Bjornson!" She pushed open the patio door and knelt beside him, listening for other sounds in the house. Clutching his left wrist she felt for a pulse. Weak. "Dr. Bjornson, can you hear me?" she said, checking the rest of him. She rolled him, and saw the pool of blood hidden beneath him. A gunshot wound in his right side bled freely.

"Cliff, Cliff." Ariana knelt beside him and took his hand.

Dr. Bjornson's lids flickered as he came to. "You're going to be okay, sir." Kayla called an ambulance. There was a lot of blood loss. "Ariana, I need to stop the flow. Can you find me a clean towel?"

"They didn't get it," he muttered.

"Kayla," Ariana cried out.

She ran for the living room. A man lay face down on the carpet. No movement. Mace came through the front door. "Stop the kids from coming in here, Mace. Ariana, we need you to keep the children outside." Kayla toed the weapon away, and Mace picked it up and checked him.

"He's dead."

She ran back to Dr. Bjornson, grabbing a cloth draped over the handle of the wall oven on her way. She knelt down and put pressure on the wound, making the doctor flinch. "Sorry, sir. The ambulance is on its way. Where's the weapon you shot him with?"

Before he answered, she saw it underneath the kitchen table. "I know you're in a lot of pain, sir, but I have to find the vaccine to the second virus. Dafoe has released the new strain."

Dr. Bjornson's eyes opened a smidge. "Who are you?"

"I'm Kayla Austen. I work with the United States Navy. A friend was with Dr. Carmichael when he died. He told her about the virus and Dafoe, and you. We've been trying to find you. Dafoe has infected three towns. He put the second strain of the virus in the water. How long will it live if it gets into the underground water systems?"

Bjornson groaned as he stuffed his fingers into his pocket. He pulled out a piece of paper, and with a shaking, bloody hand, held it out. "It doesn't mutate, but it can live in water or air. It won't die off."

Kayla took the paper and read the numbers on it. "We thought it mutated after thirty-six hours."

"Didn't work," he whispered.

"What is this?" she asked, looking at the paper.

"Where I hid the vaccine. I didn't believe Dafoe would..." Bjornson's eyes closed for a second, and his breathing was becoming shallower. "I didn't think he'd do it without the serum. I found it." He coughed. "I created the vaccine for Ebola."

"Where is it?"

"Center—"

Oh shit. "Doc, come on, what center? Please." Mace hunkered down across from her. "What center?" she said loudly.

"Center for Virus..." Bjornson exhaled, and his hand went limp.

Mace felt for a pulse and shook his head.

"Jeezus," she yelled and jumped to her feet. "Another fucking piece of the puzzle. Now we have to run this down. We don't have enough time."

"Easy, Snow White," Mace said grabbing her. "As soon as the ambulance gets here we'll go."

"Go where?"

"Center for Virus Research. It's at the University of California, Irvine campus."

"You know this place?" Hope sprouted a leaf.

"Sure. One of my sisters went there."

"How far away is it?"

"About an hour and a half."

"Can we get a helo to fly us there faster?"

Mace gave her a raised brow. "You're married to the Commander of the West Coast Chain, and trying to stop a national disaster. What do you think?"

She blew out a deep breath. "I'll go and tell Mrs. Bjornson the bad news."

He nodded and gave her a weak smile. "We'll make it. We have to."

Within ten minutes, she and Mace were in the helo heading for the university. "Pilot, can you connect me with Base Command?"

"Affirmative, Snow White."

"Gord, I need you to find the man in charge of the Center for Virus Research at University of California in Irvine," she said without a greeting when he came on the radio. "We need him waiting for us. I'm bringing him something, and we need his help to decipher it. Don't give him all the details. Just make sure he's waiting."

"Good copy, Snow White. Base Command, out."

Kayla rested her head on Mace's shoulder.

"You tired?" he asked.

"Hell, yeah. I don't know the last time I had sleep."

"That's not good for an expectant mother."

"She'll be all right." Rubbing her stomach, she said, "Sloane is going to be an independent, strong-willed, free-thinking woman."

Mace chuckled into the commset. "Just like her mom."

Mace gripped her hand and held it for the twenty-minute flight. The pilot sat the chopper down in a football field. The practicing football team scattered as the Nighthawk descended. Mace helped her out and they ran toward a guy with a clipboard and a whistle.

"Can you show us where the Virus Research Center is?" Mace said to the balding man in his mid-forties who stared at them with wide eyes.

"Uh, yeah, sure. Follow me."

"Run," Mace instructed, and they all put it into a gallop.

Chapter Fourteen

Tony hunched in the shade of a transport truck, evading the blistering sun. He'd run six separate searches for Lumin during the night. She'd been infected around sixteen hundred hours yesterday. He placed his head in his hands and willed himself not to give way to his dwindling hope. She wasn't dead. He repeated it like a mantra, but too many missions and hard knocks on reality's door said she was. When her phone cut off last night, he felt every last cell of his body go into alarm. Was she trying to find them? She didn't want to infect anyone or take the chance of approaching the police for help. Why hadn't she found another phone? he asked himself, but he knew why. She physically couldn't and that tore him to pieces.

"Bale!" Captain Cobbs strode toward him with a sat phone in hand. "Base Command on the line," he said.

"Bale," Tony answered.

"Petty Officer Bale, it's Barry."

"Go ahead, Barry."

"Tinman, Kayla asked me to keep harassing the police departments in your surrounding area. I think I have something."

His heart scrambled to hitch itself to hope. "Go ahead."

"A small department a few miles from the Kaibab National Recreation Area just received a report of a woman, possibly suicidal. They said she appeared to be sick."

"Why suicidal?"

"She had a seat full of pill bottles beside her."

Tony closed his eyes. "It's Lumin. Thanks, Barry." He listened while Barry shared the location and directions. "We've found her," he said to Captain Cobbs as he hung up.

"Chopper is on standby for you." He lowered a harsh gaze on him. "Don't lose your head, Bale, even if you've lost your heart. Want company?" Cobbs asked.

"Negative, sir."

Tony ran for the chopper.

"Another recon?" the pilot asked as he jumped into the aircraft.

"Eastern edge of the Kaibab Recreation Area. Let's go."

The hot desert air blasted through the chopper like a well-stoked furnace. His heart hammered in his chest. If the police forced her out of the car, they'd all have to be quarantined. Within a few minutes the Black Hawk flew over the sparsely treed area. Tony couldn't miss it, but he had at three in the morning. He'd flown over this area, but hadn't spotted her car hidden by the trees. Fuck, why hadn't he looked closer? Three police cars were parked in a campsite surrounding the vehicle Lumin had taken.

"We can set her down a quarter mile to the north."

"Hover over the target. I'll fast-rope down."

He gripped the rope and waited till the Black Hawk lowered to thirty feet above the surface, skirting the tree line. He was on the ground and running within seconds. An officer spoke to Lumin while the other two stood in front of the vehicle.

"Stop," one of the cops said, raising a hand as he approached. "You want to tell us what's going on, and why the military just dropped you out of the sky?"

He stepped to the side and saw her. Oh God, his beautiful lady was sick. Really sick. He stepped up to the cop. "Tony Bale, U.S. Navy SEALs. I'd advise your friend there to step away from the car."

The cop crossed his arms. "Is that so?"

"Unless he wants to stop breathing in twelve hours, yes."

"What?" The cop's brow rippled.

"She's infected with a virus. A deadly one."

The other cop, a leaner version with shades, stood with attitude. "This have something to do with what we've been hearing on the TV?"

"Hey!" he shouted to the cop standing beside Lumin's window. "Step away from the vehicle."

"And who are you?" the cop asked, straightening up.

His buddy turned his head. "Says she's infected with a virus. Addy, think you might want to listen to him."

The cop stepped away from the car. "Seriously?"

He wasn't interested in the cops anymore, his gaze glued to Lumin. Her head rested against the seat, covered in sweat, her eyes barely open.

"No," she mouthed.

He rounded the car. "Leave, now," he ordered. The cops backed away, but only a few steps. "If you don't leave, you'll all be quarantined." He bent over. "Sweetheart, open the door."

Lumin's head swayed to look at him. She placed her hand on the window, and he reached up to mirror it. "Please, sweetheart."

She coughed and a small stream of blood slipped from her lips. She swiped it away, and tears welled in her eyes.

"Tony." She bit her bottom lip to stop it from quivering. "Please," she squeaked. "Stay with me until it's over."

"It's not over," he choked through tears and cleared the lump in his throat. "We just started."

"Petty Officer Bale," the pilot called in his comm set.

"Go ahead."

"Message from Base Command Coronado."

"Go ahead."

"They advise Luminous recovery imminent."

"Where?"

There was a pause. "Cal-U, Irvine campus."

Mace and Kayla had gone to the Bjornson's residence. They must have found a lead. "Lumin!" He swallowed hard, seeing her eyes closed. "Lumin." He jumped to his feet, grabbing a good-sized rock from the ground and smashed the rear window. The noise woke her. He unlocked the doors then yanked the driver's door open.

"No!" she yelped, and tried to crawl across the seat.

He jumped in the car, started the engine and floored it, headed for the helo.

"Come here, sweetheart." He pulled her under his arm. The glands in her neck were extremely swollen, but not broken open. Rounding a hairpin bend, he saw the chopper and stopped the vehicle fifty yards away.

"Black Hawk One, you copy?"

"Go ahead."

"I'm flying that helicopter out of here. I have to get her to the base now."

Silence returned. "Petty Officer Bale, I'll fly."

"Negative. Both you and the co-pilot need to disembark."

He jumped out and pulled Lumin into his arms. "Easy, sweetheart. I've got you." She lay in his arms like a limp rag. He ran for the chopper and laid her on the deck. Closing the doors, he raced for the cockpit. Offering the pilot and his navigator a thumbs-up, he lifted off the ground. Switching the radio frequency, he called Base Command Operations.

"Black Hawk One, Base Command go ahead."

"Incoming. ETA one hour fifteen, advise Snow White I've found the light. Need the recovery package on arrival. We'll need a quarantined area as well. Two infected. Advise CDC there's a vehicle at Kaibab National Park. It needs to be cordoned off."

"Roger, Black Hawk One."

He looked over his shoulder. Lumin was rolled into a tight ball. "Hang on, Lumin. Just one more hour. We're gonna make it." She barely nodded. When her gaze rose to meet his, he felt her pain. Every ounce of it. "It's okay, my lady. You're going to be okay."

A minute later, he heard Ghost on the air frequency.

"Black Hawk One, Base Command."

"Base Command, Black Hawk One, go ahead, sir."

"Confirm, you've got the light?"

"Affirmative. We'll both need to be quarantined. What's Snow White's status?"

"Target has not been acquired."

"Then we'll die together because I'm not leaving her, sir. If permission is denied to base, I'll fly this bird into the desert."

"Permission granted. Proceed to base. We'll have a hot suite waiting."

"Roger, good copy."

"How is she, T-man?"

He shook his head and gritted his teeth. "Sick," he spouted. "Oh God, she's really sick." He clutched the control arm to keep the helo flying straight. "She can't die. I won't let her die."

"Easy, Tinman. Get her here. We'll be waiting."

"Black Hawk One, out."

* * * *

The football coach cleared a path in the hallway as Kayla and Mace followed. Heads swiveled seeing the odd threesome running past the lecture halls. She didn't have the endurance Mace and the coach had, and she was out of breath when they reached a door somewhere in the bowels of the university.

"Professor Linden?" the coach called out as he opened the door.

An elderly man looked up from a desk littered with folders and books. Bifocals sat on the end of his nose and a cardigan draped across his thin shoulders.

"Coach Ross," he said, blinking at her and Mace. The blink turned into a wary look as Professor Linden sat the book he held, onto the desk.

"Sir, my name is Kayla Austen, United States Navy analyst, and this is Petty Officer Callahan, Navy SEAL. By that look on your face, you know why we're here."

"Please have a seat. I was contacted by your peers."

"There's no time for sitting," she said abruptly. "Clifford Bjornson gave me these numbers before he died." She waved the paper in front of the professor. "I need to find whatever it's associated with, and take it."

"Clifford is—dead?"

She strayed a look at Mace.

"Yes, he is," Mace answered, reaching for the door handle, and then stared at the coach. "Thank you." Dismissing him. Coach Ross got the idea and promptly left. Mace closed the door.

"I don't know if Dr. Bjornson shared any information with you. At this point, it really doesn't matter. This looks like a combination. We need to see it now."

"Ms. Austen, I can see you're flummoxed, but Clifford told me people may come looking. His discovery must be protected."

Every second passed like the hissing end of a lit fuse. "Flummoxed? We're looking for a way to stop a pandemic that may not be stoppable. You possess the hiding place of the only hope the people of this country have. Where is it?" she shouted. Professor Linden stared at her. "Do I look like a terrorist, for crap's sake?"

"Easy, Kayla," Mace warned.

She took a deep breath and said, "Listen, professor, we're literally on the verge of damnation. Dr. Bjornson must have shared his discoveries with you. This virus has to be stopped."

The professor stood and surveyed her. "Clifford was my friend. He thought he was working for the government."

"We know that," she said, her patience dwindling. "The virus Dr. Bjornson created was released in three small towns. We don't know if anyone left the towns before it was identified, but we do know that it had a minimum of twelve hours to work its way into the underground water table."

"Ms. Austen, I have to be sure you're not connected to the man who tricked him."

"If you want me to get the President of the United States on the phone I will."

The professor's brows rose.

"He's in his bunker, pacing the floor, expecting us to stop his country from turning into a graveyard. I need the antiserum."

The door crashed open. Mace swung around, weapon in his hand, but men poured into the room like ants, and they were all armed. They parted, and in walked a tall man of Middle Eastern ethnicity. "You're not the only one, Mrs. Austen," the man said.

"Callum Dafoe," the name stinging her tongue as she said it.

"Lower your weapon," he warned Mace.

Mace did as he asked, knowing someone would die if he didn't. One of Dafoe's men took it from him and motioned Mace to the corner of the room, separating him. She and Mace shared a look and she wished like hell they had E.S.P as a first language. Instead, she read his expression. *Stand down* was written in his gaze. She placed her hands behind her and as she did, she slipped the paper Bjornson had given her into the waistband of her skirt.

Dafoe walked up to a wide-eyed Professor Linden. "Where is the vaccine?" he asked calmly.

The professor's mouth opened and closed, and then he said, "Not accessible by me. Only Dr. Bjornson can translate his notes."

Callum Dafoe's dark eyes glistened with impatience. "Show me." He turned to one of his men. "Tie them up," he said motioning toward her and Mace.

Professor Linden glanced at a file cabinet sitting to his right.

"Get them, Professor," Dafoe ordered.

"It won't do you any good."

"Give me the key to the cabinet or I take it from you and you die."

The Professor fished in his pocket revealing a keychain.

"Open it."

The Professor took a hesitant step.

"Faster, Professor."

Professor Linden cracked the small padlock on the file cabinet and fingered through the folders, gripping one. "I'm telling you, without Clifford this will not help you."

Dafoe snatched the folder from him, opened it and flipped some of the papers. "I don't need to be a scientist. I have several in my employ."

"You selfish prick." It shot from her mouth, fired by this man's blindness to anything but revenge. "Everyone loses people they love. One way or the other, people die."

Dafoe turned his hateful gaze on her. "Is it your wish to die, Mrs. Austen?"

"Who the hell are you that you think your pain and loss is more important than anyone else's? That you have the right to act like God?"

"Kayla," Mace said sharply.

A man from Dafoe's guard cinched a plastic strap around her wrists. "Everyone battles to exist. You think because your wife and son were lost to war that you have the right to annihilate innocent people as retribution. You make me sick."

Dafoe snatched the weapon from the man standing next to him and pushed the muzzle into her shoulder. "I have every right," he yelled into her face. "The Americans think they're unstoppable. Your self-righteous husband has killed thousands of people without regard for innocence."

The end of the barrel dug into her bone, but she refused to flinch. She darted a look at the professor, who'd backed himself up against the bookshelf. Would he tell Dafoe she held the combination to where the vaccine was hidden? So close. They were so damn close. If she failed, there was nothing to stop a pandemic. Dafoe wanted to live while the rest of the world expired. His wife's life would never be vindicated, he just didn't know it.

Like him, she'd wallowed for years fighting her PTSD, only to be dragged into the light by the most unlikely of men. She'd made Thane a promise to be safe, but none of them were safe. Their son would die. They'd never hear their daughter's cry.

The corner they'd been backed into was sharp and solid. No way out but through impossible odds.

"My husband shook tyranny by the throat. Men like you. Men who don't know when to stop. Men who are sadistic bastards who want to conquer and cause pain to people who can't protect themselves. You're bloodthirsty. You're something that sticks to the toe of my shoe and smells like shit," she railed.

"Kayla!" Mace shouted. "Shut the fuck up."

The blast from the weapon rapped against the walls of the tiny office. Silence. Numbness. Chaos.

* * * *

Date: 07.27.2014
Time: 1900UTC 1100hrs PST
Mission: Code Name Luminous

Tony checked the time and willed it to stop. Fifteen minutes ETA to the base. Even through the constant rush of sound from the helicopter, he heard Lumin moan in her sleep. Sweat dripped from her forehead. He contacted Base Command and requested instructions.

"Black Hawk One, you're cleared for landing, southern parking lot. Remain in the aircraft until further advised."

The sun hung high in the sky. Seven hours past the time the virus was meant to kill its host. "SITREP on Snow White?"

"No joy."

Fuck. He'd told himself a hundred times he would save Lumin. There was no other outcome. "Where are you, Kayla?" he muttered, seeing the painted lines indicating the landing pad come into view. "Base Command, I need water." Lumin had begged for water thirty minutes ago. He'd given her his and she'd choked trying to drink it, most of it puddled on the deck. The whine of the blades changed into a slow *whip* as he put the skids on the pavement. "Base Command, Black Hawk One, shutting down."

"Roger, good copy. A vehicle is en route to your position. Standby."

Tony shut the craft down. He tossed his helmet and knelt beside Lumin, cradling her in his arms. Fear dug its biting nails into his chest, making him sway back and forth. When he'd been a kid, scared and alone in an empty house while his mother worked in the bar, he'd sit in the corner and wait for her to come home and do the same thing. There'd been no one to comfort him, and there was no one now. He closed his eyes and whispered to her, "My light. My beautiful light. Can you hear me?" Lumin's pulse barely beat beneath his fingers as he clutched her wrist.

"My hero," she breathed. Lumin's beautiful eyes shone with fever and a tear trickled from the edge.

"We're together, and I won't let them separate us again."

"I don't want you to die." She reached up and brushed his cheek.

"Wouldn't be much of a hero if I didn't rescue the woman I'm falling in love with."

She coughed and her entire body shuddered. "I thought you blamed me for Nina."

Truth pirouetted on the end of his tongue. He shook his head. "No. Your hero lost his nerve. I saw my best friend coming apart because he loves Nina so much. Truth is, it scared me. I hate feeling vulnerable, and that's what you do to me."

A smile creased her feverish lips. "Tony?" Her eyes closed, and he couldn't feel her breath on his cheek it was so shallow.

He kissed her hot forehead. "Stay with me," he urged. Cold fear gripped him. "No, Lumin. No, just a little longer."

"Don't be mad," she said in a sweet, small voice.

"Mad? Never," he rasped. "You're my forever girl. I want to hold your hand when we're old and grey. You have to live to keep me on the straight and narrow. The second I looked in your eyes, my heart pumped so hard I broke into a nervous sweat. I became a man with a future in that moment, but I need you with me." Lumin's inhale rattled and his heart skipped then stopped.

Big blue eyes filled with love and pain looked up at him. "I believe you."

He looked up and saw two transport trucks approach through his tears. Failure had been an enemy he always put aside when he became a SEAL, but in this moment he was a man. Scared that the delicate creature who'd made him laugh and his heart swell within a short time would be taken from him. Nothing he'd seen or done could harden him against the bitterness of losing Lumin. They were opposites, his darkness and her brilliance collided, and he had fallen into her dainty net, caught within her innocence. He'd lost his ages ago, but she offered hers, and he had to have her. Keep her. Protect her.

"Stupid wishes," she murmured.

"Tell me your wish, my lady. I'll move heaven and earth for you."

"I wish," she paused and licked her lips. "Wish…we had time to make dreams come true."

Three men exited the back of the truck wearing bio suits. Lumin hadn't wanted to die in an airtight bubble. He didn't either. Life, he wanted it, but not without her. He squeezed her wrist tighter, the weak beat a small, feathered flutter. "Baby, please, we're the center, remember? We're the center. Everything else is moving but us." He looked down to see her eyes closed. "Lumin!"

Her fingers released their grasp on his, and his heart broke into a million pieces with the last flutter of her pulse as her light burned out.

"Oh God, no. Hang on. Hang on to me." He rocked her in his arms, his cheek against her hot skin as his body jolted with heartbreaking sobs. "Don't take her from me," he begged the heavens. "Please, don't take her from me."

Chapter Fifteen

Thane charged through the anteroom door to Base Command. "Barry, SITREP on Snow White?"

"Negative, sir. It's been thirty minutes since she checked in."

Kayla wasn't answering her phone and neither was Mace. His SEAL sense was on high alert and it was screaming with a red warning bell. When it came to his wife, he was so tuned into her it was like half of him walked away every time she did. "Try again!" he ordered.

"Yes, sir." Barry slid his chair to another console and attempted with nil results. "Admiral, Petty Officer Bale has landed. They're transporting him and Lumin to the quarantine tent. She's unresponsive at this time."

His cell rang. It wasn't the Canadian anthem Kayla kept programming into his phone, and he tucked it back into its pouch without answering. "Unresponsive?"

"Cardiac arrest."

"Shit! Put a chopper on standby, I'm flying to Irvine."

"Yes, sir."

Thane had the pilot land next to Kayla's Black Hawk waiting in the middle of the football field of the campus. The first kid who made eye contact was motivated into showing him the way to the Virus Research Center. His heart beat fast as he ran into the muddle of people surrounding an office. A stretcher was being rolled out, the sheet covering the entire body. It's not her. Not her. He repeated to himself. He pushed through the throng of people rammed into the small office. Police and campus security all looked at him when he entered.

"Kayla?" he shouted, his eyes searching. Three men lay dead on the floor. Where was Callahan? A cop approached him. "Where's my wife?"

The cop gave him a once over and nodded. "Admiral," he paused looking at his name tag, "Austen. Kayla Austen is being escorted along with the SEAL and Professor Linden to a lab downstairs.

"Is she all right?"

"Um, not really, but she refused medical attention."

His insides turned cold. "How bad?"

"Bullet grazed her arm. She'll be fine once she gets it stitched up."

He shook his head, knowing he should have stopped her from running after Bjornson. "What happened here?"

"Trying to work that out ourselves, but it appears your SEAL, I assume he works for you, took out four men. There were more bad guys, but they escaped. We've put out an APB on Callum Dafoe."

"Take me to my wife."

"Right behind you, Admiral," Kayla said.

He swung around. She clutched a small cooler in one hand and her other palm clamped her upper arm. Blood seeped down to her wrist and through her fingers, but she was smiling. "You're going to the hospital."

"Where's Lumin? We have to get this to her first."

Mace entered the room.

"Take the vaccine, Petty Officer Callahan. I need to take care of my wife." He prodded the box from her and handed it to Mace. "And we're gonna have a little talk about keeping communications open on our way to the hospital, woman."

She scowled at him. "How about an atta-girl, Admiral?"

He pulled her under his arm and guided her out of the office. "How about I put you over my knee for scaring the shit out of me—again," he growled into her ear.

"Thane—"

"I'm rescinding my orders. You're retired. As of fucking now. Do you understand me?"

"I—"

He grilled her with a look, and she closed her beautiful lips. "I'll be talking to Callahan and if he tells me you put yourself in front of a bullet, I'll put you on a plane and secure the buckle myself."

They zigzagged down the hallway, ignoring the stares of the university students.

"Give me a break. It was that or let Dafoe win."

"Where is he?"

"Ran for it when Mace took out four of his security team."

He lifted Kayla into the back of the Black Hawk and ordered the pilot to the base hospital. The other Black Hawk was already lifting off the ground with Mace and the vaccine. He rummaged through the med kit and then pulled her hand away from the wound. It bled freely, and he darted a glance at her. Gore was something a SEAL got accustomed to quickly or he wouldn't be a SEAL for long. Kayla had endured a few injuries since he'd met her and each one had the same affect. Bile rose in his throat and his heart thumped hard. She watched him carefully, and although he could keep his composure in front of his men, Kayla unraveled him like he was unraveling the gauze.

"Thane—"

"Don't talk to me. I'm pissed at you."

She rolled her eyes. "No, you're not. You're worried."

She'd fessed up while they walked across the football field as to what she'd done in the office to throw Dafoe into a rage, giving Mace a chance to take out some of his men. It had worked, but his wife had a big chunk of flesh gone from her arm and Dafoe was still on the loose.

He palmed her cheek. "I want my wife to be safe. It's old-fashioned as hell, but I need you to be there for me when I come home. Not because I demand it. You know I'd never do that, but because we have a family to raise. You are my life. I can't even think about you standing toe to toe with a terrorist. It terrifies me."

Her gaze dropped to their hands twined together. Her blood covered his fingers. She'd spilled too much and it had to stop. She nodded.

He gently raised her chin. "Was that a yes?"

"This was extraordinary circumstances, Thane. You know that."

He leaned against the bench seat after securing the gauze with some tape and gave her a stern look. One that worked on his men, but he knew it did nothing to faze his wife. "This time, but I don't care if the world comes to a screeching halt, topples on its axis or fire ants take over the North Pole. If we live through this, we promise never to break stride again."

Her deep, beautiful eyes stared into his. "I hate those hoity-toity dinner parties."

"You think I don't? It's part of the job, and if you don't want me on the front lines, it means me in my number ones and you in silk from time to time."

She shuffled over and leaned her head against his chest. "That sounds a lot like blackmail, Admiral."

"Whatever it takes, Snow White." He kissed the top of her head and held his delicate wife in his arms. She showed her soft side to him more and more, and he loved how they had evolved from two calloused warriors into a couple who had formed a united front that no one could tear apart.

As the chopper began to descend, she turned her face up toward him and the anger melted away with the warm brush of her mouth. He loved her too deeply, but it would never dissipate, it had only gotten stronger and more entrenched with every day that passed. When her lips curved into a smile, the one she saved for him, he shook his head and rolled his eyes knowing what was coming.

"I want to see Lumin. Where is she?"

"Your arm first, then you can see her. Admiral Pennington erected a quarantined area on the southern edge of the base. Tony infected himself to save her," he said, as he gently gripped her waist and pulled Kayla from the craft. They both leaned and cleared the whirling blades of the chopper. Two attendants with a gurney appeared from the back entrance of the hospital.

"I'm walking in on two feet, Thane."

He swept her into his arms and laid her on the stretcher. Leaning over her, he said, "I'm joining up with the squad. When you're finished here, call me." A brief brush of his lips to hers made his body come to life. Her soft hand palmed his cheek, and she kissed him ferociously. With a gentle swipe, his palm stretched across her stomach, his fingers making small circles to reassure his baby girl growing in her stomach. "I love you. We'll find Dafoe, bring him down and then we're going home." He kissed her again quickly. "I'll call Nina's mom and find out how Adam is doing."

She nodded. "I'll head back to Base Command after I check on Lumin and Tinman."

"Bye, baby." He nodded at the attendants and watched as they wheeled her away. He knew she was safe, but it didn't stop his stomach from rolling over. Every time his wife was out of sight he worried about her. No matter how many years would pass, it would always be that way. Every day was a blessing, one he didn't deserve, but coveted with his soul. He turned his gaze toward the sea, and hoped Tinman would have a chance to find what he, Mace, and the other married men on the team had.

Home and heart kept them alive, gave them a place to center themselves when faced with an endless battle. Once upon a time he took up arms because of the rush it gave him, now he did it for his son and for his little girl who would soon join the world. His priorities had shifted since becoming a husband and father, but the end result was the same. There was no room for terrorism and tyranny, and if he could bring those responsible to their knees, he'd neutralize them all. Callum Dafoe was at the top of the list.

* * * *

Mace hit the base tarmac running. The cooler he carried wasn't just vaccine; it held his best friend's future. Lumin had touched Tinman like no other woman. Not even Nina had brought out the dormant qualities of Tony, long ago hidden by a harsh upbringing. Two Frogs from SEAL Team Three stood guard in front of the quarantine tent. "How is she?"

Paul Armstrong pulled aside the entry flap. "Bad, really bad," he said.

Four figures in airtight suits mulled around the mobile equipped enclosure. One of them raised a hand and passed through two small partitions to meet him. "Is that it?" the man muffled through his mask.

He handed the cooler to the guy and peered through the plastic walls where two beds surrounded by medical equipment sat. Lumin lay in one, Tony sat by her side, gripping her hand in both of his, his head bent watching her chest rise and fall with help from a ventilator. Mace read the taut, scared expression on his face as he looked down at the girl who'd swept his heart away like sand in a windstorm. "How is she?" Mace asked.

"She should be dead by now, but she's hanging on. We resuscitated her twice," the suited figure said, taking the cooler from him. "It's safer if you wait outside."

Tinman looked up and closed his eyes in relief. Mace gave him a thumbs-up. "Never give up, buddy," he yelled. Tony nodded, but he recognized the face of a man whose faith only had a few precious drops left to draw from.

As Mace pushed the plastic flap aside he came face to face with the base priest. "Why are you here?" It came out with a sharp edge.

"I was requested to perform Last Rites."

Mace shook his head. "Father, with all due respect, if you do that, you're giving her permission to die, and she can't. She has to live."

"And if she does die, she's a soul without preparation and absolution." Father Pickering gave him a sympathetic smile. "You know this, Mace."

Mace was Catholic and so was Nina, but Tony hadn't been raised in any particular religion. He wouldn't understand. "How did you know? Who called you?"

"Dr. Mallory comes to Mass. He's in there with her, and she asked for a priest."

Mace blew out his breath. "One second. Stay right here." Mace skirted the tent and got as close to Tony as he could, remaining outside the walls that kept the virus trapped within. "T-man," he said loudly.

Tony released Lumin's hand and stepped to the plastic wall. His eyes were red and tired, his features aged with worry.

"Tinman, the priest is here. I don't want you to kill a man of the cloth. Lumin asked for him."

"Why?" he said, his voice ragged.

"Last Rites, my friend."

Tony paled and his head whipped around. When he set his gaze on him again, Tony's brow was wrinkled tight. "No. She can't."

"Remember when my sister Leslie was dying? I explained it to you then. Lumin was raised Catholic. It's important to her. It doesn't mean she's going to give in, but if God makes the decision for her," he paused, "she was born a Catholic, she must die as one."

"She's not going to die," Tony said gruffly.

"Buddy, you know that's not all up to her."

"Bullshit."

"Tinman, your heart is talking right now. I know what it's saying to you, but faith is part of her life and if you want to help her, you have to help every part of her, including this."

Tony's lids snapped shut and tears ran down his face. His agony tore at Mace's heart. A hand touched Mace's shoulder, and he turned his head to see Kayla standing there. Her arm was bandaged, but there's no way she'd already been tended to by a doctor. "Did you go to the hospital?"

She ignored his question. "Mace is right, Tony. We all have to believe in something, especially in our darkest hour. Lumin is desperately hanging on for you. In the warehouse, she told Nina and me how much she loved you and what she shared with you. As a Catholic, she was raised to believe that sex before marriage is a sin, but she saw so much goodness in you that she gave you her innocence. I know this is hard to understand, but she needs to ask for forgiveness. Don't deny her this right."

Tony hung his head and nodded.

"I'll go talk to the Father, maybe he can offer a prayer for our friend as well. I think he needs one," Kayla said quietly.

Mace squeezed her hand.

"Kayla's going to tell the Father he can come in." He gnawed on his lip. "How are you feeling?"

"Doesn't matter," Tony said, still staring at the ground.

"You matter to us."

"What else could I have done? What did I do wrong?" Tears welled in Tony's eyes when he raised his head. "How can I protect her now? I've never felt so useless and empty."

"No easy day, buddy. Especially today. I hope years from now, you and Lumin will look back and say this was the hardest day."

"I've never felt like this. I hate it," he choked out.

Mace nodded, remembering when he held his sister in his arms as she took her last breath. He'd been gutted from the inside out, and nothing before or since that day hurt as bad.

"Nina?" Tony asked.

"She's recovering." Mace saw the Father step into the compartment. They'd put him in a suit for protection, but the scarf and the cross hung on the outside. He knew he wouldn't be permitted to take them with him when he left. "Be by her side, Tinman. Pray for her."

"I don't know how," his voiced stuttered. "I wish I did."

"Sure you do. You don't have to believe in God, my friend, but he believes in you."

Tony swiped at his tears and nodded. Kayla joined Mace, and together they held each other's hands, bent their heads, and prayed with all their hearts for their friend, and for Lumin.

Life could be lived in solitude, but love had a mission as well. It was as much a part of a human as any organ. Seeded at birth, it waited till it found someone to make it grow and fill the void in one's heart. Lumin was Tony's seed, and Mace prayed that God would give them the chance to fill a lifetime with challenges and happiness till the end of their days.

Lumin was injected with the vaccine and another doctor injected Tony. They both stepped out of the priest's way and exited, giving them a little privacy. Tony gripped Lumin's hand and remained silent as the Father began, "May the blessing of almighty God the Father, and the Son, and the Holy Spirit come upon you and remain with you, Lumin, Amen." He gently placed an invisible cross upon her forehead. "Lumin, your sins are forgiven."

He and Kayla watched Father Pickering administer the Last Rites. When he was finished, the Father looked into Tony's eyes and rested a hand on his shoulder. "I can see your love for this woman and your hope. God's arms are always open, son. Blessings to you both."

Tony was wide-eyed and he swallowed deeply. His lips quivered and his brow kneaded together. "Thank you for coming, Father. I wish you could forgive my sins as well, but there are too many."

"All you have to do is ask."

Tony's head jerked. A large tear trickled down his cheek. "I don't have the right to ask."

Father Pickering's compassionate brown eyes gleamed. "We all have the right to ask, Petty Officer Bale."

"I want to be a man she can be proud of."

"I absolve you of your sins in the name of the Father, the Son, and the Holy Spirit."

Father Pickering brushed a cross on Tony's forehead, and a heavy breath escaped Tinman's throat. They all saw the movement at the same time.

Her eyes remained closed, but Lumin's lips formed the sweetest smile under her mask. "Amen," she mouthed.

Chapter Sixteen

For four days, Tony sat next to Lumin holding her hand, barely moving from his chair. He couldn't sleep. Afraid if he closed his eyes, she'd leave him. After the first twenty-four hours, they removed her oxygen mask. She was weak and slept a lot, but when her eyes opened he wanted to be the first thing she saw. When the thirty-hour mark came, she sat up for the first time and ate a little soup that he fed to her. Between each mouthful he kissed her and praised her for her bravery. She was his warrior, and every minute that passed she strengthened and so did his heart. By forty-eight hours the color had returned to her cheeks. Although she was in a lot of pain, she made improvements. The doctors had done several tests assuming there was organ damage. Tony began to pray in his own way for God to protect her. There were things only he noticed, like the light in her eyes returning to a brilliant, youthful glint.

On the fifth day he woke after exhaustion pulled him down for a short nap. The feel of her fingers ruffling his hair in rhythmic passes woke him. He raised his head from her stomach to see her smiling at him. It was in that moment he knew for certain that five days ago had indeed been the hardest day he would ever know.

"Good morning," she said.

He pushed himself up and kissed her mouth with a long, slow, loving touch. "I love you," he breathed on her lips. They held each other. The constriction in his heart and the thickness in his throat were from happiness, not loss.

"You saved me again," she whispered sweetly next to his ear.

"And every day for the rest of our lives," he said, kissing her quickly, and then sat down.

"You need to eat, Tony. I'm worried about you."

"I'll get something later," he said. His body had gone into starvation mode sometime yesterday when the grumblings in his stomach had stopped.

"How are you feeling?"

"Depends."

"On what?" she asked, her brow wrinkling.

He squeezed her hand and brought it to his lips and kissed her palm. "On how you're feeling. Apparently, I can't live without my light."

She chuckled, brushing his hand against her cheek. "You're silly."

"Maybe, but I don't mind showing you that part of me, and every other part. There'll be things I won't be able to share with you in the future, but I'll explain why."

She nodded. "About your job?"

"Yeah, but I promise I'll never shut you out again."

She rearranged the bed sheet and took a deep breath. "We're making a lot of promises today."

"There's more. Like, I promise to make you happy you chose me. If you do," he paused. "Choose me, I mean."

"I'm supposed to play the field, aren't I?" she teased.

He cleared his throat. "Anyone you have in mind?" he asked, as Cracker jumped into his head and jealousy nipped him.

"No, but you've had a lot of—experience." She blushed. "Well, you know what I'm trying to say."

He laughed and played with the ends of her blonde strands. "You and I are going to learn it all over again. Together. Slow. Seductive. It's a journey that will never end because I will never stop loving you." Lumin was filled with a creative sexual energy, and he didn't doubt for one second that she'd come up with ways to surprise him. He had a dream he'd replayed in his mind many times already. He'd come home to find her wrapped in a red ribbon and nothing else, just to keep their fire burning hot. And he would be the most romantic fool she'd ever know. "I'm never gonna be a rich guy. In fact, you'll probably make more than me eventually."

She placed her fingers over his mouth. "Do you really think I care about that?"

He didn't, not for a second. "Guess it depends on how many pairs of shoes you want." He grinned at her.

"I only need one pair," she said, her gaze softening with emotion. "The ones that will let me walk beside you for a lifetime."

"Lumin—aw, shit woman, you make me so happy." He threaded his fingers through her hair and attacked her lips, nearly sucking the soul right out of her. He wanted to brand her with his mark. Branding? Hell yeah! He knew exactly what he was going to do, but he'd keep it as a surprise for now. She sighed when he finally released her lips.

"You have to leave me and rejoin the team, don't you?"

He shrugged. "Can't, I was infected. I need another day or two before they'll clear us. The rest of the team is being vaccinated too."

Lumin shuffled to the side of the bed and pulled on his hand. He slid next to her, and drew her against him. His eyes threatened to close and he gave in, comforted by the beat of her heart next to his.

"Lumin," he whispered into her hair. She squeezed him to let him know she was listening. "There's been plenty of times I've been scared in my life." She raised her eyes to look into his. "But I never knew fear, real, cold, biting fear, until you died in my arms. Promise me you'll never leave me again."

"Petty Officer Bale, are you saying you like me?"

He shook his head. "No. I'm saying something I never thought I'd ever say to a woman. I don't want to live without you."

She closed her eyes and rested her forehead against his. "What about all the good reasons for staying a bachelor? Or the seven years that separate us?"

"I stopped being a bachelor a few days ago when I saw you standing at my front doorstep. The only people that might be concerned about seven years are your parents." He kissed her soft lips, and probably held her a little too tight, but she was holding him the same way.

"I think they'll be more concerned that you're not Catholic than our age difference."

He kissed the tip of her nose and nuzzled her cheek. "Then I'll become Catholic."

She blinked at him. "You will?"

He was like two pieces of a chain, and when he met Lumin she was the missing link that made him whole. Her innocence. Her faith. Every last little cell that existed inside her made him whole. "I'd do anything for you. I *will* do anything for you." She snuggled closer and that's how they drifted off to sleep.

* * * *

Date: 08.02.2014
Time: 1800UTC 1000hrs PST
Mission: Code Name Luminous

Captain Patrick Cobbs finished his comms with Master Chief Briggs. Fox was deploying ten teams, locking down major routes in northern Nevada, Arizona, and New Mexico. Canadian and Mexican border patrol had been given Dafoe's picture and advised to detain him if he attempted to cross. Ghost gave an ETA of one hour to join the team outside of Kingman. Lumin had been found, but both she and Tony had been infected. Snow White and Callahan appeared in the eleventh hour with the vaccine. The good guys were now one up on Callum Dafoe.

The mission had acquired a minor victory, but they were all waiting for the final curtain with two scenes left; Dafoe to be apprehended or neutralized, and the lethal crawl of the virus beneath their feet to be stopped. Would it make it to a main source of water? It was a ticking time bomb, but the longer it remained within the earth, the longer USAMRIID had to vaccinate as many people as possible before it raised its head and sunk its fangs into an unsuspecting population.

He dug his cell out of his pocket and thumbed the long list till it highlighted Marg's number. He needed to hear her voice. It had been a hard decision to send her away, and where to send her. If she returned to Hawaii with their girls, she could be trapped on an island with a virus. Marg gathered all three of their daughters and went to her parents' place on the East Coast. He couldn't get her much farther away from the virus unless he put them on a transport to Alaska, which he'd considered.

"Hello."

Just the sound of her voice leveled his blood pressure. "Hey, sexy lady."

Marg laughed. "Well, if it isn't my very own hero. How are you, handsome?"

"Better now," he said, beginning to walk. His boots dug into the dry sand, and he headed toward a tent used for their field HQ. Not to mention some shade. "Did you pick up the water?"

"We did. Gallons of it. We're not turning on the taps."

"I know, I'm being overcautious. The virus can't make it out east that fast, but when it comes to you, I'm not taking chances." He halted in the shade. "How are the girls?"

"They're good. They miss their dad, and Rayanne misses her boyfriend."

"What boyfriend?" he growled.

Marg chuckled. "The one she's afraid to tell you about."

"Who is he?"

"A young man from school. He's starting his second year of structural engineering at the university in September."

He grunted. "Where does he live?"

"His parents are from L.A."

"Good part or bad part?"

"Pat." Her tone dropped by a few octaves, and he knew after spending twenty years with the woman, he had to rein it in.

"Guess I've got nothing to complain about. I convinced you to date a guy from the wrong side of the tracks."

Marg's sexy chuckle shot straight to his loins. The woman still held magic over him. He'd been caught in her spell when he first saw her, and nothing had changed. They'd struggled through years of her parents' poorly disguised dislike for him and his own demons. Marg had met Ghost first and they'd shared one sweaty roll in the sheets together. Pat had wanted to walk away, he wouldn't be second choice, but Marg wouldn't let him. She was a determined woman.

"I didn't care if you lived in a train car, Patrick Cobbs. You made me feel beautiful and loved."

"That's because you are, sexy lady. I'm standing here trying to hide a hard-on just listening to your voice. I don't know how the hell you do it, but don't stop."

"Pat—are you safe?" she said, worry icing her words.

He blinked with her sharp change of course. "We've made it this far, Marg. None of us would have guessed we'd see this type of attack get so much mileage. It was always a possibility. Hell, Hollywood has made millions on the same scenario. When we bring Dafoe down and contain the virus, you and I will head back to Hawaii, and the worst thing I'll endure is a paper cut."

"I love you forever and ever, Patrick Cobbs."

"Amen, my beautiful wife. I miss you and the girls. I always do, but I have to get back. We're waiting for a team of geologists to advise on the virus tracking underground to a major water source. Everyone is holding their breath, hoping the three towns that were hit don't connect with any subterranean waterways." The line was silent. "What's wrong, honey?"

Marg spoke through her tears. "Please, be careful."

His brow tightened. Marg hadn't cried since they said goodbye when they started dating and he was deployed for the first time. They'd broken up. At least he'd tried to break up with her. "Marg, I'm always careful because I know you want me home."

"I do. I guess I never imagined you out in the field again after you took the new posting. I didn't have time to prepare myself. I'm sorry." She sniffled.

He smiled to himself, but his heart hung heavy. "I didn't expect it either, honey, but they need as much experience as they can get on this mission. I'm doing this for selfish reasons. For you and the girls. We'll have no future if this virus unleashes itself on the population."

"I know, but it doesn't mean I'm any less scared. For twenty years I watched you leave us, and I held strong, because that's what a SEAL wife is supposed to do."

"And you did a great job. You were my strength too. Every time I left. Every close call I had, I thought of you."

It had been a long time since they'd spoken like this. After so many years of marriage, things just got comfortable. They loved each other more today than in the beginning. She was always ready and willing to love him, and he thanked heaven for its blessings, and for Marg being the woman she was. He'd seen a lot of marriages flushed down the toilet, but it took two strong-willed, determined people to stay the course. She'd fought like a warrior when he tried to walk away from her. It took a while before he realized she was never going to give in, that she loved him, not his swim buddy.

Once they'd married, Ghost would give him the gears from time to time about it. His best friend never let him forget what an ass he'd been and what a good woman Marg was. His career in the SEALs had been challenging, but he was surrounded by strength and love, and their faith kept them going whenever they faltered.

"Come home soon."

"Can't refuse that offer. I'll call when I can. Kiss the girls for me."

"Watch your feet, SEAL."

"Always. Bye, beautiful." He hung up and lifted his gaze to the desert stretching out before him. Scrubbing the three-day-old growth on his chin, he exhaled deeply. The quiet before the storm, he thought to himself. He and the team had been here many times. A SEAL learned early on the back end of a hurricane was usually the worst. His eyes felt the cool relief as he pulled his shades down. Some guys missed the adrenaline rush when they stood down from active duty, but he'd had a few months to get comfortable in an air conditioned office in Hawaii. Coming home to Marg every night with dinner waiting wasn't a hardship. Having to choke down MREs in the field and ignore the aches and pains that his service years had bestowed on him while he trudged over rough terrain, weren't missed.

He'd be a lifer in the Navy, but he wasn't planning on hanging his ass out to get it shot off anymore, and yet, here he was. Rubbing the sweat from the back of his neck, he turned his gaze into the tent. Ditz and the new team guy, Ed "Cracker" Saxton, sat in a couple of field chairs gulping back water. They'd stitched Ditz up, and he was back in the mission. A couple of Marines joined them and the guys bantered back and forth. Most of the other service personnel didn't know why they were here. Alpha Squad kept a lid on the details, but something told him it wouldn't last long.

A truck rolled up, the driver's door embossed with the United States Geological Survey emblem. The dust swirled in the air when it stopped in front of the tent. He stepped into the July sun to greet four people, two men and two women.

"Captain Patrick Cobbs, United States Navy SEAL," he said sharply.

"Captain," the tall redheaded woman greeted, stepping ahead of her team. "We need to talk."

"This way, ma'am." When they turned for the tent, he called out, "Seaman Young." Nathan jumped to his feet. "Rally Alpha Squad and the members of DEVGRU. Meeting."

"Yes, sir." Ed scattered with him to collect the team.

"Captain, I'm Dr. Sandy Clarke, director of USGS Pacific, this is Assistant Director Hamilton Koch," she motioned to the short, balding man to her left. And two of our best hydrologists, Lydia Harper and Gabe Timmons."

"Thank you for coming," he shook their hands.

"Didn't really have a choice," Dr. Clarke said. "We were ordered here by the White House, and I'd like to know why."

"You will shortly. Admiral Austen is en route."

As if summoned, a Black Hawk settled her skids to the desert floor and Ghost disembarked, but he wasn't alone. Tinman and Mace were by his side.

He intercepted them. "USGS just arrived," he reported to Ghost.

"Call out the team, I want all thinkin' heads present," Ghost ordered.

"Already done."

Pat stayed Tinman with his hand. "How is she?"

"Alive," he said. He shook his head. "I was sure I'd lost her." Tinman took a deep breath and gazed at him. "I know you told me not to lose my head, but I was ready to die beside her. There's damage to her internal tissue, permanent damage."

"Internal organs?"

"Time will tell. They gave her blood thinners to stop the clotting. Her heart and kidneys may be affected."

"I'm sorry. We're the ones that are expected to take the collateral damage."

Tinman blinked, then a small smile spread across his face. "I'm not. She's alive. She's young and strong. I don't care what the outcome is. She's my light and my lady, and we've got a whole lifetime to love each other."

Pat eyed him. "How soon before she's up and around?" They set off for the tent where the rest of the team gathered.

"Not long. They said once the symptoms disappear, recuperation starts. The vaccine stopped the virus in its tracks."

"Ten years, and I've never seen you so committed to one woman. What changed?"

"I thought I was just like my dad. Lumin wouldn't accept that. I don't know what she sees, but her vision is a lot clearer than mine." He shook his head. "Imagine me falling for a Catholic virgin. Has to be some kind of strange intervention going on there."

Pat chuckled. "Marg had some heavy-duty convincing with me as well when we first started dating. I didn't come from the best stock, but she saw something in me. I think, no I know, it made me a better man."

Tinman grinned. "I want a family of my own, with her."

"You'll get that chance, Tinman."

"I hope so, but only if we stop this bug."

"Let's do it." They fisted each other and joined the rest of the men.

"This is Dr. Sandy Clarke, Director of USGS Pacific," Pat said, introducing Ghost.

Dr. Clarke motioned to Lydia, the hydrologist she'd brought with her, and the woman opened a laptop. "We were asked to provide you with information on the underground water system from three towns in New Mexico. I've also heard the reports on the TV. The details are sparse, other than a bad flu erupted causing severe fever. What's really going on?"

Ghost shared a look with the director's team. "It's not a flu, it's a weaponized virus. Engineered for longevity and can live in air or water. The Bubonic plague was spliced with Ebola."

Dr. Clarke maintained her composure, but the ripple of shock made her blink. "Terrorism?"

Ghost nodded. "The vaccine has been located, but it will take time to reproduce. The man who released the virus deployed it in three towns. Adelino, Bosque, and Los Chaves. Before we were notified and could contain the towns, the populations continued their daily routines. All three of the town's waste systems filter out into the desert, but we need to know if any of them have underground water that connects to major rivers or reservoirs."

Lydia began typing furiously, her eyes darting back and forth as she retrieved information on her laptop. Dr. Clarke and Assistant Director Koch, shared a concerned look. "Whoever the terrorist is, he planned this out carefully." Her brow wrinkled with worry. "These towns sit right on the Rio Grande. The third longest river in the U.S. It crosses the entire state from north to south. There is a large underground lake called the Ogalala which runs from southern New Mexico to Nebraska as well."

Ghost seamed his lips, and nodded for her to continue.

"The Rio Grande supplies the U.S. and Mexico with drinking water, irrigation, and plays a huge role in recreation and ecology. If the virus makes it to the Rio Grande, our food will be tainted, there will be no clean drinking water. The domino effect will infect millions. New Mexico also has the Pecos, Gila, and Canadian Rivers. All are main waterways with thousands of tributaries."

Ghost's expression became more and more rigid. None of them had considered the far-reaching fingers and the intelligence of deploying the plague in New Mexico and letting Mother Nature do the rest.

"There's more," Dr. Clarke said, and Cobbs held his breath. The tension in the tent, and the feeling that they'd underestimated Dafoe, hit full on.

"The Continental Divide also crosses the state of New Mexico. It separates the direction in which North America's rivers flow. East of the Divide, rivers drain into the Atlantic. Rivers west of the Divide drain into the Pacific. He must have known this. The virus could make it to both coasts."

Cobbs' heart leaped in his chest. Marg and the girls! The team had to stop this.

Chapter Seventeen

Tony had served with the Admiral long enough to know the tight expression he wore meant he was nearing explosive.

"What about the drought? Haven't the water tables been dropping steadily in the west due to lack of rainfall?" the Admiral asked.

"Yes, and no," Dr. Clarke answered. "The Rio Grande is fed from the Colorado."

"Don't think that's going to happen," Ditz said, placing his sat phone on the table. "You're on speaker, Snow White, repeat your last comm."

"Admiral Austen, a CDC report just received. La Joya, a small town south of Bosque, reported their residents lining up outside the medical facility. All of them have high fevers and flu-like symptoms."

"How far south, Snow White?" the Admiral asked.

"Approximately eighteen miles."

"Do we know where their water source comes from?"

"Yes, sir." Kayla paused. "The Rio Grande. Quarantine units and service members have been dispatched. CDC is now taking water samples further downstream. No results have been issued yet."

"When was the first case reported?" Ghost asked.

"Estimated two hours ago."

"Anything else?"

Tony watched Ghost. The man knew his wife was holding back.

"Affirmative. The media must have found a willing source. Twenty minutes ago, CBN reported the possibility of a pandemic, and that unfriendlies have planted a virus in the U.S."

Ghost nodded. "Keep us advised, Snow White."

"Roger that."

"That's close enough to the first three infected towns, someone could have traveled there," Mace offered.

They all looked down at the map spread out on the table. "Let's hope so," Captain Cobbs said.

Ghost straightened to his full height and put his attention on Tony. "I doubt it. Tinman, our luck has run out."

He nodded, his nerves hopping with an internal clock that started ticking double-time. "We have to divert it, and then kill it. Can CDC confirm whether we can eradicate this bacteria with heat or some other source?"

No one had an answer.

"Dr. Clarke, where is the narrowest and shallowest portion of the Rio Grande?" Tony queried.

Her hydrologist, Lydia, turned her laptop. "Here," Lydia said, pointing at a spot near the northern end of the state. She turned her confused expression on him. "You want to hold back the Rio Grande?"

"What about all the tributaries, cracks and crevices?" Ed questioned, standing between Nathan and Stitch.

Mace snatched the phone off the table, dialed, then leaned over it, waiting for someone to answer.

"Coronado Base Command," Kayla answered.

"Snow White, patch Professor Linden into this line."

"Standby."

Professor Linden answered the phone. "Professor, this is Petty Officer Mace Callahan. We need your help."

"What can I do?"

"Sir, how do we kill this virus if it's already in the water?"

Professor Linden cleared his throat. "It's relatively easy to kill it. Even though it's been spliced with Ebola, it's still a weak organism on its own. The problem is when it merges with a host, like a human, we can't kill it without killing the person. But you've got the vaccine."

"We do, but it's made its way into a large body of water. How do we stop it?"

"Without poisoning the water?"

"Yes, it's made it to the Rio Grande."

"Oh, dear. The safest way is to ozonate the water. It has the capability of inactivating bacteria and viruses, but I have no idea how you could do that to a river as large as the Rio Grande."

Options whirled in his mind. "Deployment isn't the problem, but how do we get our hands on enough ozonated material that can be deployed?"

"I'm not sure, you'd have to talk to the U.S. Environmental Protection Agency."

"We're on it, guys," Snow White said. "I'll advise when I know more."

Tony stared at the map.

"What the hell are you thinking, Tinman?" Mace asked.

"Here," he pointed. "We need to stop the Rio Grande above the first infected town. Close the dam down here at Caballo and trap it. Ozonate it, and then open her again."

"It might work," Dr. Clarke said. "This area here." She pointed. "The river runs through a canyon. The cliff walls are over a hundred feet high on either side. We'll have to check, but I think this reservoir next to Caballo Dam is very large."

Ghost, like him, was filtering and assessing every idea placed on the table by the team.

Ghost said, "Tinman, you want to bring down the canyon to stop the water within the Rio Grande Norte area?"

"It's plausible. This looks like another dam," he said pointing to the northern part of the state.

"It is," Lydia confirmed. "There's about eight dams north of Los Chaves."

Demolitions and heavy weaponry were his specialization. "There's too much distance between those two dams even if we lock them down. What if we created another here, North of Isleta Pueblo."

"What do you mean created?" Mace asked.

"If we're able to ozonate the water caught in the reservoir near Caballo, we need to have as little flow as possible. We create another block north of Los Chaves and blow a trench into the desert to divert more of the flow, we can treat the infected water, killing the virus." He waited for the USGS team to disagree. "How long would we have, Dr. Clarke, before the water would make it over the temporary block?"

Dr. Clarke turned to the hydrologist, Gabe Timmons.

"There's a problem," Timmons said. All heads turned his way. "I've just been checking the weather. Colorado and Arizona have been experiencing a lot of summer storms. It's causing a drain-off into the Rio Grande."

"If we block it, how much time?" Tinman asked again.

"What would you put in its path?" Dr. Clarke asked.

Tinman saw it. New Mexico state highways wouldn't like the idea. "Right there." He pointed at the map. "We blow it and create a trench into the desert here. We can't stopped it, but we might bring it down to a trickle."

The doc swayed her head. "Water will always find a way around. You might have a few hours max before she'd climb up and over. You're talking about a major river with a lot of power behind it. The northern dam you're looking at is called the Cochito. If we lock that off too, it will help."

The phone rang, and Tinman answered. "Go ahead, Snow White."

"I just spoke with the EPA. They said there is a company in Sacramento that has begun production on commercial-sized canisters for ozonating large bodies of water. The plan was to use it in reservoirs or lakes. Would that do?"

"Hell, yes," Tinman said. "How much do they have in storage?"

"A lot. I called the company; needless to say, they were overjoyed hearing the U.S. Navy was interested in purchasing everything they had. We're going to need a massive airdrop. They gave me a formula to use."

"For what?" Ghost asked.

"How much water can be cleansed per hour based on the number of canisters deployed."

"What's the magic number, Snow White?" Tony asked.

"I need the volume of water to finish the calculation."

"Are you near a map?" Tinman asked.

"Satellite, I've got it sitting over the Rio Grande."

"Jesus, woman," Ghost hollered.

"What?" Snow White snapped back. "It's an emergency and it's fast."

Ghost rolled his eyes. "Faster than Google Maps?"

Tinman grinned as did the rest of the team, knowing the hell she took for cracking the U.S. Navy's satellite codes and redirecting them when they were deployed. "There's a reservoir in front of the Caballo Dam. If we drop the majority of the canisters there and in mile intervals northward toward Adelino we should cover the area," Tony said.

Snow White let out a little groan after calculating. "Not enough canisters."

"Is there another source?" Mace asked.

"Negative. I've already searched, not unless you want to go to every pet store and buy aquarium-sized ozonators."

Tinman let out a frustrated breath. "That means we have to get rid of some water."

"Infected water," Ed said.

"People die in times like this. It's to be expected. We can't save everyone."

The entire group of men looked up to see who had spoken.

Wearing a sharply-pressed work uniform, the clean, lean officer nodded. "Lieutenant Abraham Lewis reporting for duty, sir," he said, looking at Admiral Austen. "It's an honor to meet you."

The team's eyes darted around the table and then back at Lewis. Tinman didn't like judging a book by his cover, but Lewis came with a reputation. There wasn't a thread out of place or a five o'clock shadow on his face. They all looked like they'd been on a mission for weeks.

Admiral Austen sized him up as well, and his ice blue eyes radiated a thought. One the team could recognize, but probably not Lewis. "Lieutenant Lewis, lives have already been lost. More U.S. citizens will also die before the virus is contained. We will mitigate loss of life as a primary goal."

Ghost's gaze cut the rigid if not arrogant expression on Lewis' face to shreds. It changed quickly to one with a shadow of wariness. At least the guy wasn't a total idiot, Tony thought to himself.

"Snow White, get a hold of the district in Caballo. Advise them the dam needs to be closed immediately," Ghost ordered.

"They won't listen to me. They don't know who the hell I am," Kayla shot back.

Ghost nodded. "Get on the phone to Admiral Hoskins. He's still at the White House with the President. Tell him what we need."

"Will do." Kayla paused. "What the hell?"

"What is it?" Ghost asked.

"Sit down, right now," Kayla said to someone. "Nina just walked in the door." Kayla held the phone away, but she came through loud and clear. "Are you out of your bleedin' mind? You need to be in bed. You look like shit." Kayla laughed. "Nice."

Mace grinned. "She just gave ya the one finger salute, didn't she?"

"Yup. What a harpy. I'll advise once I've spoken to Admiral Hoskins and we get confirmation the dam has been closed."

Tinman disconnected the phone. "What's the chances the virus has already reached the Caballo Dam?" he asked the hydrologists.

Dr. Clarke bit down on her lip and swerved a look at her team. "We'll let CDC give you that answer, but let's hope it's negative."

"We're going to need as many men as we can muster to pull this off. Let's take Alpha Squad and ten more men from Bravo Squad to survey the area."

"I'll ride along with you on this one, Tinman," Cobbs said.

Tinman was glad to hear it; Cobbs also specialized in demolitions. "We need Fox as well."

"I'll call him in," Ditz advised.

"Tell me your plan." Lewis paused to look at his nametag. "Petty Officer Bale, you're part of my squad, is that right?"

Tony straightened and turned to the squad's newly acquired lieutenant. "Sir, you're gonna have to catch up as we go. Clock is ticking on this one."

"I understand that," he said, his eyes narrowing, "However, you'll report to me before initiating the plan. I'll approve it and then you can proceed."

The tent quieted once again, and Admiral Austen and Captain Cobbs stopped their conversation to listen. Tony stepped around the table and into Lewis' airspace. He saluted. There were a few ways to do it; he used the universal "bite me," a sign of zero respect to an officer.

"Sir, I don't have an issue with the chain of command, but I do have an issue with millions of people dying. If you want to know the plan—sir—then follow us to that Black Hawk, it's time to turf the daily dress and put on some cammo. You're going to need it."

Lewis removed his cap and swept a hand through a short regulation cut. Something he and the guys rarely did unless they were home for a while and the girlfriends made them remove the scruff.

"Bale, there is a chain of command. I'm it. I'll remain here, but before you depart I'd like to know what your intentions will be."

"We work as a team, Lieutenant. You're in or you're out. That's your decision. Everyone has their way. If you want a good example of leadership and teamwork, that's the man standing over there." He pointed at Cobbs. "He's been our lieutenant for eleven years. We have to prove our abilities. You have to prove we can trust you."

"I don't need your trust, Bale. I need you to follow orders, and with all due respect, Captain Cobbs, I have my way of doing things. It's called by the book."

He turned his stare on Tony as if it was supposed to intimidate him. Wasn't really working though. Tony shrugged and eyed the guys. "We're wasting time. You want a report, I can tell you how to fuck off in four different languages—"

"Bale," the Admiral said sharply.

"Sir."

Ghost's expression remained ramrod tough, but his eyes glinted with mirth. Lieutenant Lewis was the type of officer that remained behind the safety line, clinging to his mother's skirt and polishing his Budweiser, no doubt buying every T-shirt, belt buckle and ball cap with a SEAL insignia on it. He might have been a SEAL once; now he was bordering on bureaucrat.

Enough posturing. "Dr. Clarke, can you split your team? Half at the Cochito Dam and half at Caballo Dam?" Tony asked.

Lewis finally acknowledged the geologists and eyed the director with interest.

"Yes, Petty Officer Bale, we can do that, but there'll be resistance."

Tony rested his knuckles on the planning table, giving the map a scan. What had he missed? "Resistance?"

"Cochito is on native land. The closure would have to be approved by them."

"If you run into a roadblock, call me." They exchanged numbers. "Let's see what we're dealing with from the air. Alpha Squad, you're with me." Captain Cobbs nodded at the Admiral and made his way with the squad toward the helo.

"Ghost will speak with Lewis," Cobbs said, keeping in step beside him. "If Lewis wants it by the book, Ghost will shove the whole thing down his throat."

Tony grinned. "I know it." They both bent over, running below the whirling blades of the chopper. "Did I pass the test?" He knew Ghost had stood back to see how he'd deal with Lewis.

Cobbs gripped the bulkhead and jumped in, Tony right behind him. They were the last in and sat on the deck, each draping a leg out the door as the pilot began to lift. "Not bad, but I think Ghost expected you to know 'fuck off' in five languages."

They both chuckled. Cobbs scanned the horizon with his sharp eyes.

"You gonna miss this?" Tony asked, not able to read Cobbs' stoic rigidity.

"Nope. I did my time. I missed too much of Rayanne and Cindy's years growing up. I'll be there for Kelsey." Suddenly the harshness left the edges of his expression. "Marg has put up with this job for twenty years. I owe her my undivided attention for the next fifty."

The hot wind buffeted them as the Black Hawk flew above the desert floor toward the Rio Grande. "How long did you know Marg before you asked her to marry you?"

Cobbs' head tilted and he grinned. "A SEAL year is like comparing driving to a destination by car vs 'as the crow flies.' Calendar days, it was nine months."

"And the time you were together?"

Cobbs scratched the scruff on his chiseled jaw. "I would have asked her after the first night we spent together, but we had some things to work through, so I waited."

"Until when?"

He laughed and looked toward the horizon. "Until she asked me."

"Seriously?" *This* he didn't know.

"Never forget it. The woman didn't give me an option." He grinned. "Not that I wanted one."

A second Black Hawk flew abeam of them. Dr. Clarke with her team onboard were bound for Cochito Dam. "Lumin hasn't finished her degree and she's only twenty-four. I don't want to take her options away."

"Let her decide that. Marriage isn't about rescinding choices. It's about making them together." Cobbs leaned against the bulkhead. "A wise woman told me that once."

"Any regrets?"

"Every time I left her and the girls. Knowing they wanted me home and in one piece gave me the determination to see my way through every mission."

They sat in silence until the topography changed as they neared the Rio Grande valley. Tony's mind was a jumble of duty and Lumin, switching back and forth in high gear. She'd have to put up with his life as a SEAL. It wasn't fair to her or any serving member's spouse.

Captain Cobbs gave the order to the pilot to hover over Los Chaves and then fly downriver. When they reached Highway 85, they saw the twin bridges. "Highway Department is going to hate this," Cobbs said into his comm set.

"The water's high already," Tony said. "I'll confirm with Fox, but if we blow a trench to the west in front of the bridge, it looks like a swell in the landscape could buy us some time."

"Tinman, we have enough explosives to blow a trench back to San Diego," Cobbs stated.

"Those farms are damn close," Tony noted. The entire valley was covered with them. "Anyone have a better plan?"

"Captain Cobbs, Base Command Coronado," the pilot interrupted.

"Link her in," Cobbs ordered, waited, then said, "Go ahead, Snow White."

"I've got Origin Ozone on the line wondering if they should begin racking up canisters and where to send the bill? I've already advised Admiral Pennington and Admiral Hoskins of the plan. He says Eagle has approved whatever it takes."

Cobbs gave him a hand signal. Go or no go? Eagle was a common code word for the President of the United States. Cobbs was leaving it up to Tony to decide. "Snow White, what's the time line?"

"Standby."

Nina came on the radio. "Tinman, we've got a yellow light on transport aircraft for deploy from San Francisco. Deploy from San Diego too long."

"Earliest ETA?" Tony requested.

Nina responded. "Four hours to Albuquerque. Chopper deploy to drop point."

Tony groaned and shook his head. "We have to hold the river back for hours?"

"Several."

What choice did they have? "We're going to need civil law enforcement and the National Guard to evacuate the valley between Cochito and Caballo Dams."

"I'll advise the C.O."

"Ninja Girl, one more thing."

"Roger, go ahead."

"Stop all traffic east and west bound on Highway 85 where it crosses the Rio Grande at Los Lunas north of Isleta Pueblo."

There was a pause.

"You copy?"

Snow White came on the radio. "There's a bridge in that location."

"Negative, Snow White. There's two."

"I'll locate the closest demo depot."

"Any further reports from health authorities?"

"Negative."

"Advise ETA when the canisters are in the air."

"Roger, good copy. Base Command out."

"Pilot, sweep south down the river to Caballo Dam," Cobbs ordered.

A nod from the pilot and the Black Hawk arced in the sky.

"Ditz, radio the Admiral. The request for explosives will have to come from him."

Ditz gave him a thumbs up.

"Why is the river so damn high?" Tony asked, seeing the water was near the bank's edge.

"Must be getting rain from up north," Stitch said.

Tony's cell rang. He didn't recognize the number, but he already knew the voice.

"Petty Officer Bale, this is Lieutenant Lewis."

"Go ahead, sir."

"Admiral Austen has advised me on the mission. Caballo Dam has been locked down."

"What about Cochito?"

"Initial response from the native band is negative."

Shit. The chopper settled on the ground and the squad jumped out. "Standby, Lieutenant."

When Tony cleared, he got back on the line. "Politics are involved here. Who can talk them into changing their minds? We don't want to start a war with the local native band. We're here at Caballo, the reservoir is three-quarters full, and the river has a good rip to it. We need that dam closed."

"One of the SEALs from DEVGRU mentioned a comm gal in Coronado might be half squaw."

Tinman stopped in his tracks and the hair on the back of his neck stood out. *Did this fucking asshole just call Kayla a squaw?*

"If she's a redskin like them, she might be worth something to us."

Tony blinked. He could straighten out Lewis now, but there might be a better way to take care of this idiot. "Sir, approach Admiral Austen with your thoughts. He knows all the staff in Coronado Base Command. Tell him what you just told me." An evil grin grew on his lips; he just wished he could be there to see what happened.

"I'll do that before I order her to call them. For a change, a chugg will be a help instead of a pain in the ass. Least she'll be good for something, ya know what I mean?"

Holy fuck, was this guy for real? "Chugg?"

"Yeah, Natives. Redskins."

Tony squelched what he wanted to say to Lewis. *Keep talking, asshole, your life expectancy just shortened by about fifty years.* "Sir, I believe you're talking about Kayla, team name Snow White."

"She's got a team name?" he exclaimed. "Oh, I see, she screwed someone to make her mark."

Tony choked and shook his head. Instead of giving more away, he said, "I'll check on progress in fifteen minutes." That's all it should take before Lewis was buried somewhere in the Arizona desert.

Chapter Eighteen

Thane spoke with the captain of DEVGRU. The Development Group was the best in the country for anti-terrorism missions.

"Callum Dafoe has gone into hiding, Jake," Thane said as he led him to the coffee.

Jake Ackerman accepted the cup. "Need one of these. I got your brief. Still hard to believe General Caufield turned against us."

"Greed." Thane snagged another cup of coffee. He was living on the shit. "We squeezed everything we could out of him. Dafoe's residences have been checked, but they're clean. We need your team to roust him out."

"He's got to have another residence not registered to him that he's holed up in. These guys like their comfort."

Thane nodded. "My gut tells me he's hesitating from launching a full deploy of the virus until he figures out how not to die. He's not protected from the second virus, but with us squeezing in on him, he might launch regardless."

"Wouldn't be surprised."

Jake Ackerman equaled Thane in height. He'd been a SEAL just as long, and holding the position of commanding officer of DEVGRU meant he'd earned his metal. Thane had worked with him numerous times over the years. The man prided himself on never giving in. His wife must agree, since they had six children.

"Admiral Austen?"

They both turned to see Lewis standing behind them. "Yes, Lieutenant." He wasn't going to give Lewis the courtesy of introducing Jake. Lewis looked hungry to shake anyone of higher rank's hand. The guy was a ladder climber. He could scrape up the rungs himself.

"Lieutenant Abraham Lewis, sir," he said to Jake.

Jake barely acknowledged him. This guy's reputation must be right up there with Mr. Brocklehurst in *Jane Eyre*. Jake had to know him since both had been stationed in Little Creek.

"I spoke with Dr. Clarke. The native band at Cochito will not close down the dam, but there might be an opportunity to resolve the situation without a lot of red tape."

"And that is?" Thane asked. Lewis eyed the coffee, but Thane waited, not offering.

"A woman in Coronado Base Command. Apparently she's got some redskin in her. The natives might listen to her."

Thane's cup only got halfway to his lips. He saw Jake dart a knowing glance at him. "Redskin?"

Lewis gave a jerk of his head. "Yes, sir. One of your men, Captain Ackerman, said she's half squaw."

Jake cocked his head to one side as if stretching his neck and his expression distilled into dislike.

"I spoke with Petty Officer Bale, he called her Snow White. Oxymoron no doubt." Lewis let out a sarcastic laugh. "Regardless, he said you'd probably know her."

"Yes, I know her," he said, his blood already boiling in his veins.

Jake coughed and turned away, snagging a bottle of water from the table. He slowly twisted off the cap while taking a step back.

"She's our warfare analyst, retired, but she's working on this mission."

Lewis rolled his eyes. "I've had to deal with minority staff. All you can do is harness them the best you can. I'm sure you were glad to see her go."

Thane stole a look at Jake, who shrugged his shoulders and said, "I assume Petty Officer Bale didn't tell you her name."

Lewis flicked a hand in the air. "Don't need to know her name; as long as she looks like an Indian, she might convince them to close the dam. If they throw the war paint on, she can talk their talk. Providing she's got half a brain, which most don't."

Thane ran his finger down the seam of his cammo pants, brushing the leather on his holster. "She has a sharp mind, and she's the best analyst Coronado has ever hired."

"Why did she retire?"

Thane slammed his cup on the table. "Because..." he said, his anger turning into a hurricane force warning. "She married the Admiral of the West Coast chain."

The sarcastic look on Lewis' face evaporated as his mouth snapped shut and he paled. "Sir, I thought that was your pos—"

Thane glared at him with a hefty grip on his emotions to kill one of his own, not that Lewis portrayed a single virtue of a SEAL. He leaned into him. "I strongly suggest you pull your head outta your ass, Lieutenant. If you ever call my wife a squaw again, I'll make sure you spend the rest of your fucking career putting silencers on dog tags."

"Lewis, you are one dumb fuckin' bastard," Jake added, leaning back on the table and crossing his arms.

"Sir, I had no idea."

Jake gave him a disgusted look. "That's because you're too busy sucking some ranking officer's cock." His brow rose. "Glad he's your problem now, Ghost."

"Get your ass on the next bird back to Coronado. When this is over, I'll dispatch your next assignment," Thane said.

They watched Lewis scurry from the tent. "Think that's the closest he's ever come to dying," Jake commented.

"Think you're right."

"Aside from the prejudice, he does have a point, Thane. Kayla might be able to help."

Thane seamed his lips, ordering his temper to recede. He flicked open his cell.

"Hi, darling," she answered on her personal cell.

The rest of his ire dissipated with the sound of her voice. "Hi, baby. We've run into a roadblock and need your help."

"Hit me."

Thane turned and put a few paces between him and Jake. "Rather be doing something else to you."

Kayla laughed. "I would think so, it's been more than twenty-four hours, poor Admiral."

He coughed out a laugh. "You're a hard woman to resist, isn't my fault."

"I'm already knocked up, what more do you want?"

"I can find a secluded corner and talk you through it."

She hissed out a laugh. "Stop. What do you need?"

"I hate to say it, but your bloodline."

"Say again?"

Thane explained the hedging from the local native band, but made sure to exclude the lieutenant's prejudice.

"I can try, but I'm not like you, Thane. I can't talk people around my little finger."

"You did a fine job with me, baby. We need that dam closed or we're gonna be opposing Mother Nature the whole way." He heard the tap of her low-heeled shoes on the elevated tile floor of the ops room. Her fingernails clicked on a keyboard. "What are you doing?"

"Recon, SEAL, what do you think?" She paused. "Okay I've got the band leader's name. I don't like doing this over the phone."

"I don't want you coming into the hot zone. It's too dangerous."

"Fine. And we just spoke to Nina's parents."

"How's our boy?"

"Missing Mom and Dad, but he's safe."

A warmth he only got when he thought about his family seeped into every corner of his heart. "Kayla, I know you're sick of hearing it, but thank you for falling in love with me."

She breathed out a satisfied little hum. "I'll never be sick of hearing that from your lips, which I wish I could nibble on right now."

"Phew." He adjusted himself, glad he was facing the tent wall. "I want to find Dafoe and annihilate that bastard for too many reasons, but the most important is forcing us to be apart."

"I want us to collect our son and go home. That's all I want."

"Your wish is my command. Call me when you've spoken to the tribal chief."

"Aye, aye, Admiral."

He grinned as he disconnected. Fuck, he loved his wife, and now he had to stop thinking about her to get his hard-on under control. Damn woman did it to him every time, but his mind had its own course and it wanted to replay the last time her soft curves were in his hungry hands, especially when she was pregnant. Their sex life never dimmed, but there was something totally irresistible about the woman when their baby was growing inside her. She'd lost a lot of weight after Adam was born, but now her hips were filling out again being pregnant with Sloane. He ordered his mind to stop thinking about it. He inhaled a deep breath and turned to see Jake give a quick jerk of his head.

"Better watch it, Ghost, that's how I ended up with six kids."

"I want four, but she's putting the stopper in at two. Our little girl is on her way now."

"Congrats, man. Let's make sure we find Dafoe. Don't want anything getting in the way of that master plan."

* * * *

Callum Dafoe paced the floor of the small industrial building in southern New Mexico. In the corner, several metal crates lined the wall filled with EA2. His storage unit in Idaho had been located, but he had more than enough to create a pandemic of global proportions. Eleven men stood warily watching him. The last of his security team and one scientist waited for his instructions. They'd escaped the university but he knew the manhunt for him had begun. The American forces would be split trying to contain the virus in the Rio Grande. Something he doubted they'd accomplish.

"Dr. Palin, we have lost our chance at retrieving the vaccine Dr. Bjornson created. What are our options?" He stopped in front of the scientist. Dr. Palin was in his early forties and if he wanted to live to see fifty, he would give him an acceptable answer.

"Very few."

"Not—good enough," he said. "I'm sure your family wants to see you again. A viable option is what I need." Although Callum's wife was dead, he had other family and wanted them protected.

"There's only one option and no way to confirm it at this point in time."

"Explain," he said, glaring at the man he would sooner kill than talk to. He was American and every American needed to die.

"Researchers discovered that swine flu survivors had super immune systems with antibodies that could kill off any new flu virus, not just the H1N1. Their immune systems went into overdrive. There is a possibility this could occur with Virus EA2 which Dr. Bjornson created, since we used a strain of H1N1 and bound it to the Plague. We'd need a survivor of EA2, and I doubt there are many. It was engineered that way," Palin said, his words dripping regret.

Callum nodded. "There may be one, possibly two. If we retrieve these individuals, how long would it take to recreate the vaccine?"

"Normally months. Sometimes never, but you have his notes. I've looked through them. It's possible to reverse engineer and identify the antibodies if you can find someone who survived."

Callum turned to his security captain. "Take half those crates and deliver them to Arizona by tomorrow. I want them in place for a deployment on my word. The second shipment will be driven to California. Leave ten crates here. You, Captain, have a special mission."

"Yes, sir," the security captain nodded and motioned for his men to get moving.

"You will remain with me, Dr. Palin."

"Mr. Dafoe." A tall, lanky Arab stepped forward. "I've received a report the military have been sighted in Bosque. An evacuation of all residences near the Rio Grande has begun."

"And the virus?" Dafoe asked.

"Doing its job," the young radical said with pride, as if *he* invented it. "Reports say the clinics are lined up with the sick in the valley. Others will continue their daily business and pass it on to each other. More will leave their towns. It's spreading. With no vaccine, they will all die. The government will be forced to call their military out of the Middle East to enforce quarantines and control the population." The young man nodded in respect. "Word of you has reached our brothers across the world. Some already revere you for what you have single-handedly done, Mr. Dafoe."

Young minds filled with hate were so easy to hire. In every state, some immigrants with chips on their shoulders gorged on what America had to offer and reveled in the opportunity to stab her in the back. Even young men and women who'd never stepped foot in their ancestral homeland were ready to pick up a weapon and double-cross the Americans. He used it to his advantage. Since his wife had died, he held the same contempt. It fueled his revenge. The SEALs would not stop him.

"What is your name?" Callum asked the man.

"Adeeb."

"Remain here, Adeeb."

The young man nodded and stepped to the side of the security captain.

"Dr. Palin, wait for me in my office." He looked pale and beaten down, but the doctor had better find a second wind because Callum didn't plan on expiring with the rest of the population. He turned his attention to Adeeb and the security captain. "Find Lumin Edenridge. She was given the second virus and I believe she's alive. I think the military has the vaccine. If we can't get it, we need her. Bring her back here."

Both men acknowledged his request and left.

* * * *

"Petty Officer Bale," Tony said, answering his cell.

"Tinman, it's Kayla."

"Were you successful with the Cochito Band?"

"Affirmative, but the agreement is hardly binding and they were very resistant, and with good reason. Holding the water back means they endanger their lands. They told me there's been heavy rain the last month in Colorado and many of the underground tributaries are feeding into the Rio Grande. You're gonna be on the clock, Tinman."

"Understood. What about the canisters?"

"That's why I'm calling. Aircraft was in flight five minutes ago. ETA fourteen ten hours."

"Can you do me a favor?"

"Course, what do you need?"

"Will you check in on Lumin for me?"

"Shit, Tony, ya think I haven't already? They released her this morning. She's shaky, but she wanted out of the plastic bubble something awful."

He laughed. "I bet. I want her to stay at my place."

Kayla chuckled.

"What? Oh shut the hell up, woman."

Kayla's voice altered to something akin to a teasing big sister and said, "Picked out a ring yet?"

"What? No," he drawled and paused. "Should I? Maybe I should?"

"Tony, for frig's sake, I'm kidding."

"I'm not."

"Have you lost it? You've known her a millisecond. She almost died and that scared you, but you're going to have time to get to know each other. Well…after stopping a pandemic and finishing off your seven-month deployment."

"No fucking way," he hollered. "Kayla, you have to help me. Can we get married over the phone? Video call?"

"Whoa, Tinman, listen to me. In fact, standby one."

"Petty Officer Callahan," Mace answered.

Oh, for shit's sake. "Kayla, he's standing fifteen feet away from me."

"I know that," she said, linking all three of them together on a conference call. "But this is easier."

Mace lifted his hand in a "what the fuck" gesture. "Mace, talk to Tinman."

Mace walked toward him. "What's up?"

"I want you to go find Tinman's good sense," Kayla ordered. "He's obviously misplaced it. He wants to marry Lumin."

Mace choked back a laugh. "Nothing wrong with that, is there? She's hot, probably keep him out of trouble for the next fifty years."

"He wants to marry her now," Kayla announced.

"Now as in…now? Ah, T-man, ya want to do that before or after we blow up a major highway?"

"Now," he said.

Mace cocked his head and his brows rose. "You're not kidding."

"I'm not kiddin'."

"You haven't even asked her yet, Tony. It's not exactly a 'sweep a girl off her feet moment' you're planning."

"She'll say yes."

Kayla stammered then said, "Mace, help me out here."

Mace cleared his throat. "I think she might, Kayla."

"You're both stupid," she spit at them.

He and Mace broke out laughing.

"Can we do one thing at a time, and this is not the time, Tony."

"I want her to have my name. What if something goes wrong? She'll get all my benefits. She'll have my place. I know you guys will look after her."

"Tony," Kayla yelled. "Gaaaah. Get on the phone, Nina."

"Why am I on the phone?" Nina said, coming on the line.

"Hey, babe," Mace said, winking at him.

"I've got a ton of shit to do. Hi, hot stuff," Nina said, the sound of papers shuffled close to the phone.

"Intervention," Kayla said sharply. "Tony wants to ask Lumin to marry him, as in now. Right now. As in get the pastor, now."

"T-man," Nina screeched. "Seriously, that's too cool."

"Nina!" Kayla yelped.

"What? I think it's sweet," Nina said, siding with him.

Tony laughed knowing Kayla was gonna round out on him any second. "That's three against one, Kayla."

Kayla huffed. "Well, it's going to be two against three and Lumin's vote evens it out. You need to spend time together. You've talked on the phone, and spent some precious, if not earth-shattering, hours together, but this is an important decision. Neither of you should jump into this like crazy teenagers."

Kayla was doing a good job voicing the concerns of a big sister or his mom, who he didn't talk to enough, but maybe he should. If Lumin married him, she'd become part of his small, dysfunctional family. "What if I ask her and she says yes?"

"Then," Kayla paused. "Then you're engaged, and it should stay that way for at least a few months. She's only twenty-four, Tony. Her parents will no doubt want to be part of this. Not to mention they'll want her to finish her degree."

He hated Kayla sometimes. She always managed to find the weak point. "She can still do that while we're married. In fact, she won't have to work anymore. Lumin can concentrate on school alone."

"Tony," Kayla shouted. "Do I have to get my husband on the phone?"

"Oh sure, pull out the big guns." He rolled his eyes and Mace broke out laughing, and so did Nina. "Why the hell do you guys get to be married and I don't?"

"T-man," Nina said, still chuckling, "you have to admit, we kinda knew our husbands for more than one day. I think Lumin is perfect for you, but this is only a couple shades off a Las Vegas shotgun wedding. Don't you want to ask her when you're face to face?"

"That could be months, Ninja girl."

The looming task of controlling a virus settled on all of them and no one spoke. Everything could change if they weren't successful. He and Lumin were immune to the virus, but millions weren't, and he and the squad could be months dealing with an international disaster.

"Thanks for the words of wisdom, girls."

Nina said, "Good luck, T-man. I'll take care of the mother hen here."

He hung up and Mace gave him a raised brow. "You're gonna do it, aren't you?"

"Yup."

"Ditz," Mace yelled over his shoulder. "We need a laptop over here for a video chat."

"What for?" Ditz asked as he approached him.

"Just give it to him."

Ditz shrugged and offered his. "Use this icon," he said, pointing at the screen.

"Thanks, man." He took a big breath and hoped the stars were all aligned. He sauntered over to a sizeable rock jutting from the sand surrounded by tufts of tough grass that managed to find a will to live in the hot terrain. He hunched down and sent Lumin a text to sign on to his computer at home. Within a few seconds she answered.

Sure, standby.

A broad smile tightened his cheeks, and then the reality of what he was about to do sent his heart into thumping beats.

"Hi," she said, settling down in a chair at his kitchen table. She moved slowly and winced a little.

"Hey, my lady." She looked a thousand times better than when he'd been forced to leave her and rejoin the squad.

"Are you okay?" she asked, her smile giving him courage.

A mirage of images lay out like a portfolio in his mind. He'd never tire of waking up and turning over to see her smile and those eyes first thing in the morning. He remembered the look of lost faith when she thought she would die and he willed the heavens to let her live. Seeing her ponytail flounce behind her when she'd crossed the casino lobby and knew she was special. He clearly saw a lifetime with her and he closed his little black book on bachelorhood.

"I'm doing all right, except I'd rather be there with you."

"I'd have to agree." She gave him a sweet wink. "I'd like to know what that beard feels like on my cheek."

"That might be a while," he said and gave her a thoughtful look.

"I understand." She reached out her hand and slid a finger down the screen. "I can use my imagination."

He balled his hands, wishing he could hold her. "It won't be easy for us, but I know one thing for sure."

She cocked her head, waiting.

"I always want to come home to you. I don't need months to figure out who we are, I know it's going to be you and me." With a curled brow he said, "But if you need time, then we'll take time."

"What are you talking about, Tony? Of course we'll have time."

He nipped at his lip. "Lumin, I wanted to ask you—"

"I can't wait to introduce you to my parents. I think they'll love you."

His request took a step back and then curled itself in a corner. Meet her parents. Kayla's lecture bit him in his "do the right thing" ass. He was almost thirty-one. He'd lived. Lumin had just begun. She had milestones she needed to cross, and he wanted to be there to see them, but chances were he'd miss a lot of them depending on duty. Being a SEAL meant missing a huge portion of their life together until he retired from active duty, but he didn't know when that would be.

His gaze fell to the rock.

"What's wrong? My parents will get used to the fact that you're not Catholic. I know you said you want to become one. I promise it'll be all right, even if you've changed your mind."

He nodded and gave her a reassuring smile. "I hope so."

"Tony," she paused. "Something is wrong, tell me." Her expression scrunched with worry.

"Just concerned about you." Which was the truth. He looked over his shoulder to see the squad milling by the river bank. Duty first. He rebelled against the thought. He wanted Lumin to come first, but she never would. Not in his world, even if that's all he wanted. "We have to get moving. I just wanted to check on you."

"Okay," she said meekly. "Tony, I'm going to rest up for a few days, but I'll be out of your apartment as soon as possible. I talked with my brother today. He wants me to come stay with him and his family."

He grasped the edges of the laptop and looked into her eyes. Did she think he wanted her gone? "I want you to stay near the base. Kayla and Nina are close by. If you need anything call them. I don't know when I'll be back, but my place is yours." He swallowed heavily. "Ours."

"Ours?"

His nerves jumped like he'd drank a bucket of caffeine. He must be confusing the shit out of her. This being a gentleman shit had rough edges that were making him bleed internally. "I want you to do what's right for you. If it means you don't think we're a good fit—"

Lumin surveyed him for a moment. He didn't have to wear his heart on his sleeve when it came to this woman; it just marched on out of his chest without permission.

"You called for a reason. Are you trying to tell me in a nice way to hit the road?"

Her sweet voice reached out to him and nearly hit the detonator button on his desires. "I just want you to be safe."

She picked up a piece of paper and held it in front of the camera. A list of eight names and telephone numbers, all of them women, some of them with a short message but very definitive, made him wince. Pulling the paper aside so he could see her again she said, "That was the first three hours." She shrugged. "I'll leave it on the counter for you."

"Throw it in the garbage," he said quickly. "I didn't call to dump you. I called because I can't stand it anymore. Twelve hours without seeing you is too long." He ran his tongue over his dry bottom lip. The sun beat down on him and his body leached sweat inside his fatigues. SEAL training taught a man to ignore uncomfortable, but his feelings for Lumin seemed to grow even when he wasn't in her presence. It sat somewhere in the extreme yearning mode, or higher. He kept asking himself why. She was beautiful, but so were a lot of other women. It made no sense, except for maybe the thought that she had given her innocence to him. He had to honor that. Age-old thinking, maybe even possessive, and there was no doubt it had hit him hard when Ed had come on to her, and that was even before he'd touched her.

"Tony, stop worrying about me. You saved my life, now go save the world."

Good sense flew out the window, carried on the wings of selfish need. He needed to know she was his. Forever. "Not until you agree to marry me because I can't take on the world unless you're beside me."

Lumin's eyes grew into blue saucers. "What?" she said on a whispery exhale.

He cleared his throat, took a deep breath and said, "Lumin Edenridge, I promise I will do this right when we're together again, but I'm asking if you'll marry me."

Lumin leaned back in her chair. "You're not kidding," she said, looking shell-shocked.

Maybe he should have listened to Kayla and Nina, they were girls after all. "Ahhh, no, I'm not."

"I—I mean we, we haven't talked about things that matter."

"Like what?" he said, seeing the guys milling; he knew he had to get moving.

"Well," she said, nervously. "Like children. Maybe you hate children."

"I don't. I love Squirt and Kelsey and I want us to have a family, but only when you're ready," he added.

"What about my schooling?"

"Finish it. I can support us both until you do."

A nervous laugh escaped her and she shook her head. "I don't know what to say."

"Say yes."

"T-man, we gotta go," Mace said from behind him, then leaned over. "Hey, Lumin, how ya doing, girl?"

"I'm all right, Mace."

Mace grinned at her. "Did you say yes?"

She laughed. "Not yet."

"That's what he deserves. Keep him dangling."

"I don't think I can."

Tony held his breath waiting for the next part. Lumin quickly scribbled something on the paper where she'd taken the messages. Slowly she lifted it in front of the monitor and turned it. His blood pressure spiked and he stopped breathing until the other side faced him. He let out a huge breath and laughed, and Mace did too. It said, "Affirmative, T-man."

"I love you, Lumin." She gave him the sweetest smile. It wedged itself in his heart and that's where he'd keep it. "We gotta go, Mrs. Bale."

Her grin broadened. "Keep your center, Tony."

He nodded, feeling like he'd won a prize fight, taken out every Tango on the planet and stood in the winner's circle of life. "You're my center, Lumin. Everything else is moving but us. Bye, my lady."

She waved at him and the screen went dark. He closed the laptop with a snap and rose to his feet. Mace nodded at him. "Do I need to ask?"

Mace shrugged. "Hell no, man. I've stood beside you through a shit storm, I'd be proud to stand by you when you marry Lumin."

"Thanks, man. Let's get this done and find Dafoe." His face felt like it was going to split with the wide grin he couldn't restrain. "She said yes."

They took off at a run to join the rest of the squad already in the helo. It was time to blow shit up.

Chapter Nineteen

Date: 08.03.2014
Time: 0200UTC 1800PST
Mission: Code Name Luminous

"She's going to breach!"

They'd brought down the bridge three and half hours ago and blew a trench into the sway of land that lay on the west bank. Both dams had been shut down. The Admiral and Mace led a CDC crew at the Caballo Dam while choppers dropped the canisters into the Rio Grande to ozonate the water and kill the virus. Tony watched the water continue to rise, being fed by underground tributaries they couldn't hold back. The river lapped at the shore like a needy tongue searching for food. The area had been cleared on both sides of the river. Families who'd been extracted from their homes didn't go far, waiting by their cars behind a perimeter line manned by the National Guard. Parents held small children in their arms with worried expressions. Some folks had managed to pile suitcases and a few important belongings on the roofs of their cars. These people had little but their farms. It was the only way to put food on the table, and if the squad took that away, beating the virus would be a win, but life would be a struggle.

Tony stood on the east bank. Fox was ready to set off the charges to blow the blockade they'd created with the highway bridge and concrete dividers that had been used to hold the Rio Grande back. "Come on, man," Tony said to himself, watching Ed work with the last charge on top of the rubble.

The rest of the squad stood to his left, Captain Cobbs flanking him.

Cobbs glanced at his watch and his brow furrowed. "Thirty minutes too early," he advised.

"Don't have a choice," Tony said. "If that water breaches, it'll flood the farms."

The water had risen fast. Gravity doing its job. Holding back Mother Nature had only worked for a while, the force would create another path, one with devastating results.

"Cracker?" Tony called into his comm set.

"Done," Ed said, rising to his feet and jumping to the toppled edge of the bridge, balancing as he made his way toward them. The water splashed only inches from his feet.

"Hold, Fox," he ordered.

"Standing by," Fox responded.

"Alpha One," Tony called on his portable radio.

The Admiral answered. "Are you set?"

"Affirmative, the water is about to breach the east bank. We need to let her go," Tony answered.

"Last test was clear of the bug. CDC wants another test in two minutes. Can you hold until then?" the Admiral asked.

Tony's eyes watched the water as it lobbed with a gentle sway. "Two minutes." He wanted to pace. Move. Do anything. He sure as hell would have never made a good sniper. Mace had the patience, and although he'd suffered through being his spotter on missions before, the whole time his mind worked like a big man trapped in a small space, desperate to escape.

The land owners began to mutter and some yelled out, "Blow the bridge." He understood their fears. They didn't know he had the same ones. To the families, they were as bad as insurgents, taking away their independence. His cell rang.

"Dr. Clarke, what's the water height at Cochito Dam?" he asked, recognizing her number.

"Tony, the dam operator reports the reservoir is at full capacity. They need to bleed off some of the water or she'll find another way around."

"Doc, we're almost there. We've got the same problem down here. We're going to blow the block. The Admiral advised they need a couple minutes for one more test."

Dr. Clarke covered the phone and Tony heard her strained but muffled voice speaking with someone. "We don't have two minutes," she said coming back on the line. "They're going to open the dam, you have to clear out of there. The force pushing behind the water is going to make it surge."

"We're going to lose the farms, aren't we?"

"Yes, a lot of them. Flood warnings and evacuations have been in effect for hours. The force of the water will intensify as it reaches the block taking out the banks of the river as she sweeps down and slams into the Caballo Dam. You have to open it now. Get out of there." She paused. "Just wait," she yelled at someone. "Tony, they won't wait any longer. You don't have much time."

"Friggin' hell." He hung up. "Blow the god damn thing, Fox." He held down the press-to-talk on his portable radio. "Alpha One, we're out of time. They're opening the Cochito Dam. The doc says the surge is going to be like a tidal wave. Get everyone to high ground. She's going to be packing a punch when the water reaches you."

"Copy, Tinman. We're clearing the area."

"What's the matter, Fox?" Tony watched him pressing the detonation button.

"Jesus, fucking crap," Fox swore, shaking the remote detonator. He popped the back. Surveyed the components and looked up at him. "Problem has to be out there."

"Cracker. Did you jury rig that last charge?" Cracker had taken longer than the norm to set the last one in the line.

"No, it's got to be the detonator. It should be working."

Tony's anger bloomed. "Does it fucking look like its working?" A deadly wall of water was on its way and picking up power as it went. "Tell the Guard to get those people moving out of the area or to higher ground." Cobbs knelt beside Fox, both of them inspecting the remote once again. "I'm going out there."

"No, Bale," Cobbs ordered. "She's live."

"And we're all dead if we don't blow this blockade," he said, already running backward.

"Bale, get the fuck back here."

Tony ran full out, jumped to the first broken piece of concrete and scrambled, grabbing as he went, till he reached the top of the bridge. Was it his imagination? Hell no, the water seemed to breathe a big sigh and it jumped over the bank on the eastern edge, hundreds of gallons galloping toward low ground. He tottered, found his center and dropped to his knees when he reached the furthest charge, the last one Cracker assembled. It looked good. He replaced it in the crack of cement and back tracked to the next. It was a race; man's technology against Mother Nature's need to bring balance back to her element.

Tony heard Cobbs in his headset. "Fox, check the remote again," he ordered.

They'd been in enough close calls, shaving seconds down to win or fail missions had taught him to keep his cool, but not this time. His pulse came in short, gasping shots and his adrenaline spiked.

"Sir, it's functioning. I'm getting a green on the connectivity. It has to be out there," Fox reported.

Tony checked the second charge. Cobbs put it into high gear, taking long, running strides, and vaulted onto the bridge to join him. "What the hell are you doing, sir? Get off the block," Tony said.

"Work faster, Bale."

He shot a quick look and saw the river running into the low lying area, headed straight for the nearest farm house. Captain Cobbs and he checked each charge. One left.

"Oh, shit," Fox yelled in his ear. "Get clear. Get clear. The remote went green. Get outta there!"

Both of them stood on a mountain of a bomb. Tony met his captain's gaze. Only one place to go. The explosion deafened him. The heat burned him. Cement catapulted around them, but through it all he saw Cobbs vault toward him. The impact of Cobbs' body hit him hard, protecting him as they both fell into the river. Rebar and debris exploded into the air. Before Tony closed his eyes, he saw a band of steel lash out at them.

The pull of the river swept Tony away as he powered his arms to control his direction. He surfaced, and fought hard against the current. Cobbs broke the surface but he wasn't swimming.

"Captain!" he shouted and stroked hard, only ten feet apart. "Captain!" Cobbs' eyes were closed. He'd drown if he'd been knocked out. The team ran, arms and legs pumping hard along the bank, trying to keep pace.

The distance narrowed between them and Tony snagged his captain's arm, drew him close and hung on for dear life. Up ahead he saw the bank wasn't as sheer with a bay and an easy grade. He kicked hard and used one arm to direct himself. His feet touched ground but he couldn't keep a footing. They rolled several times.

Thrusting hard, his feet found purchase on soft ground as he neared the small bay. He crawled, knees sinking deep in the muddy bottom. His arms strained, the river trying to take his captain. Every muscle burned but he refused to let go, yanking them both into the shallows.

It had been no more than a minute of struggle, but the struggle had exhausted him. "Captain," he said loudly, before opening his eyes but when he did, ice coated his spine. "No." The blood. Too much blood. He sat up and saw they were sitting in a pool of it. It mixed with the color of the river, darkening the brown to a murky black. Captain Cobbs' lids opened.

"No pain, T-man."

"Sir." He drew Cobbs into his arms just as the rest of the squad reached him.

Stitch jumped into the water and yanked at Cobbs' jacket. He blinked hard and paused as if not believing what he saw. Tony refused to believe what was written on Stitch's features. "What? Stitch? What is it?" Stitch dropped to his knees and closed his eyes as if he couldn't face what he was seeing. Tony ignored him. "It's going be okay, we're gonna get you out of here, Captain."

"Tinman," Cobbs said quietly.

Tony choked down a lump which he knew was a roar of disbelief, an all out assault against God to keep his fucking angel of death away. He strained against the reality wanting to steal this moment and make it final. He held his Captain against his chest. "Jesus, Jesus," he said, raising his gaze to the rest of the team who stood with dismay and shock on their faces.

Cobbs' life force drained out of him, and nothing would stop it. The metal had cut deep into his back, severing arteries and flesh. His warm blood gushed over Tony's hands like a waterfall into the Rio Grande.

Cobbs closed his eyes. "Don't let Marg cry too many tears," he said quietly. "I'll be waiting for her, forever and ever."

No sound except the soft wash of water rushed by them. No explosions. No yelling or confusion. The sounds of war were silent. Peaceful. They watched as a great warrior's soul slowly drifted away from them. A hurricane of sorrow slammed into him as Tony rocked Cobbs in his arms. Fox, Nathan, then Ed and Ditz kneeled around them. They surrounded their captain, gripping his shoulder, his hand and an arm, a sentry of safe passage waiting for his last breath.

It came and went without a sound. The tumblers of fate ceased to turn. Its task complete.

"Fox, SITREP?" The Admiral's voice cracked from his radio. "Fox this is Alpha One, what's going on up there?"

Fox slowly pulled his radio, but before he could answer Tony reached for it and Fox gladly gave it over. He swiped his sleeved arm across his eyes and said, "Alpha One this is Tinman, the block is open."

"Zodiak isn't responding on his radio. Is he with you?"

"Yes, sir, he's with us."

"Roger, we'll rendezvous with you in ten minutes."

"Roger, out."

They carried their captain to higher ground, and Stitch called for a medical evac. Tony sat next to Cobbs and watched as the Admiral's helo descended ten minutes later. Mace was with him. With every step the Admiral took, dread should have filled Tony, but he was numb. The Admiral had trusted him. Put him as lead on this mission. Ghost had never lost a man while he was in charge, but now he stood vigil over the Admiral's best friend.

Admiral Austen's step began to quicken, and then it was a full-out run. "What's happened?" the Admiral barked as he approached. He kneeled down on one knee beside his friend. "Pat?" The truth stared back at him, but he resisted. "Pat." He gripped his shoulder.

Captain Patrick Cobbs wore a peaceful expression, but it was obvious he was gone.

The Admiral shook his head. "What...the...fuck," he choked the words out. He turned unbelieving eyes on Tony and although there was confusion and anger, the anguish took hold.

"We—there was a fault. I went on the blockade to find it. Captain Cobbs joined me, sir. The fault was in the remote controller. The bridge went up with us on it. Debris cut through his back. He bled out." Tony was only whispering as he watched the Admiral's brows knit together. "I told him to get off the block, but he wouldn't do it. We both went into the river."

Tony's mind numbed, playing the moment over again in his head. In that split second, fate took charge. A mistake. It had to be a mistake.

The Admiral swiveled on his haunches when the sound of the medevac chopper landed. Ghost bit down on his emotion and said, "I'll carry him the rest of the way." He shoved his hands under Cobbs' body and pulled him into his arms, rose to his feet, and walked toward the helo.

The team remained where they were. Tony would never forget the sight as long as he lived, watching the Admiral's slow steps, the weight he bore in his arms inconsequential to the one in his heart. Two friends who had survived twenty years of combat because of one another were now parted. Every moment, now a memory. Ghost carefully placed his friend on the deck of the chopper. He leaned over Cobbs and spoke to him. When he was done, Admiral Austen backed away and kept his gaze on the chopper as it rose into the air. Tony finally looked away when he saw the Admiral's shoulders shake with heart-wrenching sobs.

* * * *

Lumin rested on the couch in Tony's apartment. Although her body still ached, she felt safer being here with his things surrounding her. Her cell rang and she quickly swept it up, but it wasn't Tony.

"Feeling a little better?" Kayla asked.

"Hello, Kayla. I'm not on death's door. I guess that's better."

"How about some company? Nina and I took an hour for dinner."

"Sure." As soon as she said it there was a knock on the door. "Is that you?"

"Yup."

Lumin got to her feet, took a step and paused to get over the wave of dizziness before leaving the safety of the couch. Kayla and Nina gave her a quick hug when she opened the door and then they both helped her back to the couch.

"Sorry, shouldn't have made you get up," Nina said, sitting next to her.

Kayla pulled three plates from the cupboard and opened up the take-out they'd brought.

"I'm so glad you're okay, Nina." She squeezed her hand and found she didn't want to let go.

"You too, kiddo," she said, and smiled at her. "It was a real bitch, wasn't it?"

She nodded. Kayla handed her and Nina a plate.

"Drinks?" Kayla asked.

"There's some soda and water in the fridge," Lumin said.

Lumin had a creeping feeling of unease where there shouldn't be one. "Is everything all right?"

Nina darted a glance at Kayla. After putting her plate down and chewing her mouthful of food slowly, Kayla said, "No." She stalled and shook her head. Nina wrapped an arm around her friend's shoulder.

"Captain Cobbs died this afternoon. He and Tony had to release the block in the river. There was a malfunction."

Lumin didn't know the man at all, but the short time she'd been in his presence, she'd liked him. "I'm so sorry," she said kneeling in front of the women and holding their hands. "Did something happen to Tony too?"

Nina shook her head. "He's fine."

"Captain Cobbs is the Admiral's best friend, isn't he?"

"Yes," Kayla said and dried her tears.

"Does Marg know yet?"

Nina nodded and her tongue jammed into her cheek as if trying to control herself. "That's one call I couldn't make. Kayla did it."

Lumin put her hand on Kayla's knee. "I don't know how you could have done that, Kayla. I would have fallen apart."

"They are both my friends. I wanted Marg to hear it from me, not have a uniformed SEAL approach her door and rip out her heart."

"Is she coming back?" Lumin asked.

"Not yet. She can't. Not until Dafoe is found and the threat is over."

Lumin plucked two tissues from the box and handed one to each of the girls. "Does this happen a lot?" Her heart strayed to Tony.

"It happens," Nina said. "We used to think if only love could shield them from bullets, everyone would come home. This wasn't a bullet."

Even though both Kayla and Nina seemed to accept what happened, the worry in their eyes wasn't as easily hidden. "How did he die?"

Kayla sputtered. "That's the stupid part. Captain Cobbs has been a warrior for over twenty years. Hundreds of missions and deployments. Close calls, a few injuries, but—" She took a deep breath and shook her head. "It was an accident. Tony and Cobbs were working to blow out a block they'd placed in the Rio Grande. The remote detonator malfunctioned."

Lumin held her breath. "And Tony?"

Kayla gave her a quick smile of reassurance. "They both went in the water when the charges exploded. Debris caught Cobbs across the back. He bled out. Tony pulled him from the river. He's okay, at least physically."

Lumin struggled to her feet and sat down across from the girls, then wedged her hands between her knees. They sat in heavy silence. Lumin prayed for Marg and for the rest of the squad. When her mind touched on Tony's image, her heart spoke the loudest.

This wasn't the time to tell the girls Tony had asked her to marry him but she wanted their opinion, desperately. Earlier she'd thought about calling Star, but although she was a friend, Star's attitude about marriage was less than stellar. Lumin hadn't known what to say when Tony popped the question every girl dreams of hearing from a man like him. Stunned silence followed. When the clatter in her head stopped, she stuttered, "Tony asked me to marry him."

"We know," Nina said solemnly.

"I said yes."

Kayla nodded. "Know that too. You can be engaged for as long as you want, just promise us before you walk down the aisle that you understand what a life with Tony will be like. You'll be alone for months on end and often no or little contact."

"He could be injured," Nina added. "Or worse, and you will always have that fear, but have to keep it under control and hidden away. He'll come home and the first weeks will be difficult while he assimilates back into your lives."

Kayla and Nina's warnings scared her.

"What we're trying to tell you is that you have to be sure before you take the next step. Tony has never fallen in love before. If you can't be brave and committed, you need to let him go," Kayla said.

Suddenly Lumin felt like the outsider again. The girls were protecting Tony. They weren't turning against her, but preparing her. "I don't doubt myself. I'm worried that I came across Tony at a time when he's reflecting on what he doesn't have, and that it could have been anyone."

Nina darted a glance at Kayla and shook her head. "Doesn't work that way, Lumin. In fact, it's just the opposite. Tony boasted a 'I'm going to be a bachelor forever' flag. For the SPECOP guys, it's easier. They're not vulnerable to worry or doubt. They leave a girl in rumpled bed sheets and live for the moment. Your relationship will be strained by separation and tested by living with a man who has to keep secrets from you. Love is the hardest thing these men can endure."

"I won't let him down," Lumin assured them.

The girls stayed for a while longer and left her to slowly pace the living room. Her aches and pains were nothing compared to what Tony and the rest of the team had to be going through. They couldn't stop. They couldn't grieve. She reached for the phone and put it down three times. Pushing open the patio door, she gazed around. Her nerves were on edge, but there was no reason for it. Sitting down at the patio table, she watched the children on the playground and then stared at the phone, willing it to ring She needed him to know she was thinking about him and worried for him. She picked it up and dialed.

"Petty Officer Bale."

He sounded tired. "Tony." She hesitated when the line went quiet. "Kayla and Nina were just here. They told me about Captain Cobbs. You don't need to say anything, but I wanted to tell you how sorry I am. I'm praying for you. I don't know all the details. I just know you're probably hurting right now, and I wish I could be with you and hold you."

"My lady, I wish you were here too," his voice gravelly with restrained emotion. "This is my fault, Lumin."

"How can it be your fault? Kayla said it was a malfunction. An accident."

"He shouldn't have been up there with me. The charges were live. I should have set them myself. I'm the explosives specialist, but I ordered Ed to set them."

"Tony, you can't second-guess this. You could have been killed just as easily."

Tony let out a deep breath. "I don't know what to say to the Admiral."

"Nothing until the moment is right, and you'll know when that is."

"Admiral Austen just finished talking with Marg. She's flying back to San Diego tonight."

"I can pick her up."

"You're supposed to be resting, sweetheart."

"I'm okay. I can pick her up. What time is she coming in?"

Tony spoke to someone and then said, "Nine o'clock. United flight."

"Can I use your car?"

"Of course you can. There's a spare set of keys in the basket on top of the fridge. Maybe she can stay with you."

"I'll convince her." There was a pregnant pause on the line. "Can I do anything else?"

"Let Kayla and Nina know. You're gonna need them."

"I think you're right. I've never known anyone who's died before."

"In a way that's a blessing," Tony said quietly. "But it won't stay that way, Lumin, if you walk beside me. Maybe you should think about that. I shouldn't have asked you to marry me. It was selfish."

Talking about this had a time and place, but not now. "No, it wasn't," she blurted, then paused fiddling with the edge of the table. Had she really thought it out? Her fear wasn't how much she loved Tony, it was if she could be strong enough for him. "When this is over, you can ask me again, if you want to."

"I've got to go. The team's leaving New Mexico. We have to find a lead on Dafoe."

"He's disappeared with the virus. How can you possibly find him?"

"Don't know yet, but we'll figure it out. I miss you, sweetheart. I miss you too much."

"I'll be waiting for you, Tony. Please come home as soon as you can."

That evening Lumin experienced the true meaning of grief for the first time. Tony had been right. She needed Kayla and Nina, and she thanked God when they walked in the door. The tears seemed endless after the shock subsided and Marg let down her guard. She'd brought her three daughters, and although they put Kelsey to bed, Rayanne and Cindy remained at their mother's side. They were amazingly strong girls, and Lumin saw the binding love between them.

There were moments of utter silence and periods of gentle words. They reminisced and held Marg when the memories wanted to sweep her away, but Kayla and Nina brought her back from the edge every time.

"Somehow I knew," Marg whispered to the circle of women around her. "Over the years, every time Pat left us, I had to be strong. I had our girls to raise, and a home to run." She blinked away the endless tears. "When I talked to him the other day, he promised me that this would be the last mission. I knew he was right." Marg hid her face in her hands. "I will always love that man. I don't want to face laying my head on the pillow and looking at his, knowing he'll never be there again. He's gone. He's really gone this time."

Lumin twined her fingers with Marg's. "I don't know either of you very well, but I know he's not far from you, Marg. The Captain adored you. Every time he looked at you, those silver eyes were filled with love. I don't believe he'll ever leave you. You just can't see him right now."

Marg smiled through her tears and touched Lumin's cheek. "Thank you, sweetheart. I know he does. We all signed on to love our warriors knowing this moment could come." She swiped at her eyes. "I think I'm going to lay down with Kelsey and get some rest. Tomorrow is soon enough for more tears."

Rayanne and Cindy followed their mother.

Lumin looked for reassurance. Nina and Kayla were both reeling from the loss. "I think I'd be a crumbled mess on the floor if I were her."

"You'd be surprised what rubs off over the years," Nina said, laying back and covering her forehead with her hands. "Although Mace and I have just started a life together, I know it's a possibility I could lose him."

"We almost lost you, both of you," Kayla said. "Every single military spouse, whether man or woman, has to stand beside their warrior. Hiding the worry and being strong every time they walk away is our challenge." She paused. "I hate war. Thane will never turn his back on his duty, and he won't stop now until he finds Dafoe. None of them will."

"I just realized something," Lumin murmured to herself, but she had the women's attention. "Tony and I have talked more on the phone than we have in person."

They both smiled at her and nodded. "Sometimes it's like that," Kayla admitted. "A lot, actually, but when his voice is all you have, you seize it and make sure when he hangs up that he doesn't have to worry about you."

Lumin swallowed the lump in her throat. "What if I'm not strong enough?"

Nina patted her hand. "Don't worry. Although you two have started your relationship in the middle of a firestorm, the smoke will clear. You'll have time to get to know each other."

"That's what I'm afraid of. High adrenaline. Rescue mode. Whatever you want to call it. What if I'm not who he wants when all the action recedes?"

Kayla tried to hide a grin and rolled her eyes to look at Nina. "If you're doing things right in the bedroom, the action won't be receding any time soon. If I'm not mistaken, Tinman is a needy kind of guy."

Nina chuckled. "Aren't they all." She winked at Lumin. "You'll do fine. And I think I've had my fill of tears. Let's hit the road, boss."

She walked Nina and Kayla to the door. "Thank you—for everything."

"We stick together. Stand strong. Alpha Squad and the others will end this," Kayla said.

"I hope you're right. I'm probably putting too much heart into Tony's basket, but I can't seem to stop thinking about him. I want him home."

Nina eyed the coffee table. "Phone's over there. SEALs don't sleep much. He could probably use a pick-me-up"

"I don't want to seem like a needy female."

"I'm not talking about your need." She grinned. "I'm talking about letting him know what he can look forward to when he finishes this mission."

Lumin's eyes grew. "Do you mean—?"

Kayla nodded. "But make sure the curtains are closed." She laughed.

"But his mind is on the mission and he's so upset about Captain Cobbs."

"Rule number two," Nina began. "Life goes on, and although we will cherish every memory we have of Patrick Cobbs, those who are left need to be reminded they are alive and to keep living. T-man is beating himself up over this. He needs a distraction."

Nina pecked her cheek, and Lumin closed and locked the door behind them. Once again, she stared at the phone. She snatched it up and walked down the hall into Tony's bedroom. Opening the door, his scent eased her fears. She smelled his aftershave when she lay down on his sheets. As she thumbed the button on his bedside lamp, darkness draped the room. His cell rang once before he answered.

"Hey, are you working?" *Working, was that even the right term?*

"Hi," he said quietly. "No, taking fifteen minutes to get a rest."

"Where are you?"

"In a tent." The sound of him rolling elicited the image of him on his back and settling with an arm behind his head, looking up at the canvas. "How is she?"

He didn't have to say her name to know who he was asking about. "Strong. Rayanne and Cindy are too. We talked and we cried. I hope it helped."

"I'm sure it did."

"Get some rest. I just wanted to call and tell you how proud I am of you."

Silence.

"I am."

"Would it bother you if I didn't go through with the officer's training?"

"Yes, but not for the reasons you're probably thinking."

Tony's voice rumbled with a low timbre. "What should I be thinking?"

"That you can twist fate's arm behind its back, but it will never say 'uncle' or change the outcome. Bad luck exists. Accidents happen. Most of all, you are a leader and men die in war."

"But we weren't in the sands of the Middle East or in the jungle under fire, and I lost one of the most prominent mentors of my life."

"Did you order Captain Cobbs onto the bridge?"

"No. I told him to get off."

"Did he listen?"

"No."

"Why?"

Tony sighed. "Because we work as a team. The water was breaching the banks and time had run out."

Lumin clung to the phone and spoke calmly, but her heart hurt for Tony. "He did his job, and he died in the line of duty helping to save the people of that valley. Marg understands this. She accepted the risks long ago when she married him. They both wanted forever, and they'll have it. I don't believe love dies, Tony. Not when you're with the right person."

"Our team hasn't lost a single man in eleven years, Lumin. Not when Ghost ran the show. He gave me an ounce of responsibility and his best friend is dead."

"The Admiral will come to terms with it, and I'm sure Kayla will be there in case he stumbles."

"You're going to be a good lawyer. Being an enlisted SEAL doesn't really add up to that."

Lumin shook her head and her gaze darted to the moon, almost full, out the window. "You can be whatever you want to be, Tony, but men will follow you whether you decide to be an officer or not."

"I don't know what I want anymore."

"Doubt can lick at your toes, Petty Officer Bale; it does for all of us, but I won't let it consume you."

"I let you consume me, and the word 'lick' coming from your mouth shouldn't be said unless we're in the same room."

She smiled. "I'm lying on your bed, staring out the window."

With a husky voice he said, "Are you wearing anything?"

"No, I like the moon casting its light on my skin."

He let out a deep breath. "So do I."

"Are you alone in that tent, Petty Officer Bale?" she asked, feeling a flick of excitement catch in her belly.

"Wish you were here."

"I don't have to be. I feel you near me even when you're not."

"Hmm. Is my pure light trying to seduce me over the phone?" She smiled.

"You're smiling. I can see it." His voice was raspier.

"I am."

"So am I. My hands are sliding down your hips and around to your amazing ass, drawing your warm skin against mine. You are so beautiful, Lumin."

She closed her eyes and imagined his warm rough hands instead of her own. "Wet," she whispered, as her fingers reached the moist lips of her sex.

"I'm kissing your inner thigh, running my palms along your gorgeous legs. You can feel my warm breath."

She imagined his broad shoulders bowed before her, his mouth making her flesh ripple with each kiss. The roughness of his unshaven cheek grazed her as his strong tongue flicked at her bundle of nerves.

"You smell so good. My tongue wants to taste all of you."

"Tony?"

"Right here, baby, I'm turning you over. With a gentle grip around your wrists I'm holding them above your head. I kiss the sway of your spine. The sway of your cheeks. Lift that beautiful ass in the air."

A short gasp escaped her mouth, but she wasn't embarrassed. "I feel your chest. Your weight on me." Her face was pressed into the pillow. She felt him. Smelled him. "Please, I want you inside me. Slowly. Deeply."

"Oh, Jesus, help me, I love you."

"Come inside me, please, oh please," she begged. "Harder, Tony."

They both moaned, orgasming at the same time.

"Petty Officer Balc?"

"Oh crap," he hissed. "What is it, Nathan?"

"Sir, the Admiral wants us in the HQ tent. Five minutes."

"Roger that." He paused and then spoke quietly to her. "I think I actually feel guilty over sex for the first time in my life."

"Don't. We have to keep living, Tony."

"I know, and I know it was an accident, but it doesn't hurt any less."

"Nor should it, but we'll be there for Marg and the girls, and I'm here for you." She heard him shuffle and a zipper being pulled up.

"Lumin, I meant everything I've said to you. I know I don't have a great track record, but I don't want anyone else but you. Just you." She heard the flap of canvas.

She sat up in the bed and curled an arm around her legs. "Be careful, SEAL."

"Think I've found a good reason to do that. I can't wait to see you again, my lady."

"I'm not that girl anymore. The virus left scars. Ugly ones."

"Doesn't matter, as long as I have you to come home to. That's all I need."

"Tony—faith is something that doesn't only apply to the heavens. I have faith in you. If you ever lose yours, I'll keep some in spare for both of us."

"How did you get to be so smart, and how the hell did I get so lucky?"

"You're hot." She burst out laughing, and then muffled it remembering she had guests.

"Keep the light on inside that beautiful heart of yours, and I'll find my way home. Bye."

She flopped back on the bed and smiled up at the ceiling. These were the moments the girls told her she had to hang on to because the darker ones would swarm to rip her heart out. Down the hall, Marg had to face every day from now on without the man she loved beside her. It was a sobering thought. One she would never forget.

She shivered a little now that Tony's voice wasn't keeping her warm. Staring around his bedroom, her eyes landed on his closet, and she smiled to herself as she slipped off the bed and walked toward it.

Chapter Twenty

Date: 08.05.2014
Time: 1700UTC 0800hrs PST
Mission: Code Name Luminous

Thane stood in front of a collage of maps—New Mexico, Nevada, Arizona, Colorado, and California. He'd stared at them for an hour, but couldn't focus. Two days had passed since Pat died. The teams had reconvened in Kingman. No one looked him in the eye, and he fought every minute to bite down on his grief. He couldn't let his men see it had cut so deep he could barely think straight, because if they did, they'd all lose their motivation. Every once in a while he'd turn and swear he saw Pat out of the corner of his eye. Once he'd even called his name, the patterns ingrained for so many years, his swim buddy by his side. He felt the loss, but refused to acknowledge it until Dafoe was brought down, and he hoped to God it was by his hand.

A vibration against his hip grabbed his attention and he yanked his cell from its case. He viewed the number and took a deep breath. "Marg, hey sweetheart, how you holding up?"

"Thane," her voice rippled with panic. "Lumin is gone."

His brow wrinkled. "Gone?"

"She didn't get up so I went to check in her room. The window was open, the lamp knocked over and the sheets were pulled clean off the bed."

He swiveled to locate Tinman. He sat with the rest of Alpha Squad taking cover from the heat. The normal banter between the men silenced. Possibilities swirled in his mind, and they kept landing in the same place. "Dafoe."

"What does he want with her?" Marg asked.

"I don't know."

"Find her, Thane. She's so young and naïve. Don't let her die too." Marg choked off a gasp of emotion. Her voice tightened. "I'm sorry, I didn't mean that—"

He had to hold himself in check, her words fed the guilt weighing heavy in his chest. Could he have saved his friend? Tinman wore every bit of the accident, but Thane couldn't put the blame at anyone's feet except Murphy's Law. "I know you didn't." He cleared the tight ball from his throat. "We'll find her. I'll send someone from Lieutenant Manchester's NCIS office to investigate."

"I have to do something. I just can't sit here. Maybe I should ask the neighbors if they saw anything."

"Stay until someone from NCIS shows up, and then I want you to take the girls and go to our place. You remember where I keep the spare key?"

"Yes."

"Call me when you're about to leave."

"Thane—are you going to tell Tony?"

"I don't know, Marg."

"Oh shit."

"What's wrong?" The hackles stood up on his neck. Marg and the girls were his responsibility now that Pat was gone. He was too far away from them. His gut twisted.

"Kayla and Nina just walked in."

"Don't tell her," he ordered.

"You want me to lie to her? Thane, I can't—"

"Yes, you bloody can or she'll be putting her nose to the ground to find Lumin."

"Morning, ladies," Marg greeted them with a steady voice.

He heard Kayla ask where Lumin was.

"I gotta go, Thane."

"Don't tell them." He hung up.

Why would Dafoe want Lumin? Dafoe knew Bjornson was dead. Kayla had said he'd stolen his notes from the university. What more was there, unless Dafoe thought he could trade Lumin for the vaccine?

Five minutes later he got off the phone with Manchester, who agreed to send two of his agents to Tony's apartment. He gave him the summarized version, and Manchester listened quietly without going into cop mode and asking a thousand questions. Thane also hoped like hell his wife would be gone when they showed up or she'd be on high alert instantly.

The desert wind rippled the canvas at the edge of the tent, his team sitting in quiet reflection. They'd had two days waiting on Jake Ackerman's team to find leads to Dafoe's hiding place. Base Command rooted through Dafoe's background looking for a direction. Just a single crumb of information to find his trail, that's all they needed. The United States was a big country, but DEVGRU's skills could reduce that to quadrants and cut away the edges narrowing the search.

Walking into the group of grieving men, he snagged a chair and sat amongst them, clutching his hands together.

"Any word, sir?" Tony asked solemnly to break the silence.

"Yes, but I'm waiting for a report from Lieutenant Manchester."

"Manchester?" Tony's gaze landed on him. "Why Manchester?"

Thane breathed out a shallow gust of air. "He's sent two men to your apartment, T-man."

"What?" Tony stiffened.

"Petty Officer Bale, Lumin is gone, we—"

Tony jumped to his feet. "Gone!" he shouted, his hazel eyes sparking with alarm.

"Sit, T-man."

"Where's Lumin?"

"We don't know. Marg went to wake her up this morning and she was gone."

Tony's shoulders relaxed a little. "She probably just went for a walk, or to get groceries."

Thane struggled with the right words. "No, I'm afraid not. There were signs that indicate she was taken."

"When did this happen?" Tony's anger radiated out of every pore, his fists clenching.

"A few minutes ago." His cell rang with the Canadian anthem and he answered it, keeping a wary eye on Tony. "Kayla."

"Lumin has been taken. Lieutenant Manchester's officers are here."

"And I want you to let them do their job. You stay with Marg. I told her she could stay at our place. Take her and the girls there."

"She's knows the way. I'm going—"

"No, you will not," he growled into the phone. Tony leaned over and said something to Mace. Mace shook his head, but Tony had already turned away from him and was running for the clutch of pilots standing near the helos parked in the desert. "Bale! Shit."

"What's going on?" Kayla asked.

"What do ya think? The guy's lost his focus. He's coming."

"Could anyone have stopped you when you were looking for me? Let him go."

Mace and the rest of the team sat like sprung coils ready to follow Tony. "Fox. Ed, Mace. Go with him," he ordered. All three of them vaulted out of their chairs. "Anything from Manchester's men?"

"No, but Lumin definitely put up a struggle," Kayla said.

He heard Kelsey in the background as Kayla walked through Tony's condo. "It has to be Dafoe, but why does he want her? All I can think of is a trade, Lumin for the vaccine."

"Will you? If it comes to that?"

"I will, because if that's what he wants, he'll have to come out of hiding and that's when I'm going to kill him."

Kayla began to say something and then stopped herself. "I'll call you later."

* * * *

Tony threw open the front door of his condo and thundered inside. Kayla stood in his living room with Manchester.

"Tony, what—" Kayla took a step toward him but stopped. His gaze pinned itself to the hallway and that's where his feet took him. He faltered at the entry to his bedroom. The lamp was broken and lay in pieces on the floor. One curtain was ripped from its rings and sat limp against the window frame. His gaze settled on the bed sheets. They lay strung out from the bed to the window. He read the room. She'd clung to them as her only salvation. Right here, last night, he'd made love to her. Hundreds of miles apart, but he was here with her. Loving her. When had they taken her? She didn't have a chance to call out for help.

Mace pulled him from his thoughts, brushing by him and entering the room. Ed and Fox remained in the hallway.

"Petty Officer Bale," Manchester queried as he joined them. "Don't get involved in this. You have a bigger mission. I will find Lumin."

He stared at the bed sheets, his mind working on what he saw before him. There was no other mission, but he didn't voice it.

"Admiral Austen sent us to assist if we could," Mace said. "Kayla, where are Marg and the girls?"

"Nina took them to our place. She'll stay with them."

Anger seeped between the cracks of numbness, bringing him back to life and giving him a direction. Tony grabbed Kayla's hand and drew her into the room. "Where—is—she?"

"Tony." She looked to Mace for help. "I don't know. There's no clue. Manchester's men searched the grounds and in here. They took prints from the lamp, but it's probably only going to be yours and Lumin's."

"Mace, what do you see?" he demanded.

Mace crossed his arms and let out a long, slow breath. "A struggle." He darted a wary glance at him. "She was probably sleeping and they came in quietly this time." He wandered to the window and leaned over it. His head cranked to look at Manchester. "Is this blood?"

"What?" Tony vaulted across the room and looked at the frame.

Manchester nodded. "We've taken a sample. If we're lucky, it will belong to one of her abductors. The lab is working on it now."

Tony's anger peaked and he smashed a fist through the drywall, slamming into a metal stud.

Fox squatted by the broken lamp. He didn't touch anything, just surveyed the shattered shards of ceramic. He turned his attention to the bed, then up to him. "Is everyone who was here a sound sleeper? This would have made a racket when it broke on the wooden floor."

Lieutenant Manchester's eyes narrowed. "Marg is under a lot of duress."

Fox put his hands on his thighs and pushed himself to his feet. "T-man, is anything missing?"

He closed his eyes, trying to concentrate over the thunder of his pulse. Opening them again, he glanced at every surface. He had the typical "guys" bedroom, the bare essentials and a couple pictures on the wall. His dresser held a few framed photos of him and Mace graduating from SEAL training, and a picture of him, Nina, Mace and Squirt at the beach. He pulled the drawer open on the bedside table. Nothing was missing, there were a couple books and the case with his SEAL trident. He swallowed deeply and remembered when Kayla began wearing Ghost's. Nina wore Mace's. Any brother knew when they saw a woman wearing it, she had given her heart to a SEAL.

"Everything is here," he said, closing the drawer. He walked to his closet and slid open the door. His clothes hung undisturbed on the hangers, jeans, shirts, his shoes on the floor where he left them. His dress uniform hanging neatly pressed, reminded him he'd soon wear it again to his captain's funeral. Three spare sets of fatigues, except...he pulled the hangers apart. Where was his third cammo jacket? He hadn't packed it.

Months ago, they thought the Blood Shark had bugged them to find Kayla. Manchester's NCIS team had taken their clothes. The investigators had returned their uniforms and he'd brought his spares home. He'd only kept a couple at the base, and then he remembered. "Kayla," he said, turning on his heel. It had been Kayla who had bugged the team when they'd gone into Syria for a black op.

"What?" she asked, blinking.

"The satellite tracker you put in our uniforms last year."

"What about them?" She blushed.

"Did you put them in all of our cammos?"

"Yes," she said, looking embarrassed. "What about it?"

"My jacket is missing."

Everyone looked at him with a blank expression. "My jacket is missing. I think Lumin put it on."

"Not surprised," she said with a reminiscent smile. "I did the same with Thane's clothes every time he left." She shrugged. "His scent was still there."

Ed, who had been silent, but present said, "You wear our clothes when we're gone?"

Kayla gave him a look as if it were the stupidest statement she'd ever heard. "Well, duh!"

"I had this set in my locker at the base," Tony interjected. "Manchester, your agents never found Kayla's trackers, only the one the Blood Shark had put on her. Kayla, where did you hide it?"

Kayla let out a gasp, catching on. "Under the right hand chest button pocket. It needed to be close to the heart to pick up vitals."

"Come on," he shouted, and gripped her arm. "We're going to the base."

"Tony, it's a long shot. I mean we don't even know if she's wearing it," she said, running behind him.

"She is. She has to be."

Mace put it into double-time beside them. "Would the battery last this long?"

"It's dormant until it senses motion," Kayla confirmed. "If it's been hanging in Tony's closet, it might still have some life left."

"You bugged the team?" Ed asked as they crossed the front lawn at a fast clip for Tony's car.

"Long story," Kayla said, and hopped in the front seat when Tony unlocked it.

"Wouldn't mind hearing it some time," Ed, ever the Casanova, said.

"I'm married, Cracker." She grabbed the seat belt and clicked it into the buckle.

Ed leaned over to look inside the car while Mace and Fox jumped in. "You're as hard-assed as we are?"

Kayla gripped the door handle. "Worse," she replied and slammed the door shut.

* * * *

All of them thundered past Captain Reddings' office, making him look up. "What the hell is going on?" He rose from his desk, and Ed detoured into the captain's office to update him.

Kayla hit a chair running, and it rolled fifteen feet to stop in front of the satellite monitoring station. She tapped furiously, entering a sequence of letter and numbers. He and Mace hung over her shoulder while Fox stood back with an intense but hopeful expression. "Barry, any more reports on outbreaks?" she asked at the same time.

Barry nodded.

"Where?" Mace asked.

"San Francisco and Crescent City."

They all shook their heads. No matter what they did, people would become infected either from the first or second virus. People were going to die and infect more of the population before the CDC gained control of the virus.

The satellite feed blacked out and a new image filled the screen. In the right hand corner Tony saw his name and a blinking green light. He couldn't breathe. "Is that her?" He leaned even closer, pushing Kayla forward, squishing her against the tabletop. "Sorry," he said backing off.

Kayla typed more info on the keyboard and the image zoomed in. She looked up and he looked down, meeting her gaze. "The signal is intermittent, but your jacket is traveling at eighty kilometers per hour along the I-5 toward Los Angeles."

"Yes, it's her!" He whipped the chair around and planted a huge kiss on Kayla's cheek. "I love you, woman." He grabbed Mace by the shoulder and practically dragged him toward the door. "Let's go get her. Kayla, keep me advised."

Mace blew her a kiss and Fox winked at her. Kayla leaned back in the chair with a worried expression. "Should I call Manchester and advise him?"

He held the door open, letting Mace and Fox pass him. "No, I'm going in to get her. If we need help, I'll advise."

Kayla gave him a salute.

Mace and Fox followed him outside. "I'm going to the Loadout Room first."

"Right behind you," Fox said, keeping pace.

Tony was punching the code into the door when it swung open. Lieutenant Lewis glanced up then stopped short. "Petty Officer Bale."

Oh, for fuck's sake. "Sir." He went to walk past him and Lewis gripped his shoulder.

"I want to talk to you now, Bale."

Mace and Fox slid by. "Sir, we're on Dafoe's tail. I don't have time to talk." He said it respectfully, at least as much as he could muster for the bigoted jerk.

Lewis slammed the door shut, leaving them on the outside. "You set me up. Made me look like a shit in front of Admiral Austen."

"I'm not the one with racial issues. Unless I go in there, you'll have double the trouble. You're already in neck-deep with the Admiral. You'll never dig your way out."

"I can draft just about any complaint I want, and it will have to be investigated. In fact, I could call the Men-at-Arms right now and have you detained."

Tony debated giving him a basis for his complaint and laying him out flat on the cement. "You want to come after me, then do it once we've neutralized the threat."

"I'm riding along with you on this. To keep an eye on you and regain some lost ground with the Admiral."

"Like fuck you are, sir." Tony watched as Lewis pulled his phone. He stopped him. "There's more at risk than just the virus being released by Dafoe."

"As in?" he asked, eyeing him.

"Dafoe has my fiancée." Was it his imagination or did a look of ill-disguised satisfaction sprint past his eyes?

"If we find her, we find Dafoe." Lewis contemplated for a moment. "Do you know where she is?"

The door sprang open and Mace leaned out. "You getting in the saddle or hiding behind a desk? Because it's time to gear up," he said.

Lewis gave him a nod and followed Mace into the Loadout Room. Hindrance or help, either way, Tony would not let Lewis stop him from saving Lumin.

Chapter Twenty-One

Five o'clock L.A. traffic jammed seven lanes to the hilt. Even the HOV *High-occupancy vehicle* lane crawled. Mace drove, and Tony wanted to wrench the wheel and take the emergency lane. "We gotta get off this." He pulled his phone.

"Base Command Coronado," Nina answered.

"Ninja Girl, we're running slow in traffic. Find us a way around it."

"You're on the I-5?"

"Affirmative."

"I was just going to call you. The vehicle Kayla is tracking just stopped."

"Where?" Tony took note of the next exit.

"It took Highway 133 toward Laguna Beach."

"We just passed San Clemente. They had a few hours lead on us. What do you think the delay was?"

"No idea. Maybe they were waiting for someone. Here's the neighborhood and address. It's a residence."

Tony pulled open his glove box and grabbed a gas receipt and a pen, writing down the address she gave him. "Did you give the Admiral a SITREP?"

"Yes."

"We've got one more on this mission," he said, adding the address into the GPS.

"Who? Wait. Standby." Nina took a departure report from one of the base vessels then came back on the line. "Who's with you besides Ed, Fox, and Mace?"

"Lieutenant Abraham Lewis."

"That's Alpha Squad's new lieutenant, right?"

"Roger that."

"I heard he's an asshole."

"Worse. I'll call you on arrival."

"Good luck, T-man."

Lewis hadn't said much for the last two hours, then again, none of them had. "Was that the Admiral's wife?" he asked.

Every head in the car turned. If Lewis was about to say something racist, Tony was pretty sure he'd be rolling behind the car's dust somewhere on the off ramp Mace had taken to get out of the traffic. "No, it was Nina," Tony said, keeping his eyes ahead.

"Guess I owe the Admiral an apology sometime soon."

"Why don't you meet Kayla first before you judge?" Tony suggested.

Lewis cranked his head and stared out the side window. "I'll make a point of it, but I doubt my opinion will alter much."

Tony and Mace exchanged a glance. He hadn't shared Lewis' misguided opinion of ethnicity with his best friend. Both he and Mace had grown up in San Diego where many different races converged. Mace's mother was Mexican, but his father's European roots worked to remove most of his Spanish features. If the lieutenant made a slur now, Mace would probably let him have it with both barrels. Tony wanted to avoid that from happening.

"What opinion?" Mace asked, before Tony could change the subject.

"One I'll keep to myself," Lewis said.

The guy wasn't as dumb as he thought. Tony eyed the mileage meter that kept reducing on the GPS, but it wasn't dropping fast enough. Mace took feeder routes running along the I-5. It meant more stop lights, but the traffic was lighter. After fifty minutes, Mace was heading south on 133 toward the Coast Highway, taking Cliff Drive where the car had taken Lumin.

"You're not wrong," Mace said, slowing down.

His swim buddy read his mind. What if she wasn't here? They'd just wasted precious time following a lead, and he could be getting farther away from her rather than closer. Mace drove past the address. Most of the homes on the seaward side had street level entries. The car wasn't visible, more than likely inside the three car garage. Palm trees and lush foliage obscured their view. The homes took advantage of the real estate they were perched on with the windows looking out over the Pacific.

Mace drove another quarter mile and parked in a grocery store parking lot. When Tony turned in his seat, Lewis said, "Callahan, you and Bale wait here. I'll take Fox and Ed in to find Dafoe."

"I want Lumin clear first," Tony warned.

Lewis settled a hard look on him. "I told you we do this by the book. Dafoe is the target, your fiancée is secondary."

"Bullshit."

"T-man," Fox gripped his wrist, and gave him a silent message. "Wait here."

Ed remained silent, but while Lewis watched him and Fox, Ed gave him a slight nod. "Everyone test their comms," Fox ordered.

They each confirmed, and the guys slid out. "Lieutenant." Lewis' feet had just hit the ground. "If Lumin dies because of your decisions, the Admiral is the least of your worries."

"Don't threaten me, Bale. We'll have time to do that later. As you pointed out, our country is in jeopardy and the man responsible is in that residence. He's the priority."

Lewis slammed the door, and Tony watched him saunter to catch up with Fox and Ed. "As soon as they've rounded the corner, we're gone," Mace said.

Tony didn't take his eyes off the figures as they walked through the parking lot at a leisurely stroll, but he lifted his fisted hand and Mace thumped it.

* * * *

Lumin pressed her ear to the locked bedroom door. She heard the men's low rumble as they spoke. Dafoe's men had abruptly woken her from her sleep and dragged her out the window. She hurt one of the kidnappers when she grasped a piece of broken pottery from the lamp and cut him. She gently touched the back of her head and winced. He hit her with something and she'd passed out. Swallowing down the nausea, she pressed her ear tightly against the door once more, then gave up.

She'd woken up in the car. While she'd been passed out, Dafoe had joined them. They wouldn't talk to her or answer any questions. It was as if she were invisible. She wrapped Tony's jacket around her and padded with bare feet to the window. They'd locked it from the outside. It was the first thing she'd tried when they'd pushed her into this room. The ocean cast itself against the rocks below, and she closed her eyes and buried her nose in Tony's jacket. His lingering scent gave her a little comfort, but no hope of him ever finding her unless she could get a message to someone.

The door opened, and she pushed herself into the corner of the room. "Go away," she said, seeing Dafoe step inside and close the door behind him.

"I'm not going to hurt you, Lumin, even though you've caused me nothing but grief. I just need something from you."

She shook her head. "I have nothing you want."

"You do," he said slyly as he approached her. He was a daunting figure. His dark features and sharp eyes focused on her as if she were some kind of lab rat. "You're going to make a donation."

"For what?" She slid along the wall, her escape thwarted by the bed.

"Your blood. It holds the antibodies to the virus, and I need them."

"So you can live? People are sick and you deserve the same end for the damage you've done"

"Not near enough, but soon it will be in the millions. That's when I will be satisfied."

A deep baritone bell reverberated throughout the house, signaling a visitor.

"See, Lumin, even the door-to-door salesmen aren't smart enough to find a safe place to hide. Americans exist believing no one can cause them harm, but I'm going to give them a great cause to learn they are not invincible."

He clenched her arm and thrust her ahead of him. They reached the entryway as one of Dafoe's men was closing the front door. "Help me. Please send help, I'm—" Dafoe's fingers clamped over her mouth and he twisted her arm behind her, his hand muffling her scream of pain.

"Not a wise thing to do. You just ended that man's life."

He jerked his head at his security man, and the guy pulled a weapon from his waistband and hurriedly opened the door chasing after whoever had knocked on it. She twisted a look over her shoulder to see a tall, broad, blond-haired man halfway down the front path. She knew that gait. Her fear was short circuiting her brain and giving her a flicker of hope with an illusion. Dafoe aimed her toward a stairway leading to the lower floor.

The sound of shattering glass made her jump. The house alarm blared. Dafoe released her and pulled a weapon from beneath his blazer. Instead of running away from the confusion, she ran toward it. The wood floor was covered with splinters of glass from the broken patio doors, and she leaped onto the couch as she crossed paths with a man in fatigues. She didn't recognize him, but she didn't care. A man in uniform meant salvation. Someone behind her snatched a handful of her hair and jerked her back. Grabbing above his hand, she wrenched her head away leaving a fistful of her strands with him. The warrior tackled Dafoe's security guard and she scrambled to the other end of the couch. From there she jumped to a sturdy dining table. She snapped the latch on the window and swung it open. One long step and she was balancing on the window ledge. The front door opened with a crash and she saw Fox and Ed. It had been him.

"Run, Lumin," Ed yelled at her.

She didn't wait for a second order and jumped to the balcony. One look over the edge of the railing gave her a clear view of the cliff they were perched on. It wasn't a sheer drop, but almost. The *crunch* of glass behind her made her pause. Dafoe! He held his weapon steadily aimed at her.

"Don't do it, Lumin."

She backed up and didn't give away the fact that another SEAL crept over the far edge of the balcony, but men like Dafoe survived on a sixth sense and he whirled. She knew the man under the helmet. Tony! Dafoe and he faced off, their weapons couldn't miss if they both fired.

A slow smile crept over Dafoe's expression as he turned the weapon on her. "Go ahead, SEAL. I've got great aim."

The weapon was pointed at her, but Dafoe's attention was on Tony. She quickly slid over the edge of the railing and found a foothold on the rock below. With a quick prayer she released the balcony deck and gripped the rock face. Just before disappearing she saw Tony's gaze lock with hers and he smiled.

"Thousands of people are going to die because of you, Dafoe," Tony accused. "Because of you, a great SEAL will never come home to his wife and girls. Do you expect a fair trial?"

Lumin scrambled across the cliff's outcroppings, making sure every hand hold found solid rock. She could still hear Tony. Stopping for a breath, she spared a look over her shoulder. Dafoe edged sideways and spotted her. "You are going to drop your weapon, SEAL, and I am going to walk out of here or you will watch her fall to her death."

Tony's head cocked a little. "Lay down your weapon, Dafoe, or you won't have a court date."

Tony was stalling to give her time to make it to safety. Her toes were bleeding, but she stuffed them into a crack and pulled with her arms and thrust with her legs. Almost there, she winced and pushed herself to reach the edge of the cliff. The rocks began to crumble in her hand. Near the top there was too much sand mixed in. The spit of something ricocheting off a rock splintered a piece and hurtled stone at her cheek. Another shot rang out, but this time it didn't come close. She held her breath and looked over her shoulder. Her foot slipped, and she clutched a lump of grass. Tony was gone from the balcony and Dafoe lay on his back.

Sweat rolled down her face and coated her skin. She balanced on her left foot, the only solid surface holding her up. She rested her forehead against the rough surface. A hand gripped her wrist and she screamed before looking up.

"Come here, baby."

Tony gripped both her wrists and pulled her over the edge. They fell backwards with her landing on top of him. He didn't hesitate, placing his hands around her face, and kissed her. A hard, desperate kiss. He sat up, bringing her with him perched on his lap, but he wouldn't stop kissing her. She pushed a little at his shoulders, and he finally fell back. She slipped his helmet off and ran her hands through his hair, stopping to embrace his neck. He fell back to the grass, keeping her clutched tightly to him.

"Would you do me a favor and stop getting kidnapped? I don't think my heart can take it." His thumb brushed her cheek and followed her top lip with a gentle touch.

"How did you find me?"

"A SEAL can't divulge his secrets," he said, giving her a wicked, lusty grin.

When her hero smiled, he was the most handsome man on the planet. "Tell me," she whispered. Being this close to him made her skin tingle and it didn't help that she could feel his arousal between her thighs.

"Maybe just this one secret," he said and kissed her.

"What's the secret?" She brushed her cheek against the stubble on his face and nearly purred.

"You're the woman I'm going to cherish for the rest of my life, and that means you're right here," he said, touching his heart and then hers. His gaze intensified, the smile gone replaced with a soul shaking sincerity. "I won't allow anyone to hurt you or take you from me. Marry me, Lumin, and I promise to love you and never stop."

* * * *

Tony carried Lumin back to the house, and gently set her on her feet near the front door.

Lieutenant Lewis stepped forward. "Petty Officer Bale, I'll see that Lumin returns to San Diego and make the report we've located Dafoe. Take these men back to the base with your team."

Tony didn't give a shit that Lewis wanted the glory. A real SEAL didn't strive for visibility, only success, but he wasn't going to let Lumin out of his sight. Not ever. "Is Dafoe dead?" he asked, not giving the lieutenant a confirmation on his order.

"Gone to meet his Allah and hopefully his wife and son," Mace said, stepping through the broken patio door to join them.

Fox and Ed had Dafoe's security men under guard. "I'm taking Lumin back to San Diego," Tony said, keeping her tucked safely next to him.

"Are you disobeying a direct order?" Lewis growled.

"I would be if you were my lieutenant."

"Did you just receive a promotion in the last few minutes that I'm not aware of?" Lewis asked, his eyes revealing his dislike and the chance to form that complaint he'd threatened before.

"Up to you, Lewis. You can live up to your rank, make amends with the Admiral and say you led this op and accept the 'atta boys,' or you can keep fucking around worrying about who does or doesn't respect the gold on your sleeve and climbing a ladder. At some time in the past you earned your Budweiser, but it doesn't stop with a handshake and the pin."

Lewis took a short step toward him. "Are you trying to teach *me* what it means to be a SEAL?"

Lewis glared at him, but his stare was only half-filled with certainty. Being a warrior left no room for doubt. "I am. You lucked out, Lieutenant. You've joined Alpha Squad, a team of men who will have your back, if you have theirs. This isn't a pissing contest to see who makes the highest mark on the tree. We're judged as one unit and we've got a track record of success, but no man in this squad has ever stopped training or learning or carrying each other when things get fucked up. Two men taught us that, the man you're replacing, Captain Cobbs, the other you still have an opportunity to know, Admiral Austen."

Lewis blinked at him. The rankle in his expression had melted. "You're talking like you're not part of the team."

Mace's brow quirked and he glanced at Lumin and back at him. Tony didn't answer his question. "I'll see ya back at the base."

Mace followed them out the front door, then stepped in front of them to stop their progress. "What are you doing?" he said with concern.

Lumin stared up at him with a questioning expression as well.

"Making a decision about my future," he answered. Mace's head jerked back, hearing but not believing. "I've done my time. Cobbs told me something before he died and a few minutes ago I wrapped my head around it." Mace waited with his arms crossed, but looked like he already knew what he was going to say. "He missed all the growing years with Rayanne and Cindy. Marg had to live with the fear he wouldn't come home for twenty years." He shook his head. "I'm not doing that to Lumin. I'm going to be there when she graduates law school. I'm going to be there when she wins her first case." He slid his hand to her stomach and looked into her big blue eyes staring at him with surprise. "I'm going to be there to watch our baby grow, every one of them." He put his attention back on Mace. "While my paperwork goes through for officer training, I'm going to take that position in the BUD/S training department. I might even stay, but I've done all the active duty out in the theatre I'm ever gonna do. My family was as dysfunctional as it can get. I'm not repeating that when I have a choice, and I choose Lumin."

"Tony," Lumin squeaked, and threw her arms around his neck, squeezing the life out of him. He curled a satisfied smile at Mace, and Mace's shoulders lifted with a chuckle.

"Don't think there's a better reason on the planet than what you just said, T-man." Mace gripped them both in a hug. "I'll go get the car and drive you guys back to the base. Besides," he cocked his brow. "I need to see my wife and tell her something important."

"What?" Tony sputtered.

They began to walk toward Cliff Avenue. "There's plenty of good men out there. They won't miss us."

"Are you saying what I think you're saying?" Tony asked, stopping at the end of the walkway.

"I almost lost her," Mace muttered.

"It's because you're a SEAL that you saved her."

"Yeah, and I know Nina's accepted that being away from home is part of our profession, but Alpha Squad hasn't been the same since Ghost and Cobbs left us. There are two holes and nobody will fill them like they did." Mace surveyed the neighborhood and they all watched a high-end Mercedes park across the street in front of a luxurious home. "We're never gonna live at an address like this one. But guys like us make it possible for these people to have it all. We've earned our stripes in the dirt. It's time to pass on the torch. I heard there were two spots available in the training department."

"Let's do it." Tony extended his arm and Mace gripped it. "Think the only thing I'll miss is blowing things up."

Lumin laughed. "Men and their big guns."

"Hey, you said you like my big guns," he teased, giving her a cocky smile.

"I said you have nice buns, Tony. I think you should wear better hearing protection."

Throwing his arms around his beautiful nymph, he gazed into his fiancée's eyes. "Yes, dear."

Tony couldn't stop the grin from stretching his jaw taut. Neither he nor Mace would leave the Navy. Like Ghost and Cobbs they would go the distance. They'd find and train the men who had the right stuff to be a SEAL, and if he went through with the officer's training, there would be plenty of opportunities but he would make sure it meant coming home every night.

He looked down into Lumin's brilliant smile, and knew he'd made the right choice. "Let's go home, my lady."

Date: 08.06.2014
Time: 0300UTC 1900PST
Case: Closed. Threat neutralized
Mission: Code Name Luminous deacitivated

Epilogue

Friends, family, and warriors surrounded Captain Patrick Edward Cobbs' casket. Lumin stood shoulder to shoulder with Nina on one side and Kayla on the other. The August sun mingled with the breeze of the ocean as they stood on the green grass at the grave site. It had only taken a few minutes to drive from the Catholic church that had overflowed out the enormous doors, down the stairs and filled the parking lot with people who wanted to be present when the priest performed the service. Tony had sat beside her, but now he stood with the squad across from her and to the right of Marg, Kelsey, Rayanne, and Cindy. Cobb's mother sat in the chairs provided for family and Marg's parents stood behind them. She'd seen the same soul wrenching scene in movies, but the depth of sadness never connected the dots in her heart until today.

Admiral Austen's expression remained emotionless; an enormous warrior standing regally in his officer's uniform watching his best friend being interred. Lumin couldn't imagine the willpower it took to do that without shedding a tear. Some people had suggested he not do the honorary presentation of the flag to Cobbs' widow, but he refused. Lumin clutched Nina and Kayla's hands tightly, and fought back the tears, but they surfaced anyway, and she wasn't alone as she glimpsed at Nina, but Kayla remained as stoic as her husband. Stitch and Fox stepped forward and folded the draped flag from Captain Cobbs' casket, their faces sheer rock, set in impassive reserve. Fox took the triangle into his hands, placed himself in front of Admiral Austen, saluted, released it, and stepped back.

The Admiral glanced into the heavens for a moment and his lips parted, taking a breath, then he took the few steps to stand before Marg. She sat noble and beautiful, looking straight ahead. The Admiral kneeled before her and they stared into each other's eyes for the longest moment. Before the Admiral said a word, Marg's strength broke and tears slipped over her lashes and down her cheeks. She rested a hand over his as if seeking courage and giving it.

"On behalf of the President of the United States and the Chief of Naval Operations, please accept this flag as a symbol of our appreciation for your loved one's service to this Country and a grateful Navy," the Admiral said. His eyes snapped shut and his jaw went rigid.

"Uncle Thane?" Kelsey slipped off her chair and the Admiral's brow wrinkled tight.

"Yes, Kelsey," he uttered, resting his gaze on her concerned six-year-old expression.

"Daddy still loves us, right?"

She placed her little hand on his cheek and a deep breath escaped him. The innocent touch of her hand depleted his reserve and a ragged cry escaped his throat. "Yes, baby girl, he does."

He swept her into his arms and a harsh sob escaped him. The powerful legend known as Ghost, who led men into battle, broke with a little girl's words. Lumin's heart pained for Kelsey who would have to walk through the milestones of her life without her father beside her. Ceremony, pomp, expectations of what a military service meant, didn't mean a thing to a little girl who needed reassurance from the man she'd known as her uncle. Ghost buried his face in her hair and reached his muscled arm to encompass Marg in a moment of grief and loss so strong no man or woman present that day would ever forget. No one breathed or uttered a word to break the moment, until the moment had had its say.

The Admiral gently put Kelsey back in her chair. The priest gave his final words to bless Patrick Cobbs' body and affirm his soul to heaven. There was silence, then the priest moved back and Lumin waited. She expected the crowd around her to fall out, but they didn't. In unison, Alpha Squad reached to their pockets and unhooked something. She watched with rapt attention and her insides froze as Master Chief Mason Briggs stepped up to the coffin and pounded the pin he'd taken from his uniform into the glossy wood of the casket. Mace, Ditz, Ed, Stitch, and Nathan each did the same. With each pin hammered into the wood, Lumin jumped. They all watched as Tony stepped up. He stared down at the line of pins, his brow furrowed. "You are my mentor. My Captain. It will always be that way," He paused as his eyes filled with tears and he bit down hard to hold them back. His powerful hand came down and sunk the pin to the hilt, then he joined his squad who lined the foot of the casket.

Admiral Austen was the last in line. He palmed the beautiful wood, deep in reflection. "I will take care of them as long I have breath. I vow to you, my best friend, they are my family as are you. Till we meet again, brother." The last pin dug into the wood and the Admiral took his position at the far left of the line. The squad, in unison, saluted as Admiral Austen gave the command to the honor guard, who stood fifty feet away, to fire. Three rounds broke the silence. A final salute for a warrior who protected his nation, and his team, to the end.

* * * *

Lumin sat under the sun. The brisk wind filled with the scent of the sea lifted her hair. She wiggled her toes in the warm sand. The wake for Captain Cobbs wasn't what she expected. They gathered on the shore in front of the Hotel Del Coronado, hundreds of people, all from the base. Accompanied by their families, the children played with each other in the surf. The gathering looked more like a beach party. Kayla and Nina's words sprang to mind. 'Life goes on'.

Moira and Steven Porter had come and brought the twins. "Lumin, will you help us build a sand castle?" they asked, a plastic shovel in one hand and a bucket in the other.

"Take your pails down to the water. I want to talk with Lumin for a moment," Moira said, and watched them run toward the wet sand. "Steven spoke to your mom and dad last night."

"I did too," Lumin said, tucking her knees to her chest and watching Tony talk with Steven a little ways down the beach. "I told them everything."

Moira's concern was evident. "Are you sure, Lumin? You're only twenty-four. There's a lot of life you could live before all the responsibilities of marriage."

Lumin wasn't bothered by Moira's comment because it came from the heart. "And I will live it." She turned a smile on Moira. "With Tony."

The man she knew more and more as the days passed convinced her he was the man she would live her life with. She watched as Tony's strong, muscled legs striding toward her sparked lustful thoughts in her mind. The white shirt he wore open billowed out around him. Steven walked beside him and she and Moira looked up when they stopped in front of them. Steven knelt on one knee.

"Tony asked me, since your parents can't be here, for your hand in marriage." He grinned. "He's a good man, Lumin, and I gave him our blessing, but I'm concerned, as your father is, about your future."

She peeked a look at Tony, and he winked at her. His tanned skin accentuated his hazel eyes and she had begun to learn to read them, but the easiest to see was how much he loved her. Doubt had nowhere to settle in her thoughts. She reached out a hand and Tony pulled her to her feet. "My future isn't set in stone, but I know it's with Tony."

Tony's cheek brushed against hers, and he whispered. "I love you, my lady."

"Lumin's parents will arrange to return in seven months for the wedding," Moira said, pushing herself to her feet and giving her husband a sign they should give Lumin some space.

Lumin sighed. "I wish you didn't have to do this last deployment," she said.

"I offered him a job any time he wants one," Steven said, as his youngsters tackled him from behind. A huge laugh broke from the man, and he swept one under each arm and stood up.

"Maybe you should consider it, Tony?" Moira suggested.

"Thank you," Tony said as he wrapped his arms around Lumin, "But I'm not leaving the Navy. I have a position in the training department waiting for me, and I'm going to finish this part of my combat service as promised." He tilted his head and his gaze fluttered across her face. "I'm coming home, Lumin. I promise that too."

Moira and Steven took their little ones down to the water to give them some privacy and Tony urged her to sit down in the sand beside him. "You okay?" he asked with concern.

She held her hair out of her face and smiled at him. "I've never seen such a big family," she remarked, looking at all the people scattered about them.

He nodded. "I guess we are a family," he said, gazing over the hundreds of people on the beach and in the water.

"How is Marg?"

Tony turned and put a finger to her chin, raising it so she'd look at him. "Kayla and the Admiral are with her and she has all of us." He pulled a strand from her mouth. "You have them too. If anything ever happens to me, they'll stand beside you."

She flung her arms around Tony's neck and squeezed him tight. "I'm scared."

"I know you are, but I'm coming home, Lumin. Nothing will stop me from coming home to you."

He kissed her sweetly, and she burned the moment into her mind. Tomorrow he would be gone, and she would remind herself every time fear threatened her that the grace of God would protect him. Tony was strong. Smart and courageous enough, he would look death in the eye and order it to go elsewhere. He told her every day, she was his center. Her light would always show him the way home—and she believed him.

The End

A Warrior's Challenge Book Five
Code Name: Forever and Ever
Excerpt

July 2ⁿᵈ, 1992

"Margaret Celeste, where are you going with that bag of clothes?"

Marg turned to see her mother fuming on the other side of the ballroom-sized entryway of their mansion. "To the Veteran's Service Center, Mother."

"Those clothes are worth thousands of dollars," Claire Stines declared.

"Laurene will certainly never wear my hand-me-downs and someone can put them to good use. Women who leave the service need clothes for job interviews."

Her mother marched across the entry, grilling her with an angry stare. "Then they can buy their own."

Heat stroked up Marg's neck. "If they don't have a job, they can't buy clothes, Mother. You and Father support causes all the time. Is there a difference?"

Her mother huffed. "There is! We don't support war or those who participate in it. You're nineteen years old and easily influenced. I was dead against your school allowing the military to lecture the students with false propaganda about fighting for this country. We are not at war. This family supports organizations with worthy causes. War is not one of them." Claire's gaze fell to the bag and she gripped a dress that had slipped from the opening. "This is your debutante ball gown," she said with a shrill pitch. "What's it doing in here?"

"I'm not going, Mother. I told you that."

Claire's eye narrowed in anger. "Ungrateful! Do you have any idea how many months it took for me to get you accepted? Only the best are included in L.A.'s premiere ball. Your father expects you there, and so do I. You—will—go."

Marg thought for the umpteenth time that she must have been adopted. She reached into the bag, snagged the dress and thrust it at her mother. "The rest I'm giving to the center," she announced, and walked out the front door. Her mother could throw a fit if she wanted, but that wouldn't stop her.

After tossing the bag onto the passenger seat of her car, she took a deep breath and gazed at the elegant landscaped grounds of her home. She'd known nothing other than her Beverly Hills surroundings. Mansions lined the hills and vied for spectacular gardens and well-heeled parties. She hated the falseness of it all, even though she'd been raised in its claws.

"Marg," Laurene called, running across the stamped paved driveway to catch her.

"Don't start," she said, knowing her mother had sent Laurene to talk to her. She loved her sisters but they did her mother's bidding with just a shrewd look. Laurene was the closest in age to her, being only a year younger.

"You're pissing Mom off again," Laurene said, giving her a pleading look to give in to their mother's open hatred against anything military.

"She's going to be even more pissed when she finds out I'm moving."

"What?" Laurene's big brown eyes rounded. "Oh, my God." Her hands covered her cheeks. "You got the modeling contract, didn't you?"

Marg smiled at her. "I did, and I'm moving to San Diego."

"San Diego? Why there, of all places? It's a Navy town. You know what they'll say."

"Because it's two hours farther than Mom or Dad will drive."

"They are going to freak out."

"Dad's withering contempt is because of Grandfather, Laurene. Men die in war. They die to protect us but Dad can't see past his heart, and it's riddled with grief even after all these years."

"You sound like an enlistment poster, Marg. Dad has a point. He lost his father in the Vietnam War. Of course he hates anything military. He was only eight years old."

Their grandmother had married a wealthy man from L.A. after their grandfather died. She'd had one more son but she never stopped loving Petty Officer Braden Stines. He had enlisted in the Navy and was killed in the last year of the war. Marg, nor her sisters, ever met him but reminders of him sat on her father's bookshelves in his private office at home.

Marg slid into the white convertible her parents had given her for graduation. She remembered feeling like she'd accepted a deal from the devil when her father handed her the keys. "You'll look beautiful driving this, darling," he'd said. "Driving the right car attracts the right men."

He'd been wrong. Her status, her address and her car attracted nothing but the sons of wealthy families. Most of them were pompous assholes who were looking for trophy wives without a brain. She was born with a good one, and she intended on using it. That, and the long legs and attractive features God had bestowed on her.

"Can I come and visit you in San Diego?" Laurene begged.

Laurene loved her life of pretty things and being surrounded by wealthy friends. She didn't mind their father bringing home the next "future husband du jour." Marg was sick of it, and it made her feel like a side of beef for sale to the highest bidder.

"You're my sister, Laurene. You can come any time you want."

"When are you going to tell Mom and Dad?"

"Tonight." Pulling out an envelope from her bag, she turned it in her fingers. "I'm mailing the contract back today."

Laurene closed the driver's door and bent over, kissing her cheek. "You're going to be famous. I know it."

Marg smiled. "I don't really care about famous, but I do need a job, and this pays pretty good. I can't live here under their roof and their rules anymore. Every time Dad brings one of his wanna-bes home from the studio to ogle us like well-groomed chattel, it makes my skin crawl." Her eyes gazed up toward the mansion, its brilliant front pillars and rounded façade a glorious tribute to her father's success in Hollywood. "Maybe I'm delusional, Laurene, but I want to marry a man who loves me and respects me. Whether he has money or not doesn't matter, but I'll never find him in the hills of Hollywood. There's a big, undiscovered world out there. I have to leave the protection and façade L.A. offers. I want to prove I can live on my own. San Diego will be a good start."

* * * *

The music in the nightclub thumped with a deafening beat. People yelled at each other just to make out every second word. Bodies ground together and crushed Marg against the bar. The L.A. scene wasn't very different than this favored San Diego hangout. The only difference was the guys and gals weren't wearing thousand-dollar outfits.

Tonight was her first night off from a stringent modeling schedule. The hours were long, but she had this weekend all to herself. She gazed over the crowd. There were a lot of short haircuts on the men and since she was in a heavily populated Navy town, she guessed they were sailors. Her parents would shudder at the thought, which made her smile even more.

"A man can't resist a smile like that," a low timbre said next to her ear.

She turned. Being six feet, she was surprised to have to raise her gaze, but it walked up the hulk of muscled chest bulging against a white cotton shirt until it reached tropical blue eyes, making her legs weaken.

"Hi."

He wasn't just good-looking, he was a fucking god. Her heart turned a triple somersault staring into his face. A wicked little smile graced his full lips and his angular jaw made her heart leave skid marks in her chest. His short blond hair and rugged features left her unable to stop gaping.

He leaned over and brushed her ear with his lips. "Thane Austen, and I am most definitely going to buy you a drink."

She breathed out a shallow gasp of air as the sexy rumble coursed through her. Thane only leaned back far enough to look into her eyes. The heat in his was her undoing. Whether this man wanted forever or not, she knew they were going to be in each other's arms before the night was over, and the drum of her pulse told her it couldn't happen fast enough. Her eyes locked with his and she smiled.

His jaw careened into a tight angle. "Aww man, you are beautiful," Thane said. "Where did you come from?"

She leaned toward him and said, "It's where I'm going, not where I'm from that counts. How about you?"

"Short term, I hope it's making you a satisfied woman. Long term, wherever the Navy sends me."

"So you are a sailor."

He gave her grin. "A SEAL, not a sailor. There's a difference."

"There is?" She'd read an article in the newspaper once about SEALs. They were a special fighting force the Navy used on dangerous assignments.

"My swim buddy and I just passed BUD/S. It's a night for celebration."

"Where is he?"

Thane's eyes remained on her, eating every inch up as he watched her. "Zodiak's on his way. He had some family stuff to take care of."

Her lips quirked. "Zodiak? That's a strange name."

"It's his team name. Patrick Cobbs is his real name."

"And do you have a team name?"

"Not yet. And thank God for that, since it usually comes from something stupid we've done during training." He laughed. "So are you here with anyone? Pat's single, but since I saw you first, he's just gonna have to deal with it."

She swallowed her excitement when his finger brushed small circles on her bare shoulder. "I came with some of the modeling crew from my shoot. They're off having fun. Do you want to wait for your friend?"

"You're a model?" He nodded. "Not surprised." Thane's sexy timbre lowered even further. "Why don't we get out of here? Wouldn't want you tempted away from me."

She doubted that could ever happen. Thane's confidence and hotness left her in a puddle of lust. Acting like a cheap tramp crossed her mind but not even the A-list guys from her school had Thane's magnetism. Marg couldn't control her impatient hand. It had to touch him and she slid it down his powerful arm, coiling her fingers in his. "Sounds like heaven."

A perfect white smile broke from his full lips and the dimple in his chin deepened. "I promise you heaven, sweetheart. You can count on it." With the sweep of his powerful arm, he drew her close and pushed through the undulating bodies in the bar. Instinct told her this man was one of a kind. Life had just become very interesting.

About the Author

I grew up on the beautiful West Coast of British Columbia with the Pacific Ocean on my western doorstep and thousands of acres of forest on the other. After finishing school, my life took a drastic twist, and a lifelong working relationship with the marine industry began.

After a twenty-year hiatus from my creative writing, the stories swirling in my mind began to swim hard to surface, and I threw them a life ring. I juggle my creativity during my days off, and then get back down to business serving in the Coast Guard. My life is a mix of creativity vs. black and white procedures. With a lifetime of working in the marine community, there's plenty of stories to tell. It's a different world, different language, unsung heroes and heroines aplenty, heated moments, and blissful silence when all is well. Reading and writing is the way I turn down the loud hum that my work causes, and after thirty years of humming, it's time to vent.

http://nataszawaters.com/

https://www.facebook.com/pages/Natasza-Waters/311286078885026

Other books with Secret Cravings Publishing
A Warrior's Challenge Series
Code Name: Ghost
Code Name: Kayla's Fire
Code Name: Nina's Choice
Code Name: Luminous

Message from Natasza

Thank you for spending time with Alpha Squad. If you've been following along with the series you probably realize that each story focuses on subject matter specific to the life of a warrior and those who love them.

Code Name: Ghost and Kayla's Fire were about PTSD and the challenges our warriors face to live half their lives in conflict and half at home. Code Name: Nina's Choice highlighted the struggle involved with a serious injury during combat and separation from family. Code Name: Luminous touched on two very delicate subjects: faith and loss.

This book in particular was difficult for me to write for personal reasons. Although not mentioned at the beginning of the book, I dedicate this story to Thomas Shelby, a young man I knew a long time ago, who died during his service to his country. His little girl grew up without having her wonderful father beside her through the milestones of her life. If I could turn back the hands of time and change fate, I would. But we can't change what is, so we move forward and remember with gratitude and sorrow. Above all else, we must remind ourselves that life is for the living, although we'll never forget those who sacrificed their lives to save others.

Standby for Code Name: Forever & Ever. We'll travel back over twenty years in time when Thane Austen and Patrick Cobbs join the Navy SEALs. The war against terrorism hasn't openly struck the world changing it forever. When Marg looks into Patrick

Cobbs' eyes for the first time, two thoughts strike her. She's made a monumental mistake by sleeping with his best friend, and secondly, she's pretty sure she's fallen in love with the tall, dark, silent warrior that makes her tremble with just a look. Introducing Patrick to her parents will mean immediate exile from her family, but she doesn't care. She has more to lose than her family. She could lose Patrick, if he learns of her stupid mistake.

Please continue to leave reviews on Goodreads, Amazon or wherever you have purchased the book. Join me on Facebook https://www.facebook.com/pages/Natasza-Waters/311286078885026 Visit my blog http://nataszawaters.com/ or drop me a line at Nataszawaters@gmail.com.

Please continue to help Paws and Stripes. A nonprofit organization providing service dogs for wounded military veterans with Post Traumatic Stress Disorder and Traumatic Brain Injury. http://www.pawsandstripes.org/ and Operation Gratitude who annually sends 100,000+ care packages filled with snacks, entertainment items and personal letters of appreciation addressed to individually named U.S. Service Members deployed in hostile regions, to their children left behind and to veterans, first responders, wounded warriors and their care givers. http://www.operationgratitude.com/

88's

Natasza

Secret Cravings Publishing
www.secretcravingspublishing.com

CPSIA information can be obtained at www.ICGtesting.com
Printed in the USA
LVOW04s1554160615

442682LV00016B/923/P